THE HEAT WAS RISING

The impact of his lips upon hers staggered them both. Rebecca groaned and wrapped her arms more tightly around his neck as he pursued the kiss. When her mouth parted beneath his and she let him come in, he felt the room tilting.

Blood pounded through his body in a blinding roar, blocking out all sense and sound, save that of the woman in his arms.

He heard her soft gasps for air when they moved apart. Then he felt her hands moving urgently around his back and up his neck, trying to pull him closer. Tracing the pulse in her neck with the tip of his tongue, he groaned, then began covering her entire body with kisses.

It was all too much . . . and yet not nearly enough.

———

JACKSON
RULE

Dinah McCall

HarperPaperbacks
A Division of HarperCollinsPublishers

This is a work of fiction. The characters, incidents, and dialogues are products of the author's imagination and are not to be construed as real. Any resemblance to actual events or persons, living or dead, is entirely coincidental.

HarperPaperbacks   *A Division of* HarperCollins*Publishers*
10 East 53rd Street, New York, N.Y. 10022

Cover illustration by John Ennis

First printing: July 1996

Printed in the United States of America

HarperPaperbacks, HarperMonogram, and colophon are trademarks of HarperCollins*Publishers*

❖ 10 9 8 7 6 5 4 3 2 1

The world is full of heroes. The teacher who made a difference in a small child's life. An organ donor who thought of someone else's life rather than his or her own. The person who had the guts to speak out against injustice or abuse. The child who does not make friends by the color of skin. The deaf and the blind, who do not believe themselves to be handicapped. And the dying, who do not lose faith in God.

I dedicate this book to those people, and the many, many others like them, who go through life making the small, quiet differences.

JACKSON RULE

1

The urge to run was overwhelming. But Andrew Jackson Rule had not survived the past fifteen years in a maximum security prison by running, and so he walked through the last set of locked gates leading to the outside world as if he didn't care that this was the first breath of free air he would be taking since his sixteenth birthday.

The security guard accompanying him seemed jittery. Jackson knew that he'd garnered a reputation inside for being a hard-ass. But he didn't care. It had kept him alive and more or less in one piece, if you didn't count the scars, both inner and outer, that he was taking with him.

Jackson Rule had been convicted of only one crime, but it had been an unforgivable act against God and society—even in the minds of the most hardened of inmates—and one to which he had calmly confessed without blinking an eye.

Finally, they were at the gate. The guard paused, eyeing Jackson Rule's new denim pants and jacket—compliments of the state of Louisiana—and the plain white T-shirt he wore beneath it. He glanced down at Jackson's shiny new boots and then handed him the duffel bag containing all of his worldly possessions.

"Here you go, Rule. Don't forget to write," the guard said, and then snickered at his own joke.

Jackson took the bag, but the look he gave the guard silenced the man's chuckle. Then Jackson turned, squinting against the searing heat and the barely stirring, thick sultry air. He stared through the massive iron bars, waiting for the gates to swing open and give him his first unimpeded sight of Louisiana in almost half of his life.

When the gates began to move, Jackson's heart began to pound in rhythm to the movement, but he didn't take a step. Finally they stood ajar, and he moved through them as swiftly as he'd passed from his mother's body on the day he'd been born.

At thirty-one, Jackson Rule was birthed anew in the bright light of day. He had lost his youth inside the high walls of Angola State Penitentiary, but he had not lost himself.

Unfortunately, his sister, Molly, who was four years his senior, could not say the same. She was as lost as a woman could be. According to her doctors, who had been the source of Jackson's only outside contact for the entirety of his sentence, she went through the motions of living, but without truly participating. But it was to be expected. Nearly all of the patients in the New Orleans home where she lived were missing a few active brain cells.

Tunica, the city nearest the prison, was located just off the banks of the mighty Mississippi. If one looked carefully, remnants of the Old South and the grandeur it once stood for could be seen, but not on the dusty path that led to the bus stop. Louisiana dust coated Jackson's new boots with a dirty brown pall, and in honor of his arrival, the sickly breath of wind managed to lift the long hair hanging down the back of his neck. It whipped wildly in the wind like the wings of a hovering crow. So shiny. So black.

His expression was bland, but his mind was in turmoil. Now that the long-awaited day of his release was at hand, the memories that came with freedom were more than he'd bargained for. He tried, without success, to remember Molly in happier times, but he couldn't get past his last image of her, covered in the blood of their father and screaming until there was no breath left in her body.

Angry with the morbid thoughts, he lengthened his stride. When he finally looked up, he was at the bus stop. An empty bench beckoned. But Jackson had no intention of spending his first free minutes outside of the penitentiary on his ass. He had places to go and a sister to see. And as he thought of her again, he knew that theirs would not be a simple reunion.

Ah God, Molly, how can I let you see me like this? But there were no answers, and he expected none. He hadn't had a break since the day he'd been born.

When the bus finally arrived, Jackson walked up the steps to begin the first day of the rest of his life. There were two people on the bus, and neither one dared look him in the face. It was common knowledge that this particular bus stop was for inmates waiting to be transported back into free society.

Jackson didn't notice the other travelers' reticence, but if he had, it wouldn't have deterred him. He had a goal, and, so help him God, no one was going to stand in his way. The plan was a good one. But Jackson had been behind bars just long enough to forget how fate had a way of changing one's plans.

After spending long hours on Highway 61 South, staring at countryside he had almost forgotten existed, Jackson sighed as the bus pulled up to a small country store just outside of New Orleans to refuel. His stomach grumbled, and he remembered that he'd refused breakfast that morning. He'd had no intention of starting his first day of freedom with prison food in his belly. And then he looked out the window and got another dose of reality. If memory served, the bus had stopped only a mile or so from the place where he'd grown up. Impulsively, he changed his mind about riding into New Orleans in favor of a reunion of sorts.

•   •   •

Rebecca Hill's ten-year-old pickup truck was as hot as she felt. Her pink T-shirt was sticking to her body, and the needle on the temperature gauge was rocking in the red as she pulled up to Etienne's Country One-Stop. A fresh head of steam boiled out from under the front grill as she killed the engine and popped the hood. She glanced back once at the flats of wilting seedlings in the back of her pickup and then headed for the front of the truck. Her petunias and periwinkles weren't the only things in desperate need of water. There was enough hot water coming out of the radiator to cook a batch of crawfish.

She yanked a rag from the hip pocket of her Levi's and did a dodging little two-step as she tried to remove the radiator cap without scalding her hand and arm in the process. By the time she had succeeded, her face was as red as her hair.

"Damn, damn, double damn," she muttered, and leaned over the fender, impotently pushing at the dangling radiator hose that had blown off.

She poked around the engine, looking for the missing clamp, and then sighed. The chances of this store having such parts for sale were slim to none. If she expected to get these plants delivered before they died on the spot, she had no choice but to call the greenhouse and have Pete come rescue her.

Suddenly the wind gusted, blowing steam from the engine into her eyes. She took several steps backward, instinctively covering her face with her hands to keep from being burned.

From out of nowhere, the strident blare of a car horn blasted her eardrums. She had inadvertently stepped onto the road and into the lane of traffic. In fear she spun around, her heart racing, only to come face-to-face with an oncoming car.

Before she could react, a hand suddenly clamped around her arm, yanking her backward and out of danger. She had a vague impression of being slammed against a wall of muscle and sweat before the world began to spin. A hot blast of air from the passing car seared what was left of her nerves as she swayed on her feet.

"Oh my God!"

At the moment she spoke, the grip on her arm was released. She turned to thank her guardian angel, but there was no one there. All she saw was the back of a tall, dark-haired man, with a duffel bag slung over his shoulder, walking toward the store. "Well, for goodness' sakes!"

She swiped again at her unruly hair with shaky hands and then pressed them flat against her stomach, just to make sure that whatever was in there stayed put. She'd never been so frightened in her life.

A door slammed, and she looked back at the store, unable to believe that someone would so unexpectedly appear to save her life and then not wait around for as much as a thank-you.

Rebecca regarded the man's lack of manners as a slap in the face. She frowned, and when she did, her expression went from pixie to harpy—one her father would have recognized as the disrespectful impudence he'd been unable to leach out of her personality. Being a preacher's daughter had its drawbacks, and being born with a less than perfect disposition had branded Rebecca Ruth Hill as the thorn in her reverent father's side.

Drying her sweaty palms on the legs of her jeans, she walked toward the door of the store. "The very nerve," she muttered. She had a man to thank, whether he wanted to hear it or not.

Jackson was still shaking when he walked into the air-conditioned store. He didn't know what had frightened him more, seeing the woman stumble blindly into traffic or what he'd felt when he grabbed her arm and pulled her out of danger. He decided it wasn't seeing someone die that had scared the hell out of him. It was the realization that this was the first woman he'd touched in over fifteen years. His palms were sweaty and his heart was racing faster than the cars on the highway outside the store.

Soft. Her skin had been so damned soft.

He headed blindly down an aisle with no sense of purpose, and then his stomach grumbled, reminding him of why he was here. He began to search the shelves for something . . . anything . . . to satisfy his hunger. He stared in amazement at the strange assortment of snack foods on the shelves. Things had certainly changed in the last fifteen years. He picked up a box of candy labeled ATOMIC ROCKS and almost smiled, then set it back on the rack and headed for the cooler housing the beverages, which was right where Rebecca found him.

"Hey, you!"

The grip on his jacket was just shy of rude, but there was no mistaking the tone of the woman's voice. And when Jackson turned and stared down into a doll-baby face framed in dark red curls, he did well to hide his shock. It was her! He hadn't seen her face, but he'd know that hair anywhere. Only moments ago it had been all over his face, and the scent of her was still with him. Hot and dusty, with the faint, but lingering, scent of lemon. Somehow it fit her.

Jackson shrugged out of her grasp and took two steps backward. At this point, putting as much distance between himself and this woman was all he could think of to do. Lust was hell on an empty stomach.

Rebecca tried a smile. After all, she'd come to thank a man for saving her life. But she hadn't expected him to be so handsome . . . or so cold. The expression on his face was just shy of frightening, as were the cold blue eyes glaring down at her.

"I came to say thank you for what you did out there."

Rebecca watched his nostrils flare and the perfect cut of his lips forming an answer.

"You're welcome."

She shivered. His voice rumbled across her shattered nerves like imminent thunder. Suddenly, the bus engine roared to life outside, and the driver began grinding gears as he pulled out of the lot.

Rebecca pointed toward the door. "You're missing your ride."

Jackson didn't answer her, nor did he move, and the longer she stared, the thicker the tension between them grew.

Rebecca's toes curled inside her tennis shoes, and she had the oddest urge to turn and run and never look back. But he had saved her life. He couldn't be that dangerous.

His mouth curled, just enough to warn her that he was either going to talk, or smile, and her stomach turned. *Please let it be a smile.*

It wasn't.

His voice was deceptively soft as he raked her body with a gaze that was as hot as the temperature outside. "You should be more careful, lady."

Her thoughts were in turmoil. He was telling her to be careful? But it was too late. She had just met her dear-departed mother's worst nightmare–an unsuitable man.

Although she nodded in agreement, she imagined that he was warning her of more than staggering into traffic. As the man finally looked away, she had a sudden vision of what her father would say if he saw her conversing with a total stranger, especially one who looked like this man. And because she knew he would object, she heard herself offering him a ride.

"I see I made you miss your bus. As soon as I get my truck fixed, I'd be glad to give you a lift into the city."

Jackson's restraint shattered. She'd just offered him heaven, and at the same time hell, and he had no idea how to respond except defensively, with the same force that had kept him alive inside the joint. He glared at her.

"If you know what's good for you, lady, you'll get the hell out of my face."

It was hard to say who was more shocked, Jackson for having said it, or Rebecca for being on the receiving end of the undeserved remark.

Her expression froze and her cheeks flushed. Had he known her better, he would have recognized the warning signs by the green fire in her eyes and the thrust of her chin, but he didn't.

"Listen, you jerk! My life may not mean squat to you, but it means a hell of a lot to me. I made a mistake in thinking you were a hero. I don't make the same mistake twice."

She spun on her heel and stomped out of the store before Jackson had time to react. Then he followed her out and saw her slam her fist on the fender of her truck and bury her face against her arm.

His belly rumbled again, but guilt overwhelmed his hunger.

"Damn it," he muttered. He hoped to hell that she was just mad and frustrated, because if she was crying, he was a goner.

The steam spewing from the overflowing radiator was down to a spit and a hiss. Jackson leaned over, staring down inside the guts of the truck, then dropped his bag in the dust near his feet.

"Got a screwdriver and a pair of pliers?"

Startled by his presence, Rebecca looked up. She was still angry with his hostile manner. An apology would have been nice, but she suspected this half-assed offer of help was the only one she was going to get.

Without speaking, she pulled a small toolbox from behind the seat and thrust it into his hands. As he turned away, she stepped up and into the cab, then dropped into the seat wearily. Considering the fact that it wasn't even noon, this had been one hell of a day.

Ignoring her, Jackson selected a couple of tools and leaned under the hood to inspect the engine. A few moments later he spied the missing radiator clamp in the dirt below and went down on his knees, fishing it out of the mud that the spill had made.

Heat radiated from the engine, searing his face and running sweat from every pore. To cool off, he removed his jacket and T-shirt, dropping them carelessly on top of his bag, before going back to his work.

Rebecca was in the midst of her third silent recitation of the Ten Commandments, which had been her punishment as a child for losing her temper. Although her father no longer had direct control of her life, the habit had stuck.

Right in the middle of *Thou shall not covet,* the stranger appeared at the open door on the driver's side. Rebecca glanced at the bag and clothes in his hands, and then focused upon his broad, bare chest. At that moment, she realized she was breaking the very commandment she'd just recited.

He was hard and lean, and the urge to touch him almost overwhelmed her. But the look on his face was warning enough to do nothing but get out of his way.

"If you'll steer, I'll push your pickup closer to the pumps so we can fill the radiator back up."

Rebecca's eyes widened. "You mean you fixed it?"

"We'll see. Take the wheel, lady."

"Rebecca."

He knew he shouldn't, but he couldn't quit staring; memorizing her upturned nose, a heart-shaped face, and the gouges in her cheeks that he suspected were dimples, then counting exactly five tiny gold freckles across the bridge of her nose. He was sorely tempted to touch her face to see if the skin was as soft as it looked, but instead he handed her his belongings.

When she dropped the duffel bag into the seat beside her, she was surprised. Then she swung her legs inside and gripped the steering wheel with both hands.

She looked into her rearview mirror, watching as he positioned himself at the back of the truck and awaiting his order. But when he centered his hands in the middle of the tailgate, she forgot what she was supposed to do. His muscles bunching in his arms and across his chest were more fascinating than the gas pumps directly in front of her.

When he lowered his head and started to push, she finally focused her attention on the business at hand, aiming for the water hose dangling from the post. Slowly, but surely, the pickup started to move.

When he shouted, "That's good!" she braked automatically. Then he yelled, "Pop the hood," and she obliged.

But she jumped out of the truck and beat him to the pump. She had the water hose in one hand, and was struggling with the radiator cap when he reached over her shoulder, removing it with an easy twist.

Dodging the water running between their feet, he pulled the hose from her hands and poked it into the radiator as he shoved her aside. "You're making a hell of a mess," he muttered.

Rebecca hated to be wrong. And she hated it even more when someone felt the need to point out that fact. But when he stepped in front of her, the scathing remark she'd been about to make died on her lips. In that moment, she saw something so shocking that, for a heartbeat, she forgot to breathe.

His back was broad and strong and evenly muscled to the point of perfection. But it wasn't the shape of his body that caught her attention, it was the scars. They cut the symmetry of his shoulders in hellish, intermittent patterns. Some were perpendicular, some horizontal. Some even crisscrossed the others, almost like a wild man's version of ticktactoe.

Sensing that he would resent her sympathy even more than he had her gratitude, she choked back a gasp and quickly turned away. Her legs were shaking as she slid behind the steering wheel and stared through the windshield at the upraised hood.

Then he slammed it shut, and there was nothing between them but a piece of glass. His face was expressionless, but there was a glimmer of emotion in his eyes that hadn't been there before. For one long minute, they stared at each other. Her fingers curled around the steering wheel as she bit her lips and squinted her eyes to keep from crying although, to save her soul, she didn't know why she should be feeling this way. Suddenly, he broke the tension with an order.

"Start her up!"

She did. The engine grumbled, but it spun and caught on the second turn. Rebecca watched the gauges as everything came on-line, and when the needle on the thermostat registered back in the black, she sighed with relief. Now she could make her delivery.

Lost in thought, she was unaware that he was standing at her window.

"My things?" he asked, pointing toward the bag and clothes.

She thrust them into his hands. Even though his body language said leave me alone, every manner she'd been taught urged her to try just one more time.

"I don't suppose you would accept a . . . ."

He stepped back, then lightly slapped the edge of the window with the flat of his hand.

"Drive carefully, lady," he said softly.

Rebecca glared.

"It's Rebecca!"

She slammed the truck into gear and drove away, telling herself she wouldn't look back, reminding herself that she didn't care that she'd just left a man afoot who'd not only saved her life, but had fixed her truck at no charge. But no sooner had she pulled out onto the highway than she found herself looking up into the rearview mirror.

He was still standing where she'd left him, staring at her pickup with a look on his face that she didn't want to consider. She told herself that she was being foolish. She told herself that she was romanticizing him because he had saved her life. But it didn't help. No matter how hard she tried to make herself believe it was something else, the look on his face was one of such utter loneliness that it made her want to cry.

And because there was no one looking, she did.

The distance from the store to the road that led to his old home was shorter than Jackson remembered, but he walked it with trepidation. By all rights, the trailer should not still be standing. Yet when he turned the last curve in the road, then stopped at a broken-down gate that was the entrance to an overgrown driveway, he started to shake.

It was there! Way back in the trees and nearly covered in kudzu vines. All but obliterated by waist-high swamp grasses. Just like a bad memory that won't go away, the rusting, rectangular can that had once been their home had withstood the forces of time.

Jackson considered walking through the grass and kudzu to get to the trailer, and then quickly discarded the notion. It would be stupid to spend fifteen years behind bars and then die of a snakebite on his first day out just to visit his father's ghost.

"Maybe another day, Stanton, you son of a bitch."

His curiosity had been satisfied, but an oppressive weariness came upon him as he turned away. Stanton Rule had abused his wife until she died, and then turned his anger upon his children. Jackson had no remorse for what he'd done, nor would he ever be sorry that Stanton Rule was dead.

Then Jackson's thoughts turned to Molly, and he started out toward New Orleans the same way he'd come in, one foot in front of another. There he would find himself a new life, and resurrect what was left of hers.

Only once did he let himself think of the redheaded woman he'd just met, and only for a moment. Jackson Rule had not survived Angola State Penitentiary by being a dreamer.

When he finally reached the city, it was long after dark. He took a good hard look at the street to which he'd been directed, and knew that if he was going to stay alive, he would have to use the mind-set he'd learned in prison: keep to yourself and trust no one.

Somewhere a few blocks over, he heard a woman's shrill scream, and then the sounds of loud, angry voices. In the distance behind him, a car backfired, and he spun without thinking, imagining that it was gunfire, knowing that the next time it very well could be.

His stride lengthened as he walked down the block, and when he came to 1313 Solange, he entered without hesitation. Walls, no matter how thin, were better than being out in the open alone. Especially down here.

The first door to his right bore five of the seven letters that should have read *Manager*. That they read *Man ge* instead, made him smile. It *was* a mangy place.

He knocked.

Fifteen minutes later, Jackson Rule had something he hadn't had in years. An address.

It wasn't much. Four bare walls and a floor that matched. A bathtub that was more gray than white, and a shower that dripped. But the toilet flushed, and the refrigerator in the other room worked. A small television opposite a run-down easy chair was the entertainment portion of his new abode. The dim glow from the light of a single lamp beside a narrow twin bed could not disguise the dinginess, but in Jackson's mind it was fine. It was a damn sight bigger than a 9 x 12 cell . . . and he didn't have to share it.

"I'll take it," he said, handing the manager a twenty-dollar bill. He started to close the door when the man abruptly stuck his shoe in the crack.

"That's only good for two nights," he warned.

Jackson shut the door in his face and then locked it. Ignoring the growl in his belly, he crawled into bed without undressing.

The next thing he knew it was morning.

2

Jackson sat in the back of a small café, unmindful of the loud chatter of the other customers, or the sun streaming across his table and into his eyes. His entire focus was upon the food the waitress was putting before him. The warm scent of the deep-fried fritters was enticing, and when he lifted one to his mouth and took the first bite, a light dusting of powdered sugar sifted from the fritter to the table. Beignets. He'd dreamed of them for years. As the taste rolled across his tongue, he groaned with satisfaction.

"Good, aren't they, cher?"

The waitress's grin was as wide as her hips, but at the moment Jackson noticed neither. All he could do was nod in agreement as he took another bite.

For Jackson, it seemed strange to be making choices. The last time he'd been free, he'd been too young to vote and too young to buy beer. Knowing that he could now make his own choices was empowering, when before, his days and nights had been controlled by the state of Louisiana.

As he absorbed the busy street scene beyond the café, he thought of the nightmares that he'd had for weeks before his release. Of getting to the last day of his sentence, only to have someone tell him they'd made a mistake, and that he had to serve it all over again.

He took a deep breath and tried to relax, reminding himself that things were getting better. He had a room of his own and control of his life. And then he thought of Molly. In his haste to get on with his plans, he practically inhaled the last three beignets on his plate and washed them down with a large cup of steaming coffee.

When he went back onto the street, he didn't know whether the satisfaction he felt came from a full belly, or just the simple fact that he could walk out that door, or any other, anytime he chose. Never again would he allow himself to be locked up. He would die first.

Live oaks, thick with Spanish moss, shaded most of the sidewalks within the city. Jackson drew a deep breath, tasting, as well as smelling, the damp river air that came from the great Mississippi. Traffic was thick in the narrow streets and the noise level from long-forgotten sounds was overwhelming.

Laughter filtering out of an open doorway.

The loud blast of a horn from an impatient taxi driver.

The water trickling from the fountain in the square.

A child crying.

It was so unlike the world he'd just left that, for a moment, Jackson could almost imagine himself in a foreign city, struggling to understand an unfamiliar language. Then a crowd of young men came toward him five abreast, sweeping the sidewalk with their presence, and moving everyone and everything aside as they passed. Jackson didn't move from his place against the wall, and with the rude arrogance of youth, the young man closest to him would not sway from his own path.

Inevitably, they bumped.

The young man glared and then cursed. Jackson took a long look at the faint whisker stubble on the kid's cheeks and the loose, baggy clothes he wore and then smiled. The boy obviously thought he was tough, but Jackson had come from a place that would eat that kid alive within a week. He didn't even acknowledge the youth's glare, and because he ignored the group, they moved on in a jittery pack.

Jackson resumed his walk. The sun warmed his back, but the stiffness of his new jeans chafed his thighs. He took a look at himself as he passed by a window and frowned. There was something else he had to do. He began searching the stores he passed until he found the one he wanted.

It was a secondhand clothing store called Once Around The Block. Jackson entered, then stood at the doorway as his eyes adjusted to the dim light.

"Somethin' I can do for you, sir?"

The soft, melodic voice of the dark-skinned woman behind the counter drew Jackson farther inside.

"Do you buy clothes?" he asked.

She nodded.

"What would you give me for these?" he asked, then stood back to let her get a full view of his new jeans, denim jacket, and the stiff, brown boots.

"What for you wanna be sellin' your clothes?" she asked, unable to mask her astonishment.

The smile on his face never reached his eyes. "Let's just say they're not me."

The woman shrugged, then waved her arm toward the stacks and racks. "I take it you wanna trade," she said. "Just walk on back and pick out what you like. Then we'll talk."

It didn't take him long. When Jackson exited, his step was fifteen years lighter. He'd just shed the last of his link with Angola.

The jeans he had chosen were faded to near-white and moved with him, not against him. He'd traded the white T-shirt for an old dark blue one that mirrored the same deep color of his eyes, although he had not chosen it for that reason, but rather for the Mardi Gras graphics on the front. The new denim jacket had been replaced by an older version of the same, and one step after the other, his Justin boots took him farther from his past and deeper into his future. It didn't matter to Jackson that the boots were scuffed and worn. So was he.

He walked like a man with a purpose, which in fact he was. And after asking directions twice, he finally turned a corner and came face-to-face with an imposing white structure of marble and granite that proclaimed itself to be the First State Bank of Louisiana.

Jackson took a deep breath and ran a hand through his hair, absently pushing the thick, black length away from his face. Then he started up the steps.

"My goodness, but you've had this a long time," the teller said, as he eyed the old bankbook Jackson handed over. "And I see you haven't made a deposit in years. It's just been sitting here accruing interest. Where on earth have you been, out of the country?"

Jackson's smile never reached his eyes. "You could say that."

"So, do you want to withdraw it, sir?"

"Only a couple of hundred," he said. "I want the rest transferred into a checking account."

The teller nodded. "If you'll just fill out this form, including your new address, your new checks will be mailed to you, and check here if you want an ATM card. I see you never had one before."

Jackson started to write. He had a lot to catch up on. And the irony of all this did not escape him. When he'd opened this account at the age of fourteen, he had expected to use it one day for college, or maybe for his first car. Certainly not to get him back on his feet after doing time.

Thanks to correspondence courses in prison, he had a high school diploma and several semesters of college credits to his name, but he feared that in the long run they would do him little good. An ex-con was an ex-con, no matter how well educated.

A short time later, he exited the bank a slightly solvent man, albeit an unemployed one. Finding a job was going to be the task that tried his endurance.

With a newspaper in hand, he headed for the shade of a park bench, and by the time an hour had passed, Jackson had read every want ad twice, only to come to the same conclusion. Even if someone had the guts to give him a chance, he had no experience and very few skills that would land him a job. He sighed. Another hurdle to overcome.

But in spite of his determination to get his life back on track, he was taking first things first, and seeing Molly came before finding a job. After asking directions to Azalea Home, he went half of the way on foot, and then got lucky and finished the trip on the tailgate of a fisherman's pickup.

For years, he'd dreamed of coming for Molly, and now that the time had come, it had been easier than he'd imagined. He was here . . . and yet he wasn't. Getting permission to be admitted at the front gates had taken more time than the entire trip out. By the time Dr. Michael Franco had been located, and instructed the guard to let Jackson in, he'd wasted nearly half an hour. And when the gates swung open and then clanked shut behind him, Jackson had a terrifying sensation of déjà vu. He had to make himself remember that he could leave here anytime he chose, that *he* wasn't the one incarcerated, although he suspected there were many similarities between these inmates and those he'd known in jail. A lost soul was a lost soul, no matter where it was housed.

After being ushered through the halls by an orderly, he found himself inside Dr. Franco's office, waiting for him to appear.

The doctor wasn't long in coming.

Jackson stood, facing the door as it opened. Habit forbade him to let anyone walk up behind him unannounced.

"Dr. Franco?"

The small man nodded, and then broke into a smile, crinkling the neat dark mustache above his upper lip. "You must be A. J.," he said. "You and Molly have the same eyes, you know."

The mention of his sister's name, as well as the nickname that only she used, made him relax.

"Welcome to Azalea Hospice," Dr. Franco said, waved for Jackson to take a seat, then sat down in his own chair behind the desk.

"So, A. J., we finally meet."

"If you don't mind, Doc, I'd just as soon answer to Jackson. Molly is the only person who calls me A. J."

Dr. Franco nodded, letting a smile hide his quick assessment of Molly Rule's brother. He knew where Jackson Rule had been. He knew what he had done. But Michael Franco did not judge, he healed. And he hoped that this man had healed enough to help his patient, because he couldn't, though Lord knew he had tried.

"How is she doing, Doc?"

"As a beautiful, thirty-five-year-old woman, she's physically fine. But, mentally, she's locked in some never-never land that does not exist. As you know, I came on her case after my arrival at Azalea Hospice seven years ago. She is my Waterloo. She smiles. She laughs. Sometimes she even cries. But never about anything pertinent. It's as if her life began with her arrival here. She has no memory of anything or anyone from her past . . . except you."

Jackson's heart dropped. The news was always the same. "Does she know I'm out?"

Dr. Franco sighed. "She doesn't even know where you've been. When she mentions your name, it's as if she expects you to return from school any moment, or from some place called Wally's."

"Damn," Jackson muttered. "That's the grocery store I worked at when I was fourteen."

"I suspected as much."

But there was one more thing Jackson needed to know before he could proceed. He took a slow breath, and then spit out the question before he changed his mind.

"Does she ever ask about our . . . uh . . . "

"Your father?"

Jackson's expression never wavered as he nodded.

"Never."

Jackson sighed. He'd expected as much.

Dr. Franco leaned forward across the desk. "You came to see her, I assume?"

"I want to see her more than anything on this earth, but there may be a problem in that, Doc."

Franco's thoughts were in turmoil. He suspected that there was much more going on with these two siblings than was visible on the surface, but if Jackson Rule was as impenetrable as his sister, it might prove impossible to discern.

"How so?" Franco asked.

"Things have changed. I have changed. I don't look like a kid anymore. I look like a man." Jackson shuddered, then went on. "What I'm trying to say is . . . I look like my goddamned father. The last time she saw this face, he was wearing it. I don't want to make things worse by showing up like some ghost from the past."

"I see."

Franco's remark was noncommittal, as he realized that Jackson's revelation opened up a whole new set of problems. The shock of seeing her brother like this could trigger a recurrence of unresolved emotions that might be healthy. On the other hand, it could set Molly Rule so far back inside herself that she could become lost forever.

"What do you think, Doc?" Jackson asked, and then knew from the expression on the man's face that he wasn't going to see his sister today.

"I think that you might be the most caring brother I've ever met," he said quietly. "Few people would consider another's feelings over their own. I know from your letters how close you two were. I suspect that her presence in your life helped you get through doing time, am I right?"

Jackson managed to nod.

"I think that after what you've revealed, we need to take some time with the first meeting. I want to try to lay the groundwork with Molly before we proceed."

Jackson slumped with disappointment, but in his heart he'd known from the start that this would be the case.

"Where are you staying?" Franco asked.

Jackson scribbled an address and then slid the paper across the desk.

"Here for now," he said. "And I don't have a phone—or a job—but I will. If I move, I'll let you know."

Dr. Franco nodded. "Fair enough," he said. "And you have our number. Call anytime. I'll let you know how things are proceeding, is that okay?"

"It'll have to be, won't it, Doc?"

Fifteen minutes later, Jackson was standing on the outside looking in as the metal gates swung shut with a clank. The only satisfaction he'd come away with was hearing the doctor tell the guard to admit him anytime he chose to come.

It was a long walk back into New Orleans, but Jackson didn't care. He had too much on his mind to worry about physical distances. It was the emotional distances that threatened to bring him and Molly down.

The ensuing three days were vicious, trying every ounce of patience Jackson had. Part of him acknowledged that there could be truth in rejection, but it was the other times that let him know how serious his situation was going to be. He'd known it would not be easy to get a job. But there is no way a man can prepare for the constant rejection that Jackson suffered.

The first job he'd applied for was simple. Delivering fresh produce to local groceries and restaurants.

"Got a driver's license?" the manager had asked. Jackson shook his head and set about rectifying that lack. But when he returned five hours later to reapply, the manager was the one to shake his head. "Sorry," he said, "the job has been filled."

The next seven jobs he applied for required less skill and brainpower than the delivery job. But each time they got to the question of where he'd worked last, the answer had turned each employer off like a light. No one wanted an ex-con.

Each night, he went back to his rooms feeling like a failure. The bitter lines around his mouth grew deeper, and he began to wonder if he was fooling himself by thinking he could ever regain a firm foothold in normal society. But then he would think of Molly and get up the next morning, ready to try again.

It was nearing noon nearly a week later when he passed by a junk shop that promised to have one of everything for sale. Jackson wondered if that meant jobs, too, and then looked more closely at the upheaval of goods for sale in the yard. A glitter of sunshine against chrome caught his eye.

The old Harley wasn't exactly on its last wheels, but it, like Jackson, had seen better days. As he squatted down to get a closer look, the owner came out, sensing a sale.

"Does it run?" Jackson asked.

"Like a charm," the owner replied.

Jackson squinted up against the sun and grinned. "Do I really look that dumb?"

"Well, it started last time I tried it, which was . . . oh, maybe two or three weeks ago."

"Got a key?" Jackson asked.

The man had come prepared. He fished one out of his pocket.

"Needs some gas," Jackson said.

The owner frowned and hitched his pants over his bulging belly. "Damn neighborhood kids. They're always siphoning off my fuel."

"I'll wait," Jackson said, and stood up.

The owner hustled back inside and came out minutes later carrying a small can. As he filled the Harley, the scent of gas was strong in the air, and vapor from the fumes danced between the men like a mirage. But when Jackson swung a long leg over the dusty saddle, kicked back the stand, and turned the key, there was nothing fake about the rumble, or the spit and roar of the engine as it came to life.

"Take it for a spin. But only around the block," the owner amended.

Twice as Jackson circled the block it coughed and died, but each time he managed to start it up again. When he turned the corner to head back to the junkyard, his heart was racing faster than the engine. By God, he wanted this bike. With the wind in his hair and the broken white lines on the pavement below running into one single streak, he knew he'd come into his own. Riding this bike gave him the feeling he'd been missing. Now he truly felt free.

Jackson pulled into the yard, feeling as if he'd never wanted anything as much in his life as he wanted the Harley. He was ready to negotiate.

"What do you want for it?" he asked.

"Five hundred."

Jackson snorted, and tossed the keys toward the old man. "Lord have mercy, if it means that much to you, then you keep it. It's not worth half that, and we both know it." He started to walk away.

"Wait!" the man shouted.

Jackson paused and turned. "Yeah?"

"What would you give me?"

"Two."

"Two hundred? Two hundred dollars for a Harley? You've got to be kidding!"

"Nope," Jackson said softly, and kept on walking.

"Two-fifty," the old man called after him.

Jackson shook his head and stuffed his hands in his pockets.

The old man sighed. He knew a hard-ass when he saw one, and this man was as bullheaded as they came.

"Fine. It's yours for two hundred dollars."

"I want the title and a bill of sale," Jackson said.

The old man rolled his eyes. "I don't take checks," he grumbled.

Jackson grinned. "Neither do I."

That night in his apartment, Jackson slept with the scent of gasoline and grease for a bed partner as the bike rested against the living room wall near the door. But the smell was not enough to make him regret the purchase. It was, after all, the honest flavor of his first personal belonging, and it was to become the spark that changed his life.

Rebecca's hair was flying as she made a run for the wall phone mounted beneath the porch of Hillside Greenhouse and Nursery. Breathless from her sprint, she slumped against the wall, trying to talk without gasping.

"Hillside Nursery, Rebecca speaking."

"Rebecca Ruth, you are wheezing. Are you ill?"

She rolled her eyes and dropped into a wicker chair beneath an arbor of budding bougainvillea.

"Hello, Daddy. No, I'm not ill, I was loading some bedding plants for a customer. I had to run to get to the phone."

She heard his snort of disapproval. In Reverend Daniel Hill's eyes, ladies not only did not do manual labor, they did not run to do anything, let alone answer a phone. She decided to get him back on course before he could deliver another one of his lectures that went in one of her ears and out the other.

"Did you need something, Daddy?"

"Oh! Yes! I called to tell you that we're having a potluck supper at church tomorrow night, and I wanted you to bring that casserole your mother always made."

Rebecca sighed. Here came another fight.

"I'm sorry, Daddy, but I can't."

"Well, never mind then, bring whatever you choose. At any rate, there's someone I want you to meet."

Ah! Rebecca thought. *The crux of this call—another matchmaking stunt.*

"No, Daddy, you don't understand. It's not that I can't bring the casserole. I can't come at all. I have to work. End of the month statements and payroll, remember?"

This time, Daniel Hill made no pretense of hiding his disapproval.

"I know you pride yourself on doing your own thing, Rebecca. You always have. But can't you hire an accountant and simply be what you are . . . which is the boss?"

Rebecca sighed. "That's just it, Daddy. Because I am the boss, I am responsible for everything. And until the nursery starts making a bigger profit, I do what I have to. Besides, I love my work. I like seeing things grow. Just like Mother, remember?"

"Then hire some extra help. Surely you can afford that," he grumbled.

"I've been running a want ad for a week and a half. No one's showed up yet that's been worth their salt. Unless . . ." Her eyes twinkled, and she bit her lip to keep from giggling. " . . . unless you know some unattached, single, white male who's desperate for a job and would be willing to date me as an added benefit?"

"That's not funny, Rebecca."

"Your matchmaking certainly is. The last man you introduced me to turned out to be married."

Daniel flushed. That faux pas still rankled. "Okay, fine, I get the point! But you can't blame me for wanting what's best for you."

Rebecca wanted to scream. "That's just it, Daddy. You can't choose what's best for me. Not any longer. I'm twenty-nine years old. If I want a man, I'll find one . . . by myself. Okay?"

The sound of someone pulling into the driveway was her ticket out of this conversation.

"Daddy, I've got to go. More customers. I'll talk to you soon, okay?"

"Whatever," he grumbled. "Take care of yourself, and I'll see you in church Sunday."

The line went dead in her ear. As always, her father had gotten in the last word, and an order, all in the same breath.

She slammed the phone back on the cradle and darted into the office to wash up before facing a customer. Because she was in a hurry, she didn't see the long-legged biker in the act of parking an old Harley beneath the twin magnolias that flanked her front door.

Even if she had, there was no guarantee she would have recognized him as the man who'd fixed her truck and saved her life. There was nothing left of the wary man in stiff new denim. This man's chin was thrust out at the world, and he all but swaggered when he walked. And this man didn't look lost; he looked dangerous.

3

The bell over the front door jingled, and moments later a man's deep voice called out, "Anybody here?"

"Be with you in a minute," Rebecca shouted, as water ran down her elbows and onto the floor. When the paper towels in the dispenser tore in half in her hands, she groaned and instead used the backside of her blue jeans to finish the job as she hurried out to greet her customer.

"What can I do for . . . ?"

The question died on her lips.

"I came to apply for the . . . "

Jackson was so stunned to see the same redhead from the country store that he couldn't remember what he'd been about to say.

They stared at each other from across the room, then both said in unison, "You!"

Jackson was the first to regain control of his emotions. All he could think was that he'd hit another brick wall before he'd even started. It was a safe bet that this woman wouldn't hire him. Not if she knew the truth.

Rebecca took a deep breath, and when she absently swiped at wayward curls dangling near her eyes, she realized that her hands were shaking.

"Did I understand you to say that you came about the job?"

Jackson's mouth firmed. He could either walk out without trying, or spill his guts to this woman, which, at the moment, seemed impossible. And then he thought of Molly and relented. This woman meant nothing to him. Molly was all that mattered.

His head tilted up. "Yes. I came about the job."

"Do you have a driver's license?" Rebecca asked.

He nodded.

"Good," she said, and began digging through the top drawer on her desk. "Here's an application. Fill it out, and then we'll talk, okay?"

Jackson's gaze was fixed upon Rebecca's face. He took the paper from her without looking at it, then all but wadded it in his fist as he tried to find a way to say what had to be said without stripping away what was left of his dignity.

"Maybe we better talk first and save us both some time."

Something in his voice gave Rebecca the urge to run, but because she was boss, she stood her ground.

"I thought you wanted a job."

When her assistant manager, Pete Walters, walked into the room, she hated herself for the relief she felt. *Now I am safe,* she thought, and then wondered where that had come from.

Pete grinned as he scratched at the sparse gray hair on his round and balding head. "Sorry, Rebecca, I didn't know you had a customer. I was coming to ask what you wanted for lunch. I'm going to make a run into the city. Thought I'd bring us both something back."

"Thanks, Pete, but this fellow's not a customer. He's applying for a job."

Pete sized the man up in one swift glance, noting his muscular strength and size with approval. "Been needing the extra help," he said. "Got any greenhouse or landscape experience?"

Jackson shook his head.

Pete cast a quick, but telling, glance at Rebecca.

"Where did you work last?" she asked.

"Angola."

Pete grinned. "I've got relatives in Angola. By any chance do you know Huey and Macie Walters? He runs the . . . "

Rebecca was not prepared for the distant expression that froze the man's features as he interrupted Pete.

"The penitentiary, not the town."

Startled into silence, there was little Pete could think of to say. He tried to find a way back to the conversation.

"So . . . did you work as a guard or . . . ?"

"Inmate."

Rebecca's legs gave way and she collapsed into the chair behind her.

Pete frowned and then took a deep breath, puffing his chest. "Well now," he began, when Rebecca started talking.

"So, uh . . . you're a, I mean you've been . . . "

"Look, lady, the word is . . . ex-con."

Rebecca absently corrected him, just as she had on the day he'd saved her life.

"Rebecca. The name's Rebecca, remember?"

It was nearly unnoticeable, but the bitter expression on his face shifted slightly as he shrugged.

"You two know each other?" Walters asked.

"This is the man who saved my life last week . . . and fixed the truck."

"Well, I'll be damned," Pete said.

"So you want a job Mr., uh . . . ?" Rebecca suddenly realized that after all the history between them, she still did not know his name.

"Rule. Jackson Rule."

Rebecca nodded, and tried not to stare, but it was impossible to ignore the underlying rage that seemed to be a part of him.

"You still need to fill out the application for withholding purposes, Mr. Rule."

"Rebecca!" Pete cried. "You're not gonna . . . "

The look she gave him was all the warning Pete was going to get. He cursed beneath his breath, and stuffed his hands in his pockets to keep from throttling the woman. In all his life, he'd never known a more hardheaded female.

When it was evident that no more arguments were forthcoming, Jackson took a seat and started to fill out the application. His hands were shaking and his pulse was racing. If he wasn't mistaken, he was about to get himself hired. He couldn't quit thinking . . . *Molly, honey, we're on our way.*

Rebecca leaned back in her chair, blatantly ignoring Pete, who was glaring at her from across the room. She hated being told what to do. And she hated prejudice of any kind.

Because of an ingrained reluctance to meddle in other people's lives, she was a bit surprised at herself when she felt the urge to question him further. Maybe it was a combination of nerves and curiosity. Maybe it was her inner voice warning her that she was about to make the biggest mistake of her life. Before she thought to quell the urge, the words spilled out.

"Mr. Rule . . . "

"Jackson."

"Jackson," she amended. "I was wondering . . . "

His hand paused above the application. *Here it comes. She's going to reconsider, and I'm out on my ass.*

"Yes, ma'am?"

"What exactly was your crime?"

Jesus! This kicks it. But he wasn't going to lie.

"I killed a man."

Pete jerked, accidentally bumping into the chair at his back while Rebecca stared at a single muscle jumping near Jackson's jaw.

"I see."

She gripped the pen she was holding until her fingers turned white. *Say it now*, she urged herself. *Don't let this go any further. Get yourself out of the mess you've created before it's too late.*

But Rebecca Hill had been running on her own set of rules her entire life, and nothing could stop her from asking the unforgivable question.

"Uh . . . exactly who were you accused of killing?"

Every muscle in Jackson's body went still, while rage flared deep in his eyes. His nostrils flared, and he spit out the answer in a short, angry breath.

"My father."

Rebecca reeled. An image of her own father's face flashed through her mind, and then she suddenly thought of the scars on Jackson Rule's back.

"Did you do it?"

Pete couldn't stay quiet any longer.

"Damn it, Rebecca, drop it and let him go!"

Jackson heard the fear in the man's voice, but his gaze remained fixed upon Rebecca Hill, watching for the first signs of disgust that usually signaled his dismissal. When he realized she was still waiting for an answer, he almost smiled. She might be lacking in good sense, but she had a hell of a lot of class.

"Yes, ma'am, I did."

Shock suffused her, and for a moment she couldn't have formed a word to save her soul. And then she remembered an old phrase her father quoted religiously. "Never judge a man until you've walked a mile in his shoes."

It was that single thought that gave her the guts to speak.

"If you've finished filling out the form, Pete will show you around the place. I hope you're not averse to hard work, because that's all there is here. I pay six dollars an hour and payday is every other week. You get Saturday afternoon and Sunday off, as well as an hour for lunch. When can you start?"

Jackson blinked in surprise. He thought she'd been about to show him the door, and here she was issuing orders before he'd signed on the dotted line. His pulse steadied, and the steel in his voice softened.

"Whenever you say."

Rebecca nodded. "Now is good. We have a big shipment of trees due in today. I'd say Pete will be happy for the help. Right, Pete?"

Pete's eyes narrowed, but he'd known Rebecca Hill all of her life, and knew that bucking one of her decisions would prove futile.

"Yeah, we need the help all right. Business has been real good." Then he eyed his new work partner, wondering if he should start carrying a gun.

"Then that's settled," Rebecca said, and jumped up before she could talk herself out of the decision she'd just made. "Oh, and you'll need gloves. Pete will lend you a pair. You two can talk on the way into New Orleans."

Rebecca sensed Pete's reluctance and winked at him. "If you're still buying lunch, I think I'll have a super po'boy and a large anything to drink."

"Lord, deliver me from feminine wiles," he muttered.

Rebecca grinned. "You love me, and you know it. Run on, you two. I've got the place covered until you get back. Besides, I'm suddenly starving."

Jackson thought about smiling. The woman's personality was almost charming, when she wasn't reaming someone out. It would seem that she was impossible to ignore, but ignore her he must. Any hope of having a relationship with a decent woman was, for him, out of the question.

Rebecca turned to get some money for her lunch and sensed Jackson's gaze raking her body. Valiantly, she hid a shudder. But she'd already made her decision, and going back on her word was something Rebecca Hill did not do.

She handed Pete the money for her lunch and then made herself smile at the tall, dark biker.

"You have a good afternoon, Jackson. Quitting time is 5:00 P.M., and we open at eight in the morning. Don't be late, okay?"

"Yes, ma'am," he said softly.

"Rebecca," she corrected, and walked out the side door without looking behind her.

Only after she was yards away from the office did she start to shake. She dropped down onto a stump and buried her face in her hands.

"My sweet Lord, what have I done?"

Quitting time had come and gone, and not until Rebecca heard the roar of the Harley's engine fading as the bike disappeared down the driveway did she relax. He was gone! Now she could quit looking over her shoulder.

Working alongside Pete had always been a part of the job she enjoyed. He was one of her father's oldest friends, and although they were not related, she considered him a loving and trusted confidant. He'd worked for the city of New Orleans until his retirement a few years earlier. Less than two months after Rebecca had opened her greenhouse, Pete came begging for a job, claiming retirement was going to be the cause of his death. He'd been with her ever since. With her love of growing things, and Pete's love of the outdoors, they had a lot in common. But working beside Jackson Rule was going to be a different proposition entirely.

As far as she could tell, they had absolutely nothing in common, and yet his presence had been so overwhelming that when he was at a task, she found herself looking to see where he had gone. Then just when she'd been on the verge of forgetting he was around, he would suddenly appear, taking something out of her hands that he must have thought too heavy for her. Then he would heft it against his chest while waiting for her orders, all the while watching her with those cold blue eyes.

While one day was no guarantee of faithfulness, she could find no fault with the way he worked. There was no stopping him and, it seemed, no tiring him. Even Pete could hardly complain about the man's work, though he felt obligated to remind her about the risk she was taking.

"You may have bit off more than you can chew," he muttered, as he gathered up his things to go home.

She shrugged. He wasn't telling her anything she didn't already know.

"And you know that your daddy is gonna have himself a ring-tailed fit," he added.

Rebecca glared. "Not unless someone sees fit to tattle."

"It wouldn't be tattling, girl, and we both know it. Your old man is like a dog with a bone. He won't let up until he knows the whole story about everyone you come in contact with."

"Oh pooh . . . and that's not entirely true. He can be swayed by a good suit and a stable bank account, remember? I'm not about to let him forget that the last suitor he kept touting turned out to be a married man."

Pete grinned. "Yeah, that did curdle his stomach, didn't it?"

She nodded. "I love my father, but he's overprotective. Not unlike others I know."

Pete flushed, but refused to give ground. "I care for you, girl. I don't want to see you hurt."

"Oh Lord, Pete! Now you're sounding like Daddy. I'm not a girl; I'm a grown woman, and I can take care of myself. Go home. I'll see you tomorrow."

"I'll be here bright and early . . . just in case," he warned, and headed for his car.

She did not try to hide the sarcasm in her voice. "I'm sure that you will!"

And then Pete was gone, and she was finally alone, her head swirling with what ifs and might-have-beens. Finally she sighed, gave herself a mental kick in the pants, and locked the office door before heading for her own home just beyond the stand of trees a little way down the road.

Living near the premises of her own business was convenient, especially at the end of a day like today. Her back ached and her feet burned. Their faithful clientele was good for business, but hard on bodies, and hers was due a long soak in a hot tub. She headed for her car.

°   °   °

Darkness enveloped Solange Street. Jackson had a full belly and itchy feet, and was having a hell of a time trying to sleep. He missed not having anything to read and made a mental note to himself to rectify the situation tomorrow. The urge to walk the streets of New Orleans was almost irresistible. The walls of his apartment were drawing in around him. While the need to test his newfound independence was strong, his will was stronger. He had to remember his responsibilities. His new job . . . and Molly.

So he flopped from his side to his back, shifting upon the mess he'd made of the sheet and blanket, trying to find a more comfortable position. People of the night were thick on the sidewalk beyond his bedroom window, and the couple who lived in the room next door to his was driving him mad. He didn't know which was getting to him worse, the laughter and the occasional quarrel outside, or the groans and sighs coupled with the squeak of bedsprings from the bedroom on the opposite wall, as the lovers made use of their time together in an age-old tradition.

"Son of a bitch," Jackson groaned, thinking of soft women with sweet-smelling bodies and capable hands.

He crawled out of bed, leaving a tangle of sheets and pillows to fall where they might and staggered to the window, parting the curtains, then standing in the shadows to hide his nudity while watching the prostitutes on the corner plying their wares. His groin ached with longing.

The memory of his fifteenth birthday and an older and obliging woman who'd lived in a trailer near theirs came swiftly, along with the lessons that she had taught him. By the time he'd reached sixteen, Jackson had been well versed in the ways of making love.

He swiped shaky hands across his face as he turned away from the window, well aware he didn't need to be thinking about screwing some whore just to get a release. He'd learned the hard way how to do without.

Even though long legs and short skirts were enticing, especially to a man who'd been where he'd been, Jackson's lust was tempered by the men he'd known in prison who had died from AIDS. The memory of their pained faces and rotting bodies was enough to cool the hottest of blood, especially knowing that he was unprepared, from a safety as well as a mental standpoint, to crawl into a female's bed. Going out and jumping the first willing woman's bones wasn't going to get his—or Molly's—life back in order. And Jackson had paid too dearly to mess up just when things could be going his way.

He headed to the old refrigerator in the corner of the room. The low rattle and hum of its motor was comforting—another noise to live with other than the sounds of his own breathing.

He opened the door and leaned in, peering through the darkness, trying to distinguish the cold bottle of soda from the tall bottle of ketchup.

"I've got to remember to get a lightbulb for this thing," he said, as he pulled out the two-liter bottle of Pepsi.

Unscrewing the cap, he tilted the bottle to his mouth for want of a glass. The cold, carbonated drink went down fast, burning his throat, as well as the back of his nose, and bringing tears to his eyes. Yet he sighed with relief when the liquid hit his stomach. It gave his body something to think about besides sex. Forgoing a second swig, he screwed the cap back on the bottle and replaced it on the shelf. The door swung shut with a soft thump as he went back to bed.

In spite of the window air conditioner, the apartment was hot, almost stifling. The unit obviously needed some sort of repair. All it did was stir the air inside the room without cooling it.

Jackson rolled over onto his belly and hammered the pillow into a comfortable lump, then dropped his head with a weary sigh. The day had been grueling, but also the most satisfying one in a long, long time. Today he had taken a step up and out of obscurity.

Soon he began to relax, and sometime later he finally fell asleep.

The dream. It always came when he was at his weakest. When his back was turned and his eyes were closed. When his body was at rest and his conscious mind asleep.

The sound of sirens was coming closer, breaking the silence of a Louisiana night, and still it did not drown out the sound of Molly's screams.

Blood dripped. From his hands. From what was left of his father's face. The cocky smile and handsome face that had been Stanton Rule was splattered in bits and pieces on the wall and on the couch where he'd been reclining. A nearly full bottle of beer lay spilled and soaking into the green shag carpet at Jackson's feet.

"It's over, you son of a bitch. Never! Never again."

And then there was the sound of running feet, and the police burst into the trailer, guns drawn, shouting at the top of their lungs. Jackson turned, as if in slow motion. Blood covered his face and hands and ran down his arms as he staggered, then stretched them toward the ceiling.

"What the hell happened here, boy?"

"You said it, Sheriff. Hell happened. But it's damn sure over."

The lawman looked down at what was left of Stanton Rule. Even though it was obvious the boy had been beaten nearly to death, he couldn't help but gasp.

"My God, boy, what have you done?"

"I shot the devil."

"That's no devil, that's your daddy. How could you do something like that?"

Jackson's eyes turned cold as the second bracelet on the handcuffs snapped around his wrist.

"It was easy. I just pulled the trigger."

And then everyone got quiet. Even Molly's screams stopped in the middle of a gasp. As she fainted, the lawmen scrambled to catch her before she fell in the puddle of her father's blood.

Jackson woke with a groan. It was always the same. His

memories of the trial and the days that came after were always a blur. For Jackson Rule, his own life had ended the night his father had drawn his last breath.

He rolled over and then sat on the side of the bed, staring down at his hands, imagining that he could still see the blood, then cursing himself for being so weak.

With little more than a sigh, he pushed himself out of bed and headed for the shower. By the time he emerged, day was beginning to break. He pushed the Harley out of his apartment and onto the sidewalk, then threw a leg over and settled on the seat, bracing the big bike with his outstretched legs as he took a deep breath of fresh air.

His belly grumbled, reminding him that breakfast was a near necessity, and with the assurance of a man who knew where he was going, he reached down and turned the key.

The engine kicked over like a charm, and Jackson's belly settled. It was a good sign, he thought, that everything, including the engine on his bike, was running smoothly for a change. He shifted gears, then guided the Harley through the early morning traffic, feeling a sense of release as the first gust of wind caught the hair hanging out from under his helmet and lifted it off his neck.

It was 7:35 A.M. Rebecca was deep in compost and potting soil, with a garden hose in one hand and a pair of gloves in the other. The sun was up and already warming her face, and the birds in the surrounding trees were chirping madly in spite of the traffic whizzing by on the highway beyond the fence. Droplets of water spewed upward from the steady stream pouring from the hose, dotting her bare legs, as well as the tops of her tennis shoes, but she didn't care. It felt good to be cool, and in her job, that was a rarity.

Then suddenly the birds in the tree above her head took flight. Rebecca jumped from the unexpected noise, then spun, unintentionally showering more than her work with a wide

spray of water as the deep, angry grumble of an idling motorcycle engine broke the morning ambience.

He's here!

In the back of her mind she'd thought he might not return.
She dropped the hose and turned off the water, then, when he
started toward her, she suddenly wished she'd kept it in her
hands. At least she would have had something to do with them.

"Good morning, Jackson. You're early."

"Yes, ma'am."

Once again, she corrected him.

"Rebecca."

Jackson looked at her, from her upturned nose and the
freckles he knew were there, to the slim, tan arms and legs
peppered with water. She glittered in the sunshine.

"Tinker Bell."

Rebecca's mouth dropped open, and she wondered if he
were drunk. "Excuse me?"

Jackson smiled. Only a little, but it was enough to change
his face completely. It went at once from forbidding to appeal-
ing, and Rebecca caught herself staring at the sensuous cut of
his lower lip.

Jackson shrugged. "Sorry. I guess I was thinking out loud.
You're not all that tall, you know, and from here, you sort
of . . . uh, sparkle. It reminded me of . . . "

"Tinker Bell," Rebecca said, feeling an odd sense of relief.
Suddenly she got the joke. He wasn't drunk. He wasn't crazy.
But his vivid imagination was unexpected.

He continued to stare, seemingly mesmerized by the sight
of her. But when Rebecca moved, he looked away, as if realizing that their conversation was too familiar for one between
boss and employee.

Rebecca watched the light die in his eyes and felt a wall go
back up between them. She sighed. It was just as well. She
had no business becoming personally involved in her employees' lives, especially this one's, no matter how innocent it
might seem.

"Sorry, ma'am . . . uh . . . I mean, Rebecca. Where do you want me to start?"

Her smile was bright and cheerful, but in her heart she felt a funny ache as she turned and pointed toward the far lot, where Pete was working.

"Out there, I guess. Pete is balling some trees we need to deliver, and it's at least a two-man job."

He started past her.

"Oh! Jackson!"

He stopped, then turned, as always, waiting for someone else to speak first.

"I see you brought gloves, but you'll need a pair of heavy-duty work gloves for this job. Take mine. I'll pick up another pair in the office."

Jackson took what she offered, and long after she had disappeared around the building, he was still there, staring at the supple leather gloves she'd laid in his hands.

It was simple really. All he had to do was part the cuff and slip his hand inside. But the image of sliding somewhere else inside that woman wouldn't go away.

"Get the hell over this, you stupid bastard," he muttered, and jabbed his hands inside the leather, instinctively sliding fingers into the proper slots, promising himself all the while that tonight he was going to get himself a woman.

But when his hands settled inside the gloves and the lingering warmth of Rebecca moved from her to him, he shuddered, then headed for the back lot where Pete was working.

She might look like Tinker Bell, but he was damn sure no Peter Pan.

4

After a week and a half on the job, Rebecca and Pete were wondering how they had ever managed without Jackson. His willing nature and strong back had become indispensable. And, to their surprise, the customers liked him. He was helpful, quiet, and quick.

No one, including Rebecca, really knew what went on inside Jackson's mind. In her presence he was all but mute, and yet more than once she felt him watching her intently when he thought she wasn't looking. His contribution to conversations came only when necessary, and the rest of the time he left the talking up to Pete. It should have suited Rebecca fine. But as each day passed, she found herself wondering more and more about the brooding ex-con that she'd hired.

It wasn't until the opening day of the summer sale that she got her first glimpse into the heart of the man himself.

Pete was beneath the arbor just outside the office door, taking refuge from the hot summer sun while on his break. He was just getting comfortable enough to appreciate the sweet-smelling, apricot-colored bougainvillea hanging in cascades above his head when another car began slowing down to make the turnoff into the nursery. Jackson was on his knees nearby, setting up the cactus display that Pete had started in the rock garden.

"Wouldn't you know it. Here comes another customer," Pete groaned, and made a face as he started to drag himself out of the lawn chair.

Jackson shoved the last pot into place and dusted his hands as he stood up.

"I can help them," he said, and was gone before Pete could think to disagree.

When the occupants of the car began unloading, Pete sank back down, thankful that someone besides him would be dealing with this customer. The woman was young and pretty in a haphazard sort of way, but she had more on her hands than a need for grooming. She got out of the car with two young children at her heels and one on her hip.

Even from where he sat, Pete could hear the beginnings of an argument between the two eldest boys, who looked to be about six and seven years of age, as well as the shrieks of a small toddler, who obviously wanted down from her mother's arms. He leaned back and closed his eyes, thankful for the reprieve.

Jackson, on the other hand, was wondering what had compelled him to speak up. This customer had more kids than she could handle, and she thought she was going to shop for plants? But he'd offered to help Pete out, and now he was stuck with the job.

"Can I help you, lady?" Jackson asked.

Preoccupied with issuing last-minute warnings to her unruly children, the young mother jumped at the sound of his voice, and then turned around.

"Oh! I didn't hear you coming," she said, and then shushed the boys one more time for good measure. "And it's no wonder. Jimmy—he's my husband—was going to baby-sit while I came out today, and he got called to work."

Jackson nodded, letting his gaze drift down to the pair of boys, who were eyeing his boots.

"My daddy has boots like that."

"Does he now?" Jackson asked softly.

"Yeah!" they chimed. "My daddy is tall, too. Almost as tall as you."

"Hush, boys," the mother said. "Quit bothering the man. Now come help me pick out some flowers, okay?"

The baby, a tiny girl who looked to be less than a year old, squirmed in her mother's arms.

"No, sweet pea, you can't get down. You'd be all over mud in no time." She pressed a soft kiss on the little girl's cheek and then turned her attention back to Jackson, who was waiting quietly for her requests.

"What kind of flowers would you be wanting, ma'am?"

She sighed and tried to smile. "I want to look at the bedding plants that are on sale, for the border along my front walk. It's not all that long, so it shouldn't take more than three or four dozen."

"Yes, ma'am. Right this way," Jackson said, and started toward the open doors of a nearby greenhouse, unaware that Rebecca was already inside in an alcove at the back watering some potted palms.

Color abounded within the Plexiglas building, as did the warm, rich scent of damp peat moss and potting soil. A couple of butterflies had managed to find their way through the doorway and now flitted from pot to pot, from flowering flat to flowering flat, unable to settle on the abundant smorgasbord.

"Oh! Isn't everything beautiful," the woman cried, and shifted the baby to her other hip.

Rebecca turned at the sound of voices, then saw Jackson, looking almost overwhelmed by the family. She smiled in spite of herself and, when she realized that he didn't know she was there, decided to watch for a moment . . . just to see how he would cope. It wasn't really spying, she thought. If he needed help, she would come forward. Motionless, she stood in the shadows in the back of the building and watched Jackson Rule do his stuff.

"Everything in here is on sale. You show me what you want and I'll carry them out for you," Jackson said.

But all hell soon broke loose. What the boys didn't handle, they tried to unearth, and every time their harried mother tried to discipline them, the baby took a grab at anything within arm's reach and tried to bring it to her mouth.

Lord have mercy, Jackson thought. And yet in spite of the trouble the kids were causing, he couldn't help but enjoy watching the way their quick little minds worked. He suspected, if left alone, they could have disassembled an army tank without losing a bolt.

Rebecca stifled a giggle as she watched her customer's lack of progress and thought about coming to help. At the same time, she realized that Jackson, touchy as he was, might interpret her interruption as lack of faith in his ability. And while she was trying to decide what to do, Jackson suddenly took control of the situation . . . and the unruly boys.

"Lady, why don't you let me worry about the boys?" he offered. "That way you can pick out what you want, and I'll carry it all out to the car later, okay?"

The mother wasn't in the habit of letting total strangers approach her children, but by this time, she was on the verge of giving up. She nodded in agreement as she unwound a string of ivy from the baby's small fist and tossed it on the ground.

"Sorry about that," she muttered, referring to the dismembered ivy, then eyed the boys, who'd suddenly gone quiet. "They're all yours."

Jackson put a hand on each boy's head to get their attention. They froze at his touch, their eyes glued to the somber expression on his face.

"Okay, you guys, I need your help standing guard outside while your mother looks at the flowers. Will you come with me, and I'll show you what to do?"

Their eyes grew wide and round as they listened to the deep, even timbre of the big man's voice. Then the boys exchanged nervous glances and looked back up at the man who was towering over them.

"We'll help," they chimed.

"Okay, here's the deal . . ." Jackson began as he led them outside, lowering his voice to make it seem like a secret.

A few minutes later he quickly walked back inside the greenhouse before he started laughing.

"What did you say to them?" the mother whispered, unable to believe how quiet her rambunctious boys had become.

"Told them they needed to stand guard."

She frowned. "Why?"

"To help me watch for the flower thief."

She chuckled. "How did you get them to stand so still?"

He glanced back at the door, then almost smiled. "Well . . . for now, they're undercover statues."

This time she gave him an outright grin. "You have a wild imagination, mister."

Jackson shrugged and tried not to let her know how pleased he was by her approval.

"So do they. Now let's get your flowers. I don't know how long that tale I spun will last."

The woman quickly picked out the remaining flats that she wanted to buy, and Jackson carried them, one by one, to the trunk of her car, winking secretively to each boy as he went in and out. To his delight, neither one of them winked back. They were too preoccupied with being statues.

Rebecca was stunned. During the last fifteen minutes, Jackson had talked more to that woman and her children than he had to Pete, or to her, in the last week and a half. Somehow from that knowledge came hurt. She sighed and made her way out of the back door just as Jackson came in for the last load.

He started out the door. "Okay, boys, the shift is over. Your mother is ready to leave. You did a fine job. I don't believe that there's a flower missing."

They nodded seriously and followed Jackson to the car like little soldiers.

"I don't know how to thank you," the mother said.

"It's no big deal," Jackson said.

"Now, all I need to do is pay for these, and I'll be out of your hair." She looked around. Since their game was over, the boys were sidling away from the car, seemingly bent on inspecting Jackson's Harley. "Boys! Get back over here now. If you'll be good for momma, we'll all have ice cream before we go home."

"Yea!" they shouted, and began pummeling each other in delight.

She rolled her eyes and shifted the baby to her other arm.

Jackson pointed toward the office. "Please pay inside, ma'am."

At this point, the baby started to shriek. Then the younger boy tripped and fell, and blood began to ooze from a scrape on his elbow.

"Oh Lord," the woman muttered. "Would you please hold Lisabeth for a second while I see to the boys?"

Without waiting for an answer, she thrust the baby into Jackson's arms and made a dash for her injured child.

Jackson froze, and so did the baby. Startled by the suddenness with which they had been introduced, the little girl's demeanor changed from displeasure to delight. Something new had been added to her day.

Jackson held her, stunned by how fragile she was and how light she felt in his arms. He should have felt awkward, but the wide-eyed delight in the little girl's eyes was impossible to ignore. When her baby hands reached out to touch his face, he started to shake, but not from the unfamiliar fear of holding so small a child. It was her innocence and the unabashed trust she was giving that did him in.

Her touch was as soft and fleeting as the lost butterflies out in the greenhouse. The sunlight caught and held in the mass of tiny blond curls on her head, and her rosebud mouth kept sucking in and out over four perfect teeth, as if testing their unexplained presence. The baby laughed as her hands played pat-a-cake on Jackson's cheeks. If only life could be seen and lived through the eyes of a child.

Inside the office, Rebecca froze. The childlike shriek of pain was impossible to ignore. She came out of the office on the run just in time to see the woman hand the baby to Jackson. For a moment, she didn't know where to run first. Should she save Jackson from panic, or go to the child who had been injured on her property? The injury won.

"Is he all right?" Rebecca asked as she knelt by the child, who had already stopped crying and was now inspecting his wound and blood with interest.

The woman sighed. "He's fine. If he hadn't been running, he wouldn't have stubbed his toe. It's just a scrape."

Pete came around the corner in a hustle. "Anyone need a hand?" he asked.

The injured child sidled up to his mother, who was digging in her pocket for a tissue. He sniffed loudly, while his brother admired his injury.

"I need to pay for my flowers. I bought four flats of the bedding plants that were on sale," the woman said.

"Come on inside," Pete said. "You can wash up the young'un while I write your ticket. How's that sound?"

The mother hurried away, anxious to be gone before anything else happened, while Rebecca sauntered toward the shade tree where Jackson had taken the baby. It looked to be a case of love at first sight. Jackson was caught between trying to console a wiggling child and fear that he'd do something wrong.

Rebecca touched Jackson on the arm. "Isn't she cute?"

Jackson's heart skipped a beat. He didn't know that Rebecca had been around. Good sense told him just to hand the baby over and get the hell back to work while the getting was good. But something—maybe it was the easy way the baby fit in his arms—wouldn't let him give her up.

Not just yet.

Mesmerized by the tiny perfection of the baby's features, he finally managed to nod in agreement.

"I think she likes you," she said.

"She doesn't know me," he said, and hated the fact that his voice was shaking slightly.

The underlying meaning of his words was quite clear. Rebecca paused before she spoke. And when she finally answered, it rocked Jackson to the toes of his boots.

"Oh . . . I don't know," she said softly. "You can't fool a child, Jackson. Maybe she knows something about you that we don't know."

Jackson stilled. His gaze went from the baby's face to Rebecca's, wrecking her peace of mind with a deep blue stare.

"You don't know what you're talking about," he said quietly.

The baby's wiggles slowly ceased. Her head dropped onto Jackson's chest as she poked her thumb into her mouth. Lulled by the deep rumble of his voice against her ear, she closed her eyes and began to suck.

"Oh my! Just look at her. She's probably done all the shopping she can take for one day," Rebecca said, and gave the baby a comforting pat.

Jackson couldn't see. He could only feel. One tiny body, clasped fast in his arms, trusting . . . because she was too new to know how cruel life could really be.

Well damn, he thought, and cradled her close to his chest.

When the mother came back to reclaim her child Jackson found himself handing the baby over with reluctance, then watching as they drove away. The excursion might have been hell for the woman, but it had been heaven for him. For a moment he'd felt worthy, truly worthy, of being alive.

"I'll be out back if you need me," he said curtly, and walked away.

"Jackson."

He paused, but did not turn.

"You did a good job. You handled a problem customer with great finesse. Thank you."

For a moment, Rebecca didn't think he was even going to acknowledge her praise, and then he finally nodded.

Just don't be too nice to me, Rebecca Hill. I can't afford to care, he thought, before moving on.

But Jackson was on a high. He felt so good inside that he almost smiled. It would have been all right, as Rebecca would not have been able to see his face. She would not know that he absorbed her praise and appreciation like a man starving for water. Keeping his weaknesses to himself was all that had kept him alive thus far. Revealing himself now would be a disaster. If no one was aware of what he thought and felt, then no one could hurt him. It was the only way he knew.

Rebecca stared at the stiff, unyielding set of his shoulders and sighed. So much anger in such a big man. All she could do was hope to God that he didn't explode and destroy all of them along with himself.

"Are they gone?" Pete asked, as he ambled out of the office.

Rebecca nodded. "Thank God."

Pete grinned. "Maybe I'd better see if there really is a loose stone on the walkway. I'd hate to have another customer trip out there."

He was heading for the sidewalk when Rebecca stopped him.

"Pete, what do you think about Jackson's progress?"

"Hate to admit it, but he's been a damned good employee. He's always on time. Doesn't shirk any work, no matter how dirty or hard, and he doesn't talk my ear off, neither." He shifted his stance, eyeing Rebecca as he continued. "That doesn't mean I think he's got any business out in society mingling with regular folks. He may have served his time, but his father is dead. He's still a killer. There's no getting around that."

But Rebecca wasn't ready to give up the discussion.

"Ever wonder why he did it?"

"Well hell, no. I don't think there *is* a good reason to kill the man who gave you life. Or the woman either, for that matter. There can't be anything bad enough to do that."

Rebecca leaned forward and caught Pete's hand in hers. "Pete . . . you read the papers. You hear the news reports. Just because someone becomes a parent doesn't mean they instantly become saints and angels. Bad people can give birth just as easily as the good ones."

"Still . . ."

"Still nothing, Pete Walters. He's paid the debt society demanded, and it's not up to us to judge. As long as the man does his work, I don't want to hear another word about it."

Her chin jutted, her eyes were flashing. And when both hands went to her hips, Pete gave in. Rebecca was as stubborn as they came. And until Jackson Rule gave him a reason to say "I told you so" to Rebecca, he would have to bide his time.

"Whatever you say. After all, you're the boss."

Rebecca knew that Pete's compliance was little more than lip service, but for now she would take it. She didn't want any dissension on the job, and Pete needed the help.

Another string of cars turned off of the highway and into the lot. The sale was going to be a success. It remained to be seen whether or not the working relationship among the three would survive.

Late in the afternoon, Rebecca wandered out to the back lot, where the men were transferring some heavy shrubs for a landscaping job the next morning.

"About got it all loaded?" she asked.

Pete grinned. "You know we do, or you wouldn't be out here yet."

"Are you saying I shirk my work?" she asked, trying hard to be indignant about the teasing remark.

"Not me," Pete drawled.

Jackson smiled to himself. If only he felt comfortable enough to joke with these two. He envied them their easy camaraderie.

And then Pete slapped his leg. "Darn it all, Rebecca, I forgot to tell you. That new shipment of azaleas will be here today as promised, but it will be late. When the company called, they said the driver had called in with some sort of trouble, but was back on the road about an hour and a half behind schedule."

Rebecca rolled her eyes. "Oh great. That means I can't go home at six o'clock after all." She flopped down on the tailgate of the delivery truck and sighed. "My aching muscles are so ready for a good soak."

Jackson lifted the last potted azalea into the back of the truck and tried not to imagine Rebecca Hill getting into a tub. It wouldn't do to think of her naked. Not ever.

"Want me to wait around?" Pete asked.

"No. I was just feeling sorry for myself. I'm sure it won't be long."

"I don't mind."

"No, really, Pete. If you two have the truck loaded, then why don't you hit the trail before someone else comes. I've already put out the CLOSED sign on the office. I'll get myself a pop and enjoy my own flowers for a change."

Jackson fidgeted with a clump of dirt on the side of his hand. *Say it,* he urged himself. *Don't be such a chump. All she can do is tell you the same thing she told Pete, and he didn't take offense.*

"I don't mind waiting if you think they'll need help unloading," Jackson said.

Rebecca jumped. His voice was so quiet, she almost hadn't heard him speak.

Pete looked wild-eyed, afraid to say what was on his mind, that he wouldn't drive off and leave Rebecca here alone with this man.

Rebecca ignored the look on Pete's face and smiled. "Thanks, Jackson, but there's no need. Really. It's not like this has never happened before. I'll be fine."

He shrugged. At least he'd offered, he told himself as he followed Pete to the office to clean up before going home. They started home simultaneously. Pete turned east; Jackson went west toward New Orleans.

The familiar growl of the engine between his legs was comforting as Jackson accelerated into the sun hovering along the horizon. His sunglasses broke most of the glare, but muted the dark, rich green of the trees bordering the highway to a sepia-brown. It was like looking at an antique photograph of the world. The wind cut past his ears with a roar, stinging his cheeks and lifting the hair from his neck as the sweat on his body dried instantly beneath his shirt.

Five minutes into the ride, a truck turned a curve in the road up ahead and then aimed itself toward Jackson like a two-ton bullet. In the space of seconds, the driver had swerved across the yellow line twice, and each time, it seemed as if the speed increased.

"Stupid bastard," Jackson muttered, and guided his bike closer to the shoulder of the road. He had no wish to become a statistic.

The truck passed in a rush of hot air and burning rubber, and Jackson let out a slow breath.

Something . . . he would wonder later what it was . . . made him stop and look back at the disappearing truck. There in plain sight in the back of the bed was a bouncing shipment of shrubs. Rebecca's missing azalea bushes were about to be delivered, and if Jackson wasn't mistaken, the driver was either drunk or sick. Either way, she was going to need help.

Without giving himself time to change his mind, he spun the cycle back toward the nursery and gunned the engine. The Harley shot down the highway in swift pursuit of the trucker, who was already out of sight.

"Thank goodness," Rebecca muttered, as she saw the truck swerve into the drive. She waved him toward the back of the building and then followed on foot.

The driver skidded to a halt just shy of a chain-link fence and then rolled out of the cab and stood, watching Rebecca's approach with anticipation.

Whaley Smith was drunk. It wasn't the first time he'd gotten drunk on the job, but he suspected when he got back that it would be his last . . . at least on this job. He was willing to bet good money that his ass would be fired when he returned with the truck.

At this point, he didn't care. He felt too good and too cocky to worry about paychecks. At thirty-six, he considered himself in the prime of life and didn't want to waste a minute. He hitched his pants up a notch, slid his hand down the front of his fly in a comforting gesture, and swaggered his two-hundred-pound bulk to the back of the truck, where the woman was inspecting his load.

Rebecca didn't pay much attention to the driver. She was too intent on pointing out the damage already done to the goods.

"Two of them have turned over," she said, pointing toward the side of the truck bed. "If they're ruined, you'll have to take them back and give me credit," she said.

Whaley grinned and slid his hand across her backside. "I'd be willin' to give you more than credit, darlin', if you know what I mean."

Rebecca froze. She couldn't believe what was happening. In all her years of dealing with this company no one had ever crossed such a line. She spun indignantly, and then her belly drew tight with fear. With the truck at her back and this man in her face, she was trapped . . . and alone. Panic mixed with fury as she reacted by striking out.

When he caught both her hands in his own and then slid them down the front of his body in a suggestive manner, she kicked at his legs and ankles and then began to scream.

"Don't be that way, darlin'," he said, and leaned forward, trying to catch that gasp on her lips.

His breath was hot on her face and his bulk pressed her harder and harder against the truck bed. He circled her neck with one hand, choking off her scream as the ground tilted at her feet. God help her, she was going to faint.

Fear gave way to hysteria as she continued her struggles to get free. One button on her shirt gave way . . . then another . . . and another. The harder she fought, the rougher he became. A three-day growth of whiskers raked the tender skin on the side of her throat, and when his hand dipped between her legs, she screamed even louder, clawing at him with both hands in a futile attempt to get free.

"Mister, you better find a new place to put your goddamned hands, because I'm about to break your neck."

The sound of another man's voice was just enough to pull Whaley Smith out of his drunken fugue. He spun around, his fists doubled, and then staggered when the horizon shifted before his eyes.

Rebecca sagged against the truck, feeling weak with relief. It was Jackson . . . and she hadn't even heard him come back.

She grabbed the front of her shirt to cover herself up as unshed tears shimmered across her vision. She'd never been so afraid in her entire life. "Thank God," she said, and then everything started going black.

"Who the hell are you?" Whaley asked.

"Trouble."

Whaley never saw the fist coming. He went down like a sack of wet meal at the same time Rebecca's legs gave way. Jackson caught her before she hit the ground. For several moments he held her without speaking until she began to regain her senses.

"Oh God, oh God!" She covered her face with her hands as Jackson held her upright. "I've never been so scared in my life. He almost . . . "

"Hush," Jackson said quietly. "It's all right. He can't hurt you."

"How did you know? What made you come back?"

Jackson groaned, trying not to think of how soft she felt in his arms. How perfectly their bodies fit. She was as relaxed in his embrace as the baby girl he'd held earlier, and it took everything he had not to let the feelings go to his head . . . and places south.

"I passed him as he was coming out here. He was all over the road. I figured he was either drunk or sick, so I came back."

She shuddered, then looked up. "Now I owe you twice for saving me."

He took one look at her bruised and shaking lips, then took a deep breath and three steps back, trying to put some sanity back into his head.

"You don't owe me anything. It happened. I was here. It's over."

"No, it's not," Rebecca muttered, nudging at the lump of man at her feet with the toe of her tennis shoe. "It's not over yet." She started toward the office.

"Where are you going?" Jackson asked.

"To call the police. I have no intention of letting that creep off the hook. If you hadn't come, he might have raped me and who knows what else. The least I can do is get him for assault and DWI. Right?"

Jackson started to panic. *Oh God. The police.* But his fear was never voiced. Instead, he stood guard as Rebecca disappeared into the office, wishing to hell that he was somewhere else.

5

Sirens.

The sound made Jackson sick. As long as he lived, he was never going to be able to tolerate the electronic scream and the flashing lights.

Old memories. Bad memories. They all came with the sound of sirens. While the skin on his body crawled from the intermittent wail, he glanced down at the truck driver, who was slowly regaining consciousness.

While Jackson stood guard, Rebecca waited a few yards away outside her office. When the parish police pulled into the driveway, she breathed a shaky sigh of relief.

"Here!" Rebecca called, and waved her arm to get their attention.

A pair of uniformed officers emerged from the police car, pausing first to look at her, then at the two men who were standing near a truck.

Rebecca sensed something odd in the behavior of the taller officer, who suddenly frowned as he stared intently toward the truck. But when he sent his partner in that direction and then approached Rebecca, she dismissed the thought.

"Ma'am . . . I'm Officer Wayne. You reported an assault?"

The simple act of retelling the story made Rebecca shake all over again, and because she was so rattled, everything she said came out all wrong.

"Everyone was gone, and I was waiting for a delivery and then when it came, the man was drunk . . . and when I was talking to him he started putting his hands . . . "

She trailed off as she remembered how swiftly everything had gone from sane to insane. She shuddered, trying to regain her train of thought, unaware that her omission of certain pertinent details was going to give the officer the wrong idea.

"Just take a deep breath, ma'am," the officer said.

She nodded, wrapping her arms around her waist for lack of anything else to hold on to. Her mind jumped past the ugliness of the actual assault to the end of it.

"Jackson came out of nowhere . . . I didn't know he was anywhere . . . I didn't even hear him come back. All I know is, if it hadn't been . . . "

She knew the moment the officer visibly jerked and then started toward the truck, that she'd said something wrong, but she didn't panic until he headed for Jackson.

"Miles! Cuff the big one!" he shouted, and pointed toward Jackson.

Jackson's heart sank. He told himself this was no more than he should have expected, and yet when the other officer slapped the cuff across his wrist, he wanted to run. Not again. Not again.

When the officer grabbed Jackson's wrist, Rebecca bolted.

"Not him!" she shouted. "Wait! You've got the wrong man!"

"I don't think so, lady," Wayne said. "Do you know who this man is?"

Her eyes were flashing an angry green, her words were short and breathless from running, but there was no mistaking her intentions when she stopped him from fastening the other cuff on Jackson's wrist.

"Of course I know who he is. He's the man who saved me. Now, would you please take those handcuffs off of him and put them where they belong?"

To say the officers were surprised would have been an understatement, and yet in the face of Rebecca's claim, they could do no less than obey.

"You're saying that this man is the one who assaulted you?" Wayne asked, and pointed toward Whaley Smith, who was rubbing the swiftly spreading bruise on his chin and wishing he could have started this day all over again.

"Yes, of course! Please turn Jackson loose!"

Her eyes implored Jackson to forgive her for something she couldn't understand, and yet he wouldn't meet her gaze. She couldn't imagine how he must feel. He'd done the right thing and still he had been assumed guilty . . . and all because of her.

When the cuff came off of Jackson's wrist, it felt as if a hundred-pound weight had been lifted from his chest. He gave both men a bitter glare, then smiled. It was not a friendly sight.

"Thanks for the vote of confidence, boys," Jackson drawled, and leaned against the truck bed as Whaley Smith was led to the waiting patrol car.

Rebecca sighed. She hadn't considered what the arrival of police would mean to him. She'd been so frightened and so angry that seeking justice had been more important than tact.

Wayne made no attempt to hide his contempt for Jackson. He'd been a rookie cop, only a few years older than Jackson Rule had been when Rule had been arrested for murder.

"So you're out," he said, making it more of a statement than a question. "I guess all good things finally come to an end."

Jackson didn't bother to answer. He turned to Rebecca instead. "I'll just unload these for you while you give the Lone Ranger here your statement, okay?"

Rebecca wanted to cry. He'd saved her from God knows what, and this was the thanks he was getting.

Wayne grabbed Jackson's arm. "Look, Rule, why don't you move along. If she needs any help, I'm sure she will call one of her . . . "

Rebecca interrupted. "I would appreciate it, Jackson. You know where they need to go, and we'll consider it overtime, okay?"

Jackson nodded, then shrugged off the officer's hand and crawled up into the truck bed as Wayne led Rebecca a distance away.

"He works for you?"

Rebecca nodded.

"Do you know that he's an . . . ?"

"Ex-con? He told me the day he applied for the job," Rebecca said.

"But do you know he committed . . . ?"

Once again, Rebecca silenced the officer before he could make his revelation.

"Murder? He told me that too. And . . . that it was his father he killed."

Mark Wayne had been in law enforcement all of his adult life, and he'd never seen anyone so blasé about such a fact. He gave Rebecca a closer look, wondering if she and Rule had a thing going, and if lust had blinded her to the truth.

"So it's no big deal to you?" he asked.

"Yes, it's a big deal to me," Rebecca said between clenched teeth, unwilling for Jackson to know what they were talking about, although she could have saved herself the worry. He'd known from the outset what was bound to happen. She glanced at the truck. The bed was nearly empty. Obviously, Jackson wanted out of their sight as badly as they wanted him gone.

"Of course it's a big deal," she repeated. "It's a horrible fact, but the way I see it, the state of Louisiana says he's served his time. You people turned him loose. I advertised for extra help. He applied." Once again, she felt herself wanting to cry. "He's the best worker I've ever had. He's prompt and he's patient and polite . . . and actually, he's saved my life twice now. At this point, I'm beginning to consider him my lucky charm. Now do you want to know the particulars about the man who assaulted me and tried to rape me, or would you rather hash over old news?"

Wayne frowned. He could see that it would do no good to try to dissuade her any further. He'd done his duty by warning her. After that, she would be responsible for the mess she made of her life. He flipped his notepad open.

"Okay . . . now when did the driver arrive?"

Rebecca started talking, and fifteen minutes later, when the police car pulled away with Whaley Smith inside, she felt weak and drained. She staggered toward her office.

"Oh God." She dropped into the nearest chair, cold and shaking from the inside out. Shock had set in, replacing the earlier fear and anger. And, as before, Jackson was suddenly, and unexpectedly, at her side. His voice rumbled in her ear, deep . . . concerned . . . gentle.

"Are you all right?"

Her stomach lurched. "I don't think so," she whispered.

Jackson got her to the bathroom with no time to spare and, to Rebecca's humiliation, held her to keep her from falling on her face as she threw up. When it was over, he propped her up and calmly and competently washed her face with a handful of cold, wet paper towels.

"Feel better?"

Rebecca nodded. She couldn't look him in the eyes.

Jackson sighed. *Damn. Why did this have to happen? And why now?*

He'd almost convinced himself that he thought of her only as his boss. But one look at the stark expression in her eyes and the tremble on her lips, and he knew he'd been lying to himself all along.

"My neck burns," she mumbled, and reached beneath her collar with shaking hands, testing the fiery skin beneath.

"Let me see," Jackson asked, and moved the torn edge of the shirt collar aside.

The son of a bitch! The deep, bloody runnels in her soft white skin made him sick. Rage swamped him all over again,

just as suddenly and fiercely as it had when he'd ridden up and
seen that man with his hands on Rebecca's body, crossing
boundaries that no man should cross. He would hear her
frightened screams in his dreams for days to come, and he
knew it.

"It looks like scratches . . . probably from his fingernails,"
he said. "Where's the first aid kit?"

Rebecca knew he was talking. She could see his mouth
working around the words. She knew also that she was still
alive and breathing, because she felt the gentleness of his
hands upon her body. But she couldn't find it in herself to
answer. All she wanted to do was cry.

Jackson sighed. He could tell that normal conversation was
beyond her. And the tears shimmering in those wide green
eyes were about to do him in.

"Just sit down before you fall down, okay? I'll find the antiseptic, and we'll clean up those scratches."

Gently, he pushed her down onto the closed lid of the com-
mode, then left the bathroom before she had time to argue.
Seconds later, she heard him rummaging through the shelf
behind the front desk.

"I found it," he yelled, and she closed her eyes and trembled, wondering if this day was ever going to be over.

When he came back, Rebecca was standing at the sink
splashing water upon her face again and again. He paused in
the doorway, giving her the space and time that she needed to
regain her sense of self. He knew only too well that violence
made one feel dirty.

"You can take all the baths you want when you get home,"
he said quietly. "Right now I need to doctor those scratches
before they get infected."

Rebecca looked startled. *How had he known what she was
feeling? How had he known she wanted to wash and wash
until there wasn't a trace of that man's touch . . . or scent . . .
left on her?* Suddenly she remembered where he'd been, and
what he must have endured. She stared at him while water

dripped from her face and hands onto her clothes and the floor.

Jackson's heart sank. The shock on her face had nothing to do with what had happened to her, and everything to do with what she was thinking. He'd seen it before, on other faces, in other places. But seeing it on hers was the ultimate shame. And because it shamed him, his words were coarser and harder than he would have liked.

"Yeah, I know what the hell I'm talking about, don't I? I must. After all, you've got to remember where I've been." He yanked the cap from the antiseptic bottle, his hands shaking with an emotion that had nothing to do with rage. "Unbutton your top button again, or this stuff will get on your shirt."

Again unable to make eye contact with him, she did as she was told, and then grimaced when the antiseptic made contact with her burning skin.

Jackson's voice softened. "Does it burn?"

She bit her lower lip and nodded.

"I'm sorry, Rebecca. Stand still. I'll blow."

When that dark head dipped toward her breasts, her heart stopped. She found herself holding her breath as his mouth pursed. And when the first gentle gust of his breath hit her skin, she swayed on her feet.

Without thinking, he steadied her as he continued to blow. And when his hand closed around her arm, Rebecca closed her eyes, willing herself not to think the things that were flying through her mind. Reminding herself of this man . . . and his past . . . and the danger he could be to her future.

"Is that better?"

Unaware that he'd moved away from her and was now in the act of putting the top back on the bottle, she began to stammer, "Uh . . . yes, thanks to you," she said, and willed herself not to cry.

Jackson's eyes narrowed thoughtfully as he handed her the bottle. Something was going on behind those bewitching green eyes, but he didn't have the guts to pursue it.

"You're welcome," he muttered, and stepped away.

The distance he kept between them was more than bodily, and yet, as nervous as Jackson made her, Rebecca couldn't quit remembering that were it not for him, things might have turned out entirely differently.

"I don't know how to . . . if you hadn't come back he might have . . . "

Jackson shook his head. "Don't say it, Rebecca. I did come back. It's over. You're safe."

Yes, I'm safe. And all because of you.

The fear that had been inside of her moments earlier suddenly disappeared. Something settled within her heart—some nameless thought that had been with her since the day she'd hired him. She didn't know what had caused it, and she didn't know why, but Rebecca Hill had just experienced a revelation. No matter what came next, she knew she would never be afraid of Jackson again. She shuddered, then sighed as an odd weight lifted from her shoulders.

"They told me I have to go to headquarters and sign a complaint, but I need to go home and change first."

Jackson frowned. "You're not going alone?"

"I don't need anyone to . . . "

"Call Pete. Call your father. Call someone, Rebecca, just don't go alone."

"But I . . . "

"Take my word for it. Whether you're the victim or the offender, you will want moral backup."

He stood aside, then breathed a quiet sigh of relief when she finally left the bathroom and went to the phone.

Her fingers shook as she punched in the numbers, and when he pointed toward the chair behind her, she willingly sat down before her legs gave way again. Her eyes closed as she counted the rings, and when the man answered, she began to speak.

"Pete, are you in the middle of supper?"

Pete had known Rebecca nearly all of her life, and when he

heard that shaky quaver in her voice, he knew something bad had happened.

"What's wrong, girl?"

The sympathy in his voice was, once again, her undoing. She tried to tell him, and then started to cry.

Jackson took the phone from her hands.

"Pete, it's me, Jackson. Forget what you're eating and come back to the office, okay? That damned delivery man finally showed up, but he was drunk. He assaulted Rebecca."

Rebecca hid her face, trying not to listen to the ugliness of the words. Just hearing it said aloud made her sick all over again. She could tell by the way Jackson was answering that Pete's response had been quite vocal.

"No . . . no, I met him when I was on the way home and came back to help them unload," Jackson said.

Rebecca struggled to shake off the feeling of humiliation. By God, what had happened wasn't her fault. She shouldn't feel obliged to apologize or explain. She took the phone back from Jackson before he could finish.

"Pete, it's me," Rebecca said softly. "Jackson saved me again." She tried to smile. "Yes, it's beginning to become a habit of his. Anyway . . . I'm all right. He's already unloaded the truck, but he says he won't go home until I call someone to come with me to go sign the complaint."

"And right he is," Pete said. "Tell him not to leave. You're backup is on its way." Then he hung up.

"He's coming," she said.

Jackson nodded, satisfied that matters were well on their way to being worked out. But the next person to arrive, fifteen minutes later, was not Pete.

When she heard the sound of a car Rebecca ran to the window. The expression on her face went from disbelief to dismay.

"Oh no! Pete called my father."

Jackson frowned. "And that's bad?"

"You don't understand," she muttered. "But you will."

Moments later, Daniel Hill burst into the office and started talking before the door closed behind him.

"Rebecca Ruth, are you all right? I couldn't believe it when Pete called. As for that, I'd like to know why you didn't call me yourself!" He threw his arms around his daughter.

He continued his tirade without giving her a chance to respond to one question, let alone the lot he was throwing in her face.

"This is nothing more than I've been expecting," he said, and held Rebecca at arm's length to give her a closer inspection.

Rebecca fought back tears. "Dad, I don't need to hear this right now. If you want to go with me to sign the complaint, I would appreciate it, but if you're going to preach at me all the way there and back about changing my lifestyle, I'd rather go by myself."

Daniel frowned. The ongoing disagreement between his daughter and himself regarding her work was never going to be reconciled until she came around to his way of thinking.

"Now, Rebecca . . . you know I'm right. You need someone to take care of you. I won't live forever. If you would only pursue the issue of finding a good man to marry before you are too old to . . . "

The walls began closing in around Jackson. He couldn't stand in the corner and listen to any more of this and know that he could never be the kind of man she would consider.

"Rebecca, if you don't need me for anything more, I think I'll be going now," he said.

Startled by another man's voice, Daniel spun around and then frowned, surprised by the man's presence. Judging by appearance, this man was not his idea of a suitable associate for his daughter. His old jeans and dusty boots, the smudges on a once-white shirt and hair in need of a cut did not sit well with Daniel, who prided himself on cleanliness being next to godliness.

"I didn't know anyone else was here," he muttered, and slipped his arm around Rebecca's waist.

"Dad, I'd like for you to meet my new employee, Jackson Rule. If he hadn't had the foresight to come back to the greenhouse when he passed the truck on his way home from work, I don't know what would have happened to me."

Daniel Hill relented in his harsh assessment of the man's appearance. At least that explained his unkempt clothing. He'd been on the job. Sorry that he'd judged without waiting for an explanation, he crossed the room with his hand extended.

"Young man, I want to shake your hand for saving Rebecca. She means everything to me."

Jackson gripped the preacher's hand with reluctance, well aware that if Daniel Hill knew the truth about him, the last thing he would do was willingly shake it.

"I'm glad I could help," Jackson said, as he headed for the door.

"Jackson?"

He paused and turned. "Yes, ma'am?"

She smiled and corrected him. "Hunh uh . . . we've been all through this before."

He almost smiled back and then waited for her to continue.

"Thank you again. For everything."

Jackson felt like someone had pulled the plug on his life, and it was emptying at his feet. He wished he could be casual about it, but he needed to put some distance between them before he made a total ass of himself.

"You're welcome."

Moments later, the sound of his Harley could be heard as it roared from the yard of the greenhouse and back onto the highway. Daniel Hill frowned.

"Odd man," he said.

"No, he's not," Rebecca said. "Let's go, okay? I want to get this trip over with and get home before dark. I'm getting sick to my stomach."

∘   ∘   ∘

That night, Rebecca's house seemed way too large and empty for one person to inhabit. The moonlight was lost in the clouds flying across the sky before the oncoming storm. Rain was imminent, and so, she suspected, was a sleepless night. The wind whipped the trees and shrubs around her house and aggravated her nerves to the breaking point. When the phone rang, she was so startled she almost choked.

"Hello?"

Her voice was hesitant and uncertain. Nothing like the Rebecca that Pete knew and loved.

"Am I forgiven?" Pete asked, as he heard her sigh.

She knew he was referring to the fact that he'd called her father instead of coming himself. "I suppose," she muttered.

"He would never have forgiven either one of us if I hadn't, and you know it."

"I know . . . and thanks for calling. I was feeling sort of goosey. Now that I hear the sound of another voice, I think I can finally settle down."

Pete nodded to himself. "Yeah, when Jackson called, he told me to be sure and call you tonight. He said that you'd be jumpy."

A wash of emotion swept over her so quickly that it had come and gone before she knew to prepare, leaving her weak and speechless.

"He told you to call?" she asked finally.

"I was going to anyway," Pete hastened to add. "After all, I needed to hear for myself that you're really all right."

Tears sprang to her eyes, and Rebecca pressed a fingertip against the bridge of her nose to keep from letting them spill.

"Thanks to Jackson, I am," she said quietly. "It's starting to rain now. I think I'll go sit on the porch awhile. You know how I like to watch the storms."

Pete grinned. "Yes, girl, I do at that. Sleep well now. If you feel like taking a day or so off, Jackson and I will manage just fine."

By now the tears were rolling down her cheeks. "I don't think so, Pete, but thanks. I'll see you tomorrow."

"Bright and early," he reminded her and hung up the phone.

She laid the phone back in its cradle and went to get a jacket before going outside.

The moment she opened the door, the breeze swept through the opening and into the room, blowing papers from a table and lifting the curtains from the rods like the sails of a ship. She took a deep breath, pulled her jacket a little closer around her neck, and walked out onto the porch.

Rain hammered upon the roof and blew across the porch in a hard, wet spray. It matched Rebecca's mood—wild, unsettled, and a little bit angry. Pellets of rain peppered her face, mingling with the tears on her cheeks and washing them from her eyes. She lifted her chin and inhaled the storm, savoring the cleansing that came with it, not caring that her slacks were becoming plastered to her legs and her jacket was getting soaked. She took one step down from the porch and lifted her face, then as she'd done so many times as a child, closed her eyes and opened her mouth and drank the water from heaven.

It felt good to be clean.

But the storm did nothing for Jackson's restlessness. His thoughts jumped from Molly to Rebecca and back again. He needed a steady income and a good home before he could consider taking care of his sister, and that meant keeping the job, and staying in daily contact with a woman who was getting under his skin. He stared through the muddy tracks the rain made on his window and then shuddered and turned away. It was too much like looking at the world through iron bars.

A used copy of *For Whom the Bell Tolls* lay open on his bed, while an intermittent flash of a red-and-blue neon sign from the club across the street made a crazy pattern on the wall behind him. It, like the place in which he lived, was typical of

the area. Garish, run-down, dangerous. It was the neighborhood in New Orleans that the cops called Central City, and the
place Jackson Rule called home.

Somewhere a few streets over, the sound of a police siren
could be heard, accompanied by the familiar squall of a fire
truck. Whatever had happened couldn't be good. Jackson
dropped into a chair, staring at the floor without blinking until
his eyes burned from dryness. He'd spent the last five hours
reliving the entire incident, from the time he'd pulled Whaley
Smith off of Rebecca until the minute he'd walked out of the
office. And each time the ending remained the same.
Someone else had stayed with her and comforted her and
wiped the tears from her eyes while he'd ridden away.

"Ah God," Jackson groaned, and finally pulled himself out
of the chair. He grabbed his keys from a table and walked
out of his apartment, wearing the same clothes he'd come
home in.

The rain was cold, but not nearly as cold as his heart. He
was thoroughly soaked within seconds as he looked up and
down the street, but he could not have cared less. With no
purpose in direction, he put one foot in front of the other and
started walking. Streetlights gave the falling rain a glittering,
gilded appearance, and the puddles accumulating on the sidewalks became silver pools that constantly split and shattered
with each drop that fell into them.

"Hey, honey, wanna party?"

At the sound of the woman's voice, Jackson stopped and
then stared intently into the alley by which he was passing. The
woman was shivering, her thin clothes plastered to her lanky
body, wet hair clinging to her head and the sides of her face
while cheap mascara ran like black tears from the corners of
her eyes. He wished to God he could "party." He wanted . . .
needed something to take his mind off of Rebecca. But letting
this woman put her hands—or her mouth—on his body
seemed dirty, and he'd been dirty enough already to last a lifetime.

He shook his head and walked away without answering her question.

A cop car cruised by at the corner and still he kept moving, farther away from his room and the memories, and finally lost himself in the storm and the night.

6

Rebecca had never been allowed to sleep in on Sunday mornings. Attending church was so much a part of her life that forgoing her father's sermon never even crossed her mind. Even when she was angry at him, she was still able to separate the man from the pulpit. No matter what he did to her personal life, she could still admire him as a minister. And so she hurried through the house on her way out the door, her skirttail flying and the curls on her head bouncing with every step.

The church parking lot was almost full, and she had to circle it twice before she found a place to park. People were visiting out on the lawn, as well as moving in groups toward the church. She waved at one couple, and nodded to another as she made her way up the steps. Sunshine warmed her face as well as her heart. When she took her seat on the first pew at the front of the church, for a moment she could almost believe that the world had not changed and she was still eight years old, fidgeting for having to dress up and sit for hours while her father preached, when a beautiful day beckoned her to come out and play.

The moment was bittersweet. Rebecca could almost hear her mother's voice whispering for her to sit up straight and, not for the first time, wished that she were still alive. Besides the fun they used to share, she missed her mother's presence in the family. She'd always been the perfect buffer between Rebecca and her father's overprotective, stifling sort of love.

Daniel Hill entered the pulpit and stood there, gazing out across the sea of faces that was his congregation. His benevolent smile belied his rather singular view of the world. She counted to five, then hid a grin as he casually ran a hand over the crown of his hair, patting it to assure himself that everything was in place.

Her father was a man of routine. He'd done the same thing for as long as she could remember, and she knew that within another few seconds he would tap the microphone at the pulpit with the end of his finger, then step away and clear his throat.

When he did so, she wanted to laugh aloud. There was comfort in the familiarity of loving one so dedicated to routine.

And when he glanced over at the pew where she was sitting and then winked, she smiled and opened the songbook to the first hymn. Whether she liked it or not, she was well aware that in his eyes she would always be daddy's little girl.

While everything was unusually smooth between her father and Rebecca, it was not the same at work, however. The next day, Rebecca found herself stumbling over Pete and Jackson at every turn she took. No matter what she did, one of them was offering to help. They acted as if she might break, shadowing her every move, chipping away at her patience by tiny bits and pieces.

Finally, during a lull in trade, it broke.

A dragonfly darted past Rebecca's nose on its way to a nearby birdbath. The thick, sweltering air was refusing to stir, adding to the day's aggravation, and as her last customer was driving away, she suddenly realized that no one else was in line waiting for service.

"Thank goodness," she muttered. "I've been dying for a break." And then she remembered the office refrigerator was empty and checked her pocket for money as she started toward her pickup.

"Pete! We're out of pop. I'm going to the quick stop down the road. Do you want anything special?"

Pete dropped the garden hose and turned off the water.

"I'll go," he said quickly. "You just take it easy. Jackson can stay here with you. It won't take me a minute."

"No thanks," she said. "I'd rather go myself. I need to get away for a bit."

Her easy smile did not sway either man from the path that he'd chosen. She could see the argument coming.

"Hey, Pete, why not let me go, instead?" Jackson said. "It would be better if you stayed with her."

She sighed. They were at it again, talking about her and not to her.

"Hey!" she yelled.

Both men turned, shocked by her outburst.

"Dammit, I'm over here. Talk to me. I won't break. I would dearly like to get over what happened to me, but when you insist on treating me like glass, all it does is remind me that I was a victim."

Jackson was the first to relent.

"I'm sorry," he said, and started to back off, but Pete wanted to argue.

"Now see here, girl, I wasn't trying to do anything of the . . ."

The spray of water hit him squarely in the chest. It was hard to say who was more shocked, Pete for having been hosed down, or Jackson for being too close to the spray. Both men stared, mouths open, water dripping, as Rebecca calmly turned off the spigot and dropped the hose back to the ground.

"I think I'd better go after all," she said calmly. "You're both all wet."

She got in her pickup and drove away, leaving both men behind to make what they chose of her behavior.

Jackson grinned. The more he was around Rebecca Hill, the better he liked her. He swiped at the water droplets on his face and arms, then grinned at Pete. "She's right. You are all wet."

"Damned moody woman," Pete grumbled. "Just try and do her a favor and see what happens." He looked down at the water dripping from his chest. "Hells bells, look at me! I look like I went and peed my pants."

Jackson grinned. "You don't look so bad. Maybe you'll dry out before another customer comes."

Pete snorted. "In this humidity? Not a chance." He stomped away to the back of the premises, leaving Jackson alone to deal with whatever customers happened to come by.

A short while later, Jackson was busy loading some camellia bushes into the trunk of a woman's car when Rebecca returned. He watched from the corner of his eye as Rebecca made peace with Pete by way of a cold Pepsi, a Snickers candy bar, and a kiss on the cheek. It was the closeness between two old friends that did him in. He swallowed a knot at the back of his throat and returned his attention to the customer. No need dwelling on impossibilities.

When the customer drove away, Jackson turned to find Rebecca at his heels. If she had not been so close—if he hadn't been able to see those damned five freckles on her nose so clearly—then he might have restrained himself. But when she handed him a Coke and then offered him a choice of the candy bars she held in her hand, he almost said the wrong thing.

"Take your pick," she said lightly.

"I'll have what you gave Pete," he said.

Her breath caught in her throat. She could almost make herself believe she was imagining the inference he just made. She looked up. His expression was bland, and his gaze focused on her face, as if he were waiting.

She shuddered. Waiting for what? But in her heart she knew.

"What are you saying?"

Jackson's fingers slid across the palm of her hand, then centered on the candy bar in the middle.

"That I'll have the Snickers. Always did like chocolate and caramel."

He smiled slightly, then walked away, well aware that he'd almost crossed a line, and telling himself that it didn't matter. He'd never consciously do anything about it, and neither, he knew, would she.

Rebecca froze. It was all she could do not to gawk at his backside, those long legs, and that slow, easy saunter. He gave new meaning to the phrase "animal magnetism." But, she reminded herself, he was more of a domesticated animal gone wild!

And the moment she thought it, she felt the need to run in the opposite direction. It was common knowledge that strays were the most dangerous animals of all. Once they'd been someone's treasured pet, and then they'd been abandoned, tossed aside like last week's garbage. Like Jackson, they had no fear of man, only hate.

"But I'm not afraid of you," Rebecca said, well aware that he couldn't hear. It didn't matter. She was only saying it to remind herself.

The day passed without further incident, and when she arrived the next morning to unlock the office, she found Jackson finishing off the last of a coffee and a sack full of beignets as he waited beneath a shade tree in the front yard.

"Morning, Rebecca."

His drawl was slow and easy, just like the look in his eyes. She nodded and smiled, while an antsy feeling began to resurrect itself down deep in her stomach. She reminded herself that she had too vivid an imagination where this man was concerned, and decided to play it cool.

"Did you save one for me?" she asked, as he wadded up the empty paper sack and followed her into the office.

When he looked startled, then sheepish, she grinned.

"I was only teasing. Besides, I don't think I'd look as charming with a powdered sugar mustache as you do."

Her remark sent him into the bathroom and then back out again seconds later. This time she laughed out loud.

"Gotcha," she said.

There hadn't been anything on his face when he went in, but there was something on his face now, and he could feel it coming no matter how hard he tried to stop it. Everything inside him was warming. Because of Rebecca, the wall he kept between himself and the world was crumbling.

He smiled.

Not the tentative, careful smile he saved for pauses in their conversations. This one came from the heart. It broke the hard, fixed planes of his face and shattered the bad-boy image in one motion, lighting the blue of his eyes and making him appear younger than his thirty-one years.

Rebecca was stunned by the difference, and for the first time since the day he'd pulled her from the path of the oncoming car, knew she was seeing the real Jackson Rule. Not the hard, embittered ex-con with a yard-wide chip on his shoulder. This must have been what he was like before . . .

She couldn't finish what she was thinking, because having to remember that Jackson Rule had killed seemed suddenly obscene.

"You are really full of it today, aren't you, lady?"

Rebecca cocked an eyebrow and pursed her lips, as if giving the matter some thought.

"I suppose you might say that. Last night was something of a milestone. I didn't once have that nightmare about . . . you know."

His smile disappeared. "I know about nightmares." Then before she could think to react, his cool persona slid back into place as he picked up a pair of gloves from the bathroom shelf.

"Where do you want me first?"

The seriousness of his expression made her angry, both with him and herself. Every time she opened her mouth around him, she said the wrong thing.

Where do I want you first? I wish to goodness I knew. And then, the moment she thought it, wanted to kick herself back down the steps. Her wayward thoughts were getting entirely out of hand.

She dug through the lower shelf below the counter for the clipboard where she kept the scheduled job orders. Frowning slightly to read Pete's scribbles, she scanned the top sheet.

"It looks like we've got a couple of small landscaping jobs today. If I'm reading this right, the first one is the Brownley place, then another just across the road at the Osters'. Those two women have a real case of 'keeping up with the Joneses.' What one woman does, the other quickly copies, only in a more flamboyant fashion."

He nodded, and started out the door when Rebecca's parting remark gave him cause to wish he were another sort of man.

"Jackson . . ."

He paused, expecting further orders.

"You have a very nice smile. You should use it more often."

To say he was startled would have been putting it mildly.

"I have a what?"

"Smile. You have a nice smile."

Oh damn.

Rebecca grinned. "You're supposed to say, 'Thank you, Rebecca.'"

But his response was not what she expected. When he answered, his expression was grim.

"Don't, Rebecca."

"Don't what?" She couldn't believe she was being taken to task for the light remark that she'd made.

"Don't be nice to me."

"But I . . ."

He didn't stay around long enough to hear her answer. She could only stare at the door swinging shut between them and wonder where she went from there.

By the end of the day, Pete was nursing a mashed thumb and Jackson was nursing a grudge against life. Rebecca wanted nothing more than to put some distance between herself and the two of them. She locked the door to the office and stood on the steps with her hands on her hips, trying to find the best way to tell them what was on her mind. Finally, she blurted it out.

"Do you know what?"

In the act of washing the potting soil off of their hands and arms, both men looked up, waiting for her to continue.

"You two are a miserable pair to be around. I don't know who put a burr in your pants, or why you feel like you do . . . and furthermore I don't want to know. All I can say is, get over it. If you need to howl at the moon tonight, then let 'er rip. If you feel the need to run naked through the bayous, have at it with my blessing. But so help me God, if you come back here tomorrow with those long faces, I'm going to scream."

Pete reacted like a scolded child by ducking his head, and Jackson withdrew inside himself, wishing he knew how to hide his inner self from the outside world. Both men knew that they'd been taking their personal miseries out on a woman who didn't deserve such treatment, especially after what she'd just endured at another man's hands.

"I'm sorry, Rebecca. I will go home and soak my thumb . . . and my head," Pete said, giving her an apologetic smile.

"Apology accepted," she said, and then looked at Jackson, waiting to hear what he had to say. The look on his face never changed, and the longer she waited, the more she wished she'd never pressed the issue.

Her hands were shaking as much as her voice as she combed the straggles of hair away from her face with her fingers.

"Damn you, Jackson. Why is it every time I talk to you, you always make me feel like I've trespassed on sacred ground?" Frustrated, she pivoted toward her pickup. "Never mind. Maybe you just need a good night's sleep."

Jacksons' spirits slumped. The least he could do was respond. She had no way of knowing that his carefully balanced world had taken a big plunge today when he'd called Molly's doctor.

Though he'd hoped to get a go-ahead on a visit, he'd been

told instead that during her regular session, she'd suddenly started to cry. She'd gone from hysterics to withdrawal, and Dr. Franco had informed him that her regression was substantial. At this point, she was in no shape for an unexpected visitor with a frighteningly familiar face.

"Rebecca."

She stopped in mid-step and then turned, waiting for him to continue.

"I'm sorry."

She smiled. "I know. So am I, for making such a big deal out of it, okay?"

She drove away, leaving the pair alone in the yard, studying the ground beneath their feet. Pete was the first to break the silence.

"She's a hell of a woman, isn't she?"

Jackson's heart ached too much to talk. All he could do was nod. He headed for his bike, desperate to put space between himself and this place, at least for tonight.

"See you tomorrow, boy," Pete called, then watched as the man and bike became one, spinning out of the yard and onto the highway as if the devil were at his heels. He looked down at his thumb and winced. It was black-and-blue all over and twice the size of the other one. This was going to play hell with a good night's sleep.

The weight of the world was on Rebecca's shoulders as she pulled into her yard and got out of her truck. The flowered border along the walk from her drive to her house was alive with color. Butterflies dipped in and out of the open blooms like tiny kites flirting with gravity, while a late evening breeze rustled the thick, waxy leaves on the magnolias in her yard. The spearlike fronds of some sword grass dipped and swayed with the breeze, rattling in mock ferocity.

Inside the house, the cool blast of air from the central unit soothed the outer heat on her skin, but did nothing for the turmoil within her soul. She slammed the door behind her, locking it out of habit as she dropped her purse and keys on the hall table. Shoes came next, and by the time she was in her bedroom, she was carrying her shirt in her hands. The full-length mirror hanging from her closet door reflected her condition most admirably. Her shoulders drooped, her hair was a mess, and there were tears shimmering in her eyes.

"You have nothing to cry about," she warned herself, and stripped out of the rest of her clothes.

Moments later, the hard, peppering spray of a refreshing shower was stinging her skin and giving her something to think about besides the look in Jackson Rule's eyes. But when she emerged, the memory came back, along with the knot in her belly.

Later, dressed in a pair of white cotton shorts and a tank top, she headed for the kitchen to fix herself some supper. But there was no joy to be had this night in the house that she loved so much. Satisfaction in the perfectly matched furniture and drapes was lost in the lonely sound of her footsteps on the cool, hardwood flooring.

She stood in the middle of her kitchen and, for the first time, saw her existence for what it really was. Yes, she had successfully realized her dream of owning a greenhouse and landscaping business. And yes, she had a fine home and a comfortable bank account. But Rebecca Hill had no one to share any of it with. She dropped into a kitchen chair and buried her face in her hands.

Maybe her father was right. Maybe it was time she found herself a husband.

As that thought entered her mind, the face of a man who had no business there came calling. A man with hard blue eyes and a bitter smile. A man with more scars on the inside than the obvious ones on the outside of his body. A man who had killed.

Tears ran between her fingers and across the tops of her hands.

"Why, Jackson Rule? Why can't I get you out of my mind? Why do you haunt my nights and ruin my days? And why on earth did I ever hire you?"

But there were no answers for Rebecca, because Jackson had them all. He knew he was treading on uncertain ground every day he spent in her employ. It was only a matter of time before he did something unforgivable, and she would send him away. And yet he didn't have it in him to quit.

For Jackson, there were few options. She'd suggested he "howl at the moon." And while finding a woman to warm his bed was tempting, he knew it would be a lost cause. He didn't want just anyone . . . not anymore. He wanted one about average height . . . with red, curly hair and exactly five small gold freckles across the bridge of her nose. Making love to that woman until her green eyes closed in ecstasy would be easy. Finding another woman to fill Rebecca Hill's shoes would be impossible.

He rode his Harley down a tree-lined street and stopped at the small café on the corner. Running naked through bayous was out of the question. He would have to settle for a solitary meal and a long sleepless night.

But the best-laid plans often have a way of changing, and Jackson's changed just as he was about to take his first bite.

The woman stood outside the window of the café, clutching her child's hand with something close to desperation. The little boy pointed toward the café, as if begging to go in. And when the woman shook her head, then looked out into the street, Jackson paused with the fork halfway to his lips. He couldn't remember the last time he'd seen such hopelessness on a child's face. He looked down at the food, all but overflowing his plate, and then back at the woman and child.

She was thin to the point of emaciation, and the child's legs protruding from a pair of oversize shorts seemed too spindly to hold him up. The bag on the woman's shoulder seemed to be dragging her down, and yet she clutched it as fiercely as she did her child.

Because it's all that she owns, Jackson thought. A waitress walked by his table, and before he could talk himself out of the notion, Jackson flagged her down.

"Miss, I see some friends of mine," he said, pointing out to the street. "I'll be right back. I want to catch them before they get away."

The waitress nodded as Jackson bolted out the front door. Without considering what he was about to do, he hailed them just as they were about to cross the street.

"Lady! Wait!"

She spun. The fear on her face shamed him.

"I mean you no harm," he said gently, and pointed back inside the café. "I saw you from my table. I'm eating alone and thought maybe you and your child would like to share my meal."

Shock mingled with fear on the woman's face. She understood all too well what a man alone might want from her in return. Jackson answered the question in her eyes before she had to ask.

"No strings attached, lady. I swear. It's just that . . ." Emotion caught him unawares as his voice cracked. He took a deep breath and then managed a smile. "I've been where you are," he said. "I'd like to help."

"Momma, can we eat with the man?"

Jackson squatted until he was on the boy's level. The child's eyes were dark and round, almost begging for the food he sensed was being offered.

"My name is Jackson," he said, and held out his hand.

The boy looked up at his mother, who nodded warily.

A slow grin spread across the child's face as he laid his hand in Jackson's palm.

"His name is Billy," the woman said, and then she smoothed her hand down the front of her shirt and brushed at the legs of her pants as Jackson stood. "My name is Esther."

Jackson nodded, giving her the space that she obviously needed. When he opened the door, and then stepped back to let them enter, the woman walked into the café with her chin up and her head held high. She might be destitute, but she had not lost her dignity.

Ignoring stares, he led the way back to his table and offered them a seat.

Esther Thibideaux had been on hard times before, but until last week, she'd never been homeless. It was the hunger on her child's face that had prompted her to accept the stranger's offer. But it was the kindness in his eyes that let her relax enough to eat something herself.

When they were nearing the end of the meal, Jackson asked, "Do you and your boy have a place to stay?"

Fear swept across her face. "Why, we've been doing all right so far. I know of a . . . "

"You misunderstand," Jackson said gently. "I want nothing from you other than to help. Have you tried the missions?"

She slumped. "Sometimes they feed us, but they don't have any beds."

Jackson's eyes narrowed thoughtfully. During his search for work in the city, he remembered passing an old building that had been renovated into a shelter for the homeless. He was pretty sure he could find it again.

"I might know of a place. It's called the Jesus House." Then he grinned. "Have you ever ridden a motorcycle? Think you can hang on?"

"I've been hangin' on to life for thirty-seven years. I reckon I can hang on a little while longer," she said, and for the first time since he'd dragged them in from the street, she smiled.

"Momma, are we gonna take a ride?"

Esther Thibideaux stared into Jackson's eyes, judging by what she saw as much as by what she sensed. Finally, she swept her hand across her son's head, brushing at the unruly hair that kept falling into his eyes, and nodded.

"Yes, Billy, I believe that we are."

Long after Jackson was at home and in bed, he kept thinking of the profound relief on Esther's face when they'd been accepted into the shelter. Like most children, Billy adapted better to his new surroundings than his mother. But given time and a little help, he suspected that Esther would find a way to reestablish her life. If only it was that simple to reestablish his own.

He rolled over in bed, bunching the pillow beneath his cheek, and closed his eyes. There was one thing from their encounter that Jackson hadn't expected to feel. It was a sense of satisfaction for a job well done.

Finally it was the weekend . . . and payday. The half day had been hectic, but it was drawing to a close. Rebecca was in the office making out a deposit while the men were outside putting everything under wraps.

The sound of laughter drifted through the open door. She was glad that at least Pete and Jackson got along. She supposed it shouldn't matter that for the time being, they were giving her a wide berth. After delivering the ultimatum she had, she'd more or less asked for it.

The laughter got louder, and then she could hear the sound of footsteps as someone ran around the building.

"What on earth?"

She dumped the bank bag inside her purse and walked out of the office, intent upon finding out what was so funny. All she got for her trouble was water in her ear.

The slender stream of water that came from her right was unexpected. If she'd been a little slower, it would have just cleared her nose, but she wasn't, and it didn't. It splattered along her cheekbone and into her ear with unerring accuracy.

"Hey!" she yelled, batting her hands at the oncoming spray too late to stop its progress.

Pete was clutching a hot pink water gun. His shirt, pants, and hair were splotched and dripping, and he was red-faced and puffing, obviously out of breath from his dash around the building. The look on his face was somewhere between embarrassment and disgust.

"Well damn, Rebecca. I'm real sorry, but if you had let us know you were coming out, we would have held our fire."

She knew she must be staring, but for the life of her she couldn't stop. Pete Walters was at least sixty-five years old if he was a day, and she'd caught him in a water fight.

"Come on, Jackson!" Pete yelled. "We've been found out, and I'm not taking the rap alone."

Jackson was still grinning when he emerged from the left side of the building. His shirt was splotched, but his hair and pants were almost dry, proving him either the better shot, or the faster on his feet.

"I can't believe my eyes," she muttered. "Where on earth did you two find those, and better yet, what possessed you?"

"We found them on the picnic table in the back," Jackson said, and rolled the neon green water pistol in his hand, admiring the sparkles embedded in the plastic. "And he started it," he said, aiming his gun over her head at Pete.

Pete's eyes danced. "And I'm about to finish it, too."

Before Rebecca could duck, both men let loose, catching her squarely in the middle of the war. While she squealed, they emptied their guns on her.

Dripping wet and laughing like children on a playground, the trio finally collapsed into lawn chairs beneath a wide patch of shade provided by an ancient row of live oaks.

"Oh Lord, but I needed that," Rebecca said, and groaned when a muscle in her side pulled a stitch. "I can't remember when I've laughed so hard."

Pete grinned. "I don't doubt it," he said, well aware what he was about to say was going to get another rise out of her. "If you'd get yourself a man before you're too old for bait, you might be a little more friendly."

She glared. "I don't suppose you've been talking to Daddy again?"

Jackson listened to their verbal sparring and tried not to care, but for him, the fun was gone. He didn't want to think about Rebecca and "some" man doing anything, let alone laughing together.

"Speaking of the devil," Pete drawled, and pointed toward the driveway.

Rebecca looked up. Sure enough, her father had driven up and was getting out of the car. And if memory served, that look on his face meant trouble. She wondered what had set him off now.

"Hi, Daddy. You're too late for the fun . . . but at least you're safe." She pointed to the guns in their hands. "They ran out of water."

Daniel Hill was shaking, both with anger and disgust. What he'd learned today had set him on edge. He could hardly remain calm while his daughter sat beside the heathen that she had hired. He raked Jackson Rule with a cold, judgmental look, and then aimed his attention at the gun in Jackson's hand.

"Well, at least one of you knows how to use that thing."

Rebecca gasped. Jackson paled, then looked at the toy that had suddenly become an icon of something evil. He took a slow, aching breath and laid it carefully on the ground at his feet.

"I'll be going now," he said, and walked away before anyone could think what to say.

By the time Rebecca got to her feet, she was trembling with rage.

"How dare you, Daddy? How dare you? I have been mad at you plenty of times in my life for a number of things that in the long run were inconsequential. But I have never, and I mean ever, been ashamed of you until now!"

Daniel staggered from her unexpected attack. He'd expected almost anything but this.

"But you don't understand what he is," he argued.

"No! It's you who doesn't understand something," she said. "This is my business; therefore, what goes on here is *my*

business, not yours. I don't come to your pulpit and tell you
how to preach. How dare you say something so vile to one of
my employees?"

"He's an ex-con. And although the legal system chose to call
it manslaughter, the truth of the matter is . . . he committed a
murder. His father is dead because of him."

"We know that," Pete said, feeling an obligation to put in
his two cents. "He told us the day he applied for the job."

Rebecca's father was stunned. "He told you? And you still
hired him? Rebecca Ruth, what on earth were you thinking?"

She counted to ten while trying to find an answer that
would not destroy what little was left of her relationship with
her father.

"I guess, Reverend Hill, that I was doing what you'd taught
me to do." Her voice was shaking as angry tears threatened to
overflow. "It was something about . . . let's see, how did it
go . . . *judge not, that ye be not judged,* and there was the
other . . . um, oh yes, *he that is without sin among you, let him
first cast a stone* . . . remember those bits of heavenly wisdom
you drilled into my head?"

He blanched. Never in his life had anyone thrown the scrip-
tures back in his face, and in such a condemning fashion.

"You're not being fair," he said.

"No, Daddy, you're the one who wasn't fair."

Rebecca turned to look as Jackson rode away. The sound of
the Harley's engine finally faded, but the look on his face
would never fade from Rebecca's memory.

"It isn't the same," Daniel argued. "It was my duty to tell
you what I felt was an endangerment to you."

"In a public forum?" She was as close to screaming at her
father as she'd ever been, and yet she managed a disgusted
accusation. "Why didn't you just whip out the tar and feathers
and get it over with at once?"

"Why are you defending him?" Daniel asked. "How dare
you accuse me of wrongdoing, when he's the one who committed the unforgivable sin?"

At that moment, Rebecca hated her father for reminding her of Jackson's crime. She knew only too well how heinous the act had been. The fact still remained that her father didn't believe her capable of making any adult decisions on her own and continued to meddle in her business. That he'd insulted one of her employees in the process was the final straw. She pointed a shaky finger at him.

"Until you apologize to Jackson, you are not welcome on these premises again."

Daniel gasped. "You can't mean that!" Then he panicked. How had something he thought so right have been so terribly wrong?

She spun away, tears running down her face, and headed for the office. All she wanted was to get the purse that she'd dropped, put her money in the bank, and put as much distance between herself and her father as she could.

"Well, Daniel, you went and did it now," Pete grumbled, and picked up the gun Jackson had laid in the dirt. "We were just having ourselves a little fun. Rebecca has been real uptight ever since she was attacked, and you've gone and made the situation worse. Sometimes you're just too self-righteous for your collar, if you know what I mean."

Having said his piece, Pete got in his car and drove away, leaving the father and daughter to thrash it out as best they could.

Daniel was thunderstruck. He'd seen himself playing the role of a savior, and now he was faced with being something considerably less. He kept remembering what his daughter had said, and he didn't like the way it made him feel. He *did* preach forgiveness. He *did* preach to turn the other cheek. He *had* taught his daughter what he believed to be the right way to live, and when she'd done as she'd been taught, he'd been the first one to cast doubt on the wisdom of it all.

"Oh Lord," he muttered. "Help me find a way to make this right."

Rebecca came back out with her purse on her shoulder and her keys in her hand. She locked the door behind her and started toward her car without looking her father's way.

"Rebecca, wait!"

She paused. Her lip was still trembling, but there wasn't a sign of a tear anywhere on her face.

"Why are you still here?"

He blanched. "Don't do this to us, honey."

"I didn't do anything, Daddy. It was you, not me, who broke one of your precious rules. The way I look at it, you're the one who needs to fix it."

"I'm sorry," he said.

She shook her head. "I'm not the one who deserves the apology."

She drove away, leaving him alone beneath the shade of the live oaks to ponder the frailties of man.

At the same time, Jackson tried to outrun a past that would never go away. Long after dark, he was still on the highways, riding nowhere, unwilling to go back to his apartment and listen to the ghost of the preacher's voice echoing inside his head.

It was sunup when he rolled the Harley into his apartment and locked the door behind him. It was all he could do to walk to his bed before he fell facedown on it in exhaustion. Sleep came without effort, but there was no rest for the wicked. His dreams were full of Molly, covered in blood and screaming until she had no breath.

When Rebecca's face was suddenly superimposed over Molly's, he woke with a start, and made it to the bathroom just before he threw up.

It was a hell of a beginning for a Sunday.

7

Twice as Rebecca was dressing for church, she almost talked herself out of going. And each time, she kept thinking that she couldn't let her father's rules interfere with her life. She liked going to church. It gave her the moral and spiritual boost she needed to start a new week. And just because her father was blind to reality, didn't mean she had to be. This morning, she would focus on the sermon and not the man delivering it.

The sign on the church lawn announcing the text of the Reverend Hill's sermon was, as usual, to the point. He didn't go for the cute, catchy phrases that were a biblical play on words, but preferred to get straight to the point, and today's sermon was no exception. It was just a plain and simple, *Ministering to a friend in need.*

Rebecca parked, gave herself a last glance in the rearview mirror, and then got out of her car. A puppy from the house across the street ran through the maze of cars, his tongue lolling, his nose to the ground.

"At least you're having a good day," Rebecca muttered, sidestepping the dog. She fidgeted with the collar of her best pink suit as she walked up the steps and took her usual seat in the pew down front.

She felt guilty about harboring anger, especially on the Lord's Day, but forgetting about her father's meddling was impossible, never mind his cruel words toward Jackson.

When Daniel Hill walked onto the podium, the first thing he did was look to see if Rebecca was there. When he saw her he seemed to relax. She knew that in his mind, her presence meant that all was forgiven, and that she'd finally come around to his way of thinking.

"Good morning," he said to the congregation, absorbing the sound of his echo as well as the smiles of welcome on his parishioners' faces. "I had planned my sermon around the use of faith in our daily lives, but I feel compelled to deliver a different message to you this day. One that I believe you have need of remembering. I'm speaking of God's commandments."

At that point he stared pointedly into Rebecca's face. She froze, her mouth slightly agape as he calmly turned and announced the number of the first song to be sung. Throughout the singing of the hymn, she kept thinking that he couldn't possibly mean what she thought he meant. But when he began to preach, she realized she was wrong. He'd meant that . . . and more.

With every rule he quoted, he delivered a scathing accusation to accompany it. An accusation directed at her.

"God does not suffer fools!" he shouted, pounding his fist on the pulpit. "He gave us rules to live by. Rules that were meant to be followed . . . not bent . . . not broken!

"Yes, He taught us to forgive . . . but there are some things that are unforgivable! Heinous acts of vengeance are not ours to take." Daniel leaned over the pulpit, his voice strained, his eyes glazed with the passion that the words of God evoked within him. He lifted a finger and pointed right at Rebecca. "Vengeance is mine, saith the Lord! It's His right to take vengeance . . . not ours! Do you understand?"

Being singled out and then chastised before everyone present was more than she could take. Past caring what the parishioners might think, or of how her father might react, she stood, and without a by-your-leave, turned her back on the pulpit and walked down the aisle and out of the church in a silent rage.

Stunned by her actions, Daniel clutched the podium in silence, while the congregation looked to him for an answer. But when the door slammed behind her in a loud and abrupt manner, he was at a loss for words. Shaken by her behavior, he managed to bring the sermon to an end, then slumped into his chair as the choir began to sing.

Too late, he remembered another of God's rules.

Judge not, that ye be not judged.

The clock on the office wall was ticking away the better part of Monday morning, and Jackson had still not shown up for work. Rebecca waited on her customers with a smile that was a stranger to her face while trying to ignore the sick, empty feeling in the pit of her stomach. She just wasn't sure what hurt her most. Her father's betrayal, or the fact that Jackson might be gone. She kept telling herself that he wouldn't just quit without a word, and yet she really didn't know Jackson Rule well enough to know what he would do.

Maybe he was sick. Maybe she should try calling the manager at his apartment again. But she couldn't bring herself to pick up the phone. The last time she'd asked the manager to knock on Jackson's door, he had seemed to think her concern for Jackson was blatantly sexual. What bothered her most was that the suggestion hadn't offended her nearly as much as it should have.

The bell over the back door jingled. She spun around in anticipation, but it was only Pete.

"I'm loaded and ready to go," he said. "There are three small jobs on the truck, so it'll take me until at least midafternoon to get back. There's that lot of shrubbery to be planted at

Widow Fontenay's, four trees at the new house that sold in that new development, and then I've got to lay that bit of sod in front of a new beauty shop. Are you sure you'll be able to manage on your own?"

"I'll be fine. I brought my lunch, and you know it always slows down around noon. Don't worry."

Pete lifted his cap and combed a hand through his hair, readjusting the remaining sparse growth in frustration.

"This isn't like him," Pete muttered. "I can't help thinking something's wrong."

There was no need asking to whom he was referring. Jackson's unexplained absence was on both of their minds.

Rebecca sighed. "And we both know what it probably is. After what Daddy said, who can blame him?"

Pete shook his head. "No, somehow I don't think that would put him off like this. This can't be the first time he's experienced that sort of condemnation. Remember the police the day of your attack? How you said they were ready to arrest him on the basis of his presence alone? You said that didn't seem to faze him."

"But this was so personal."

"Killing is a personal business, girl," Pete replied. "The man is not a fool. He has to know that most people will always judge him and assume the worst."

She sighed. "I suppose you're right. At any rate, you run along. I'll be fine."

Minutes later, Rebecca was alone with her thoughts and wishing for customers to distract her. Remembering the breakfast that she'd skipped that morning, she headed for the refrigerator in the other room. No need making herself any sicker than she already was.

The soft drink was cold in her hands. She unscrewed the bottle top and turned to toss it in the wastebasket beside the desk when she noticed that the phone was off the hook.

"Great," she muttered. "No wonder it hasn't rung all morning."

The moment it hit the cradle, it began to make up for lost time. Rebecca grabbed it on the first ring.

"Hillside Nursery."

"Rebecca! Thank God! I was beginning to think you'd never quit talking."

Relief swamped her as she clutched her drink and leaned against the desk. It was Jackson.

"The phone was off the hook. I just found it." And then she sighed. "It's been a rough morning."

"Tell me about it," he said. "I ran into a little trouble on the way to work. I ruined a tire, then had to wait until a store opened before I could replace it." He paused, then took a deep breath. "So . . . do I still have a job?"

"Look, Jackson, you need to understand something now. I run this business, not my father. Had I known what he was going to say I would have . . . "

"Save it," he growled. "He didn't say anything that a thousand others haven't already said."

"Nevertheless . . . "

"No! Let it go, Rebecca. Your father cares about you, which is more than mine did for me. Just tell me, do I have a job or not?"

She found herself grinning and was thankful he couldn't see her.

"Only if you can get to Pete before he has to lay that order of sod. He hates that more than anything. He just left with three jobs on the truck, but I don't know where he's going first."

He sighed audibly, obviously relieved. "Just give me the addresses. I'll find him."

Rebecca read him the list of names and addresses, and when he disconnected she sat back and smiled. Her world was back in orbit.

One day ran into another and then another as customers came and went, and while no one was looking, the wall around Jackson Rule's heart began to crumble. It became easier for him to laugh and to accept praise for a job well-done. In the back of his mind, he wanted to believe that he was no different from any other man, but facts were hard to ignore.

And the facts were that he was an ex-con and the woman he wanted was the daughter of a man of God. It was an impossible situation, and Jackson knew it. And because he lived with a troubled soul, he found himself gravitating back to the Jesus House and the people there, who, like him, had lost their way in this world.

Clark Thurman stood across the room, watching the children, who ran to greet Jackson Rule. It wasn't so much the children's reactions that amazed him, because children would love anyone who'd love them back. What Clark noticed, time and again, was the peace that settled on the big man's face when they clamored for their place in his lap.

"He's an angel, isn't he, Mr. Thurman?"

At the sound of Esther Thibideaux's voice, Clark turned and smiled. He knew that in her eyes the man could do no wrong, although he suspected that Jackson Rule had existed on the side of wrong a lot longer than he had on that of right.

"They sure think so," he said, pointing toward the children, who were thrusting their favorite books in his face to be read.

And as Clark watched, Jackson took them one by one, stacking them in order on the table in front of him, and then began with the first. It was, after all, why he'd come.

Jackson hadn't expected to find a place for himself in this house, but when he did, he'd embraced it, and the children, with open arms. Like the baby who'd been thrust into his arms at the greenhouse and then fallen asleep against his chest, these children accepted him for who he was, not where he'd been.

"Read mine first!" Billy Thibideaux cried, as he crawled into Jackson's lap.

Jackson grinned. *The Little Engine That Could* was the boy's favorite book.

"Are you guys going to be quiet?" he asked.

All seven nodded in unison.

"Don't make promises you can't keep." He laughed, and tweaked Billy's ear.

When the child's blond head shifted beneath Jackson's chin and then grew still, the frailty of his body brought a lump to Jackson's throat. For a child so small, like most of the others present, Billy Thibideaux had already seen the worst side of life.

A small dark-skinned girl of no more than four crawled onto his other knee, claiming her place in his lap by her age alone. She gave Jackson a wide smile, stuck her thumb in her mouth, and leaned back against his chest, her eyes riveted on the pictures of the pages before her.

Jackson took a deep breath and began to read, unaware of Clark Thurman's intent observation. Twelve books later, parents began to intrude, claiming their children to be put to bed. As always, it took a promise from Jackson to get them to leave.

"Will you wead to me tomowwow?" the little girl asked.

"If your mother says it's all right," Jackson replied, aware that he was treading on thin ground with these people. They had few people they trusted, especially with their children. He lived in constant fear that someone would find him out, and then he'd be barred from coming back.

As the last child left, Clark called to him from across the room. "Jackson, come into my office before you leave. I'd like to speak with you."

His heart sank as he nodded. Convinced that he had just been found out, Jackson entered the director's office and closed the door behind him.

Clark smiled. "You've got quite a following out there," he said.

Jackson's gut clenched, and he shoved his hands in his pockets so that Clark wouldn't see them shake. "I'm only reading to them. I would never hurt them."

Ah, Jackson, just as I thought. You do have some secrets of your own, don't you? And then he smiled.

"You misunderstand me," he said. "This isn't a complaint. It's praise."

Relieved, Jackson dropped into an empty chair.

"The reason I called you in was to ask you a question," Clark said. "What would you think if I asked you to counsel some of these children? Not so that it would conflict with your job, you understand. Only when you had the time to give."

The question was a shock to Jackson, but what surprised him even more was the excitement that he felt at the thought. But he could only list the reasons why he shouldn't.

"I don't have any training. I took several semesters of college, but by correspondence. I have no skills that would equip me for anything like that."

Clark shook his head. "You don't understand where we're coming from here, do you? Most of this house runs on volunteer services. We do what we do because we've been where they are. Because we understand their fears . . . and because we don't ever want to go back to the streets. Our cook, Marion, is no chef. She's a widow who raised seven children; therefore, she knows how to cook. The woman who comes in twice a week and teaches people how to read isn't a teacher. She's someone who cares . . . and who knows how to read. As for you, I don't know why, but you seem to relate to the children better than you do the adults. And it's obvious that they relate to you. That's all it takes. A little faith and a little trust. And when we get in over our heads, we call in the experts, okay?"

Jackson's fingers tightened around the arms of the chair as he considered the wisdom of telling this man the truth about himself. And then he knew, if this thing was ever to work, he would have to tell the truth.

"I spent the last fifteen years in prison," Jackson said.

Clark took a deep breath, but held his tongue. It was nothing he hadn't expected.

"Are you on parole?"

Jackson shook his head.

"Why, Jackson? What were you accused of doing?"

A bitter expression moved across Jackson's face. "It wasn't an accusation. I was guilty."

Clark shifted in his chair, but held his gaze firmly fixed on Jackson Rule's face.

"Of what?" he asked. "I don't ask for my sake, but for theirs," he said, indicating the people who temporarily resided beyond the door.

Jackson's eyes glittered with unreserved hate as he stared the director in the face. "My father beat the hell out of me for sixteen years. The bigger I got, the worse the beatings. One day it came down to him or me. I shot him point-blank with a shotgun, and if I had to, I'd do it again."

Stunned by Jackson's rage, Clark exhaled slowly, then began to nod. "That explains a lot," he said.

It was the last thing Jackson expected him to say. "What are you getting at?" he asked.

"You notice that there are several single-parent families here. Everyone here isn't automatically homeless because they have nowhere to go. Sometimes it's because they're afraid to go home. The shelters for abused women are often full. And even then, the men know where to find them. Sometimes it's fear that makes people leave home, not a loss of job and money."

Jackson was quiet, absorbing the truth of what he already suspected. More than one child had seemed frightened at the idea of leaving the shelter.

Clark got up from his chair and began pacing the floor. "Maybe you didn't know that a lot of the children here have been in abusive situations. For that matter, some probably still are. I suspect that's why you relate to each other. You sensed their pain because you've been there. And while I understand what happened to you, I'd like to think you would not recommend the same solution to them, right?"

Jackson shuddered. "Hell no," he said softly. "I wouldn't recommend my life to a snake."

Clark grinned. "Point taken. So . . . what do you think about my suggestion?"

Jackson shook his head, but there was a light in his eyes that hadn't been there when he'd come in. "I think you're nuts, but I'm willing to give it a try."

Clark leaned over the desk and offered Jackson his hand. "Thanks, friend. Then we've got a deal."

Jackson's heart surged. Except for Rebecca, this was the first person who'd been willing to trust him since his release.

That night, when he entered his apartment, it didn't seem quite as dingy, and the road to reclaiming his sister didn't seem quite as long. If there was hope for Jackson to change his life, then there was hope for Molly, too.

And yet, as positive as he felt about reuniting his family, he felt hopeless about his feelings for Rebecca. She had been raised to believe in the good in people, and he'd seen nothing but bad. He didn't relate to her world, and she didn't belong in his. To be able to bear the disappointment, he had to convince himself that it was all for the best.

It was only at night, when the dreams came, that he let himself pretend that theirs was a different relationship. In his sleep, there were no barriers between them. In the dark, alone in his bed, she was always with him—beneath him. As when he dreamed, he became lost in a woman he could never have. That was what got him through the night . . . and the next day . . . and the next.

And then, once again, everything changed.

Heat waves danced above the pavement, caught between the thick, humid swelter of the atmosphere above and the hot concrete below. It only added to the misery of the task the two men had to perform. Jackson moved without thinking. Laying sod took strength, not brains, and he was beginning to have the same opinion of the job that Pete Walters had.

Behind him, Pete's constant grunts and grumbles were so commonplace he had almost blocked them out of his mind. A few streets over, somebody honked their horn, and seconds later, the loud, intermittent squawk of a car alarm sounded. Jackson pushed the raw edge on the thick roll of grass and sod firmly into the ground and then stomped it into place.

"That's the last one," he said as he turned to Pete.

"It's about damned time, too," Pete grumbled, and staggered to his feet.

Pete's face was flushed, and sweat was running profusely upon his body. Jackson noted the white ring around Pete's mouth and the short, gasping breaths he was taking. Concerned for the older man's welfare, he patted him on the back. "How about some shade and a cold drink?" he said.

Pete nodded, cursing sod beneath his breath as he bent down to pick up his tools. And then he suddenly swayed and grabbed at his chest as he came upright in a sharp jerk.

Every nerve in Jackson's body went on alert as Pete turned pale.

"Pete? Are you . . . ?"

Pete's mouth crumpled. He groaned and began clawing at the front of his shirt as he started to fall. Jackson caught him before he hit the ground and rolled him onto his back.

"Tell me!" Jackson begged.

"Pain, pain . . . chest."

"Hang on, buddy," Jackson whispered. "I'm going to get some help."

Without hesitation, he dashed across the parking lot to the nearest store in the small shopping complex, thankful this hadn't happened yesterday, when they were on a job miles out of the city and nowhere near a phone.

The lady behind the counter looked startled when Jackson burst into her store, but it didn't take her long to figure out what was wrong. Even from where she stood she could see the man on the ground across the parking lot. He wasn't moving.

"Call an ambulance!" Jackson shouted. "I think my partner is having a heart attack." When he saw that she was doing as he asked, he bolted back across the lot, then knelt at Pete's side.

"Pete . . . Pete, can you hear me?"

There was no answer. *Don't you dare die*, Jackson thought, and bent down, praying that he would feel Pete's breath upon his cheek.

He felt nothing.

He yanked open Pete's shirt and began CPR. Blocking out the feel of cold, clammy skin beneath his hands, he sealed Pete's nose with a pinch and began breathing for him. He didn't want to remember how much he enjoyed the older man's company, and tried not to think about having to tell Rebecca that her best friend had died before his eyes.

Mentally counting breaths, then chest compressions, he repeated over and over the steps that he'd learned in prison and wondered if he was doing it right.

"Come on, Pete, don't die on me," he muttered.

For the first time since the death of his father, he began to pray for the sound of sirens. Long minutes went by, and he was so lost in what he was doing that he was unaware of the gathering crowd. When help finally arrived, he hadn't even heard it coming. It was only after the ambulance was pulling away that he realized it was over. Whatever happened now was out of his hands.

"Jesus," he whispered, and swiped his hands across his face.

"Good job, mister," he heard someone say.

Had he not been so worried about Pete, he would have laughed. It was a cop. The last thing he had ever expected to hear come out of a cop's mouth was praise.

"Where are they taking him?" Jackson asked.

"Pendleton Memorial on Read Boulevard."

Jackson nodded and started back across the street. He needed the use of a phone, just one more time.

It wasn't often that one of Rebecca's customers fell into the shallow goldfish pond near the greenhouse. It had happened before, but usually to children. She had signs posted everywhere warning people to stay back, so she knew that as far as liability was concerned, she was more than covered. But the overweight, matronly woman had been so intent on inspecting the size of the nursery goldfish in comparison to the ones in her own little pond at home, that she'd leaned too far over.

As splashes went, it had been a doozy. The woman bellyflopped onto a nice arrangement of lily pads and grounded two of the smaller fish on impact. When she landed, the waterspout that went up drenched her husband, as well as a couple of nearby customers. It was all they could do to get the landlocked fish back in the water and the woman out, without going into hysterics. Everyone, except the doused woman, thought it was funny. Even her husband was so overcome he couldn't talk. But laughing at customers was not in Rebecca's best interests, and so she wound up being the one to help her out of the pool and into the car.

The smile was still on Rebecca's face as they drove away. She was halfway back to the office when she heard the phone ringing and ran to answer it.

"Hillside Nursery."

The breathless, happy quality of her voice made Jackson sick. Within moments, he was going to ruin her day.

"Rebecca . . . "

"Oh hi, Jackson, what's happening? Have you finished with the shopping center? If you have, then tell Pete to . . . "

"Rebecca, listen to me!" Then realizing that he had all but shouted at her, his tone softened. "Please."

"I'm sorry," she said and started giggling all over again. "But you should have been here. One of the customers just . . . "

"Pete had a heart attack. The ambulance just left. They're taking him to Pendleton Memorial on Read Boulevard. If he has any family that need to be notified, I would suggest that you call them now. He didn't look so good."

She gasped. "Oh my God! What happened?"

Jackson frowned, then closed his eyes, remembering all too well the ashen quality to the older man's face.

"He just grabbed his chest and collapsed. I don't know any details, but I'm on my way to the hospital now."

"I'll be right there," she said.

"What about his family?" Jackson asked.

Rebecca's chin began to quiver. "He doesn't have anyone but me . . . and Daddy."

Jackson knew when he said it that it was going to cost him, but it had to be said.

"Then call your father before you leave. Just because you two are on the outs doesn't mean Pete won't want both of you there."

She was too quiet, and a silent Rebecca was not a normal thing.

"Did you hear me?" he asked.

"Yes," she finally answered. "I heard you."

"Then do it, lady. I've got to go."

"I'll see you there," she said, but she was talking to herself. He'd already disconnected.

Cool air circulated antiseptic odors throughout the waiting area, mingling with intermittent blasts of outside air, as people came and went from ER. Jackson paced the floor, trying to distinguish what they were doing to Pete beyond the constant noise of other patients being cared for, as well as the comings and goings of the health care workers.

It was impossible. Somewhere down the hall a woman was crying. Behind the curtain behind him, a child screamed in terror as stitches closed the gap in his scalp. A couple of policemen stood guard outside another area while a patient under arrest cursed loud and long while being given first aid.

Jackson shuddered. It reminded him too much of prison chaos. Never quiet. Always in turmoil. On the edge of disaster at all times. And then someone touched his arm. He flinched, and then spun.

"Rebecca."

There was relief in his voice, and for a moment, she thought he was going to throw his arms around her. And then he didn't.

"How's Pete? Is he . . . ?"

"They haven't told me a thing," he said, and then suddenly grabbed her by her arms and moved her out of the way just in time to avoid being run down by a crash cart being wheeled into an adjoining room.

"Damn," he muttered. "This hallway is a hell of a place to stand. There's a small waiting room a couple of doors down. We can talk better in there."

She nodded, then glanced over her shoulder at the door. Jackson caught a look on her face that made him wonder.

"Did you call your father?"

"There was no one at home," she said. "But I left a message."

Jackson wanted to hold her so badly he could hardly think. Her hair was nothing but a jumble of curls, and there was a slight smudge on her white T-shirt and a small rip on the knee of her jeans. Tears shimmered in her eyes, and her chin was trembling.

"Oh Jackson . . . is Pete going to die?"

When the tears started sliding down her cheeks, he lost it.

"Come here," he said roughly, and held out his arms.

She went without hesitation, laying her head against his chest and wrapping her arms around his waist. The top of her head was just beneath his chin and her curls were tickling his throat.

"Don't cry, honey," he said quietly, unaware that he'd called her by a name that he saved for his dreams. "Pete's tough, and I'm told the doctors here are good. He's got as good a chance as anyone could have."

"I should have hired more help," she said between sobs. "I let him do too much."

Jackson brushed her hair away from her face and then dug a handkerchief out of his back pocket. He tilted her chin and began wiping at the tear tracks on her cheeks.

"I haven't known Pete Walters as long as you have, but I don't think he's the kind of man who *let* anyone do anything to him. Isn't he pretty much his own boss?"

Lost in the gentleness of his touch and the concern in his eyes, for a moment Rebecca forgot why she was here.

When Daniel Hill burst through the doors of ER, the first thing he saw was his daughter in the arms of that man and felt sick to his stomach. *Oh Rebecca! No, no!*

But as badly as he wanted to shout, he kept his reaction to himself. As it was, he'd spent days in prayer, afraid that their relationship was irrevocably ruined. Yet as he stared at the couple in each other's arms, he wondered how, in all conscience, he could still remain silent. He took a deep breath and headed toward them with single-minded intent.

"Rebecca!"

They both looked up at the same time. Jackson dropped his hands and took a step back in reflex as Rebecca turned. She took one look at her father's face, and, believing that his concern was directed toward Pete, she hugged him.

"Daddy, Pete had a heart attack. They're working on him now."

"I know, honey, I know," he said, patting her awkwardly on the back and trying not to glare at the man who'd been holding her only moments earlier. "After I got your message, I called the hospital before I came. They said he's holding his own."

Relieved by the news, Jackson collapsed into an empty chair and tried to ignore the disgust on the preacher's face.

"They haven't told us a thing," Rebecca said.

Daniel hugged her. "I'll get some answers. I have a little pull here, you know," he said, referring to the countless times he'd been called to minister to sick church members and grieving families.

Jackson stared at a spot on the floor across the hallway. With the arrival of Rebecca's father, he was, once more, on the outside looking in. He knew that the Reverend Hill was the proper person to be comforting Rebecca, but when she'd turned from his arms to her father's without even looking back, he'd felt empty, from the inside out.

Then a nurse approached them. "Excuse me. Are you members of Pete Walters's family?"

"Yes," Daniel answered. "Rebecca and I are all the family he has."

"Then come with me," she said. "The doctor is in his office and would like to speak with you."

They began to follow the nurse down the hall when Rebecca realized that Jackson was not behind them. She stopped and turned.

"Jackson."

He looked up from the chair.

"Aren't you coming?"

"Now, Rebecca, I don't think . . ." Daniel began.

She gave her father a long, hard look. "He was with him when it happened," she said, then turned back to Jackson.

He followed without a word. Refusing that woman a thing was not a possibility. Even if her father hated the sight of his face. Even if he had no place at Pete Walters's bedside, he went where she wanted him to go.

The doctor was at his desk, nursing a much-needed cup of coffee when they entered.

"Dr. Pittman, how is Pete doing?" Daniel Hill asked.

"Daniel! I didn't expect to see you," Pittman said.

"Pete Walters is a part of our family," he explained.

The doctor nodded, then drained his cup before surveying the trio before him. "All I can say is, he's a lucky man. Someone had the foresight to do CPR on him until the ambulance arrived. It saved his life."

The hair stood on the back of Jackson's neck. What he'd done had been on impulse, not out of heroism. He'd worn the brand of a murderer for so long that being called a hero seemed out of place.

Rebecca stared at the look on Jackson's face, and in that moment, she knew. She slid her hand up his arm. The muscles jumped, then relaxed beneath her touch.

"Oh, Jackson, it was you, wasn't it?"

JACKSON RULE   107 –

He shrugged, then nodded.

Daniel was shocked, yet couldn't bring himself to add to Rebecca's praise. *Jackson Rule's sin was so heinous. How does one reconcile to accepting the fact of such a terrible crime?*

Jackson fidgeted, uncomfortable beneath so much scrutiny. Anxious for the conversation to take a different turn, he asked, "What's the prognosis, Doc?"

"He will be hospitalized for at least a week. The next forty-eight hours are critical. In these cases, there's always a danger of a second attack. But, barring complications, and with a change of pace, he should be fine. Once he's released, I recommend he take it easy for a month or so before resuming work."

Rebecca sighed with relief. "That might be hard to enforce, but I swear we'll do our best. Pete doesn't like being told what to do."

The doctor smiled. "Reverend Hill, if you need to make any phone calls regarding Mr. Walters, feel free to use my office. I've got to get back on the floor."

He left, and the silence in the room was almost oppressive.

"Well now," Daniel began, when Rebecca stunned both men by throwing her arms around Jackson's waist in a fervent hug.

"Pete means the world to Daddy and me, and you saved his life. How can we ever thank you?"

Jackson looked over Rebecca's head, straight into the fierce, angry gaze of her father, and froze. Judgment was written all over the preacher's face.

"You don't thank me for anything," he said harshly, and thrust Rebecca away from him. What he saw in her eyes was something he knew he'd never be able to live up to. "And don't go making me out to be a hero, either," he growled. "Don't forget what I am, Rebecca! Don't forget what I've done."

"Don't be ridiculous!" she said, feeling her temper get the better of her. "I'm not about to forget what you did. You heard the doctor. You saved Pete's life."

"So you think that balances the scales back in my favor? You think that saving a life makes up for the one I took?"

She blanched and would have looked away, but he kept on talking, refusing to let her glorify what he'd done.

"Don't make me into something I'm not, Rebecca, because if Stanton Rule was standing here today, I'd kill him all over again, do you understand that?"

Daniel was staggered by the venom in Jackson's words. Never in his life had he felt such anger or hate. But Rebecca took his words a different way. She glared at him, her fists doubled, her voice trembling.

"Then why? Tell me why, Jackson Rule. What did he do that was so terrible? Is he responsible for the scars on your back? Did he beat you all of your life? If he did, why didn't you ask for help?"

Still shaking with misplaced anger, Jackson ignored her. "I'm going to take the truck back to the greenhouse now."

"Fine!" She tilted her chin. It was an I-let-you-win-the-argument look that almost made him smile.

He started out the door when she called him back.

"Jackson."

"What?"

She tossed him a set of keys. "I locked up before I left. You'll need these to get in. If any customers come before I get back, you can handle them, can't you?"

The keys burned the palm of his hand. The implications of what she'd done . . . and in front of her father . . . were too obvious to ignore. She'd said, in the only way she knew how, that she trusted him implicitly.

Everything around them, including Daniel Hill, suddenly faded as Rebecca became Jackson's sole focus. Her eyelashes were still wet and clumped together from crying. The smudge was still on her shirt, and those damned, all-seeing green eyes held him pinned to the spot. She saw too far inside him for comfort, but there was nothing he could think to do but answer her as truthfully as he knew how.

"Yes, ma'am, I can handle anything you tell me to do."

"What did you call me?"

He grinned slightly. "Rebecca."

She nodded, her curls bouncing across her forehead as she accepted his half-assed apology.

"That's what I thought you said."

When the door swung shut behind him, Rebecca went limp, as if he'd taken all of the life and energy from the room. Her father's hand was firm upon her elbow as he turned her toward him.

"You're playing with fire, Rebecca Ruth."

Her heart was heavy, but her words were firm as she answered.

"No, Daddy, I'm not *playing* with anything . . . or anyone. Whatever I do or do not feel for that man has nothing to do with games. Now let's go see if we can sneak into Pete's room. I'm not leaving here until I know he's stable."

Daniel Hill followed his daughter from the room without saying another word. He'd said what was on his mind, and if it meant sticking around to pick up the pieces of his daughter's life afterward, he would do it. His main fear was that there would be no life left to pick up.

Once a killer, always a killer, kept twisting through his mind. *Please God, no!* he prayed. *Not my daughter.*

8

The dark of a moonless night was interrupted only by the muted glow of streetlamps along the sidewalk. Traffic had slowed to the occasional car, and foot traffic on Solange Street consisted mostly of local hookers on the prowl for johns. Although it was nearly midnight, the air was still thick with daytime humidity.

The window unit in Jackson's bedroom, having now been fixed, churned out a respectable blast of cool air that didn't quite reach his bed. A nearby table fan oscillated from side to side, stirring the air across Jackson's body as he slept.

Although the curtains were drawn, they were sheer from age, not design, and let in more than the normal amount of nighttime light beyond the windows. But Jackson had spent the last fifteen years in a place that was never completely dark, so the streetlights did not impair his rest at all.

It was the dreams that took his peace . . . and his sanity . . . and left him worn-out and weary each morning when he awoke. And tonight, like every night since his release, he lived and breathed in a nightmare with no end.

o   o   o

She danced across the grass in a halo of sunlight. The closer she came, the more clearly he could see her face. Rebecca! She came with arms outstretched, a wide, beckoning smile, and green devils dancing in her eyes that promised him heaven if he only had the guts to take her there.

He called her name and she laughed, her body moving in slow motion, fluid with grace. Her breasts bounced lightly with every step she took, and her smooth, tanned skin begged to be touched.

She ran into his arms, catching him around the waist and halting his breath on impact. She fit perfectly within his embrace, just as he'd known she would. Her head tilted back, pleading for the kiss she knew was coming.

Jackson tossed in his sleep and groaned at the moment their lips met. The taste of her was on his mouth and the faint sheen of perspiration on her body felt like warm honey beneath his hands.

Make love to me . . . love to me . . . love to me . . . love to me.

Her plea echoed inside Jackson's subconscious like a prayer. He could no more refuse her in sleep than he could awake. Without thought of the consequences or the impossibility of making love to a ghost, he took her kiss and her body and made them his own.

They joined, bodies hammering against and into each other with relentless passion, burning, using each other up in the heat of an all-consuming emotion. She took what he gave and begged him for more. Jackson gasped, then laughed, and drove himself down, down, down. At the point of climax, she started to scream, and he tried to pull back. But it was too late! The harder he fought to regain his sense of self, the more poignant her cries, and then she disappeared beneath him, leaving nothing behind but a mind-bending wail.

When he looked again, Rebecca was no longer there, it was Molly, and she was covered in blood. It was then that he realized the screams he heard were hers.

A tear trickled from the corner of one of Jackson's eyes as he thrashed upon the bed.

Don't Molly! Don't cry!

But she couldn't hear him any better now than she had the day Stanton Rule had died. He started toward her with outstretched hands and then stumbled. When he looked down to see what he'd kicked, the faceless body of Stanton Rule was staring up at him.

Jackson's eyes flew open and he sat straight up in bed. Sweat was pouring down his face and every muscle in his body was shaking.

"Jesus Christ!" Jackson muttered, and swiped a shaky hand across his face. "Damn you Stanton . . . why can't you leave me alone?"

As he staggered toward the bathroom to wash his face, the echo of screams still ringing in his ears, he suddenly stilled, then listened. The dream had disappeared, but the screams had not. They were real and ongoing.

The echo of a child's shrill cries drifted from upstairs and down the hall to his door. Plaintive cries for help that had nowhere to go but out. Accompanied by the child's short, piercing shrieks, were the harsh, ugly sounds of a man enraged. Jackson listened to the sound of furniture falling and glass breaking as the child kept crying . . . begging . . . for help that didn't come.

Jackson paled. He knew what he was hearing. His stomach rolled in reflex as he heard the distinct sound of hand against flesh in the room above his head. He didn't know the man, of course, but he sure as hell knew the type.

"You son of a bitch," he whispered, and yanked a pair of jeans from a chair as he started toward the door.

He had no plan in mind, no cognizant thought of the trouble he might cause by meddling in someone else's business. All he could remember was that when he had cried out for help, no one heard. No one came.

The hall was dark as he headed for the stairs. All the bulbs in the lamps were missing; either burned out or stolen for use in someone's room. The floor beneath his bare feet felt gritty, and he grimaced as he took the stairs two at a time.

The child screamed again as Jackson rushed to the door just ahead. He banged on it with his fist, rattling it on its hinges like a clap of thunder, and then took a slow, deep breath, trying to calm his racing anger.

Suddenly there was silence. He interrupted it with another vicious thump that quickly got results.

"Who is it?" a male voice yelled out.

"Santa Claus, you son of a bitch, now open the door before I kick it in."

"I'll call the damned cops!" the man shouted, slurring his words just enough that Jackson knew he was drunk.

"That's fine with me," Jackson said. "Call Child Welfare while you're at it, buddy."

Jackson heard a string of muffled curses. He held his breath and waited, then flinched when he heard a lock turn, suddenly realizing that he might be facing the muzzle of a gun. Instinctively, he stepped back into the shadows and waited as the door began to open.

"What bleedin' heart is crawling around in my home in the middle of the night?" the man growled, peering out into the dark hallway.

Jackson would have bet good money that the man had been wearing his clothes for the better part of a week. The pants were stained and sagging below a bulging gut, and the shirt was missing all but two buttons, leaving far too much of a hairy belly and unwashed skin to be seen. He stood barefoot in the middle of the doorway, swaying to an alcoholic rhythm running through his veins. The half-empty bottle in his hand banged against the doorframe as he peered outside.

Good. No gun. Only a bottle, Jackson thought, and stepped forward.

Startled by the figure emerging from the shadows, the man jerked back, accidentally banging his bottle against the door. He had good reason to fear. Jackson Rule towered over him by a good six inches.

Jackson pushed the door wide and, less than politely, shoved the man inside.

The odor of filth was nearly overwhelming. Scraps of uneaten food lay in pizza boxes, days old and molding by the hour. Unwashed plates were everywhere, and garbage spilled from the top of overflowing trash containers. In a corner, just beyond the circle of lamplight, Jackson could see a child cowering in the shadows.

"Come here, boy," he said softly. "Let me see your face."

"You stay where you are," the man warned, and pointed the half-empty whiskey bottle toward the child.

Jackson grabbed the man lightly beneath his chin, twisting his shirt collar just enough to get his message across. "No, you stay where you are," he warned. "I want to see the boy, and I mean now." He softened his tone. "I'm not going to hurt you, boy," Jackson said. "What's your name?"

"Freddie," the child whispered, unsure which man he should fear more.

"How old are you, Freddie?"

"Six."

Jackson shuddered. "Nice to meet you Freddie, my name is Jackson, and I guess we must be neighbors."

The boy got to his feet and took one step into the light.

Bruises, both old and new, mingled with a steady stream of bright red blood that ran from a cut over his eye as well as out of his nose. His lower lip was so swollen that Jackson wondered how he was able to talk, and the clothes he was wearing hung on his thin, bony frame.

"You ride the Harley," the child muttered, and swiped his arm beneath his nose, smearing blood across his cheekbone.

Rage overwhelmed Jackson as he stared long and hard at

the child. Then he looked back at the drunken man he held fast in his hand.

"I don't know what your name is, mister, but I know where you're gonna wind up if you don't stop beating the hell out of your boy."

"I ain't doin' nothin' to him that my old man didn't do to me," the man replied, and swung the bottle in his hand at Jackson's head. He missed by a mile, then staggered and fell on his ass when Jackson shoved him backward. "You don't know shit," he muttered.

"Oh, but I do," Jackson whispered, and squatted down until they were eye to eye. He pointed back at the child, who was staring fixedly at the scene being played out before his eyes. "You see little Freddie there? Well one of these days, Freddie is going to grow up . . . just like I did. And when he does, you're going to come in drunk once too often, and take a swing at a man, not a boy, and little Freddie there just might blow your damned head off . . . just like I did my old man's."

Even in the pale yellow glow from the lamplight, Jackson saw the man stare at the child and then pale.

"You don't know . . ."

Jackson smiled, and the man quit talking in the middle of his sentence.

"That's where you're wrong, buddy. It cost me fifteen years of my life, but I sent my daddy to hell where he belonged, and I'd do it again for free."

The man swayed where he sat as the words soaked in. Suddenly Jackson stood, unwilling to stay in the filthy environment a moment longer.

The drunk looked up, and it seemed as if the man above him were ten feet tall.

"I better not hear that boy cry again," Jackson warned. "If I do, I'll call cops, social services, and every bleeding heart in New Orleans. You won't be sucking on any more whiskey when they're through with you. The only thing you'll be sucking on is your thumb."

Behind him, a floorboard squeaked, and he spun in a half crouch with his hands fisted as a door opened across the hall. When he saw it was a woman, he relaxed. Her brown face wrinkled with concern as she spoke.

"I heard. I'll take Freddie in with me for the night. It won't be the first time."

She smiled gently, moving past Jackson into the room. When the child saw her, he suddenly gave in to his suffering and began to shake, crying in soft, broken sobs.

"There, there, little man." She gathered him into her arms. "You come spend the night with Martha. We'll wash you up good, and you can sleep with me. How will that be?"

The child literally wilted in her arms, sobbing against her neck as she quickly retreated into her room and shut the door.

Jackson paused in the doorway, giving the drunk one last look. "I meant what I said, you son of a bitch. Don't make me hurt you."

As he pulled the door shut behind him, he heard the familiar sound of retching and knew a moment of satisfaction, although it was still less than the man deserved.

Jackson went downstairs much more slowly than he'd come up. His muscles were tight from unreleased anger, and when he entered his room, car lights swept through the window and across the opposite wall, momentarily blinding him. Without thinking, he locked the door and turned on the lights.

He stood without moving, his mind locked on what he'd just seen and heard. It was daunting to realize that the cycle of abuse seemed to perpetuate itself from generation to generation. *Nothin' my old man didn't do to me.*

The words made him sick. Would every abused child grow up to be an abusive parent? Jackson groaned. If so, what in hell would that make him?

Disgusted with the entire episode, he started toward the shower. Even if it was only symbolic, he felt a sudden need to be cleansed. With only the living room light for guidance, he entered the bathroom and then stopped short at the shadowy figure of the man staring back at him from the vanity mirror. His heart skipped a beat, then hammered into overtime.

"Stanton!"

It took him several seconds to realize that he was staring at himself and not his father's ghost. In a panic, he turned on the light and then leaned over the sink until he was eye to eye with the man in the mirror. He'd known the resemblance between them had been great, but he'd never known how remarkable until he'd seen the hate and rage on his own face that he had always associated with his father.

"Oh my God," he groaned, and turned and threw up into the toilet. Like the man upstairs, he'd had the hell scared out of him in more ways than one.

A long while later, he lay faceup with the lights still on, staring at the ceiling over his bed, afraid to close his eyes and see the truth of what he could easily become. In that moment, he realized that a home and family might never be for him. He'd rather die than put a child through the life that he'd led. Look at poor Freddie. He was the butt of someone else's pain, just like his father had been before him.

Somewhere between midnight and dawn he finally slept. When he awoke, it was morning. Memories of the night before were all too real. To avoid looking at himself in a mirror, he decided to forgo a shave. Just then, the fear of seeing Stanton Rule in himself again was more than he could handle.

He arrived at the greenhouse nearly an hour early, and sat outside beneath one of the live oaks, listening to the birds singing in the trees overhead, letting the peace and solitude of the countryside seep into his soul. By the time he saw Rebecca's truck turning off the highway, he had himself and his fears well under control.

Rebecca's eyes were burning from lack of sleep, and the clothes she was wearing were the ones she'd put on the day before. Refusing to leave Pete alone in the hospital, she'd spent a miserable night alone on the ICU floor, dozing off and on in a waiting room chair. Every time she was allowed, she slipped into the ward for a brief, five-minute visit to her oldest and best friend.

Only after the arrival of her father an hour ago had she been able to leave the hospital. The morning sun hurt her eyes, and her stomach rolled. Whether from lack of food, sleep, or both, she didn't know. But she did know she was going to be late for work.

It took all her remaining strength to drive out of the city toward home. Instinct got her as far as the greenhouse. She barely remembered turning off the highway or parking the truck, but when Jackson suddenly appeared at her door, she wasn't surprised. Somehow, he kept turning up when she needed him most.

He took one look at her pale, drawn expression and red-rimmed eyes, noted she was still wearing the same smudged T-shirt and torn jeans from yesterday, and yanked the door open. His fear for her took the form of anger.

"Damn it, Rebecca, you could have had a wreck."

"I'm fine." Her chin trembled, belying her claim. "But I need to go home and clean up. I knew you could open up because you have my keys, but the deposit bag is still in my pickup. I never made it to the bank. If I . . ."

He took the bank bag from the floorboard of the pickup and guided her toward the office.

"Shut up," he muttered. "Just shut up and come with me."

She did as she was told.

The building smelled stale until Jackson switched on the air-conditioning. He pulled her toward the single room off the main room that served as break room and office combined. With one sweeping motion, he cleared a double stack of land-scape books from an old cot and then pointed.

"I can handle whatever comes for a while. Lie down, Rebecca, before you fall down."

She tried to find the strength to argue, but it didn't seem worthwhile in the face of such an offer of luxury.

"I'm so dirty," she mumbled.

Jackson glared, wishing he had the right to kiss her piddling arguments from her lips, and then sighed with frustration.

"So's the damned cot," he muttered. "You'll match."

With one gentle push, she was on her back. While he watched, she took a deep breath and then rolled over on her side. Seconds later, she was asleep.

Jackson took out the smaller bag that she kept for daily cash, and dropped the one meant for bank deposit into her lower desk drawer, shoving it far to the back.

She sighed and moaned softly in her sleep. Drawn to the sound as well as the woman, he squatted down until he was nearly on a level with her face. Those five small freckles stood out against her pale skin, and her curls were even more unruly than usual. But the curve of her cheek and the intermittent trembling of her chin did him in. He felt himself leaning forward and could no more control himself than he could stop wanting her.

His lips grazed her cheekbone, then strayed across her face until they came to the edge of her mouth. Gently, without taking a breath, he closed his eyes and tasted heaven.

She twitched and stretched, and he stood with a jerk. The last thing either one of them needed was another confrontation.

"Sleep well, baby," he whispered, and gently moved a layer of curls from her cheek before leaving the room in darkness and the door ajar.

Soon he had the key to the money drawer in his pocket and a portable phone nearby as he pruned, clipped, and watered. The customers came and went while Rebecca slept, unheeding of their cheerful voices in the adjoining room and unaware that while she rested, her own guardian angel hovered very nearby, waiting for the sound of her voice.

o   o   o

Daniel Hill drove with his eyes on the traffic while his thoughts were elsewhere. He'd seen the condition Rebecca was in when she'd left the hospital, and assumed that she'd had the good sense to go home and get some rest. In his opinion, that business of hers could go begging for a day or so. It wouldn't hurt her to close it down in an emergency, and this was certainly an emergency. After checking on Pete, as well as making the rounds of other sick parishioners, he'd made up his mind that he would see for himself if she'd gone home as she should.

But his dismay deepened as he saw her company truck parked at Hillside Nursery.

"Still a willful child," he muttered, and, with a quick twist of his wrist, turned his car off the highway and into the parking lot.

When he saw the motorcycle parked nearby, his heart skipped a beat. The last thing he wanted was to confront that man face-to-face. His scathing condemnation of Jackson Rule still hung between them like a festering sore, and as hard as Daniel tried, he couldn't find the words to tell the man he was sorry, because he still believed that he was right.

He parked and then started toward the office with no small amount of trepidation. It was quiet, too quiet, and in spite of the presence of both vehicles, neither Rebecca nor the hired man were anywhere in sight.

When he entered, there was no one inside, only the quiet hum of the cooling unit, cutting the outside heat and humidity with blasts of chilled air.

"Rebecca?" he called, and got nothing but an echo for his trouble.

Out of habit, he closed the door behind him to keep the cool air from escaping, then continued his search. The half-open door leading to the back room beckoned, and although there was no light burning, he pushed the door aside. All he could see from the doorway was the lower half of a woman's body with legs outstretched and lying still . . . too still.

"Oh my God!" Fear hit him gut level. He went to flip the light switch when a hand cupped his elbow, restraining him.

"You!" Daniel took two steps backward.

Jackson frowned. "I work here. Who did you think it would be?" He glanced into the room where Rebecca still slept to make sure she hadn't been disturbed. "She's been asleep all morning," he said. "I didn't want you to startle her."

Daniel slumped with relief. "She's asleep? But I thought . . ." Shame silenced the last of his words.

Shock spread over Jackson's face, turning his eyes a cold, hard blue. The fact that Rebecca's father believed him capable of hurting her was almost more than he could bear. And Daniel Hill didn't have to finish saying what he thought for the truth to be known. It was there on the man's face, waiting to be seen. In anger, Jackson lashed out without thinking.

"What? Did you think I'd killed her? Hell, preacher, you have an even lower opinion of me than I expected."

"I didn't really . . ."

"Don't lie. At least allow me that damned much."

He pivoted angrily toward the bathroom, intent on finishing what he'd come to do.

Daniel flinched at the abrupt dismissal, and then suddenly gasped as he saw a deep red stain spreading across Jackson's shoulder. "You're bleeding!"

Without answering, Jackson yanked his shirt over his head, and then began digging through the medicine chest.

Focusing on the injury, Rebecca's father followed him without thought, and then forgot everything in his shock at the sight of Jackson's back.

Daniel froze, staring in disbelief as the blood from a small cut on Jackson's shoulder seeped over more scars than he'd ever seen on one person. "My goodness," he gasped, and then added, "what happened to you?"

Misunderstanding the question, Jackson grimaced as he tried unsuccessfully to clean the wound with a handful of wet paper towels.

"I backed into a broken window on the side of the greenhouse. Pete ran a hoe handle through it the other day and we haven't had a chance to replace it."

"Here, let me," Daniel said, taking the wet compress out of Jackson's hands. His own were shaking as he cleaned the blood from his back, trying to imagine what horrible injury could have inflicted such scars. Finally, curiosity won. "Did you get these scars in prison?"

There was a sardonic smile on Jackson's face when he turned.

"No." He handed Daniel a bottle of antiseptic and a handful of large Band-Aids. "You want to finish up, Doc, or shall I?"

Daniel's hands were shaking as he sprayed the antiseptic and then waited for it to dry before applying the bandages. The implications of Jackson's answer were staggering.

Those scars were old. And if he didn't get them in prison, then that meant he'd had them before he went in. How? And then he remembered Jackson's earlier claim. *I'd kill Stanton Rule all over again.*

Dear God, Daniel thought. *Could a father wreak this kind of havoc upon a child of his own flesh?*

As soon as he had asked it, he knew. Every day, a thousand times a day somewhere around the world, children died from beatings at the hands of those who had given them life. It was obscene. Almost as obscene as killing those same people for the deed.

For a fleeting moment, Daniel almost understood the act that had sent Jackson Rule to prison. And then he remembered the teachings to which he'd devoted his life, one of which rang in his ears as loudly as if God himself had just delivered it.

Thou shalt not kill.

Shuddering, he took a deep breath and finished what he was about. "There, it's nearly stopped bleeding."

Jackson knew he was making the man nervous, but damn it

all to hell and back, the man didn't have a clue about life as he'd known it.

"Thanks for the help," Jackson said, and then dipped his bloody shirt in the sink and began scrubbing at the stains.

Following the sound of voices, Rebecca walked through the open door of the bathroom, rubbing sleep out of her eyes and stifling another yawn. "What's going on?" she asked.

Both men spun, surprised by the sound of her voice, and then Jackson shrugged. "Not much, boss," he said, and continued to scrub at his shirt.

Rebecca took one look at the blood on the shirt and the bandage on Jackson's back and turned toward her father with a gasp of disbelief.

"Daddy! What have you done?"

The shock on Daniel's face was priceless. That his daughter assumed he could be capable of inflicting bodily harm upon a living soul was devastating.

Jackson looked at the preacher's face. "Doesn't feel so good, does it, preacher? Having someone assume you're guilty without checking out the facts."

Daniel's face turned red. The blow hit far too close to home as Jackson began to explain.

"I backed into that window Pete broke yesterday. Your father was helping me clean up a bit."

"Oh. Well . . ." A bit embarrassed, she quickly apologized. "Sorry, Daddy. Sometimes we all jump to conclusions, don't we?"

Before he could respond, she changed the subject.

"How's Pete?"

Daniel shifted into a word-for-word explanation of the doctor's most recent prognosis. While they were talking, Jackson slipped away.

Nearly half an hour later, he heard the sound of a car leaving the premises and breathed a quiet sigh of relief. That man made him nervous as hell.

"And it couldn't be because you covet his daughter," he

reminded himself, and thrust both arms elbow deep into a sack of potting soil.

It would be a few more days before Jackson Rule realized that covet was not the right word for what he felt for Rebecca Hill.

9

Hot air swirled around the corners of the greenhouse like eddies from hell, sucking the oxygen from the air and throwing a blast furnace of heat into people's faces. Customers did not linger at their tasks, but made quick, decisive choices in order to get back home to find a modicum of comfort.

The humidity was palpable. There was no cure for the heat of a Louisiana summer except air-conditioning. And while the cool office was nearby, there was no chance that Rebecca or Jackson would get a chance to use it, except while taking money from customers.

Jackson savored the shade in which he was standing as a customer whose car he had loaded finally drove away.

"Jackson, there's someone I want you to meet."

At the sound of Rebecca's voice, he turned, expecting almost anything except what he saw.

She came around the corner of the office hand in hand with the man at her side. He looked to be about her age, tall, tan, and blond. The light brown shorts he was wearing matched his pullover shirt, and Jackson hated him on sight. The first thing that crossed his mind was that, unlike himself, Daniel Hill would probably approve wholeheartedly of this fellow. The man leaned over and said something beneath his breath that made Rebecca laugh aloud. She punched him lightly on the arm, then hugged him to make up for the slight.

And when she did, Jackson froze. In the heat of the day, goose bumps covered his arms, and the skin crawled on the back of his neck. He tried to take a deep breath, and felt it stick in the back of his throat.

Oh God, please don't let this man be important to her.

With one hand, he steadied himself against the nearby tree and tried to pretend he wasn't scared half to death by the implications of the pair coming toward him, but it was no use. He'd been telling himself for weeks that he just wanted to take Rebecca Hill to bed. Nothing more, nothing less. But he'd been fooling himself, because he had just come face-to-face with love, and it looked as if she already had someone else in mind.

"Jackson, this is my cousin, Simon. Simon, this is Jackson Rule, my right-hand man."

Cousin! He nearly sagged in relief, but then he wondered how close their relation was. Plenty of distant cousins married, especially in the South.

Simon Andrews held out his hand. "You saved Pete Walters's life. I want to thank you. That man taught me how to fish . . . and nearly every other important thing a boy needs to know. He's been a big part of our lives for so long that the thought of losing him seems impossible to contemplate."

When Jackson didn't move, or speak, Simon's hand wavered alone in the air.

Rebecca frowned at the odd expression on Jackson's face. Had something else happened while she was out back with Simon?

"Jackson, are you all right?"

He blinked before quickly extending his own hand toward the unexpected offer. "Uh . . . sorry. I guess it's the heat. I was lost in . . . uh . . ." Once again, his voice trailed off as he stared at the way Simon's arm draped so casually and comfortably across Rebecca's shoulder.

"Thought," Rebecca finished.

"Thought what?" Jackson asked.

She laughed. "Thought. You were lost in thought."

A flush stained his cheeks. If he didn't get himself in gear, he was going to make a fool of himself.

"Oh . . . yeah," he muttered. "I was lost in thought."

"Jackson, Cecilia needs some help," Rebecca said. "Would you take the dolly to the first greenhouse and help her?"

"Cecilia?"

"My wife," Simon explained.

Wife! He has a wife! "I'll be right back," Jackson said, and wanted to shout with joy as he did what he was asked.

"Strange man," Simon remarked, as he watched Jackson pushing the dolly toward the building they'd just exited. "He seems to have more going on beneath the surface than the normal man . . . which, I suppose is to be expected considering his circumstances."

"Don't say it, Simon. Don't even think it. If I hear one more judgmental word out of another one of my relatives, I am going to scream. Except for Pete, Jackson Rule is the best worker I've ever had. Enough said, all right?"

Simon grinned. "Uncle Daniel been at it again?"

"You have no idea. I don't know why Daddy feels compelled to constantly interfere with my life, but he treats me as if I were nine, not twenty-nine. Besides, it's not like there's anything personal between Jackson and me . . . other than the fact that he's come to my rescue a couple of times, which I definitely appreciated."

They turned at the sound of laughter. Jackson and Simon's wife were coming out of the distant greenhouse pulling a huge assortment of potted plants. The ever-bubbly Cecilia had already put a smile on his face that Rebecca envied.

If only it were that easy for me, she thought. *He smiles at me, but never with me.* But trying to outguess that man was impossible , and she knew it. Even when they were working side by side, she was always aware of the mental distance he kept between them.

Simon looked at his cousin and tried not to frown. He heard what she was saying, but felt that there was more to her denial than just words. There was something about the way her eyes followed Jackson's movements, and the lilt in her voice when she talked to him . . . and about him.

"Methinks the lady doth protest too much."

Rebecca spun, her mouth slack with surprise, and started to argue when conscience struck. "I, uh . . . oh good, here they are now," she mumbled, and felt in her face a rising heat that had nothing to do with the sun.

"Where do you want them?" Jackson asked.

Simon opened the back of their Blazer and started pushing items aside. "Dang, Sissy, I didn't know you were going to buy out the place."

Cecilia ignored her husband's complaints, as she and Jackson began to unload the dolly.

"Here, let me help you," Rebecca said, and bent down to lift a couple of pots, when Jackson's hand slid down her arm and stilled her intent.

She looked up and became lost in blue eyes filled with secrets, then forgot what she'd been about to do. In the back of her mind, she could hear Simon and Cecilia arguing lightly as they made room for the plants. But for Rebecca, time seemed to stop.

Jackson's gaze was suspended upon her face, his grip on her arm just short of painful.

"Let me," he said.

Let you what?

It was almost as if he'd read her mind. His lips parted, and Rebecca could almost feel his breath on her cheeks. If she closed her eyes . . . if she moved just a little bit to the right . . .

"Jackson."

Her voice was just above a whisper, somewhere between a question and a request, and the sound of his name upon her lips was almost more than he could bear.

Rebecca stared at a muscle jerking lightly along his jawline, as if he were clenching his teeth to keep from saying something he should not.

"How many more are there?" Simon grumbled, and the moment was broken.

Rebecca blinked and found herself standing outside the trio, who finished loading the car.

"That just about does it. Good Lord, I'll have to take out a loan to pay for all of this," Simon grumbled, and then laughed when his wife poked him in the side.

Minutes later, Rebecca was on the front step, waving goodbye and wondering where Jackson had gone. Common sense told her she should check on her employee's whereabouts . . . just in case she needed him, of course. But instinct told her to leave him alone.

She went back into the office with an emptiness inside her that had nothing to do with skipping lunch, and headed for the bathroom to wash the grime from her hands.

As she began to scrub up the length of her arm, she paused and closed her eyes, letting herself remember the feel of Jackson's hand there. Wondering what would have happened if they'd been alone when he touched her like that.

She shuddered, then splattered her face with the cool running water, trying to wash away thoughts that had no business in her mind. Whatever was between them was becoming increasingly impossible to ignore.

She dried with abandon and then headed for the front office, where she flopped into a chair to contemplate the whereabouts of her runaway heart. That common sense she was so fond of using told her she already knew where her heart had gone. It was following a man she couldn't want . . . shouldn't want . . . but did.

She would concentrate on quitting time. It was Saturday, only half a day. Surely she couldn't get herself in any more trouble. She picked up a buyers' guide for Christmas trees, reminding herself that while it was at least 110 degrees outside, one could never make plans too early.

She started flipping pages. Several minutes later she realized that she didn't remember one price or shipping cost on a single page.

"Shoot," she muttered, then tossed the catalog on the counter and stared out the front window at the cars passing by on the highway beyond, all the while giving herself a silent scolding.

With the time and space of a weekend between them, she could get herself in gear. She would go see Pete. Go to church tomorrow and make peace with her father . . . and God. And in the process, maybe regain control of herself.

And then Jackson opened the door and all of her good intentions flew out of her head. Desperate for something to say, she blurted out the first thing that came to mind.

"Never was so glad to see quitting time come, how about you?"

He nodded without looking at her and went inside the bathroom to clean up.

Rebecca counted out the drawer to make the deposit, and then remembered his paycheck and laid it carefully on the counter so that she wouldn't forget it when he passed.

Water ran for what seemed like hours. From the sounds, he must be taking a bath, she thought, and then wondered why it mattered. He was probably hot and tired and hungry and wanted to cool off before going to eat.

When he came out of the bathroom, she forgot everything she'd been telling herself. He was still damp from washing and carried his work shirt in his hands. The shirt he wore now was fresh and clean and matched the blue of his eyes.

She handed him his paycheck. "Going somewhere?" she asked, and hoped that it sounded as light as it should, and not as curious as she was.

Jackson paused, the check in his hand, and almost smiled as he allowed himself one last look at Rebecca. It would have to last until Monday. Then he remembered where he was going, and what he might have to do, and the wall went back up between them again.

"Yes."

Rebecca waited for further explanation that didn't come. Finally, her pride came to the rescue. She tilted her chin and straightened her shoulders against the blow of his rejection.

"Then have a good trip, and I'll see you Monday," she said, and turned her back so that he couldn't see the pain on her face.

Jackson's heart sank. The set of her shoulders was too stiff, her voice too bright. By being so withdrawn, he'd hurt her feelings, and he knew it.

Goddamn it, lady. How do I tell you about my sister without telling you too much about me?

"Tell Pete I said hello," he said instead.

She spun, her eyes bright with unshed tears, but the smile was wide and fixed upon her face.

"I sure will. He'll be glad to know you thought of him."

Jackson nodded, and then he was gone.

When the sound of his Harley was no longer distinguishable, Rebecca turned the sign in the door to read CLOSED, went into her office, and cried.

She didn't really know why, but there was too much pain inside of her to keep. When she had finished crying, Rebecca walked around the office, checking windows and doors and turning off the air conditioner and the lights.

With her money in her hand she headed for her truck. Before she went to see Pete, she needed a bath, some food, and her head examined.

Heat waves hung just above the road surface—iridescent curtains, shimmering with color like a melting rainbow. Jackson rode the Harley through them at full throttle, trying to outrun the demons inside his mind. But as fast as the bike would go, it was still not quick enough to escape his past. *Why couldn't I have known Rebecca before . . . before it was too late?* But there was no answer for Jackson now, just as there'd been no answer for him years ago.

An eighteen-wheeler pushing way beyond the speed limit came out of nowhere and passed Jackson as if he were sitting still. Rocked by the side-draft of the big rig, it was only his skill and balance that kept him upright. When the truck was safely past, he eased off on the throttle, coming to a stop at the side of the road.

The sudden silence was overwhelming as Jackson pushed his bike to the line of trees just beyond the pavement. Heart hammering from the shock of the truck's passing, and his ears still ringing from the echo of his engine, he sat down on the grass. Bracing himself with bent knees and using the tree for a prop, he began to contemplate how close he'd come to dying.

He had to get a grip on himself, he thought as he dug his fingers through his hair. Molly was depending on him. He couldn't let his feelings for a woman he couldn't have get this out of hand.

But as easy as it was to give himself advice, it was not so easy to follow. Closing his eyes, he inhaled slowly, reminding himself that he'd gotten along for fifteen years without a woman. All he had to do was get back into the mind-set of out of sight—out of mind, and he'd be all right.

"And dogs don't howl at the moon," he muttered.

Long minutes passed as he regained his composure, then nervously checked his watch as he remembered that he had less than three hours before Azalea Hospice was closed to visitors for the day. He jumped to his feet and began pushing his bike back to the road. The Harley came to life between his legs as he slipped it in gear and accelerated.

"Ready or not, Michael Franco, here I come."

Less than half an hour later, he braked at the entrance gate and started to give the guard his name when he noticed that the parking lot beyond was full of cars, and the front lawn was crawling with people.

"What's going on in there?" Jackson asked.

"They're having a party," the guard said. "Watermelon on the lawn and lemonade beneath the shade trees. It's the first Saturday of the month . . . family day, you know. Isn't that why you're here?"

Jackson felt sick. Family day? Poor Molly. How many family days had she endured alone? And how many more before her doctor would let him see her?

Jackson's shoulders drooped. "I think you better try and get Dr. Franco on the phone. Ask him if it's okay if Jackson Rule comes in. He didn't know I was coming."

The guard picked up the phone while Jackson parked his bike against the gatehouse and then walked up to the gate, watching the festivities going on inside.

Once again, in spite of his proximity, he was on the outside looking in. Yes, those people were locked up, and he was free to do as he chose. But what price freedom when you had no one with whom to share it?

"Mr. Rule, Dr. Franco says for you to wait here. He'll come and get you."

Jackson shrugged. Whatever it took, he still needed to talk to Molly's doctor. He needed to hear something positive. And he needed to hear her name. He wanted to hear someone else acknowledge that she existed outside of his own mind.

A few minutes later, a man in a golf cart came up the drive toward the gate.

"That will be Dr. Franco," the guard said. "You can leave your bike here. I'll watch it for you."

Jackson nodded and waited impatiently for his ride.

The smile on Dr. Franco's face went a long way toward alleviating some of Jackson's tension as he crawled into the cart and took a seat.

"Jackson! Welcome! I'm glad you came."

Jackson's heart skipped a beat. It sounded like good news.

"How's Molly? Is she better? Has she come out of her . . . ?"

Franco laughed. "One thing at a time, man. One thing at a time." He turned the battery-powered cart and headed back toward the hospice. "Yes, I believe she is better. The setback we talked of awhile back has all but disappeared. She seems to be her smiling self again."

"Does this mean I can see her?"

Franco frowned, and as they neared the busiest part of the lawn, he chose a less-traveled path. "Let's just take the back way inside . . . for today. Okay?"

It wasn't what Jackson wanted to hear. This meant Franco didn't want Molly to see him coming, and that could only mean one thing.

"You don't think it's time, do you?"

The cart stopped near a sidewalk. "We can walk from here," Franco said, and motioned for Jackson to follow him inside. The cool air that met them at the door was a welcome relief from the sweltering heat outside.

"Isn't it kind of hot for an outdoor party?"

Franco laughed. "Yes, but our facility isn't large enough to handle that many people inside. So . . . it's outside or nothing. The faithful families that come would rather be uncomfortable than miss a visit."

"What happens to the ones who never have visitors?"

Franco could hear the guilt in Jackson's voice and patted him on the arm as he led him through a maze of corridors to his office. "Most of them never know who belongs to whom. They are all so excited to see new faces that, in a way, it becomes one big family reunion."

Jackson tried to tell himself that was good. That Molly couldn't tell family from strangers, but the idea that his sister was so lost inside herself made him sick.

"Have a seat, Jackson. Can I get you something cold to drink? I have all kinds of pop. Help yourself."

He opened the door of a small tabletop refrigerator and waited for Jackson to take first pick. Then he chose one for himself.

"That must be a hot ride out from the city," he said, while watching the intense expression on Jackson's face as he stood at the window overlooking the lawn party. He sighed as he realized Jackson was searching the crowd for a glimpse of his sister.

Jackson took a long drink from the cold bottle and then
turned away from the window.

"Talk to me, Doc. I need to hear some good news."

Franco shrugged. "For the last two weeks, I've been trying
to get Molly to talk about her childhood. She will, up to a
point."

Jackson's gut kicked. "What does she say?"

"Not much. The only thing she seems intent upon sharing is
that your mother died when she was about eleven and she
likes peanut butter and pickle sandwiches."

In spite of his disappointment, Jackson laughed. "Oh Lord,
I'd forgotten that. I used to tease her about it, telling her that
she was going to turn into a sour-puss squirrel."

The doctor smiled. Jackson Rule wasn't officially his
patient, but he had a feeling that the man didn't often open up
like he had just now, and that it would do him a world of good
if he'd try it more often.

"Tell me more about your sister," he encouraged. "Maybe
with your input, I can go about her sessions from a different
angle."

The smile on Jackson's face became fixed, and the light in
his eyes went out.

"There isn't anything good to talk about," he said, and
turned back to the window, draining the bottle in one big gulp
before tossing the empty into the trash.

"Look, Jackson. I'm not trying to get you to talk about yourself, honestly I'm not. And I don't need to hear anything
you're not comfortable saying. But maybe if you could think
of . . . "

"Where is she?" Jackson asked, his gaze fixed upon the constantly moving crowd.

Franco sighed, then set his pop down on the desk and
moved to the window. The brother was just as closemouthed
as the sister. Somehow it figured. He knew both children had

been physically abused. Molly bore several small scars to prove the fact, and he'd read Jackson Rule's file as well. The boy who'd been incarcerated for murder would forever bear the marks of the abuser, although he'd long since rotted in the ground. Franco knew that in severe cases of child abuse within a family, one child often protected the other by never revealing a thing. The fact that Jackson and Molly were now adults mattered little, because they'd never had a chance to recover emotionally from the childhood assaults.

"Let me see," Franco said. "I don't know if I can find her in all that, but let me look awhile. Maybe I'll spot her."

"Do you know what she's wearing?"

Michael Franco smiled. "We had a session this morning. She was wearing a pink-and-white-striped thing then, although she might have changed for the party. It was one of those divided skirt outfits . . . like pants, only shorter."

"Her hair. Is it short . . . or long . . . is it up or down?"

Franco smiled. "I have a picture of her in my file. Let me get it for you."

He turned away to fumble through his files, wishing his secretary would quit rearranging his system, and missed seeing Jackson stiffen, then lean forward.

"Here it is," Franco said. "Now let me see if . . ."

"Oh God . . . oh, Molly."

Jackson's voice was so soft, Franco almost didn't hear him speak. But when he turned to look, it was obvious that Jackson had spotted someone whom he thought to be his sister. He dropped the file upon the desk and hurried to the window. Chances were that Jackson had made a mistake. Fifteen years was a long time for instant recognition.

"Where do you . . . ?"

"There!" Jackson said, and pointed to a trio of women who were up near the serving table, handing out slices of the dripping red melon. "The one on this end."

"Well I'll be damned," Franco muttered. "It *is* her! How on earth did you . . . ?"

"She looks like Laura."

"Laura?"

"Our mother." Jackson's hands were shaking as he pressed them against the window and leaned until his forehead was touching the glass. He watched her through a blur of tears. "Molly, honey . . . when did you get so pretty?"

But it was a stupid question and both men knew it. A lot can happen in fifteen years. Young girls became women. Boys became men. Lives were lost. And hope can die.

The doctor stepped to one side, studying the intent expression on Jackson's face.

"I'm sorry that I didn't have better news for you today."

For a long, long time, Jackson remained silent. And when he finally turned away from the window, his words stayed with Molly's doctor long after he had gone.

"For today, Doc . . . this was enough."

But later, when he was on his way home, he realized it wasn't the truth. Old wounds ached. Old memories were resurrected. And a loneliness he thought he'd accepted threatened to overwhelm him. The thought of going back to that empty apartment was unbearable. In his frame of mind, the ghosts from his past would be all too real to ignore.

As he wheeled into town, he impulsively took the turn that led to the Jesus House. He needed to hear laughter. To see smiles. He needed to hold . . . and be held. And he knew exactly who would oblige.

"Jackson! It's Jackson!" a child shrieked, and, as if by magic, children swarmed toward the big man who'd just walked in the door.

He had a package in one hand, and a sack in the other. By the time the children met him halfway across the room, he was laughing.

Clark heard the uproar from his office, and when he looked out, he started to smile.

"What did you bring? What did you bring?" the children cried as they clamored for his attention.

What they wanted from him was more than what he had in his hands, and Clark knew it. It was his attention on which they thrived. It was amazing to Clark how all of the children had opened up since Jackson's visits began. The ones who'd been shy and frightened seemed almost normal. The ones who'd been angry and wanting to lash out at the world for what the world had done to them were more in control of their own emotions.

And then, out of the corner of his eye, Clark caught some movement—that of a small, stocky child with a pug nose and dark curly hair standing in the shadows, gazing with longing at the children who were flocking around Jackson.

Clark amended his thoughts. All, that is, except Taylor Monroe. In his opinion, breaking through that child's defenses was almost hopeless. Although Taylor was only eight, he never played with the others, and rarely spoke. He and a woman who called herself his aunt had arrived a month ago, and Clark had yet to see him smile.

"Taylor, don't you want to go see what Jackson brought?" Clark asked.

The boy ducked his head and disappeared, as if shocked that he'd even been seen looking on.

Clark sighed and made a mental note to speak to Jackson about the boy, but as fate would have it, they made their own acquaintance, and without anyone else's help.

After the kids had gone through the cookies Jackson had brought them and started taking turns working on the new puzzles he'd given to the shelter, he went outside to try to fix his bike, which had quit on him just as he got to the shelter.

He'd located the problem. It was nothing but a loose wire, but in the dark, it kept slipping off the connection before he could tighten it up. Frustrated and hot, he'd yanked his shirt off without thought, and was on his knees, peering through the shadows beneath the seat of the bike, trying to work his way by feel. When it slipped off the third time, he cursed softly and walked back inside the shelter to borrow a flashlight.

Clark saw him coming through the door and went to meet him.

"Trouble?" he asked, eyeing the grease streaks on Jackson's bare chest and the sweat running down the middle of his belly.

Jackson nodded. "Got a loose wire, but I can't see well enough to fix it. Do you have a flashlight I can borrow?"

"Be right back," Clark said, and hurried toward the janitor's room.

Jackson swiped at the sweat on his forehead with the back of his arm, while watching the children at play on the other side of the room. He smiled to himself, amazed at how much they'd come to mean to him. A slight breath of air stirred itself enough to come through the open doorway, and in relief, he turned, intent on letting it cool his heated body, when something else caught his attention.

He almost didn't see the small, dark-haired boy standing quietly in the corner, but when he did, he realized he didn't know him. His first intention was to speak, and then he saw the expression on the boy's face and froze. There were no words to express the horror he saw in the child's eyes.

"I won't hurt you," Jackson said, and instinctively squatted on his heels, putting himself on the same level as the child. "My name is Jackson."

"I know," the child said, and then quickly looked away. But as much as he felt the need to run, he was more intrigued by what he'd seen on Jackson's back.

"What's your name?" Jackson asked.

It took a moment, but finally he answered. "Taylor Monroe."

Jackson nodded. "Pleased to meet you, Taylor Monroe."

The child almost smiled, and then he looked away again.

"Been here long?" Jackson asked.

The child shrugged as Clark came back with a flashlight in hand. Jackson watched him closely, and when he saw that he was about to bolt, instinct made him ask, "Do you think you're big enough to hold that flashlight so I can see to fix my bike?"

Clark was close enough to hear, and wise enough to hold his ground as he stopped, waiting to see what transpired between the two loners.

Taylor eyed the flashlight in Clark's hand, and then looked back at the man he knew as Jackson.

"You could ask your mother to come, too, if it would make you feel better," Jackson offered.

The child straightened. "Ain't got no mother," he said. "Don't have to ask Edna nothin'."

Jackson held his breath. It wasn't an out-and-out refusal.

"Mr. Thurman could come, too, if you like," Jackson added.

Taylor eyed the director judiciously. Then he shrugged.

"I reckon I don't mind," he muttered.

Clark couldn't believe his ears. Jackson Rule had gotten more out of this child in three minutes than they had in three weeks.

"Here you go, Taylor," Clark said, handing the child the flashlight.

Jackson stood up, then started out the door, letting the boy follow at his own pace, aware that too much attention at this point was worse than none at all.

Taylor punched the switch on the flashlight and stalked out behind Jackson, full of importance.

Jackson was already on his knees when the boy arrived, and this time, when Jackson picked up his screwdriver and then reached for the loose wire, a bright glow came over his shoulder and down into the mechanism.

"Move it a little to your left," Jackson said, and the light shifted.

They were an odd trio. A man in charge of people who had nowhere to go, a child who trusted no one, and a man who trusted few. The wire was already in place, and Jackson was putting the last twist to a screw when he felt a light, almost nonexistent touch upon his back.

The moment he felt it, he knew it for what it was. The boy was tracing the paths of Jackson's scars, running his small fingertips up and down, and then across his back in silent fascination. Sensing that there was more to the child's reaction than curiosity, Jackson stilled, waiting for Taylor to say what was on his mind.

"It hurt real bad, didn't it?" the boy asked.

Breath caught in the back of Jackson's throat, because it wasn't curiosity he heard in Taylor's voice, it was understanding. Slowly, so as not to frighten him, Jackson turned. Still on his knees, he answered.

"Yes, it did," he said, and realized that he hadn't admitted that to a living soul in more than twenty years.

Taylor's eyes were huge. His chin trembled, but his expression never wavered.

"My grandpa hit on me," Taylor said, as calmly as if he'd admitted his hair was black. "I'm a bastard. Edna says so."

Jackson swallowed twice before he could find his voice. The cool, unemotional way in which the child spoke told him volumes. As a child, the more that life and Stanton Rule had hurt him, the less he'd been able to admit it. Taylor Monroe was a mirror image of himself at the same age. As much as he wanted to touch the child, he knew it would be wrong. All he could do was say what he'd learned to be true, even though it had taken him a long, long time to learn it.

"All men aren't bad, Taylor. There are a lot of good ones in the world. You and I just had a little bad luck."

Taylor didn't answer. He figured the man didn't know what he was talking about. He had yet to meet one who kept his word, or didn't raise his voice or hand.

"I swear," Jackson added, and pointed to Clark. "Has Mr. Thurman ever hurt you? Or lied to you?"

The child shook his head.

"Do you think I would?" Jackson asked.

"No," Taylor said, and then, with the innocence of a child, he added, "'Cause you know how bad it would hurt."

"Oh God," Clark whispered, and turned away. This was no time to let the boy see him cry.

Jackson ached to hold him. "Okay then, you know two men who wouldn't hurt you, right? So it just stands to reason that we aren't the only ones, don't you think?"

For a long while, the child was silent. And then he suddenly handed Jackson the flashlight and ran into the building, too overwhelmed by what he'd done to communicate any longer.

"Son of a bitch," Jackson whispered, and levered himself to his feet.

He put his tools back in the box on the bike and then slipped into his shirt.

"What you did tonight was amazing," Clark said.

Anger was all over Jackson's face, and in his posture, as he swung a leg over the bike. "I didn't do squat," he said harshly. "But what I'd like to do is meet his *grandpa* in some dark alley."

Clark put a hand on Jackson's shoulder. "Wouldn't we all? Unfortunately, violence isn't always the answer, and it won't help Taylor."

The faint glow of the security light in front of the shelter cast harsh, foreboding shadows across Jackson's face, giving him a dark, eerie expression.

"And sometimes, my friend, violence is the only way," Jackson said softly.

Before Clark could answer, Jackson fired up the engine and then roared away into the night, trying to outrun the image of a child's face and the memory of what he'd just said.

10

"*They're moving me out of ICU* and into my own room tomorrow," Pete said the following Saturday, as he fidgeted with the IV needle taped to the back of his hand. "These things hurt. Looks to me like they could find an easier . . ."

Rebecca leaned over and kissed Pete on the forehead, then pressed a finger across his lips, stilling the complaint before he had time to finish. He made a face as the lights in the ward began to blink, a quiet signal to all the visitors in ICU that the five-minute visit was over.

"Be glad you're here to gripe, buddy," she said softly, and began gathering her things to leave.

Pete saw the love and worry on Rebecca's face. "I know," he muttered. "But I hate being so helpless."

Rebecca looked over her shoulder at the nurse who was standing at the door, waiting for the visitors to leave.

"I've got to go before she comes after me," she said. "Do what they tell you, Pete. Jackson and I need you to be well. Without you, there's no one to tell either of us what to do."

Pete frowned. As thankful as he was for Jackson's having saved his life, he was worried sick that Rebecca was now alone with him at the greenhouse. Although he knew she was going to resent it, he couldn't let her go without a word of caution.

"Rebecca honey, about Jackson . . . "

She groaned. "Oh, Pete, not you, too? I thought you'd gotten past this."

"Now, wait a minute, it's not what you're thinking. I don't believe he'd do a single thing to harm you. In fact, it's just the opposite."

"What do you mean?"

Pete sighed. There was no easy way to say this, and the nurse was coming toward them at a fast pace. He had to spit it out or forget it altogether.

"When you're not looking, he never takes his eyes off of you. The only time I see a real smile light up his face is when you call his name. He thinks he's hiding his feelings, and maybe he is, even from himself. But there's something going on behind that silent facade of his that has nothing to do with work and a lot to do with monkey business."

"Miss Hill! It's time to leave," the nurse said, and waited at the foot of her patient's bed to escort Rebecca out of the ward.

It took Rebecca a second to find her breath. She couldn't let Pete see how much his words had shocked her, and so her answer was much more lighthearted than she felt.

"Stop fussing, Pete. I'm a big girl, remember? I can take care of myself." She blew him a kiss, then waved good-bye and left without looking back.

Pete closed his eyes and then sighed. He'd done all he could. Whatever happened now was up to her. He just hoped to God that she came to her senses before she let Jackson ruin her life.

Outside the ward, Rebecca's stomach was in knots. *He watches me when I'm not looking? What does that mean?*

But in her heart, Rebecca suspected she already knew. There'd been too many times when she and Jackson had been that close to saying or doing something to the other that would have crossed the line between employer and employee . . . between friendship and something more.

"But we haven't," she reminded herself as she crawled into her pickup truck and drove out of the parking lot. "And we won't."

However flawed the reasoning, Rebecca quickly convinced herself of their integrity, then turned the air conditioner up to high and the radio on low. Humming along with a song on her favorite country station, she made mental notes to herself as to what she needed to buy at the grocery store before heading home. She hadn't really shopped in weeks, satisfying herself with picking up the odd item now and then. But now there was virtually nothing left on her shelves, and the refrigerator had an echo when she slammed the door.

When she turned into the parking lot of the supermarket, she groaned. There were cars everywhere. The store would be packed.

"It's what I get for putting this off," she said, and headed for the door.

More than an hour later, she was helping the bag boy load her goods when a low, ominous rumble overhead surprised her. She looked up in surprise. "Hey! It looks like rain."

"Yes, ma'am," the boy said as he set the last bag in the cab. "They've been broadcasting storm warnings all afternoon." Having said his piece, he grinned and winked when Rebecca handed him his tip and made a dash for the store just ahead of the first raindrops.

Rebecca jumped into her pickup and started out of New Orleans. With one eye on the clouds and the other on the traffic, she was hoping to get home before the worst of it hit.

The sweltering heat of the day had changed too rapidly for Jackson's peace of mind. Dark clouds swirled above and behind him as he rocketed down the highway, pushing the Harley to its limit and then some in an effort to outrun the storm. He'd made a quick trip out to Azalea Hospice to talk to Molly's doctor, and then made up his mind to head for home.

With one eye on the clouds and the other on the road, Jackson wove through traffic.

It wasn't so much that he minded getting rained on, because the wind in his hair felt good compared to the earlier heat of the day. It was the heavy, hanging wall cloud that made him worry. It felt like tornado weather, and that dark green cast to the clouds could mean hail. He thought of all the tender green plants and shrubs out in the open at the nursery, as well as the fragile walls of the greenhouses, and began to worry, wondering if Rebecca's nursery stock was covered by her insurance.

No sooner had he thought of her, than he changed his destination. He had all weekend to hole up inside that damned dingy apartment, and Rebecca was probably still in the city visiting Pete. She wouldn't get home in time to put up or tie down whatever might be at risk. It wouldn't take long, he thought. Just a quick detour. Maybe he could beat the worst of the storm before it hit.

He barely did.

Wind was already howling through the trees, arrogantly pushing at the heavy branches, and making them bow in supplication to its power as Jackson turned off the highway. Small clay pots stacked four high were already rolling across the grass.

He came to a stop and jumped from the bike, grabbing up an armload of empty pots as he ran against the wind toward the potting shed. Once inside, he was momentarily protected from the wind's force, but not the sound. The metal shed rattled and popped from the impact of the storm. Jackson scooted the pots beneath a shelf and then stood in the doorway, trying to decide what needed tending first.

Only two days earlier, a new shipment of fall shrubbery had been stored in the farthest greenhouse. Even from where he stood, Jackson could hear the repeated hammering of something loose down that way.

He decided to check that first. He would hate for Rebecca to lose the whole shipment.

He took a deep breath and ran out into the wind just as the first raindrops fell. They came cold and fast and hit his body like wet bullets.

It took less than a minute to get to the building, but in that time he was soaked. Lightning flashed, and then the sound of thunder rocked the heavens, reminding him that, for the moment, nature had the upper hand. Jackson ducked instinctively, and then began circling the building, trying to find whatever was loose. Nearly blinded by the rainfall, he moved by touch as much as sight, feeling each window as he passed, testing it to see if it was locked. One by one, he traced the edges of the facings all the way down the wall, and still he found nothing to indicate the source of the noise.

"Come on . . . come on . . . where the hell are you?" he muttered, and silently cursed the rainfall pouring from the roof and down his back.

No sooner had he turned the corner than he saw it. The back door to the greenhouse was being whipped back and forth against the building. Open. Shut. Open. Shut. And each slam rocked the door on its hinges.

Jackson ran forward, grabbing at the door as it swung open, and then, with unexpected force, he was instantly pulled with it as it started to slam shut. He went with the motion, gaining entry into the greenhouse just as the door hit the frame. As the wind gathered force for a repeat performance, Jackson yanked the door up just enough to make the lock slide into place.

The sounds of rain and wind were deafening inside the greenhouse, but the relief of being inside was welcome. His clothes were dripping, his muscles shaking from cold, but for the moment, he was out of the worst of it.

"Oh man," he muttered, and leaned over, grabbing his knees, while he fought for breath and listened to the sound of something outside being ripped apart. He peered out a window, frowning as a couple of baskets went rolling across the back lot. One of the small sheds in that area must have blown down. There was nothing he could do now but ride out the storm inside the greenhouse, and then salvage what was left when it was over.

And then he remembered the fall shipment and turned. The wind had made a swath through the middle of the room, rolling pots one into the other. Ignoring his discomfort, he began working his way toward the front of the building, setting everything upright.

He was almost finished when a sound, different from the storm, penetrated his thoughts. He stopped, looking up and out. The sheets of rain blurred the image through the window, and the storm clouds had darkened the evening sky to that of a nightfall, but Jackson could see well enough to know that someone was racing toward the office. And while he could not identify the figure, he recognized the blue pickup all too well.

What on earth was Rebecca thinking? She could get hurt by being out in such heavy weather.

This time there was no hesitation when he came out of the building. Aware that he couldn't get any wetter, he made sure the door shut firmly behind him before he began to run.

The puddles had turned into small rivers. In some places, the water was nearly ankle deep on his boots. He vaulted the steps at the office and gripped the doorknob, turning and jumping in one motion as he hurled himself through the front door, as unexpected as the gust of wind at his back.

Rebecca knew before she took the turnoff toward home that the bridge over the creek just below her house would already be flooded from runoff. And while the flood stage rarely lasted long at that point, there would be no way to get home until the storm was over. Her groceries would keep, but she had no intention of sitting on a roadway in the dark and watching water rise through the glow of her headlights. Without a second thought she headed for the nursery instead. At least her office provided shelter, a bathroom, and a cot. If worse came to worst, she could spend the night there. It was, after all, her home away from home.

She parked and then stared through the windshield at the torrent of rain slashing down across its surface. Mother Nature was not making this easy for her. She took a deep breath.

"Here goes nothing."

In the few seconds it took to get from her pickup to the door, she was soaked. Her hands were shaking as she jammed the key in the lock and then turned it. The knob slipped beneath her fingertips as she pushed all of her weight against the door, then it gave unexpectedly and she fell inside onto her knees.

She rolled onto her back, kicking the door shut with the heel of her shoe and instantly shutting out the wind and rain hammering against the door. Her heart was pounding from the burst of adrenaline, her pulse was racing from the exertion, but she was out of the storm. For the moment, she was safe.

She looked up at the ceiling and started to chuckle at what she imagined she must look like. Flat on her back in the middle of the floor, wet as a rat and laughing like an idiot. Her stomach grumbled and she started laughing even harder. She was starving to death, and all of her food was back outside in the truck . . . in the rain.

"Smooth move, Rebecca Ruth," she chided herself, and groaned before rolling to her knees, then getting to her feet.

Normally, it would not be dark at this time of evening, but the clouds and the heavy rainfall had hastened nightfall. The office was shrouded in shadows, and when she tried the lights she found, to her dismay, that they didn't work.

"Pooh," she said. But she wasn't afraid of the dark. She knew this place like the back of her hand.

She headed for the bathroom, hoping to find a fairly respectable towel with which to dry. She didn't have a change of clothes, but she would settle for anything to get the water out of her hair. It was dripping down her back in the most unappealing fashion. When none was to be found, she wandered out of the bathroom on her way to the office in the back, willing to use anything as a substitute for a towel, even a spare T-shirt.

Lightning flashed and the ensuing thunder rippled overhead, rattling the windows and the floor beneath her feet. At that moment the door opened behind her and she spun toward the sound, thinking it had come open from a gust of wind. All she saw was the silhouette of a man who came flying through it.

She screamed in fright and pivoted toward the back door, running on instinct.

Jackson hadn't considered that his sudden appearance would scare her. Rebecca was already rushing toward the back when he came in the front. Without thought, he bolted after her, calling her name with every step he took.

"Rebecca! Rebecca! Don't run! It's only me!"

But Jackson's shouts were lost in the tumult of storm and the volume of her screams, and Rebecca was too frightened to stop and listen. Her only thought was to get outside, then maybe she could elude her attacker in the storm.

God help me, she prayed.

And then his arm fastened upon her shoulder and before she could scream again, she was spun around and slammed into a wall of wet fabric and muscles shaking from exertion.

"Honey, honey, it's me. It's Jackson. Stop screaming. Don't fight me. I won't hurt you. It's me. It's me."

His voice was low and shaky, the tone of his words urgent, but she recognized the feel of the man before his voice. She'd been held like this before, just as she was about to be run down on the road outside of New Orleans. And again, after Whaley Smith had assaulted her. She went limp in his arms and started sobbing.

"Jackson . . . Jackson . . . oh my God!" She thumped his chest with her fists. "You scared me to death."

His arms tightened around her as he rocked her within his embrace.

"I'm sorry. I'm sorry. I'm so damned sorry, baby. Please don't cry."

She shuddered and wrapped her arms around his waist to steady herself as his presence calmed her and his voice seduced and she let herself absorb what he'd called her.

"Why on earth are you here and not at home?" Jackson asked, and felt her body shaking beneath the wetness of her clothing. Before she could answer, he began running his hands up and down her arms in an effort to rekindle circulation. "You're going to be sick."

What it kindled had little to do with blood flow and everything to do with passion. Rebecca tilted her head back, trying to see through the shadows to the face of the man above her.

"My road floods when it rains," she murmured, and leaned a little closer, letting his hands have their way with her body.

Jackson felt her sway and thought she was faint. "You're shivering from cold," he muttered, and held her a little bit closer.

"I'm not cold, Jackson. I'm afraid."

Jackson froze. His hands ceased moving upon her body as her words pierced his heart. She was afraid of him! He couldn't bear the pain of knowing that he disgusted her that much.

"I'm sorry," he muttered, and started to turn away when her hand on his arm stopped him.

"You misunderstand me," Rebecca whispered. "I'm not afraid of *you*. I'm afraid of *us*."

Us? Us? Jackson's pulse began to race as he felt her move from behind him until the breath from her lips was warm upon his face.

"Jackson?"

"I would die before I'd hurt you," he whispered, and clinched his fingers into fists to keep from putting them back upon her.

"I know that." Rebecca found his face in the darkness, her fingers tracing the shape of his jaw, feeling the muscles in his cheek jumping beneath her touch.

"Rebecca . . ."

Urgency was thick in his voice as want surfaced over warning. As she took a step closer, her breasts brushed against his chest in a taunt he could not ignore.

"Be careful, lady." His voice was harsh as his hands raked through her wet, tangled hair, bringing her face closer to his own.

"Of what?" She slid her arms around his waist, moving her body into perfect alignment with his.

Instinctively he braced himself and pulled her close, rocking gently against her in an age-old rhythm.

"Of this." He cupped her hips with his hands and lifted her off of her feet. "Of that." His groin had swelled in one huge ache and was pressing into her flesh. "Of me."

Lightning flashed, momentarily illuminating the room inside and highlighting the passion etched upon his face. In that moment, Rebecca knew that she was loved.

"Ah God," he whispered, no longer able to restrain himself from the joy of his life, and took what she had offered.

The impact of his mouth upon her lips staggered them both. Rebecca groaned, and wrapped her arms a little tighter around his neck as he pursued the kiss. When her mouth parted beneath his and she let him come in, he felt the room tilting beneath his feet.

Blood pounded throughout his body in a blinding roar, blocking out all sense and sound save that of the woman in his arms.

He heard her soft gasps for air when their lips moved apart, he felt her hands moving urgently across his back and up his neck, trying to pull him closer, closer. Tracing the racing pulse in her neck with the tip of his tongue, he groaned, then began raking her body with kisses. It was all too much and yet not nearly enough.

She was trembling from head to toe as he backed her against the wall. The pressure of her body against his was at once a pleasure and a pain. With shaking hands, she held on as he lifted her off the floor. Wrapping her legs around his waist, she sighed with pleasure as he took them deeper into dangerous territory.

Desire shafted deep in her belly as she reeled from the onslaught of emotions his touch had triggered. And when his mouth began a journey down the front of her shirt and centered upon the nipple protruding against the wet fabric of her shirt, tears shot to her eyes. She wrapped her fingers in his thick wet hair.

"Jackson . . . Jackson . . . Jackson."

It was a plea he understood all too well. But their timing was off. Way off. This had to stop now. He had nothing with him in the way of protection, and he'd already crossed too many lines with this woman to take that unforgivable step.

"Ah damn," Jackson whispered, as he tore himself away from her.

Rebecca staggered as her feet hit the floor. The ache between her legs was so great that she could not stand, and the emptiness in her arms was too great to bear. She dropped to her knees and buried her face in her hands, then wrapped her arms around her waist in an effort to keep from falling apart.

"My God . . . why did you stop?"

"Someone had to." His voice was rough, his anger at himself overriding his sense of caution. "You would have hated yourself . . . and me . . . in the morning, lady." *And that would have killed me for sure.*

"Dear Lord," Rebecca whispered, and pressed her fingers to her lips to keep from screaming. "What are we going to do?"

Jackson's voice was full of anger. "*We* aren't going to do anything. And when I leave, lock the goddamned door behind you this time. The next man to come along might not be so willing to give up a good thing."

She gasped at the rudeness of his words, and when he spun and walked out into the storm, she crawled to her feet and followed him to the door. Rain sliced across her face and peppered her vision, but not enough to keep her from seeing the man straddle his bike and disappear into the night like a dark ghost. She stood on the threshold and shouted until she was choking on her own tears.

"Damn you, Jackson Rule! Damn you for making me care." *And damn you for making me love you*, she thought, even though she didn't have the nerve to say it aloud.

Jackson hurt in every bone and muscle of his body. But not even the storm could drown out the sound of her voice ringing in his ears, and he roared away into the night. *Damn me? Hell, honey, you're a little too late. I was damned before we met.*

By Monday, the storm was a thing of the past. Rebecca had worked all day Sunday picking up debris and hauling off things too damaged to salvage, wishing that she could pick up the mess she'd made of her life as easily.

With every step she took, Jackson's ghost was right beside her, taunting her, reminding her that he'd turned down what she'd offered without a fight. She didn't know what hurt worse, her pride or her heart.

When she turned into the driveway to open up for the day, Jackson's bike was parked in its usual place, but he was nowhere in sight.

"God give me strength," she muttered as she killed the engine and got out on shaky legs.

A slight wind lifted the thick clump of curls that she'd pinned on top of her head and molded her lightweight blouse against her upper body like the hand of a gentle lover. The brush of fabric against her skin reminded her too much of Jackson's mouth upon her breast and his hands upon her body. She bit her lip, opened the door, and walked in.

Jackson stood in the doorway between the two rooms with a cup of coffee in one hand and a pair of gloves in the other. For one long, silent moment, they stared deep into each other's eyes, trying to read each other's mood.

In all the years he had spent in prison, Jackson had never had a day when he'd regretted anything he'd done as much as he regretted what he'd done to Rebecca. He'd put that hurt, wary look in her eyes, and for that, he was sorry. So terribly sorry. But he couldn't say it, and wouldn't let her know how deeply her loving had affected him.

Rebecca swallowed a lump in her throat and blinked, telling herself that she would not cry, although she'd done little else since he had left her. The planes and angles of his face seemed sharper, as if he'd suffered greatly and slept little during the time they'd been apart. And yet the hard, warning look in his eyes said all there was to say: *Don't!*

So fine, Jackson Rule. You don't either, she silently warned. Her eyes blazed as her stomach twisted into knots.

Jackson wanted to cross the room, take her in his arms, and kiss away the pain he'd put on her face. He settled for a greeting instead.

"Rebecca."

"Jackson."

"Did you have much damage?" he asked.

Only to my heart. "Not so much," she said.

"That's good. What do you want me to do first?"

Make me understand you. "I don't know. Heaven knows we don't need to water anything right now. Maybe you could take the truck and drive into the shopping mall you and Pete landscaped and see if anything needs replacing. You might take a flat or two of flowering plants and some bedding plants as well."

"Yes, ma'am," he said, and went out the back door without looking back.

"Rebecca. Damn you to hell, Jackson Rule, it's Rebecca," she said, but he was already gone.

11

Rebecca had been taught that all good things come
to those who wait, or words to that effect. The problem was
that she wasn't exactly a patient person, and waiting for
Jackson Rule to relent was making her nervous.

In the three weeks since the storm, he had alternated
between ignoring her and answering in monosyllables until
she was ready to scream. He was treating her as if the whole
incident between them, as well as the last few months, had
never happened. For all intents and purposes, his behavior
was a repeat of his first week on the job.

She wanted to cry. She wanted to back him in a corner and
make him acknowledge her. She wanted to hate him . . . but
she couldn't. So she stayed on her side of the proverbial fence,
and he on the other, as life went on around them.

Pete was released from the hospital, and several days later
her father brought him out to the greenhouse for a visit.

Just to say hello.

Rebecca knew it was a lie. They'd come to look. To make
sure that the sinner she had hired was keeping his hands to himself. If it wasn't so painful, she would have laughed. The last

thing Jackson Rule was about to do was touch her, never mind
start a congenial conversation. The only thing that kept her
going was the memory of that night, and the way he made love
to her with his eyes. She wanted that night . . . and that man
back. What she got was another dose of her father's interfer-
ence. When they drove up, she went to the car to meet them.

"Pete! I'm so glad to see you," Rebecca said, and hugged
him around the neck, planting short, sweet kisses along his
jawline while he blushed.

"Shoot. If I'd known that's what it would take to get some
sugar, I'd have done this a long time ago," he teased, and
hitched his pants over a much smaller belly.

"Come inside where it's cool," Rebecca urged, then smiled
at her father, who stood to one side with a pensive expression
on his face. "You too, Daddy. I've got your favorite pop cooling in the fridge."

Rebecca did not know that her father was fighting the
grievous sin of envy. He would have given a lot to be able to
be that open and easy with his daughter. Every time they were
together, it seemed that one of them wound up angry, and it
was usually Rebecca.

He smiled and masked a sigh. It was hard to let go of the
fact that she didn't need protecting. In his mind, she would
always be the skinny-legged, nine-year-old crying in his arms
because someone had made fun of her wild mop of red hair.

He followed his daughter and his best friend into the office,
dabbing at the beads of perspiration that dotted his forehead
and wishing he'd worn something cooler than his professional
attire. The dark suit coat seemed to soak up the heat, and the
clerical collar felt two sizes too small.

Then he came face-to-face with the man from his nightmares. The look in Jackson's eyes was as cold and empty as
he'd ever seen on a living man. He wanted to look away, to
find something else on which he could focus his attention, but
the flat expression in those piercing blue eyes was impossible
to ignore.

"Jackson!" Pete walked toward him with outstretched hand. "Man . . . I can't tell you how grateful I am for what you did for me."

Jackson shifted his gaze to his working partner and smiled slightly, but the light never reached his eyes. "It was my pleasure. The CPR was compliments of Penitentiary 101."

Daniel Hill cleared his throat and ran a finger around the neck of his collar while Pete looked startled. He hadn't been expecting the hard, cynical attitude. Embarrassed, Pete dropped his hand without ever having touched Jackson and turned toward Rebecca, expecting her to pick up the conversation.

She seemed grossly absorbed in the papers near the cash register and never looked up.

Pete's heart hurt, but this time, from an emotional, not a physical pain.

Oh no, he thought. He had been afraid of this. He didn't know what, but something had happened between these two, and whatever it was, it wasn't good.

Pete decided to test his theory. "Hey, sweetheart!"

Rebecca looked up.

"Aren't you going to offer me something cold to drink and wipe my fevered brow?"

She tried to smile, but Pete saw past the ruse to the shadows beneath her eyes and the faint shimmer of unshed tears. *Damn. I knew it!* He turned to glare at Jackson, but got nothing but a faint glimpse of his back as the door closed behind him.

"What'll you have?" Rebecca asked as she dug through the refrigerator.

Pete stuffed his hands in his pockets and sauntered over to the refrigerator, pretending to survey the contents while he whispered in Rebecca's ear.

"I'd settle for the truth," he muttered.

She jerked upright and bumped her head in the process.

"Damn, damn, double damn," she groaned, and held the aching spot with both hands.

Daniel frowned. "Rebecca, watch your language!"

For Rebecca it was, more or less, the last straw. She turned on her father with tears in her eyes and a bitter smile on her lips.

"Oh, thanks for asking, Daddy, but yes, I'm all right."

She yanked a Pepsi from the refrigerator, removed the cap, and handed the bottle to Pete. "I'll be right back," she said, and ran out of the room before either man could see her cry.

"Well, I didn't mean to . . ."

Pete handed Daniel the soft drink and got another for himself. "You know what I think," he said, as he took the first swig. "I think you two are too much alike. You are just as hardheaded and independent as your daughter. The only problem is, she knew when to let go of your apron strings . . . you didn't."

Daniel began to pace, ignoring the condensation on the outside of the bottle that was dripping between his fingers. "When my wife died, I promised her that I'd look after our daughter. It wasn't easy to raise a girl all by myself. There's much about the female species that I don't understand, and I'll be the first to admit it. But when she constantly disobeys everything I taught her, I feel that it's my . . ."

Pete put his hand on his old friend's shoulder and squeezed. "Just listen to yourself, Daniel. You're speaking of her as if she's still a child. Rebecca is a grown woman. She answers to herself and no one else, and that's as it should be. Obey is not the right word. Understand what I'm saying?"

Daniel set the bottle on the desk and wiped his hands on the seat of his pants. It was an unseemly thing for a man of God to do and quite outside the norm of his behavior. It was also a sign of how troubled Daniel Hill was over the situation between his daughter and himself.

"What I don't understand," he muttered, "is how she can stand up for a man who took a life. There is no excuse for cold-blooded murder."

"Who says she's standing up for him?" Pete argued.

"He's still here, isn't he?"

Pete shrugged. "Right now, I'm in no position to say I wish she'd never hired him, because chances are, you would have already said the eulogy over me and stuck me in some soggy old mausoleum."

Daniel blanched. "I didn't mean that he should never have saved your life. I only meant . . . "

"Think about it, preacher man. I once remember you saying that you don't always get what you pray for, but that you have to be open enough to accept what you do get. No matter how *you* look at it, it was darn sure my lucky day when Rebecca hired Jackson Rule."

Rebecca came back into the room with a smile plastered on her face that was as false as the hope that she couldn't let go.

"I blew my nose and washed my mouth out with soap. Am I forgiven?" she asked lightly.

Pleased to be let off the hook so easily, Daniel hugged her while Pete stayed to one side nursing his Pepsi, not in the least fooled by her empty smile or her teasing remark.

Guilt that she and her father were constantly at each other's throats made Rebecca try even harder to make the visit a pleasant one. "Petey, come see what we've been doing while you were on vacation."

"Vacation, my great-aunt Fannie," Pete muttered, and pulled her nose at the frivolous use of his name.

But truth be known, looking over the place was exactly why he'd come. Pete had to check out his old haunt, expressing concern over the bits and pieces of damage still evident from the storm, as well as delight over the new array of fall shrubs and plants.

"You did a real good job, honey," he said, as he tested the topsoil on a lot of young trees waiting to be balled and shipped.

"The credit goes to Jackson, not me. I didn't have anything to do with it."

Pete sat back on his heels, studying the grounds and the neat, orderly way in which everything was displayed for optimum customer satisfaction.

"He's changed things some."

Rebecca gauged Pete's expression, trying to guess if that was a complaint. She held her breath, afraid that Pete would feel left out and unnecessary.

"But I think it's better this way. Look how he's grouped the tall bushes behind the shorter ones, and then layered the flats and pots of ground cover in front of them to give customers an idea of what it would look like if planted in this landscaped effect."

He stood and dusted his hands, then looked around. "I think I'll go look him up. It never hurts to hear a word of praise now and then."

Pete sauntered off with his hands in his pockets, whistling beneath his breath from the joy of just being alive and back in the place that he loved best.

"Well now," Daniel began, trying to find something to say that wouldn't get him in hot water all over again. "Uh . . . Pete looks good, don't you think?"

Rebecca smiled and nodded. "I'm so happy to see him up and walking, but it's going to be awhile before he can go back to any sort of regular work."

"Maybe you should hire some more help, so you and your uh . . . so you and that . . . "

"Jackson. His name is Jackson."

The tone in her voice was warning enough. Daniel didn't stutter over the suggestion again.

"Right! Jackson! Maybe you should hire another man to pick up the slack until Pete can come back."

She shrugged. "I don't think so. Business is slowing down a bit. If I get any big jobs, I'll call the university. There's never a shortage of college boys willing to make extra money."

Before he could comment, a customer arrived, and Rebecca left her father in a chair in the shade. Moments later, Pete came around the building with Jackson at his side, talking with ease and pretending not to notice that Jackson was barely participating in the conversation, answering only in monosyllables.

Rebecca stuck her head out of the greenhouse and yelled.

"Jackson, would you bring the small dolly and an empty flat?"

"Yes, ma'am."

Pete sat down in the empty chair beside Daniel and tried not to stare after Jackson. But it was impossible not to notice what had just transpired. Now he knew for sure something serious had happened between that pair. Because Jackson had called her ma'am, and she'd let it stand.

He leaned back in his chair and stared at the white-blue sky overhead, trying not to think of the dozens of scenarios that could have changed their friendly relationship to this cold war.

"Nice day, isn't it?" Daniel asked, unaware of the significance of what had just happened.

Pete decided there was no need spilling his concerns to Daniel. The way things were between father and daughter, it would only make things worse. Pete settled for a sigh.

"Yes, old friend, I'd say that it is."

An hour or so later, the two men left, and Rebecca was alone with her thoughts while Jackson was making a delivery. She told herself the visit hadn't gone that badly, after all. She'd known that Pete would be aware of the change in their relationship and had worried about how he would react. All in all, she decided that it had gone pretty well.

If she could just find a way to get back in Jackson's good graces, she would be a satisfied woman. And while Rebecca knew the smartest thing she could do was leave things as they were, her sleepless nights and aching heart told her otherwise. Just for a moment, in the darkness of night in the middle of a storm, Rebecca had caught a glimpse of another side of Jackson Rule. And it was that man . . . the loving, passionate man, that she wanted back.

What she got was another dose of her father's meddling.

"Damn you, Jackson Rule! I'm the boss! Nowhere on earth does it say I have to take that from you," Rebecca shouted, and threw a wet glove at Jackson's receding figure. It landed with a soggy thump near the middle of his shoulder blades as he kept on walking.

She sat down on a stack of sacked peat moss and counted to ten, trying to regain her control, but it was difficult to do after having been told to mind her own business.

She dug the toe of her tennis shoe into the dirt. A blue jay dive-bombed the fish pond, barely missing the dragonfly hovering above a lily pad, and then squawked angrily when it landed on the branch in the tree above her head.

"Yes, and you keep your opinions to yourself, too," she said, and glared at the bird because she couldn't glare at a man who wouldn't fight back. "Just because I asked him if he had any other family didn't mean I was being nosy."

But in her heart she knew she was lying to herself. She was being nosy because she had wanted to know more about him. As she was about to work herself into a serious mood swing, she heard another car turning off the highway and looked up.

"Oh, great! The answer to my prayers," she muttered, and made herself smile as she went to meet her father.

"Hi, Daddy, what's up?"

The look on her father's face, and the fact that another man was getting out of the passenger side of the car, were answers enough for her question. Daniel was matchmaking again. Rebecca was willing to bet good money that the stranger had come to look her over.

Daniel smiled. "I brought someone I want you to meet," he whispered, and gave her a hug. When he did he felt the tension in her shoulders.

"Should I show him my teeth first, or let him feel my muscles?"

"Rebecca! Don't start," Daniel warned.

She smiled benignly at the stranger, and then turned her back on him to hiss at her father. "Why should I have to put up with this? I've told you before, I don't like being put on display like some . . . some . . . brood mare."

"He's nice."

She rolled her eyes.

"He's Mrs. Hallet's nephew."

"She takes her teeth out when she sings."

"Rebecca Ruth! One has nothing to do with the other!"

"Reverend Hill . . . you didn't exaggerate after all. She *is* pretty."

Daniel turned with a fixed smile on his face and a warning in his eyes that Rebecca recognized all too well.

"James Wilson, may I present my daughter, Rebecca Hill. Rebecca, James is the new vice president of the downtown branch of First State Savings and Loan."

The man was strutting. And when he looked at her, he looked at her body before he looked at her face. Rebecca hated men who presumed too much. And he was too clean and too blond to suit her tastes. She liked a man who'd just as soon roll in the mud as have a roll in the hay.

After raking Rebecca's body with a look that was just this side of lecherous, James Wilson held out his hand and winked, as if to suggest that they shared a joke no one else knew.

He's presuming again, Rebecca thought. *I don't see a darn thing funny about any of this . . . yet.*

There was a small smile on her face that Daniel instantly recognized, but it came too late for him to alter her intent. She reached across the space between them and caught the banker's hand in a firm, no-nonsense grip.

James Wilson liked to get down and dirty as well as any other red-blooded man, but figuratively, not literally. The impact of their momentary union had the feel of hand-to-hand combat, not a genteel handshake from a pretty female, and the residue left behind when she turned him loose took him aback.

"What the . . . ?"

Rebecca pretended to look startled as James Wilson's hand came away with a fair-to-middling amount of wet peat moss and potting soil on it.

"Sorry," Rebecca said, and flashed him her best Sunday smile. "I just didn't think."

James had sat across the desk from too many nervous borrowers not to know a lie when he heard one. *Didn't think? Like hell, lady. You knew exactly what you were doing.*

"Oh dear," Daniel said, and grabbed the banker by the arm. "Come with me, James. I'll show you where you can wash up."

"Sorry about that," Rebecca said sweetly. "I'll just wait right here."

Her father glared at her, then apologized to the banker all the way to the office.

"Serves him right," Rebecca muttered, wondering how long it would take her to get rid of him. She sat down on a bench, wishing she were a thousand miles away, and not caught in the open, waiting for the second shoe to drop.

"I'm going into the city now."

Startled by the sound of Jackson's voice, she stood up, then turned. He was standing on the other side of the bench.

"I didn't hear you come up," she said, and tried to think of something to say that would bring a smile back into his eyes.

"Sorry, I didn't mean to scare you, ma'am."

In a day filled with obstacles that she hadn't expected to face, his steadfast refusal to call her by her given name was the last straw.

"Shut up," she said, and balled her fists to keep from crawling over the bench and laying into him just to see if she could get any emotion from him other than the poker face she'd come to hate. "Just stop it! If you call me ma'am one more time, Jackson Rule, I'm going to punch you."

The last few weeks had been hell on Jackson. Two things were obvious. He loved a woman, and he knew that making love to her would ruin her, both personally and publicly. But dealing with truths like that hurt. In fact, they'd nearly killed him. He lived with her face in his mind and her laugh in his heart. Not even the children at the shelter had been able to take his mind off of her. And just when he thought he couldn't take another step, except off the face of the earth, he would think of her and get the courage to try one more day.

He looked down at her fists and then up at the scowl across her forehead and wanted to yank her across the damned bench and into his arms so badly he didn't trust himself to speak.

"Did you hear me?"

I hear more than you know, love. But he only nodded.

"Good, because I need backup. Since I'm the boss here, I'm ordering you not to leave these premises until my father and that . . . that . . . gigolo he dragged over here are gone."

Jackson's heart sank. *Gigolo!* That meant her father was matchmaking.

"Yes, ma . . ." He froze in mid-word and then smiled in spite of himself because Rebecca had one foot on the bench and was climbing over when her father came out of the office with the squeaky-clean banker in tow.

"Hallelujah, I am saved," Jackson drawled.

Rebecca flushed and came down off the bench, brushing her grimy hands on the seat of her jeans and wishing that all men would be turned into worms.

"Daddy would be happy to know that," she muttered, and pasted on a smile that would have made any other father proud.

Unfortunately, Daniel Hill had seen far too many of his daughter's faces not to know that this one was as fake as her earlier apology had been. She'd dirtied James's hand on purpose, and he knew it.

And to his dismay, the ex-con had come on the scene. No matter how many times they met, Daniel constantly caught himself looking down at Jackson Rule's hands, trying to picture what they must have looked like when they'd killed.

James's eyes narrowed at the sight of the dark, glowering man just to Rebecca's left. And then he realized this must be the hired man that Daniel was fussing about. He gave Jackson the once-over and then dismissed his presence, unable to believe that a woman would ever prefer rough and rugged over perfectly groomed.

Had Rebecca but known—her stunt had not put James Wilson off. To the contrary, he'd been intrigued. He didn't like his women soft, giggly, and willing. He liked them wild, feisty, and fighting him all the way. Something told him that this preacher's daughter had a fire inside of her that could burn a man up. James smiled at Rebecca. He was good at starting fires . . . and putting them out.

"Now then," he said, and slid his hand across Rebecca's shoulder. "Maybe we could start over . . . say, at dinner tonight?"

The familiarity of his touch made her skin crawl. *Not in this lifetime, buddy*, she thought.

Daniel gasped. "Rebecca, I don't . . . "

He never got a chance to finish.

Jackson's eyes narrowed and it took all he had not to tear the man's hands from Rebecca. *No one touches her like that but me*, he thought, and then died inside. *Anyone but me can touch her*. That was the inescapable truth. But saving Rebecca Hill had become his quest, whether he liked it or not. Before anything happened that couldn't be undone, Jackson interrupted.

"So, which is it, boss? Do I make the deliveries, or do you?"

Jackson's question took them all by surprise. Rebecca was all primed to douse the would-be suitor's ardor, and Daniel was mentally preparing another apology. James was incensed that a hired man would presume such familiarity. He was the first to object.

"I say, Rebecca, you need to have a word with the help. There's a little matter of manners lacking here."

Jackson took a step forward and asked a little more loudly, "Well, Rebecca, which is it?"

Startled by what he'd just said, she fixed Jackson with a slow, steady gaze.

You called me Rebecca.

Yes, lady, you won. Are you happy?

She took a deep breath and then turned to her father.

"Gee, Daddy, I'm sorry, but it seems that you came at a bad time. We've been pretty busy today, and I need to get back to work." She smiled at the banker. "Mr. Wilson, it's been a pleasure to meet you. If you ever need any landscaping done, give us a call. Jackson is swift and efficient. I can promise you won't be disappointed."

"But what about dinner?" James asked.

She smiled. "I couldn't possibly. Much too busy, but thanks so much for asking." Before Daniel could argue, she kissed her father on the cheek and started walking them toward the car. "It's good to see you, Daddy. Call me sometime. I'll fix supper for you."

He brightened, thinking he might include his latest find in the invitation, when Rebecca squeezed his arm a little too hard to be anything but a warning.

"Thanks, sweetheart, I'll do that," he said, and sank into the seat behind the steering wheel, wondering all the while where he'd gone wrong. *It shouldn't have been that difficult to raise one child. One little girl should have turned into one young lady, not a defiant heathen.*

James buckled himself into the passenger seat and stared at the redhead through the windshield without smiling. It had been a long time since he'd been given such a slick brush-off. And he'd bet a year's interest that there was something going on between Daniel's precious daughter and the hired help. He didn't mind. All that meant to him was that she was already broken in.

Rebecca waved as they drove away. When she turned, Jackson was still on the other side of the bench. Waiting. She started toward him with a smile.

"I didn't think you'd ever forgive me for . . . "

Jackson took two steps back, keeping the bench firmly between them. "Do you want to make the delivery or should I?"

The wall was up again, but Rebecca didn't even care. He'd taken a big first step today, and it was one she'd almost lost hope of seeing. She wasn't going to push her luck again. Not with this man.

"You go," she said softly.

He turned toward the loaded delivery truck and was almost at the door when she spoke.

"Jackson?"

He turned, expecting almost anything but what came out of her mouth.

"Would you mind doing me a favor?"

"Depends," he muttered, gauging the wistful expression on her face.

"I'm suddenly starving. When you come back, would you bring me a candy bar and a great big something to drink?"

His smile was slow in coming, but when it did, it broke the stern planes of his face, shattering the anger that carried him through each day.

"You want a candy bar? And something to drink?

"A great big something to drink," she reminded him.

"Got any preferences?"

She inhaled slowly and then let her gaze move up and down his body in a look he could not misunderstand.

"Surprise me."

Oh lady, it would be my pleasure, and in a thousand ways.

"Yes, ma'am," he said, and swung into the truck before she could make a move.

He looked in the rearview mirror just before pulling onto the driveway. She was still standing by the bench, but he thought that she was smiling.

12

James Wilson had not become the successful man that he was by letting a good thing pass him by. And in his mind, Rebecca Hill was something to be had. Inside of three days, he was back at Hillside Nursery. Only this time he'd come alone and was waiting for her when she came to open up.

When Rebecca drove into the yard, the last thing she expected to see was the tall, blond man leaning casually against the trunk of a tree. His perfectly groomed hair and studied pose set her teeth on edge. But it was the expression on his face that made her nervous. She knew a predator when she saw one, and despite fancy clothes and a moneyed air, James Wilson was on the make. Where on earth did her father find these men?

"Rebecca! Good morning."

She gauged the tone of his voice against the glitter in his eyes and masked a shudder. There was something about him that made her think of Whaley Smith, the man who'd attacked her. He had taken without asking. And then her nerves settled as she got out of her truck. Surely a successful, prominent man like James Wilson would not cross the line of good behavior.

"Mr. Wilson. Whatever brings you this far out of the city . . . and so early in the morning?"

He smiled. "You."

She stopped in mid-step as her instincts sounded a warning. "I see you don't waste words."

"Or anything else of worth," he said, and raked her body with a look.

At that moment, Rebecca wished she had chosen a looser pair of blue jeans and a different shirt to wear that day. The way he was staring, she felt as if her well-worn T-shirt was clinging to her body like a second skin.

"I appreciate the thought, really I do," she began. "But I'm not in the market for a . . . "

James cupped her elbow with his hand and led her toward the office as if this were an everyday occurrence.

"Don't let me stop you from doing whatever it is you do to open up," he said. "I'm a firm believer in good business practices."

Gritting her teeth, she thought a thousand vile thoughts for which she had no words as she tried to ignore the man's presence. With a casualness she did not feel, she began counting money into the cash drawer and turning on signs and lights.

James watched, well aware that his presence had taken her by surprise. He smiled. The chase was half of the game.

"So, are you going to be a good girl and reconsider my offer of a date?"

Rebecca dropped the last three dimes into the drawer and slammed it shut. The placid expression on her face was not what James had expected to see.

"Why?"

The question took him aback. Explaining his motives was not something he did . . . ever. It wasn't often he met a woman who intrigued him as much as Rebecca Hill, and he wasn't sure how to gain her confidence. Did one tease and flirt, or was open and honest the best way to proceed? He decided on honesty with a very small white lie.

"I'll be honest, Rebecca."

That would be refreshing, she thought.

"At first, I was only doing your father a favor by coming with him the other day. I didn't expect to be intrigued by you. You did something that no woman has been able to do to me in years. You challenged me. I like that in a woman."

She searched the wide, open innocence of his expression and knew that she'd just been snowed. *So I challenged you, did I? And that's supposed to turn me on?*

"Since we're being honest . . . "

James bowed his head and smiled. "Please."

"I don't like being set up, which is what my father does on a regular basis. I'm sorry he dragged you into this, Mr. Wilson . . . "

"Please call me James."

Rebecca continued without acknowledging his request. "Unfortunately, I did not experience the same sort of chemistry that you seemed to feel. Thank you for the invitation, but I really don't want to get involved right now."

Her rejection shocked him. He'd been so certain that once he'd stated his case she would fall into his arms that he'd already made dinner reservations at one of the finer restaurants in the city.

"I'm very well established," he said, and hated himself for saying it. It sounded like begging.

"So am I," Rebecca said.

"I could do big things for you. Get this place off the ground in nothing flat. You could be a lady of leisure and still maintain control of the business without dirtying your pretty little hands anymore."

She hid a smile, realizing that the dirty handshake still rankled. "But I like getting my hands in the business, in every way. I don't mind a little honest dirt. It always washes off."

He stepped forward. She felt the pressure and hated herself for getting nervous. This man wouldn't dare say or do anything to harm her. He would know that she would tell . . . wouldn't he?

"A lady like you shouldn't be bothering herself with menial tasks when she's so much better suited for other . . . pleasures."

When he lingered on the word "pleasures" she went still. There was no mistaking his inference, or the small, secretive smile on his face.

"I think you'd better go now," she said. "And I'd rather you didn't come back."

A sneer marred his pretty features. James Wilson was not a good loser. "There's got to be a reason why you're not interested. Can it be because you've already got something going on with someone else? Someone for instance . . . like maybe your help?"

If she were innocent of the accusation, she should be shocked. When she reacted with anger instead, he knew he'd scored, and hated her for choosing trash over respectable credentials.

"I can't believe he's that good at satisfying a woman. After all, one has to remember where he's been. I'd venture to guess he's had a lot more experience with the male sex than a woman like you."

Rebecca was livid. "Get out!" she yelled.

He jammed his hands in his pockets and rocked on his heels, gauging her emotional outburst with sexual interest.

"You're beautiful when you're angry, did you know that, Rebecca?"

"Get out and don't come back!" Her voice was shaking. Never in her life had she ever wanted to hit a man as badly as she did James Wilson.

His low whisper made her flesh crawl. "I'll bet that you scream when you come."

The coffee cup beside the cash drawer was suddenly in her hand. An inch of yesterday's brew clung to the bottom with cold, thick persistence. It sloshed on her hand as she let it fly.

He ducked as the cup hit the wall to the side of his head and then frowned when he realized that some of it had splattered across the sleeve of his clean, white shirt.

"Like I said . . . you're a passionate little thing. In the right hands, you would be . . . "

The back door opened, slamming against the wall with loud force. Jackson was stiff with anger as he crossed the space between them and stopped inches short of Wilson's face.

"Just say the word, Rebecca, and he's mine."

The smirk on James Wilson's face wilted. Considering what he knew about Jackson Rule, as well as what he'd just implied about him, it was very unnerving now to be eye to eye with the man.

A wave of relief swept over her. "Jackson! I didn't know that you were here."

His gaze raked the banker's face, and then he smiled slowly. "Neither the hell did he."

For James, the game was no longer fun. He'd had all he wanted of this bitch and her consort.

"Get out of my way," James said, and started to push past when Jackson suddenly stepped between him and the door.

"Don't call her. Don't come back here. Don't even say her name aloud again. Not to anyone. Do you hear me?"

James was too afraid to do anything but listen as Jackson reinforced the threat by taking a step closer. When he felt the ex-con's breath on his face, he started to shake.

"The last man who touched her against her will is in jail, awaiting trial. He was a nobody, so I doubt if he cares that his reputation is ruined. But you, on the other hand, would make a real loud noise if you fell." Jackson leaned closer. "All it would take is one push. Do you understand me?"

"You bastard," James growled, and pushed past Jackson toward the doorway. "Take what you want of her! After you've had her, no respectable man would want her anyway."

Rebecca gasped, but the damage had already been done. In spite of the cool rage with which Jackson was dealing with the banker, she could tell that the words had cut deep.

"Jackson! Let him go! He isn't worth the trouble it would cause."

Jackson stepped aside, then watched as Wilson bolted out of the office. He was running by the time he'd cleared the steps. His car spun out of the yard in a flurry of gravel and dirt, leaving nothing of himself behind except the damage that he'd already done.

Rebecca dropped into a chair, shaking from the inside out at the ugliness of the man and his words. Jackson stared at her from across the room, not trusting himself to get too close.

"Are you all right?" he asked.

She nodded. "Some men can take no for an answer and some can't. It was getting ugly. Thank you."

The urge to hold her was tearing him apart, but the memory of Wilson's parting shot was still ringing in his ears.

"Maybe if you hadn't known me, this would never have happened."

Rebecca frowned. "What are you saying?"

"If you'd never met me, you would not have been subjected to this kind of scrutiny. People are the same the world over. They figure that if you lie down with dogs, you're bound to get fleas."

"I'm not *lying* with you, and we both know it."

The tremble in her voice was nearly his undoing. But he said what had to be said.

"But we both know something else, don't we, Rebecca?"

If she'd had another coffee cup to throw, it would already have hit the wall. She stood. There was no way she'd take this slam sitting down.

"Why can't you just say it, Jackson? Don't hint around at the truth. We both know what? That if you hadn't been the one to call a halt the night of the storm that I would have let you make love to me?"

"That's enough, damn it!"

"No!" she shouted. "It wasn't enough then, and it's not enough now! And don't you lie to me by pretending it didn't affect you as much as it did me! I felt your hands shaking when you touched me! I heard you groan when I kissed you back! You wanted me as much as I wanted you."

Jackson was immobile, stunned by the truth of her claim and lost in the memory of how she felt in his arms, and how her lips had trembled beneath his.

"Say it, Jackson! For once, tell me the truth!"

The silence between them was frightening until finally he answered.

"Yes."

"Yes, what?"

"Yes, damn you."

Rebecca wilted. She knew she'd pushed too hard, but loving this man was making her crazy. And the moment she thought it, stumbled backward in shock. *Love? When did that happen?*

"Are you happy now?" Jackson demanded.

She stared at him without blinking, absorbing the cold anger on his face and the pain in his eyes, and then her heart broke. *Oh Jackson, I don't know if I'll ever be happy again.*

"I'm going to work . . . unless you need to draw more blood," he said.

"I didn't mean to hurt you," Rebecca whispered. "For once, I just wanted some honesty between us."

Jackson's expression was bleak. "Honey girl, take it from me. Honesty can kill you."

The words were still ringing in her ears when Jackson closed the door after himself. With an aching heart, she began cleaning up the mess that she'd made with the coffee cup, wishing it could be this easy to fix what was wrong with loving Jackson Rule.

Her fingers trembled as she knelt on the floor, swiping at the spill with a handful of paper towels, all the while muttering beneath her breath.

"Dear God, the first time I fall in love in my entire life, and you make it impossible for him to love me back."

But it hurt too much to cry, and there was no use dwelling upon the impossibilities between them. She tossed the towels in the trash and looked out the window, uselessly searching for a man who'd already made himself scarce. All she could do was live each day as it came and pray for a miracle.

o   o   o

August had come and gone, taking the worst of the heat with it, leaving a dull lassitude behind. Days came and went with sluggish repetitiveness, draining the spirit of the impetus to do anything but search for shade and something cool to drink.

When Jackson wasn't at the hospice checking on Molly, he was at the shelter with the children. He made a point of using every spare minute of his time so that he wouldn't have to think of what he'd done to Rebecca . . . and to himself.

To Jackson's delight, Billy Thibideaux and his mother, Esther, had gotten a new and unexpected lease on life. He'd been at the shelter the evening her father drove in from Illinois to take them home with him. Esther had cried, and then laughed, and then cried some more. And it hadn't taken Billy long to bond with a man he didn't know. He'd seen all he needed to see when the man who was his grandfather had opened his arms and hugged his mother tight. He hadn't seen such joy on her face in his entire life, and in his mind, anyone who made his momma happy, was fine with him.

Nearly everyone at the shelter had rejoiced in Esther's good fortune. Everyone, that is, except eight-year-old Taylor Monroe. He'd watched the reunion with a blank expression and then retreated into his shell. To the observer, it would seem that Taylor simply wasn't interested in people he didn't know, but Jackson knew better. He saw the pain, and the jealousy, and the longing for some of the same on Taylor's face. When Taylor left the party, Jackson followed him down the hall and out of the shelter.

"Hey, Taylor, don't you want to come back and have some cake and ice cream to help celebrate?"

Taylor shrugged and kicked at a clod of dirt with the toe of his shoe.

Jackson's heart ached for the child. Taylor held so much anger inside. As hard as Jackson had tried over the past few weeks, he still hadn't been able to get him to share more than a brief and occasional conversation. He put his hand on the child's shoulder, trying not to concentrate on the small but significant scars he felt through his thin jersey shirt.

"I know it's hard to be happy for someone else when you're not happy inside. But maybe if you tried, it would make you feel better."

Tears shone in the child's dark eyes as he jerked away from Jackson's touch.

"I don't care nothin' about them," Taylor muttered. "You just wait and see. Billy's grandpa don't mean what he says. He's just pretendin' to be nice. When he gets them alone, it'll be different."

Jackson sighed in frustration. How did one teach a child like this to trust? Not for the first time, did he wish he had some training to fall back on, and wondered about pursuing more schooling at one of the local colleges. If his life weren't so messed up, if he knew where he stood with Molly and could get past the love he had for Rebecca to get on with his life, then maybe someday he would. But now, it was all he could do to get through each day.

"You're wrong, Taylor. Not everyone is a liar. Not every man beats those he says that he loves. I know it's hard for you to understand, but you have to believe me."

Unexpectedly, Taylor erupted. "You're lyin'!" He turned on Jackson with his fists doubled. "I don't believe you! I ain't no little kid! I don't believe in Easter bunnies and Santa Claus." His voice was shaking as tears poured down his face. "I don't even believe in God!" he shrieked, and then waited for Jackson to make his move.

Then how do I reach you, boy?

For a long, silent moment, neither one spoke, and then to Taylor's dismay, Jackson Rule dropped to his knees and opened his arms. The child hadn't expected acceptance. Not after the awful things he'd just said. Before, outbursts like this had earned him nothing but a beating. To be offered comfort took him off guard. His breath caught on a sob as he wavered, longing to be sheltered from the fear that constantly dwelled within him.

"I'm sorry, Taylor. I'm so sorry," Jackson whispered.

For the boy, it was too much. He fell forward into Jackson's arms, sighing with profound relief when they closed around him without causing him pain.

"I still don't believe you," he muttered, even as Jackson rocked him.

Jackson's sighed as the child trembled against him. "I know, kid. I know." And as he held him close, he realized that there was someone who might be able to help where he could not.

Jackson glanced out the office window, making sure that Rebecca was engrossed in helping the customer who'd just arrived, and then began flipping through her Rolodex for her father's number. He'd wrestled with the notion of asking for Daniel Hill's help with Taylor Monroe all night. With the bad blood between them, there was a good chance that the man wouldn't even hear him out. And then he'd think of Taylor and know that he had to try.

Checking one last time for Rebecca's whereabouts, Jackson dialed, hoping that her father was at home. What he had to say couldn't be left on an answering machine.

"Hello, this is Daniel Hill."

Jackson took a deep breath and then started to talk. "Reverend Hill . . ."

"Yes, this is he."

"This is Jackson Rule."

For a moment Daniel didn't know what to say. This was the last man he would ever have expected to call. And then something occurred that frightened him.

"What's wrong? Has something happened to Rebecca?"

"No, sir. I'm calling to ask for your help."

Daniel couldn't believe his ears. His spirits soared as he envisioned this fallen man coming to Christ.

"I see," he said. "While I think it's admirable that you recant your sins, I must say that I'm a little surprised you've asked me for help. We haven't been on the best of terms."

Jackson grinned. Like Rebecca, the man had a way of understating the obvious.

"I'm not calling about me," he said. "It's for someone else." Before Daniel could interrupt, Jackson began to explain. "Have you ever heard of the Jesus House?"

Daniel frowned. "Isn't that a shelter for the homeless?"

"Yes, sir. It's down in Central City."

Daniel rolled his eyes in silent dismay. It was one of the worst and most dangerous parts of New Orleans.

"Look, Mr. Rule, I don't know what you think I can . . ."

Jackson interrupted. "Jackson . . . not Mr. Rule, okay? And just hear me out. The director is a fine man. His name is Clark Thurman. You can call and talk to him if it will make you feel better."

"Exactly what is it you're asking of me?"

Jackson took a deep breath. "I'm asking you to teach a little boy named Taylor Monroe to believe in God."

"Dear Lord," Daniel gasped. "What on earth do you mean?"

"Look, preacher. The boy is only eight. One of the first things he told me was that his grandfather beat him because he was a bastard. It doesn't matter what anyone says to him, or does for him, he distrusts it—and them. He won't play with the kids down there. He rarely talks, and when he does, his words are full of anger. The kid hates. Not one particular thing—everything." Jackson took a deep breath, and momentarily closed his eyes against the pain of what he had to say next. "You've *got* to help him before he grows up into someone like me."

The words rang in Daniel's ears like thunder. He tried to concentrate on a platitude that would soothe this man's fervent plea, but it was no use. In spite of Jackson's intent, the preacher heard despair in his voice, and something else he'd never expected to hear. Compassion for another human being. It didn't fit the image Daniel Hill had of this man.

When Jackson got no reply he thought he was going to be refused. In a panic, he noticed that Rebecca and her customer were walking in the direction of the office. "I know what you think of me," he said. "And I don't blame you. I know you're a good man, and you've raised a good daughter. Please . . . for the child's sake . . . won't you help?"

"Give me the phone number," Daniel said.

Jackson went weak with relief and did as he was told, disconnecting only moments before Rebecca and the customer entered the office. He grabbed his gloves on the way out the back door, not giving her time to ask what he'd been doing, or where he was going.

And it wasn't until the customer was gone and she was closing the till that she noticed her Rolodex was open. Out of habit, she started to close the lid when she realized it was open at her father's name. While she often called her father at work, she knew his number by heart and would have had no reason to be looking for it.

The odd way in which Jackson had suddenly bolted from the office came back to her, and out of curiosity, she picked up the phone. Her finger paused above the redial as she considered what she was thinking, and then she scoffed at herself as she punched it. There was no way Jackson would be calling her father. In fact, Daniel Hill would be the last man he should want to call.

The phone rang four times in her ear, and then she heard the familiar sound of her father's message on the answering machine and gasped.

"What on earth?" she muttered as she dropped the receiver back onto the cradle.

She knew better than to ask Jackson, and quizzing her father would only succeed in reinvolving him in her personal life, which she did not need. With a frustrated sigh, she went back to work, and, when she got busy, forgot all about the call.

∘   ∘   ∘

That evening, when Jackson showed up at the shelter, he was carrying two sacks. One full of cookies for whatever children were still in residence, and another for Taylor Monroe.

"Where is he?" Jackson asked, as Clark handed the bag of cookies to a parent to distribute among the kids.

"Where's who?" Clark asked, trying to be heard above the din of voices.

"Taylor."

Clark paused, and then turned, staring thoughtfully at the man at his side.

"I don't know. Around, I suppose. Want me to look?"

"No, it's no big deal. I'll do it myself," Jackson said, and started to walk off, when he remembered Daniel Hill and stopped. "Hey, Clark, did a preacher call here today? A Reverend Daniel Hill?"

Surprised, Clark nodded. "How did you know?"

Jackson shrugged. "I asked him to talk to Taylor. Would you clear it with his aunt?"

"Sure," Clark said, "although I can guarantee that 'Aunt Edna,' as she likes to be called, isn't going to give a damn. What amazes me is the fact that she's still around. I fully expected her to abandon the boy here and leave the rest of his life up to someone else."

Jackson hated what he was hearing. It reinforced Taylor's assumption that Edna wasn't his aunt, and that no one seemed to care about his welfare.

"Well, for the time that he's here, I'd like to think he'll see a different side of life," Jackson said, and walked away, still carrying one of the sacks.

He found the child out back, playing a solitary game with a beetle and a stick.

"What have you got there, Taylor?" Jackson asked, and squatted down to the boy's level, pretending interest in the black, shiny beetle that repeatedly crawled off and on the stick Taylor kept putting in its way.

Unaware that anyone had approached him, Taylor flinched at the sound of a grown-up voice, and then relaxed as he recognized it as Jackson's.

"Oh, just an old bug." To show that he had no concern for it, he promptly stood and stomped it into the ground.

The deliberate way in which an eight-year-old boy had eliminated something that he'd probably spent hours playing with made Jackson sick. He wanted to hold him, and, at the same time, he wanted to shake him. He thought of what he'd brought and wondered if this was going to get the same treatment. Gauging the interest with which Taylor was eyeing his sack, he decided to take a chance.

"I brought you a present," he said.

The child's eyes grew round, and for a second, the anger that was always on his face disappeared.

"What is it?" he asked.

Jackson opened the sack and began pulling out the contents. The clay pot came first, then a small sack of potting soil, and the last thing he pulled out was a small plastic bag.

"Do you know where I work?" Jackson asked, aware that Taylor was more than a little intrigued by the objects, although it was obvious he didn't know what to do with them.

Taylor shook his head.

"I work at a greenhouse. We grow real pretty flowers and bushes and trees, and then we sell them to people to plant in their yards. When I was little, and before my mother died, she had a great big honeysuckle bush in our front yard. I used to love to smell those flowers on a real hot day. They were almost as sweet as honey tastes. Did you know that?"

Wide-eyed, Taylor shook his head, trying to imagine anyone as big as Jackson Rule ever being little like him.

"So, have you ever planted anything and then watched it grow?" Jackson asked.

"My grandpa used to plant 'taters, but I didn't do it right. I kept forgettin' to put the eyes up."

Jackson nodded. "Yeah, that's a pretty hard job. If you'd

been a little older, I bet he would have let you help. Maybe he just didn't want you to feel bad."

Taylor shrugged. "Naw, he just didn't like lookin' at me. Said I reminded him of the no'count who knocked up my mom."

Damn that old man to hell, Jackson thought, and then opened the small plastic sack and shook the contents out into his hand.

"Look at these," he said. "What do they look like to you?"

Taylor peered closely at the little brown bulbs and their soft, fringy roots.

"Kinda like onions."

Jackson grinned, and dropped them into Taylor's hands. "They do, don't they? But they're not. They're flower bulbs. And the best thing is, those little brown things can grow the prettiest flowers you'd ever want to see. They're called hyacinths, and the flowers look sort of like the blooms on a lilac bush, only not so wobbly."

"Yeah?" Taylor asked, turning the bulbs over and over in the palm of his hand.

"Yeah," Jackson echoed. "So, would you like to plant them in this pot and then watch them grow?"

"I don't know how," he muttered, eyeing the pot, the dirt, and the bulbs.

"I'll show you like my friend Pete showed me. How's that?"

"Yeah . . . okay," Taylor said, and dropped to his knees.

Jackson started to open the potting soil, when he slapped his leg, as if just remembering, though he'd been planning to involve Taylor in it right from the start.

"Dang. I almost forgot," he said, and held up the pot. "See this hole in the bottom?"

Taylor bent down and looked up through the hole and into Jackson's face, then grinned in spite of himself when Jackson winked at him.

"Pete says you've got to put some small rocks or gravel in the bottom of these kinds of pots so that they'll drain just right . . . and I forgot to bring any. Suppose you could find us some?"

Taylor jumped to his feet just as Clark came out the back door.

"What are you two doing?" he asked, as he sauntered over to where Jackson was sitting, missing nothing of the stuff on the ground around him.

"I'm gettin' rocks," Taylor announced, and darted off into the alley.

Clark nodded, and when the boy was out of earshot, whispered to Jackson.

"What are you doing?" he asked again.

Jackson grinned. "Waiting for Taylor to get the rocks."

Clark rolled his eyes. "I know when I'm not wanted," he muttered. "See you later."

That night, when Jackson was readying for bed, he could still remember the intense concentration with which the boy had planted the bulbs. From poking them in the loose, rich soil, to covering them just right and then watering them down.

"When will they grow?" Taylor had asked, as he carried the planted pot into the shelter and set it near his bed.

"Plants are sort of like children, Taylor. And you're going to have to be the parent. You have to take care of it. Feed and water it just like you would a child, and then you have to make sure that it gets enough light, and doesn't get too cold. Then, when it's ready . . . like a child that's been loved just right . . . it will grow."

"I can do that," Taylor said.

Jackson nodded. "I knew that, son, or I wouldn't have brought you the gift."

And so time passed. But it wasn't just the days that were slow, it was the slack season for Rebecca's business, as well. It was too late in the year for planting summer stock, and a little bit too early to consider late fall planting. She spent her days living for the rare moments when Jackson would laugh with her, or start a conversation for no reason other than the urge to communicate. Every day she told herself she was living a futile fantasy—one in which she was the only player.

As Pete's strength returned, his visits became a regular thing. On the days that he was around, Jackson's mood was just that little bit lighter, as if the other man's presence were the buffer he needed to keep himself under control. Rebecca watched them and hated herself for the jealousy that she felt. *Damn you, Jackson, why can't you talk to me like you talk to Pete?*

But in her heart she already knew. In Jackson's eyes, Pete represented no threat, but she did. So she pretended she didn't care, and the smile in her eyes slowly faded, and the laugh that had always been just under the surface was gone.

And when she wasn't watching, Jackson saw her pain and recognized it as a mirror of his own. He cursed himself for not having the guts simply to walk out of her life before he ruined them both. He spent sleepless nights trying to focus all of his energies on Molly, waiting for the day when he could see her face-to-face, and wondering if it would ever come.

And then a drunken man with a match changed the rules.

It slipped under the space beneath the door like a ghost hunting a place to haunt. Ashen and silent, moving at will along the floor, it was a forerunner of death.

Jackson rolled over and sat up in bed as if someone had just called his name. For a few seconds he stared around the room into the shadows, trying to figure out what it was that had awakened him. And then he saw it, inches above floor level and climbing. He rubbed his eyes, unable to believe what was before them, and in that moment, a child's piercing scream brought reality to a rude, ugly head. He bolted from the bed and found himself knee deep in billowing smoke.

Precious seconds were wasted as he quickly dressed, pulling on jeans, a shirt, and his boots. As he stuffed his wallet into his pocket, he gave his bike, as well as his meager belongings, a rueful glance. There was no time to gather up what was his. Not unless he was willing to ignore a child's cry for help. He bolted out of the door without looking back.

The smoke was thick on the stairs, and even thicker on the upper floor. People were already running out of their apartments, anxious to reach safety.

"Fire! Fire!" a man shouted, as he ran past Jackson, banging on door after door along the upper hallway as he headed for the stairs.

Gut instinct told Jackson he was crazy for doing this, but he knew he would never be able to face himself again if he left without checking on the child he'd heard.

Smoke was thickest at the end of the hallway where the boy named Freddie and his father still lived. Jackson lifted his fist to pound on the door. From where he stood, he could already feel the heat emanating from behind the wall.

"Freddie! Freddie! Are you in there?" he shouted.

Once again, the door behind him opened, and the woman who'd come to Freddie's rescue that night long ago came out on the run with her arms full of clothing and a terrified expression on her face.

"Is the boy with you?" Jackson shouted.

"No! Dear Lord, aren't they out?" she cried, dropping the clothes she was carrying as she started toward the door.

"Hell if I know," Jackson said, and added his voice to the call. No one answered, and the door was still locked.

The woman screamed at the top of her voice and swayed against the wall. Jackson grabbed her by the arms and shoved her toward the stairs.

"Get the hell out of here," he shouted. "When you get outside, find a fireman and tell him there's a child trapped up here."

"Oh my God!" she wailed, and staggered.

"Run, damn it, run!" Jackson shouted.

So she did. As she found the stairs through the smoke, the last thing she heard was the sound of splintering wood and then a loud roar, as if someone had opened the door to a blast furnace.

∘　　∘　　∘

The sweet, soulful peal of a trumpet's wail from her clock radio pulled Rebecca out of her sleep. She rolled over on her back, and hit the snooze alarm before reburying her nose in the pillow, rooting for that soft spot that had been there before. But it was as elusive as the yearned-for extra five minutes of sleep. Finally, she rolled out of bed with a groan, stumbling toward the bathroom.

Twenty minutes later, showered, dressed, and ready to face another day, she headed for the kitchen. Although the thought of food turned her stomach, common sense told her to eat. She refused to make herself sick over the love of a man who didn't seem to want her.

Sunlight spilled through the yellow sheers hanging over the kitchen sink, coating the room with a cheerful warmth that was hard to appreciate, especially before wake-up coffee. She leaned over the counter and peeked out the window, gauging the sky with a practiced eye. It didn't look like rain. If the weather held, she and Jackson could get some work done outside today.

The scent of the freshly brewed coffee made her stomach grumble, and she absently poured herself a cup from the pot that she'd readied the night before, wishing that life came equipped with automatic timers like her coffeepot. It would be a lot simpler.

Minutes later, with a plate of toast in one hand and her coffee in the other, she headed for the living room to watch the news while she ate.

Flipping past national news, she searched the channels until she found one showing local and area news, and then bit into her toast right in the middle of the broadcast of a breaking story.

Seconds later, she set the toast aside and leaned forward, adjusting the volume on the remote until the reporter's voice was so loud that it seemed he was right beside her.

"New Orleans firemen fought an out-of-control blaze for

*hours last night. The apartment building on Solange Street in
the area known as Central City was a total loss. At this time,
the cause of the blaze is unknown, but several people who tried
to help the residents of the apartment building escape are
claiming that it started in a second floor apartment where a
man and a child were living.*

*"At this time, the firemen are still searching the rubble for
bodies, although they think most of the residents have been
accounted for. Eight people have perished so far and nine others have been taken to various hospitals for treatment. Red
Cross has set up a temporary shelter at . . ."*

"Oh my God."

In a panic, she watched them replaying footage of the fire at
its worst. When they flashed to body after body being carried
out on stretchers, she began searching the faces in the crowd,
hoping to see a familiar scowl. She was pretty sure that
Jackson lived on Solange Street.

Maybe she was wrong. Desperately, she hoped so.

She grabbed her purse and keys and ran for her truck, anxious to get to the office and check her files. His address would
be on record. All the way up the road she kept telling herself
that she was making a big deal out of nothing. But when she
pulled his application out of the drawer, she blanched and collapsed into the chair behind her.

"Okay, calm down. That's a residential neighborhood.
There's got to be more than one apartment building in the
area. Any minute now he'll come riding in on that big black
Harley and smirk at me for being such a worrier."

But eight o'clock came and went, and then nine o'clock did,
too. Rebecca sat in the office with the lights out and the
CLOSED sign in place. She heard two cars drive up and then
back out without parking. She didn't care. Her focus was on
the phone, willing it to ring.

"He could have had a flat," she told herself. "Remember the
other time when he was late, and I thought he'd quit. He had a
perfectly good reason then. He will have again, I'm sure."

But she wasn't sure. And the longer she waited, the more panicked she became.

This was silly, she finally decided, and grabbed her purse and keys. She would go see for herself.

"I'm sorry, miss, but you can't go any farther here."

Rebecca's face was strained as she tried to see past the roadblock of vehicles and police cars that had barricaded the end of the street.

"But I've got a friend who lives down there. I just want to see if he's all right," she begged.

The policeman shook his head. "I'm sorry. No one's allowed down there until they're through searching for bodies."

She clutched the steering wheel to keep from screaming. "Where can I get some information? How can I . . . ?"

"Red Cross has set up a temporary shelter down at an empty warehouse about six blocks over. Injured have been transported to several hospitals. I have no idea who's gone where. Check with Red Cross about that. And the dead have been taken to the morgue for identification. That's all I can tell you, miss. Now please move on."

Rebecca did as she was told, and as she passed the street she looked down it. A thick pall of smoke hung heavily in the damp morning air. She took a deep breath, trying to calm her fears, and nearly choked on the acrid stench as she began searching for signs of Red Cross vehicles and an abandoned building. And when she finally saw it and found a place to park, it took every ounce of strength that she had to get out of the pickup and walk across the parking lot toward the entrance.

"Please, God, let him be all right."

Quiet chaos met her at the door. That was when panic set in. People were everywhere. People like her—searching for missing friends and loved ones. Now and then a wail would break the dull roar of voices echoing within the confines of the large, vaulted ceiling, and Rebecca would cringe, aware that someone had received bad news.

A woman lay sobbing on a cot near the door, clutching a pillow to her chest. Rebecca looked away, unwilling to trespass upon another's tragedy. On another cot, a man sat with his legs hanging over the edge and his head in his hands, staring down at the floor in a stupor. The devastation of what had happened was obviously just catching up with him.

Cot after cot, chair after chair, table after table, Rebecca searched the faces of the people, looking for one blue-eyed man in desperate need of an attitude adjustment and a haircut.

If he never speaks to me again ... if he moves away tomorrow ... if that is what he wants to do, I won't care. Just let him be alive.

But the harder she looked, the more hopeless it seemed. There was a list posted on a wall naming those who were in the hospital. Jackson Rule's name was not on it. That meant he was either here or . . .

She shuddered, then swallowed a sob. The alternative didn't bear considering.

"Oh God, oh God . . . Jackson, please, please, please be here."

"Can I help you, miss?"

She spun at the sound of the voice, and before she realized it, was clutching at the sleeves of the woman before her.

"I'm looking for someone. A man by the name of Jackson Rule."

The woman frowned, as if considering the name, and then shook her head. "I'm sorry, but it doesn't sound familiar. However, I don't have a complete list of the survivors. Maybe if you checked down at police headquarters, they could help you." And then her voice softened and she laid a comforting hand upon Rebecca's shoulder. "You do know that there are several as yet unidentified."

Tears slid from the corners of Rebecca's eyes and out onto her cheeks. "Don't say that! He's not in the morgue. I don't want him to be in the morgue." And then her voice broke. "He can't be in the morgue."

"I know, dear. I'm sorry."

Rebecca turned away, wiping the tears from her cheeks, and willing herself not to cry. At least not until she found something to cry about. She took a deep breath and then gasped as a man suddenly appeared beneath the archway at the end of the room.

"Jackson?"

From where she stood, he was little more than a silhouette, but the stance was familiar, and the height about right. She held her breath and started down the aisle, dodging cots and people as she walked.

Seconds later she was calling his name in an all-out run.

Jackson was weary, both in body and in spirit. His chest ached from breathing smoke, and the skin on his hands was still tender where he'd scorched them. But a little boy was alive today, and that was all that counted. Freddie's being an orphan was a definite improvement over his life before.

Talking to the authorities had taken the better part of the morning. They were finally finished with him, and he was more than through with them. Jackson was on a one-man mission to find a phone. He needed to hear Rebecca's voice more than anything he'd ever wanted in his life. As he paused in the doorway, staring across the room full of displaced people, he realized that he was now one of them. It was a sobering thought.

And then he heard someone calling his name. The voice was familiar, and, only moments ago, he'd been wishing for that very sound. It was Rebecca, laughing and crying, with tears on her face and her arms open wide.

Without hesitation, he went to meet her, and then caught her on the run, lifting her feet from the ground and spinning her around and around in his arms as he buried his face in the curve of her neck. With his defenses down, he could no longer deny himself the truth. This woman and her love were the reasons he had survived. For one more chance, one more time.

13

"You're alive! You're alive! Thank God you're alive!" Rebecca locked her hands at the back of Jackson's neck and then laughed aloud as he swept her off her feet and into his arms. Damn the consequences, but she loved Jackson Rule and was sick of denying it.

"You're a crazy woman," he growled as he covered her face and neck with swift, indiscriminate kisses, caring little for where they landed, only that she had given him the right to plant them. "If you had a brain in your head, you wouldn't be here." *But thank the Lord that you are*, he thought.

He set her back on her feet, trying hard to slow the burn in his blood, but quelling this redhead's emotions was like playing with fire. At this point, if he kissed her once more, he wasn't sure he'd know when to stop.

Joy that she'd found him was breathtaking. She laughed and then clutched his hands with delight. To her surprise, he winced, and when she looked down at the bright pink skin, she realized that he had not completely escaped the wrath of the fire.

Her voice trembled. "You're hurt."

"Not so much," he said softly, cupping her face with his hands.

His skin was hot to the touch, and Rebecca felt sick, imagining the horror of what he'd escaped.

"Be careful of your burns," she whispered.

He lowered his lips and she forgot to move. And when they connected with her lips, she forgot to breathe.

Gently. Coaxing. Taking. Giving.

His mouth moved from one pleasure to another until Rebecca lost all track of place and time. Her eyes closed, her senses completely attuned to the rhythm of his breath upon her cheeks, she felt it catch and then cease. Only then did she open her eyes. Had he not been holding her up, she would have gone to her knees.

His blue eyes had turned a dark, stormy gray, his nostrils flaring as he tried to draw breath, and a muscle in his cheek was jumping.

"Ah, God, Rebecca . . . "

"Yes."

He jerked, his eyes narrowing as he looked past her five freckles into a future he'd never allowed himself to consider.

"Be careful how you answer me, girl. You might get more than you bargained for."

She shook her head. "Never." And then the smile on her face slipped away as she held his hands in hers, palms up. "You need to see a doctor."

"Already have," he said. "The burns are minor. He gave me a prescription for some ointment, but I'm not going to use it until I can clean up."

"Then you're coming with me."

He smiled, and Rebecca swayed toward the look in his eyes. "Not yet, honey. I need to find a new place to live, and I don't have any . . . "

"We'll worry about that later."

"I don't think this is such a good . . . "

"I didn't ask you what you thought, Jackson. I said . . . you're coming with me."

He grinned. "That you did, ma'am, that you did."

Ma'am? She arched an eyebrow and then hooked her hand through his elbow. "You will pay for that later."

"I never had to pay for it, honey, even when I was a teenager. It would be a damn shame to start now."

She blushed and tried to think of a comeback, but couldn't.

"Too much too soon?" he asked softly.

She shrugged. "Probably the opposite. Not enough to brag about."

Stunned by her honesty, and the admission of lack of experience, he couldn't help but laugh. When she blushed and then grinned, he hugged her.

Several people turned toward the laughter, unable to see what could possibly be funny at a time like this, and then smiled when they saw the young man slide his arm around the young woman's shoulders and walk with her out the door. Lovers. That explained it.

They were in the pickup and on their way to her place when Jackson spoke up.

"Would you mind stopping at the first pharmacy you come to? I need to pick up some stuff."

She nodded, remembering the prescription from the doctor that needed filling, and shortly thereafter pulled into a small shopping center and parked.

Jackson looked down at his scorched and smoky clothing, then back up at the store. He wasn't exactly dressed for the occasion, but it couldn't matter. Before he went another block with this woman, there were some things that had to be done.

Rebecca saw him hesitate. "Do you need to borrow money? I'd be glad to go inside for you."

Hesitation disappeared. "No, honey, I don't need any money, but thanks for asking, and this shouldn't take long."

He crawled out of the pickup, ignoring the weariness in his bones and the hours of lost sleep, and sauntered into the store.

Rebecca shivered, remembering her first response to his embrace. Right before their lips met, it felt as if he'd absorbed her, taking away breath and sanity in one motion. She wondered what she was getting herself into, and then leaned back in the seat, closed her eyes, and sighed. Chances were, she would soon find out, and if the truth be known, she could hardly wait.

Jackson ignored the customers' startled glances as he walked to the back of the store and handed the pharmacist the prescription.

"It'll take a minute," the pharmacist said, and then frowned as he caught a glimpse of Jackson's hands. "Burns are painful, aren't they, mister?"

Jackson shrugged. "Some things hurt more."

He looked back toward the front of the store. From where he was standing, he could just see the cab of Rebecca's blue pickup. His eyes narrowed and his mouth firmed as if coming to a monumental conclusion.

"I need a few other things. Can I pay for it all back here?"

"Yes, sir," the pharmacist said.

Jackson turned and started up the aisles, on a mission. It took little thought to yank such things as razors, shaving cream, and shampoo from the shelves, but when he came to the aisle where over-the-counter birth control was displayed, he paused, his hand hovering over the boxes of condoms. Hesitation was brief, because in his heart, the decision was already made. Without a second glance, he added them to what he was carrying and then dumped the entire armload on the counter near the register.

"Did you find everything you need?" the pharmacist asked.

"All that matters," he said, and pulled out his wallet.

Moments later, Jackson was on his way out of the store and to Rebecca. In his mind, there was no turning back.

"Are you ready?" she asked, when he slid into the seat beside her.

His slow, steady gaze raked her face until she flushed. "The question is . . . are you?"

All the tension she'd been feeling suddenly disappeared. She leaned across the seat and kissed the side of his cheek, near his mouth.

"I've been ready for you all my life, Jackson Rule. Now let's go home."

A home with you? Jackson thought. *If only that were possible.*

The assurance in her voice told him more than any words ever could have that she wasn't afraid of the next step in their relationship. He took a long, deep breath, and then closed his eyes.

Have mercy, Rebecca. I'll be afraid for both of us.

A half hour later, Rebecca turned into the driveway leading to her house and felt, rather than saw, Jackson tense.

"Your father is here."

Her fingers tightened on the steering wheel, but otherwise she didn't react to the sudden panic that settled in her stomach. This was sooner than she'd planned, but at least the confrontation would be over.

"It doesn't matter," she said. "He can help me get the rooms ready."

Jackson's attention was so fixed upon the man in the swing on Rebecca's front porch that at first he didn't catch her remark. And then when he did, they were almost at the house.

"Rooms? What rooms?"

She pointed to the unattached garage near her house. "I stayed up there while I had this house remodeled. It's empty. It's furnished. You need a place to stay."

"This isn't going to work," he warned.

"It's only temporary," she said. "I'm not trying to tell you what to do, Jackson. I'm offering you sanctuary. What do you say?"

Sanctuary. Such a small word with so much meaning. He looked at her and then looked away, afraid to hope. Afraid even to pretend that anything permanent could come of this.

She parked, killed the engine, and then turned to him, waiting for his answer.

It came from the depths of his heart. "I say thank you."

She smiled. "You're welcome. Now, come with me. I'll show you how to pull a thorn out of a lion's paw."

Jackson wanted to grin but couldn't find it in him to do so. Gut instinct kept reminding him that Daniel had had God on his side, and he doubted he could make the same claim.

Daniel sighed in relief when he saw his daughter's pickup turning into the driveway, then said a silent prayer of thanksgiving.

When he'd been unable to get her on the phone, he'd only been mildly worried. He knew how much time she spent outside and how busy they often got at the greenhouse, but after coming to the store and seeing the CLOSED sign on the front door, he'd panicked. Not once in the nine years since she'd bought the property had she closed during her normal business hours. *Except the day Pete had had his heart attack!*

His imagination had been working overtime until he'd seen her coming up the drive. But relief quickly turned to horror when he saw the man in the cab beside her.

Daniel and Jackson hadn't seen each other, or exchanged a word, since their conversation about Taylor Monroe, but he was still reeling from the commendations the people at the shelter had given Jackson Rule. Hearing parents praising the man for helping their children was disturbing for Daniel. He kept wondering how many of them knew what Jackson had done, and then when he'd look around at the dismal surroundings, wondered if they'd even care.

To his dismay, the child Jackson had asked him to visit had been worse than Jackson had indicated. He and the boy were breaking ground slowly. Daniel was optimistic, however, because once in a while he saw a glimmer of a lonely child beneath Taylor Monroe's rough exterior and it gave him the hope he needed to continue.

Rebecca waved at her father as she parked. He couldn't bring himself to do more than grit his teeth, wave back, and remember to keep his opinions to himself. When they got out of the pickup, Daniel took a deep breath, forcing a smile as he walked off the porch to meet them.

"Daddy, I'm so glad you're here!" Rebecca said, and gave him a quick hug and kiss. "What a morning! I've been all over Central City, and . . . a little surprised I didn't see you there. I recognized several pastors from churches in the area ministering to the victims."

"Central City! Why on earth would I be there? What victims? And better yet, what were you doing there? It's not such a good place to . . . "

"Didn't you hear about the fire?"

"Fire? What fire?"

Now that her father's attention had been refocused, she knew it was the prime time to introduce Jackson's presence into the conversation.

"Jackson, I'm so sorry. Here we are visiting with no concern for your injuries. Come with me, I'll show you where you can clean up."

Father or no father, the gentle squeeze of her fingers around his biceps, and the look in her eyes, was impossible to ignore.

"Thank you," he said softly, and finally followed her up the steps.

"Did you get your medicine out of the truck?"

He held up the sack. "I've got everything I need right here," he said. *And from the look on your father's face, probably more than I need.*

"Medicine? Why does he need medicine?" Daniel asked, following them into the house.

Rebecca ignored the question as she led Jackson toward the hallway, pausing at the linen closet to get a set of towels before leading him to the nearest bathroom.

"You can shower in here," she said, dumping the towels on the counter. "There's soap, shampoo, and whatever else you might want in the cabinet over the sink. Help yourself. When you finish, Daddy or I will be glad to help you doctor your hands, okay?"

"Why does he need his hands doctored?" Daniel asked, and felt himself losing ground when Jackson closed the door between them.

"Oh, and Jackson . . . just throw your clothes out into the hall. I'll put them in the washer for you," she called out, and then headed back toward the front of the house.

"You're washing his clothes now? Have you lost your mind? What is going on with . . . ?"

Rebecca paused in the doorway between living room and kitchen.

"Daddy, do you remember where the breaker box is to the apartment over the garage?"

Surprised by the question, Daniel began to stutter. "Well . . . I suppose I could . . . maybe it was down by the . . . Rebecca Ruth! What's going on?"

She kissed him on the cheek. "I'd appreciate it if you'd find it and make sure that all the utilities come on in the garage apartment. Jackson lost everything he owned in that awful fire down in Central City last night. I heard about it on the news this morning. When he didn't show up for work, I knew instantly what must have happened. I suppose it was by the grace of God that he is one of the survivors. He's going to stay in the apartment until he has time to find himself another. After all, I can't have my one and only helper on the streets and homeless, now can I? Besides, it's the Christian thing to do, don't you think?"

"Well I suppose so, but maybe you could have . . . "

"Thank you, Daddy," she said, ignoring the fact that he was trying to find a way to disagree with her logic. "I'm going to call Pete and have him pick up a couple of pairs of jeans and some T-shirts for Jackson so that he'll at least have a change of clothes until he can do his own shopping."

She picked up the phone and was in the act of dialing Pete's number when she realized her father hadn't moved. In fact, he was right where she'd left him.

"Daddy?"

"What?" he mumbled, trying to remember why he'd even come.

"The breaker box . . . ?"

"Oh! Yes! Right away."

When the door slammed behind him, she settled into a chair and covered her face with her hands.

I am a weak, lying coward. But if I'd said what's in my heart, it would have given my father a heart attack. How do I tell him I love the man he reviles?

But there was no answer to be had, and, finally, she pulled herself together and began dialing Pete's number. By the time she'd finished explaining to him what she had done, she'd had to answer the same questions all over again.

Her patience was hanging by a thread as she walked down the hall to get Jackson's clothes. And then she paused, listening to the sounds of running water on the other side of the door and trying not to think of that man wet and naked.

She sighed, leaning her head against the door and splaying her hand across the cool, flat surface of the wood. Today's events had answered all of Rebecca's questions regarding the wisdom of loving Jackson Rule. For three frightening hours she thought she'd lost him. And when he'd walked through that doorway and opened his arms to her, she'd lost the last of her inhibitions as to what "people" might say. It was time to listen to her heart.

"I don't think this is such a good idea," Pete grumbled as he handed Rebecca the sack containing the clothing she'd requested.

"That's what I said," Daniel added, thankful that someone besides him could see the fault in this arrangement.

She ignored them both. "How much do I owe you?" she asked, digging through the sack for the receipt.

"*You* don't owe me anything," Pete muttered. "On the other hand, *Jackson* owes me $73.41."

"Then come inside so he can pay you," she said, surprising Pete, as well as her father, by her casual behavior.

But when they entered the house, the trio suddenly ceased all movement and simply stood and stared.

Wrapped in the bedspread from her bed, and flat on his back on the couch, Jackson had finally given in to exhaustion.

He was sound asleep, with one arm over his eyes and the other trailing the floor. His thick black hair was still slightly damp from his shower. In repose, and without the piercing blue gaze, his face was that of a young boy. Even from where they stood, they could see his fingers twitching and his feet jerking beneath the covers, and knew that he was probably dreaming of the hell he had barely escaped.

"Well I'll be . . . "

"Sssh," Rebecca hissed, and waved both Pete and her father back outside. When she was satisfied that their voices could not disturb his sleep, she turned around.

"Thank you for helping me, Daddy. And thank you, too, Pete. When Jackson feels up to it, I'm sure he will thank you himself. Until then, I don't think he's up to anything more than about eight hours of good sleep."

"But what are you going to do?" Daniel asked.

"After you two leave, you mean?"

They looked at each other in guilty silence, then looked away.

"Why, I'm going to work. What did you think I would do?"

Neither one would answer.

"Thank you for coming," she said. It was as blatant an invitation to leave as they were going to get, so they did.

The minute they were out of sight, Rebecca quietly reentered her house and then knelt at Jackson's side, eyeing the light film of burn ointment on his skin and the dark circles of exhaustion beneath his eyes.

In all her life, she'd never wanted to touch someone as badly as she did this man, but she settled with lightly brushing the hair away from his eyes.

Sleep, my love. There will be time for us later . . . when you are well.

She left a note on the kitchen table, new clothes on a chair, and the phone off the hook, then walked the quarter of a mile to work, unwilling for so much as the sound of an engine starting to disturb his uneasy slumber.

°   °   °

When he woke, he knew he was alone. The house, like his heart, felt empty. Somewhere down the hallway, a clock chimed five times, and although it was still daylight outside, Jackson sat up with a start, unable to believe that he'd slept the entire day away.

A set of new clothes lay on a nearby chair and his boots on the floor beside it. For a long, silent minute he stared at the outfit, contemplating the significance of someone laying out his clothes and humbling themselves enough to clean the boots of a man who had killed.

Angrily he swiped a hand across his eyes, telling himself that it wasn't anything more than lingering sleep that had clouded his vision.

He came up and off of the couch in one smooth motion, naked in body and spirit. Rebecca stripped him of everything, including anger, leaving nothing in her wake but an overpowering need for him to love her . . . to give back some of that which she had given to him.

In slow, painful movements, he stepped into undershorts, then jeans, wincing a bit as the new fabric grated against his palms. With socks in one hand and boots in the other, he headed for the front door. Maybe if he got some air, he could put his thoughts into perspective.

He walked out of a cool, even temperature into the start of a warm, sultry evening and dropped his socks and boots on the porch in favor of the rough, uneven texture of the planks beneath his bare feet. Before he could contemplate his next move, he looked up the road and saw Rebecca coming home . . . to him. Emotion swelled inside his chest, threatening to choke him.

When he stepped off the porch and started toward her, the dirt was warm between his toes and on the bottoms of his feet. The sun was low at her back, the air alive with insects. Somewhere to his left, he could hear the deep-throated belch of tree frogs as they tuned up for the night.

At first, her steps had been slow but steady, and her shoulders straight, but when he took that first step toward her, she picked up the pace.

Awareness of the blood coursing through his body came first, along with a focused perception of the air moving upon and then flowing around his skin. He was alive . . . felt alive . . . and all because of her. Even from here, he could see the slight bounce of her breasts against her shirt and the unconscious, but womanly, sway of her hips as she hurried toward him. Everything was contained but the wild, unruly curls on her head. They were the giveaway to Rebecca Hill's true identity.

Jackson began to burn from the inside out. He'd waited far too long for this moment, and then wondered, as they came abreast, if he'd waited long enough. She didn't speak, but simply opened her arms and let him come in.

On the verge of tears, she sighed when her arms slid around his neck. "I've been waiting all day for this."

Jackson closed his eyes, rubbing his cheek against the side of her face as he pulled her fast against the warm wall of his chest.

"You haven't been waiting for this nearly as long as I have, girl."

For a moment, both were silent, too silent, as the implications of what came next soaked in. Finally, it was Rebecca who took the initiative.

"Am I going to be the one to say it, Jackson?"

He tilted her chin until their gazes were locked, and then he lowered his head, stealing from her what she was too weak to deny. His mouth was cool against her face, but by the time he reached her lips, she felt scorched. And when he released her with a low, aching groan, she shuddered. So much passion. Would she be woman enough to survive it?

"I want you, Rebecca. I want to lie with you . . . to hold you in my arms with nothing between us but the truth, and make love to you until we both lose our minds. If you can bear the burden that loving me will bring, I will never let you down, I swear." He hesitated, then lowered his lips again, taking breath from her body before she could answer.

She moaned, swaying in his arms from the impact of his vow.

"Loving you is no burden, Jackson Rule. Only losing you can hurt me, and today . . . for a time . . . I believed that I'd lost you. Nothing, and no one, is ever going to make me change my mind about what I feel for you. Believe that, and we will both survive."

He swung her off her feet and started back to the house with her in his arms as if she didn't weigh a thing.

"You're going to hurt yourself," she said, all too late remembering his hands.

"I very well might," he said with a grin. "It's been a hell of a long time since I made love. If I fall off the bed, just climb on down and join me on the floor, okay?"

Rebecca blushed, and then grinned as she mimicked a silly Southern belle to perfection.

"Jackson, darlin', the things you do say!"

But by the time they entered the house, all the playfulness had disappeared from their demeanor. It was the sounds surrounding them that amplified what was about to happen.

The click of tumblers as the locks slid into place.

The catch of Rebecca's breath as Jackson's hands moved from her arms to the front of her shirt.

The sounds of bare feet upon hardwood floors as they moved through the house to the bedroom.

One slow, husky moan as lips touched . . . then parted.

The soft swish of fabric as clothing was removed.

Another kiss . . . this time more urgent and more difficult to break.

And then the squeak of bedsprings, a soft sigh, and a sweet, unfettered gasp as Rebecca lost track of space and time.

There was only the man . . . and the woman . . . and the love.

14

Jackson's hands moved across her body, mapping the hollows and contours of her shape. His gaze followed the path his fingers were taking, marveling at the silky perfection and the textures that were Rebecca. Listening to her soft, unexpected gasps and watching her eyelids flutter as he tested her endurance, it was all he could do not to plunge himself inside of her immediately. She would have let him, of that he was sure. But he wanted to give before he took. His head dipped, his lips parted, and he drew the hard peak of her breast into his mouth, circling it with his tongue and then testing the fragility of her skin with the edge of his teeth.

The gasp was instinctive as Rebecca arched beneath him, digging her fingers in Jackson's hair and pulling him closer, urging him on.

He inhaled slowly, trying to focus, and moved from her breasts to her neck, whispering low and urgently against her ear. "So, you like that, do you, baby?"

"Yes."

"What else do you like?" he whispered again, propping himself on one elbow while he traced the shape of her lips with the tip of his finger.

Rebecca was caught in the blue heat of his eyes, mesmerized by his touch as well as the man himself. When his hand slid across the flat of her belly and paused just above the juncture of her thighs, she shuddered.

"You . . . just you."

The light in his eyes flared as he reached behind him. With the curtains drawn and the shades pulled, there was little light inside the room, but enough for her to see the flash of foil as he tore into the packet in his hands and then protected himself . . . and her. It was that last small gesture of consideration that told her she hadn't been wrong. He cared, in many more ways than one.

And then everything began to spiral. Tentative exploration moved to staking a firm claim. Rebecca became weak beneath Jackson's onslaught. He took her so far past embarrassment and shame that denying the man anything would have been impossible. When his hand slid between her legs and then moved into tender territory, her world tilted. He was everywhere, and still not close enough.

Jackson had been in Angola far too long, with nothing but memories of a woman, to deny himself for any length of time. Covered in a thin film of sweat and shaking from the need to be inside of her, he gritted his teeth and held his breath.

"Ah God, forgive me, lady. I can't hold back any longer. It's been too long . . . too long."

Rebecca never knew when he moved from beside her to above her, but she knew to the heartbeat when he slipped inside, because he was coming apart in her arms.

The dance was timeless, and yet for them, all too new. The give-and-take of their bodies and the building pleasure was too sweet to prolong. On the brink of too much to bear, the heat burst and splintered inside of Rebecca, sending a sweet, satiated warmth shooting through her body.

No more time . . . no more . . . Jackson's thought ended with one last thrust, and then nothing existed but the mind-bending rush of completion as he collapsed in Rebecca's arms.

Harsh, shuddering breaths rocked them as he rolled, taking her with him. Face-to-face, unashamed of what they'd done in the name of love, each stared at the lingering passion on the other's face and knew that there was no going back. This could never be a one-time thing, for either of them.

"Sweet Jesus," Jackson said, cupping Rebecca's face in his hands. "How am I ever going to let you go?"

Panic thrust its way into the afterglow as she levered herself up on one arm. Wild curls tumbled into her eyes and around her neck as she glared, angry that he would distort the beauty of what just occurred with such a statement.

Tears shimmered in her eyes, changing the glow of pleasure into a pool of despair. "Damn you," she whispered. "Even after this, you still push me away?"

He groaned and pulled her back into his arms. "I'm not pushing you anywhere, baby. I'm just telling the truth." Her shoulders shook with grief as her tears sprinkled his chest. At that moment, he would have willingly died not to cause her this pain.

"I don't understand," she sobbed, holding him even tighter as he rocked her within his embrace.

He thought of his past, the ugly history that stood between them, and wanted to rage at fate for giving him this woman too late in life for it to matter.

"I know you don't," he said softly.

"Then help me . . . make me understand," she said, and pulled away. Forgetting her nudity, she rolled from his arms and out of bed. With tears streaming down her cheeks and her voice shaking, she begged. "Tell me why it's okay to make love to me, but it's not okay to love me."

Her words stunned him. She'd completely misunderstood everything about his reticence.

"I'll be right back," Jackson said, crawling out of bed and heading for the adjoining bath. The water was still running in his hands when Rebecca burst into the bathroom, unwilling to wait for him to return.

"I'm not much good at waiting," she said, and tilted her chin with a painful defiance, as if waiting for the last deadly blow to fall.

"Then it's a good thing that I was the one imprisoned for the last fifteen years . . . wasn't it?"

She grabbed the door facing for balance as he calmly turned away to dry his hands. Panic began to spread as she searched for a way to convince him that their love would work.

"If it has anything to do with what my father thinks, then I can . . ."

"Your father? You think that he's the only one who'll criticize you?" He grabbed her by the arms and spun her around until she was staring at herself . . . and him . . . in the mirror. "Look, Rebecca! What do you see?"

Her chin quivered, but her voice was firm as she leaned her head against his chest and looked squarely into the reflection of his eyes.

"I see the face of the man I love."

And I say what I do because I love you more, he thought.

Her words pierced his heart, but he couldn't weaken, not now. Not when it meant the difference between foundering on or surviving what was between them. His mouth twisted as he spit out the ugly truth.

"Well, that's damned noble of you, sweetheart. Will you still be able to say that when people begin to talk? When your business suffers? When your friends quit calling, and your neighbors turn away as you pass by?"

"That won't happen," she said, and hated him for making her afraid.

"The hell it won't," he whispered. "Loving me will ruin you, lady."

She turned in his arms and slid her hands up the wall of his chest. Face to face, body to body, she felt the tentative thrust of his manhood against her belly.

"Then what a way to go," she whispered, and took him in her hands.

Within seconds, she had him out of control and knew a sweet moment of success as he pinned her against the wall. When he lifted her feet from the floor, wrapping her legs around his waist, she shuddered, then sighed. And when he plunged, driving himself inside of her, she bit her lip as pleasure began rolling toward its peak. At the point of climax, Jackson thrust and groaned, and Rebecca's cry was nothing more than the truth.

"I love you . . . love you . . . only you," she cried, her voice low and shaking with spent emotion.

Jackson's legs were weak as he cradled Rebecca in his arms and then staggered with her toward the bed.

"God help us both, but I love you, too," he groaned.

He tumbled into the covers, taking her with him. Within minutes, they were fast asleep. Even then, Jackson's arms held her close in a protective manner. But the damage had already been done, the protection he'd so responsibly purchased had been forgotten in the second act of passion that had consumed them.

Daybreak was only a thought away when Jackson woke, believing himself to be lost in a dream. But when Rebecca stirred, and then opened her eyes and smiled, he couldn't help but smile back. Dream or no dream, he didn't ever want to wake up.

While Rebecca was in the middle of pouring a second batch of pancake batter onto the griddle, the doorbell rang. "Oh shoot," she muttered, wishing Jackson hadn't already gone across the driveway to his new apartment to look it over. Right now, she needed another set of hands.

"Who is it?" she shouted, flipping the crisping cakes neatly in place.

Pete opened the door, poking his head inside and sniffing with appreciation.

"It's me!" he shouted.

Rebecca grinned wryly. That rough voice was eminently familiar. And when he sauntered into the kitchen with a newspaper rolled beneath his arm and leered at the pancakes, she grinned again. Pete Walters didn't know the meaning of tact.

"Good morning, me, how are you feeling?"

Pete snorted. "I'm fine. Doc cleared me to go back to light work two days ago. I'm reporting for duty." And then he frowned. "That is . . . unless you've replaced me permanently with someone else."

"Do shut up. This is a beautiful, sunny morning. Would you like some pancakes? I made plenty of batter and Jackson should be over soon. He hasn't had time to get any food for his place, and I always did hate to eat alone."

"Humpf." He eyed the twin stacks of pancakes already done, laid his newspaper beside an empty plate, and sat himself down at the kitchen table without another word. He forked a stack from the warming plate to his own and began slathering butter between the cakes with serious concentration.

Rebecca rolled her eyes and resisted the urge to use the pancake turner on Pete's balding head. She was pouring more batter onto the hot griddle when Jackson entered the kitchen with one of the new shirts in his hand.

In the act of a first bite, Pete looked up, gauging the easy stance of the half-naked man in the doorway and the smile Rebecca gave him, and frowned.

"Good morning, Pete. I think I owe you some money," Jackson said quietly. "I appreciate your going to all the trouble to get me a change of clothes. My wallet is back in the apartment, but I'll get it before you leave."

Pete flushed. The last thing he'd expected Jackson to do was remember his debt, especially this fast.

"Oh . . . it's no big deal," Pete said quickly. "I know you're good for it. Besides . . . I know where you live now, don't I?"

Jackson's eyes narrowed thoughtfully. There was more behind Pete's remark than just an offhand comment.

Rebecca was trying not to stare at the bare, brown expanse of flat belly and muscled chest and arms, but it was difficult, especially remembering how many times last night she'd kissed them. The scent of browning batter jerked her attention back to the business at hand.

"Pancakes are done," she said. "Better eat them while they're hot."

"Thanks, honey," Jackson said softly, surprising Rebecca, as well as himself, by using that endearment in front of Pete. "Just as soon as I get this tag off the shirt. Have you got a pair of scissors . . . or a knife handy?"

"Here, let me," Rebecca said, remembering the tender skin on his hands, and quickly cut the label off his new white T-shirt. "You start eating."

"Not without you."

She smiled, handed him back the shirt, and quickly flipped the last pancakes from the pan to the plate while he pulled his T-shirt over his head and then sat down.

Pete's presence became lost in their gentle byplay, and it was all he could do to keep chewing. The bite in his mouth kept getting bigger and bigger, and when Rebecca leaned across the table and poured fresh coffee into his empty cup, he took a big swig without thinking.

"It's hot!" she warned, but not soon enough.

Pete would have sooner chewed glass before he'd let her know that he'd just scalded every taste bud he had off his tongue. He wasn't being hardheaded. It was simply a guy thing.

Jackson grinned. He recognized the dull flush creeping up Pete's neck and face as he poured syrup onto the stack on his plate and then handed Rebecca the syrup bottle.

"So . . . Pete, how about sharing your paper?" Rebecca asked. "I want to see if my new ad is running. They were supposed to start it yesterday, but with everything that happened, I didn't get a chance to look."

Pete eyed his last two bites of pancake and then ruefully moved his plate to the side. He'd like to finish, but he was afraid if he chewed, the skin on his tongue would go down with the food.

"Oh yeah, that's part of the reason I came," he said, and unfolded the paper to the front page and then shoved it into the middle of the table. "Looky here. Who do you think that looks like?"

Rebecca paused, a forkful of pancake halfway to her mouth, and stared at the grainy likeness of a big man who'd been caught on film, running out of a burning building. Fear was etched on his face, but it was evident that the fear was not for himself, but rather for the limp body of a child clutched tightly in his arms.

Rebecca's eyes widened and her hand shook slightly as she reached across the table for the paper. And yet as she held it closer, she knew she didn't need a better picture to recognize the man in this one.

"Oh Jackson," she said softly, and covered his hand with her own. "Did he live?"

Jackson looked stunned. He had no recollection of cameras or news crews, or anything. The only things he remembered were the faces of firemen and the urgent voices of the paramedics telling him to turn loose of the boy.

Uncomfortable with the attention, Jackson shrugged and stirred at the syrup on his plate with the fork. "They airlifted him to some burn unit because of his lungs, but they think he's going to make it."

Pete felt shamed. Each time he was ready to judge this man for his admitted sins, he went and did something like this. First Jackson saved Rebecca, then him, and now a child. Pete ran the palm of his hand across the stubble of his whiskers and wondered what it was about a man who dared you to hate him for murdering, and then kept saving other people's lives?

"It says here that they think the fire started on the second floor."

Jackson paused in the act of putting a second bite into his mouth and frowned. "There's no thinking to it. We all knew where and how it started. A drunk who called himself that kid's father passed out with a lit cigarette in his hands and fried himself. Nearly killed the boy along with him."

"How awful!" Rebecca shuddered, trying to imagine how frightening it would be to lose a parent in this way, and then, at the same time, remembered Jackson . . . and his father . . . and what he'd done.

Guiltily, she looked away, but not soon enough. He knew the moment he saw her face what she'd been thinking.

"No, it wasn't so awful, at least for the boy. If you ask me, it saved him a lifetime of hell. His old man beat him on a regular basis."

Pete frowned. "How do you know?"

Jackson looked up, his eyes wild with anger and pain. "I know, old man. Take my word for it. When a child cries, pain has a different sound. When blood runs from a kid's nose, it's one thing. But when it runs out of his ear . . . and from between his teeth, then by God, someone's been beating the hell out of him."

He shoved his chair from the table and stalked out of the room while Rebecca and Pete stared at each other in mute horror. The same thought was circling inside each other's head, yet neither could bring themselves to say it.

Was that what the child had told him, or was it the firsthand experience of another child . . . a long time ago . . . a child named Jackson, who cried and no one came?

Oddly, the greenhouse was unusually busy that day, and it was late afternoon before Pete could find a moment alone to apologize to Jackson for doubting his assessment of the boy upstairs. But it was as if the outburst had never been. Jackson was quietly solicitous about Pete's recovery as he counted out the money he owed for the clothes, but he wasn't talking about the fire . . . or the rescue. In fact, except for business, he wasn't talking much at all.

And, unfortunately for Jackson, that picture on the front of the newspaper would prove to be a huge setback in his sister Molly's recovery.

It was later that same afternoon, while Rebecca was tallying up the day's totals, that Jackson remembered that if Dr. Franco needed to contact him, the number he had would no longer be in service. It gave him a sudden sense of urgency, knowing that anything could happen to Molly, and no one would know where he was. He waited until she was through writing down a figure before he interrupted.

"Rebecca, I need to use the phone."

She looked up, surprised that he would even ask. "Sure, go right ahead."

"I'll just go in the break room and close the door . . . so I don't disturb your count."

Something was wrong. She could sense it. But knowing Jackson like she did, he wouldn't tell her until he was ready, and that could be never.

She nodded, and when he turned away, she knew by the look on his face that something was bothering him. When the door closed, it felt as if he'd shut her out, as opposed to just himself inside.

She stared back at the stack of bills yet to count and sighed. *No one said this is going to be easy*, she reminded herself. *A man like Jackson will have secrets. Just please don't let them destroy him . . . or me.*

Jackson punched in the numbers and then waited impatiently for Dr. Franco to come on the line. When he got nothing but an answering machine, he wanted to curse. He needed assurance that nothing was going to be wrong. When the machine beeped, Jackson quickly explained the temporary change of phone number and asked that the doctor call him as soon as possible tomorrow, leaving the number of the nursery for that purpose. He disconnected, anxious and frustrated, and tried to tell himself that it was just his imagination.

"Are you finished?" Jackson asked, as he swung the door wide.

Rebecca blinked. She hadn't moved since the door closed between them. She looked down at the cash, as if wondering where it had suddenly come from, and shrugged.

"I guess I'm not," she said oddly, and began to count.

A few minutes later, they were on their way out the door to drive into the city and make the deposit.

"If you want to do something by yourself later, I'll understand," Rebecca said quietly, as she maneuvered through traffic on her way to the bank drive-through. "I don't want you to feel trapped by circumstance and obligated to be with me at all times."

"No way, honey," he said softly, and pulled her hair in a gentle, teasing fashion. "I've done the solitary route. Believe me, two's better . . . at everything."

Her eyebrows arched and her mouth dropped. Just a little. She couldn't help it. The laughter in his voice and the sexual innuendo he let slip through his answer had shocked her. He'd just told her, in so many words, how he'd dealt with sexual frustration in prison.

"Shocked?" he asked.

A small smile dimpled her cheeks. "No . . . now I'm just well informed."

Laughter rolled up and out into the cab of the pickup as Jackson doubled over, and every time he looked back at her, the slight grin on her face made him laugh even harder.

Rebecca sighed. She didn't care if she was the butt of the joke. Not this time. She'd eat peanut butter standing on her head if it would make him happy. She wanted this relationship to work. But no matter how hard she tried, she couldn't forget what he'd said to her right after they first made love.

How am I ever going to let you go?

The question taunted her by the minute, by the hour.

By God, I'll show you, Jackson Rule. You can't walk away from me, because I won't let you.

·   ·   ·

The phone call came right at noon the next day. One minute
Jackson was talking and laughing about a customer who'd
flirted with Pete, and then the phone rang. Pete answered it,
glad to have the conversation changed.

"Some doctor . . . for you," he said, and handed Jackson the
phone.

When Jackson went pale, Rebecca felt sick. *Oh God, not
again. Jackson . . . Jackson . . . talk to me.*

Instead, he headed for the break room. "I'll get it in here,"
he said, and closed the door firmly between them, leaving
Pete and Rebecca to think what they liked.

Pete listened only long enough to hear Jackson's voice come
on line, and then he quietly replaced the receiver he'd been
holding and stared at Rebecca.

"What the hell's that all about?" he growled.

She shrugged. "I don't know," she muttered. "A man's got
to have some privacy, doesn't he? If we need to know, then I
suppose he will tell us."

"What if we do need to know and he keeps mum?"

The same thought had occurred to her, but she'd be
damned before she was going to say it aloud, especially to
someone who was waiting to say . . . I told you so.

"What if you go to lunch and I go water something?" she
shot back.

"Well hell," Pete muttered, and shuffled out the door.
"Want me to bring anything back?"

Rebecca shook her head. "I'm not hungry."

"I'm not surprised," Pete said, ignoring her angry glare.

He left in a huff, leaving Rebecca with a bed full of pansies
in need of water and a heart full of worry. If she'd only known
what was going on, she might have been able to help.

But Jackson was too overcome with guilt to do anything
but listen as the doctor unloaded the latest problem into his
lap.

"I was worried about you," Dr. Franco said. "I knew about the fire . . . after a fashion . . . but didn't really relate it to you until I saw the picture in yesterday's paper. Even then I wasn't sure it was you . . . but after Molly saw it, there wasn't any doubt."

Jackson's instant of elation died as he let himself absorb the tone of the doctor's voice.

"So . . . you're telling me she didn't shout with joy, aren't you?"

The doctor sighed. "Something like that, Jackson."

"Exactly what did she do?"

"Well, someone left the paper in the lobby. It's not against rules or anything, you understand, although few of the residents here are capable of caring what goes on in the outside world, never mind wanting to read a daily paper."

"I'm listening," Jackson growled, and wished he was there face-to-face so he could watch the doctor's expressions, to judge for himself how much was truth, and how much he was omitting.

"Anyway, Molly saw the paper. I don't know what she did first, because no one saw her initial reaction. All I know is, I was called in after they found her in a corner, moaning and crying and hiding her head in her lap."

"Dear God," Jackson muttered, and tried to imagine the horror that his sister lived with on a daily basis. "But what makes you think it was the picture that triggered her reaction?"

Dr. Franco sighed. "Remember your telling me that you looked like your father . . . ?"

Jackson's gut wrenched. "So?"

"She kept pointing toward the paper and repeating the same phrase, over and over again."

Jackson stood up. He wasn't sure what was coming, but he had a feeling he wouldn't want to hear it sitting down.

"What the hell did she say?" he asked, and held his breath, almost afraid to hear the answer.

"The gist of it was that Stanton's ghost was coming to get her."

Jackson felt sick. "Oh God," he whispered. "I told you what seeing me might do to her."

Franco was silent for a moment. "I know, but if you think about it, there's a plus side to this whole thing."

Bitterness coated Jackson's answer. "Just what the hell could that possibly be?"

"Well, the shock factor has already come and gone," Dr. Franco said. "Like it or not, and whether she knows it or not, she's seen you. Now if she can come out of this latest relapse, we might have just opened the window of opportunity for your first visit."

Jackson felt the floor tilt. The doctor had all but pronounced a death sentence for Molly. Because of the way he looked, he might never see his sister again. And knowing what he knew of the situation, he couldn't blame her reaction.

"So . . . if she does come out of it, what then?" Jackson asked.

"Depending on how long it takes, then, as I said, I would recommend a real face-to-face confrontation . . . with me present of course, to explain your true identity."

"And if she doesn't?"

Franco took a deep breath. "Then I would have to say you were right all along. The shock of seeing you, or your father, as she would assume, pushed her too far over the edge."

"Have mercy," Jackson muttered.

"Amen," Dr. Franco echoed. "I'll call you if anything changes."

The line went dead in Jackson's ear.

It took everything he had to walk outside and face Rebecca, but it had to be done. He didn't know what he was going to do or say until he got there, but he couldn't hide in here forever.

Girding himself for a fight, he walked out into the office only to find himself alone. Pete's car was gone, and Rebecca was nowhere in sight. He circled the building, following the sound of running water, and found her on her knees in the pansy bed.

"Rebecca."

The sound of his voice startled her, but when she turned and looked up, the look on his face frightened her even more.

"Jackson . . . what in God's name is wrong?"

"Come here."

There in the broad light of day, and in plain sight of anyone who happened to be passing on the highway beyond, he pulled her into his arms.

All the questions that had been hovering at the back of her mind were forgotten. The only thing that mattered was the man in her arms and the pain on his face. She held him tight against her body, giving him her strength and her faith to lean on.

"What would I do without you?" he whispered, and buried his face in the heat of her hair.

God willing, you'll never have to find out, she thought, and held him a little bit tighter.

That evening, she learned something about Jackson's life after work that she would never have imagined. A message was on her machine when she walked in the house. As she played it back, she realized that it was meant for Jackson, but he was in his apartment, taking a shower. On impulse, she called the number, and when a man answered, she identified herself as Jackson's friend.

"Thank God," Clark Thurman said, as Rebecca listened. "We've been half out of our minds here at the shelter, worrying about him. If anything had happened to that man, I don't know what the kids would have done. They're on such shaky ground as it is, you know. They've been pestering me all day to take them to see him, but I didn't know where he was, or how to reach him until Reverend Hill mentioned he knew where Jackson was staying."

Rebecca was at a momentary loss for words. Shelter? The Reverend Hill . . . as in her father? Kids? Shaky ground? If anyone was on shaky ground, it was she.

"I'm sorry," she said. "I'm completely lost on this whole conversation. I wasn't aware of Jackson's after-hour activities, or that the Reverend Hill is in any way involved. You are referring to Daniel Hill, right?

Clark smiled. "Right! He comes to the Jesus House to counsel a particular child that Jackson recommended to him. And I guess I have the upper hand because I do know who you are. Jackson talks about you all the time. According to him, you do everything but walk on water."

Joy filled her. "The feeling is pretty much mutual," Rebecca said, and then curiosity about Jackson's activities at a homeless shelter overcame any regret she might have had for inquiring into his private life. "About the children wanting to see him . . . if you're serious, I live at . . . "

Clark took down the address. "Look," he said, "don't tell him that I called, okay? Maybe we can surprise him."

When Rebecca agreed, Clark Thurman hung up, a much happier man than when he'd made the call. With a little help from the children, he was going to give Jackson a big surprise.

A slight breeze had sprung up just as the sun was about to set, and it was a welcome relief from the heat of the day, though the air was still thick and sluggish.

Jackson sat on the front steps of Rebecca's house, listening to the sounds as she moved around inside. He closed his eyes, letting himself absorb the knowledge that there, and for a time, he was loved. Hinges squeaked on the door behind him as she came outside, and he looked up, smiling a welcome as she sat down beside him and then handed him a tall, frosty glass of ice tea, dripping with condensation.

"Thanks," he said, and took a long drink before leaning over and kissing her firmly upon the lips.

Their mouths were cool from the drinks, but the heat of passion that hovered between them quickly melted more than the ice in their glasses. Finally, it was time to stop, or else go inside before they made a spectacle of themselves.

"I can't seem to get enough of that . . . or of you," Jackson said as he broke contact with her lips, then, because he felt empty, rubbed the ball of his thumb across her mouth where his had been, feeling the dampness that he'd left behind.

"There's no shortage of either," she said, leaning her head against his shoulder, letting the quiet of the evening and the comfort of his touch soothe her jangled nerves.

Just when their mood might have taken them further, they heard the sound of an approaching car.

"Well, damn," Jackson muttered, and started to move away. "You've got company."

Rebecca stared up the road at the white minivan. She'd almost forgotten the phone call until she heard Jackson gasp.

He set his glass on the porch and stood up, staring in disbelief as the van pulled to a stop and children and parents he recognized from the shelter began to emerge from both sides of the vehicle. "Oh my God," he muttered. "It's Clark, with the kids."

After Clark Thurman's mysterious request, she'd suspected that they might come, but she wasn't prepared for what she saw. More than ten children poured out of the van, running toward Jackson with outstretched arms, laughing and calling his name.

"We surprised you! We surprised you!" they cried, and began clutching at his arms and legs, begging to be picked up.

"Hey, you guys, ease up," Clark shouted. "Remember what I told you. Jackson might be burned from the fire."

Abashed, the children went instantly quiet, and more than one seemed on the verge of tears. They couldn't bear to think that this man, who'd become such a constant in their lives, was not the same.

One child stood at the back of the crowd, apart, but not alone. Not anymore. He held the string of a large, red helium balloon clutched tight in his fist, waiting patiently for his part in this procedure to unfold.

"Taylor! Come on, boy. Do your thing!" Clark called, and made a path for the boy to get through.

Jackson forgot that he hadn't shared this part of his life with Rebecca. He forgot to worry about what she'd think, or that someone might judge him and find him unfit to associate with them. The boy coming through the crowd sent him to his knees with his arms open wide.

"We brought you a present," Taylor said, and handed over the balloon.

Jackson's heart was almost too full to speak as he read the words on the balloon.

"Do you know what it says?" he asked, searching the child's face for lingering signs of anger. To his relief, he saw none.

Taylor nodded.

"Tell me," Jackson persisted.

The child didn't miss a beat as he swung the balloon around and pointed to the words. "I . . . love . . . you."

"Do you, Taylor? Do you love me?" Jackson asked.

Taylor didn't speak, but he wrapped his arms around Jackson's neck and held on. For Jackson, it was answer enough.

"I love you, too, boy," he said softly. And then he looked at the expectant faces of the waiting children and grinned. "Hey, you guys, I'm not that hurt. I think I need a hug."

They swarmed as Rebecca stared in shock. In a daze, she set her own glass aside and got to her feet, unable to believe that the man in the midst of those children was the Jackson Rule that she knew and loved. This couldn't possibly be the same stiff, unrelenting man who'd so often refused her overtures of friendship. "Miss Hill, it's a pleasure to meet you," Clark said, and offered his hand.

Rebecca shook it without thinking. "I don't understand," she said. "How does he know them?"

Clark stared. "You mean you don't know?"

She shook her head.

"They're from the Jesus House . . . it's a homeless shelter down in Central City. Jackson comes by nearly every evening.

The kids love him, the parents trust him. He reads them stories, and brings them cookies and puzzles." He looked back at the man in the midst of the kids and smiled gently. "Actually, he does what their parents are unable to do right now. He spoils them, and they thrive on it."

"Oh my."

It was all she could think of to say, and then while she was watching, Jackson suddenly stood. He was holding one child in his arm, and had another by the hand as he turned to Rebecca. It was odd, but as he struggled to find the right way to explain his association with them, he felt suddenly afraid, as if she might not accept these lost and raggedy children for what they were. And then, as soon as he thought it, he knew he was being foolish. She'd accepted him. These kids would be a breeze.

He took a deep breath and smiled. "Rebecca, I'd like for you to meet my friends." Then he looked down at the serious, waiting expressions on the children's faces and winked. "Guys, this is Rebecca."

"That's a great balloon," she said, pointing at the shiny red helium balloon that was now tied to Jackson's wrist.

Her praise broke the ice.

"It says 'I love you,'" they chorused.

Rebecca looked across the children between them, and into Jackson's eyes. She didn't have to say what was in her heart. He could read it on her face. Tonight was just about perfect, because she loved him, too.

15

Fog hung just above ground level, shrouding the area in a thick, swirling veil. The damp night air sifted itself through Rebecca's clothes and hair, wilting the fabric of her shorts and shirt and making her dark, red ringlets into impossible tangles.

Somewhere across the way, Jackson sat alone in the apartment with his ghosts. Something told her that he had always been alone, and the knowledge hurt her.

She drew a deep breath and then shivered, leaning against the porch post, and remembering how only hours earlier he'd borrowed her pickup and left without explaining where he was going. She tried to tell herself it didn't matter. That he had a right to privacy that didn't necessary include her. Since Clark's visit with the children, she knew what he'd been doing at the homeless shelter. If that was where he was going, then why didn't he say so?

But hours later, he'd come home a quiet and lonely man, and the near-desperate manner in which he'd held her made her ache with worry. And just when she thought he would open up, he'd walked out of her house and up the stairs to his apartment without another word.

Now, she was staring hopelessly through a thick fog, wondering what had gone wrong. *What is it, Jackson? Why won't you talk to me? You let me make love to you, but you won't let me inside your heart.*

She had no way of knowing that Dr. Michael Franco had all but broken that very heart. That he'd confessed to Jackson that he was at an impasse with Molly's treatment, and if there wasn't a breakthrough soon, he had nothing more to try.

Music drifted through the mist to where she stood. She held her breath, listening, thinking that if she could hear the tune, she could gauge his mood. She smiled, recognizing the station as one of her favorites, and wrapped her arms around the post as she absorbed the soulful sound of the blues.

Long minutes passed as the music continued to play, one song after the other—tears put to music for the whole world to hear. Fog or no fog, she wanted to walk across the yard and make her way up the apartment steps. But he knew where she was and hadn't come down, and somehow, it seemed an intrusion to go up without an invitation. Especially after the way he'd left her.

Okay . . . so I'm not going up, but maybe there's a way to get him to come to me.

Rebecca went inside her house, returning with a portable stereo that she'd tuned to the same station he was playing. She sat it down against the wall, turned up the volume, and then walked off the porch.

The fog shifted to let her pass and then drifted back in behind her as if she'd never been. Halfway between the two houses, Rebecca stood in the darkness and waited.

The way Jackson looked at it, the last two days had gone to hell in a handbasket, starting with Pete showing up for breakfast with that newspaper. Granted the visit from Clark and the kids had been great, but it was small compared to the blow he'd been dealt today. Michael Franco's news had been one crack too many in the wall he'd built around his heart. How would he cope if Molly didn't get well?

He could close his eyes and at any time remember a dozen different scenes from their childhood in which Molly was always laughing or playing. Her role in his life was one of many; usually the big sister, sometimes a mother substitute, but always his friend. He wanted that back. He needed a family, and Molly was all that he had of his past. Yet if the mere sight of his face was all it took to destroy what was left of her soul, he couldn't ... wouldn't ... risk it.

And then there was Rebecca. Dear God, what had he done to her, and to himself? He loved her more than life itself, but did he love her more than Molly? Could he risk his sister's well-being for his own personal pleasure? And if he did, could he live with himself afterward?

"Damn it," he muttered, as he struggled hopelessly with conscience and love.

For lack of anything else to do, he turned on the radio and stretched out across the bed. Closing his eyes, he let the music take him to another place and time.

Night ... and the fog ... came in while he wasn't looking. When he got up to get a drink, he was surprised and a little troubled by the fact that, although Rebecca's house was only yards away, he couldn't see it at all. It gave him an odd, isolated feeling, not unlike that of being locked up in solitary.

She's all right, he told himself. *Just because I can't see her, doesn't mean she's not there*.

He walked outside, then stood on the landing, staring silently into the dark mist, willing himself to see something ... anything, that would assure him she was okay.

The music from his radio drifted through the open door and out into the night. The notes hung in the air, and it was as if the fog were too thick to let them pass. They seemed to build, one upon the other, until Jackson was overwhelmed by the sound within the silence.

And then out of the night, like an eerie echo, came the same music, but from another direction, and he knew instantly what it meant. Rebecca was telling him, in the only way she knew how, that she was there. The gesture was so like her—too giving, and too much to ignore.

Jackson started down the steps, feeling, rather than seeing, his way until his boots touched the ground, and then he stood motionless, listening while the music played in stereo around him. And, in spite of the clear, pure wail of the trumpet in the song, Rebecca was so real to him, and so thick in his blood, that he thought he should have been able to hear her heartbeat.

Slowly, he started walking toward the sound, never noticing the moisture collecting on his face, or upon his bare chest and arms. His every thought was to get to her. To hold her, to feel her, to be with her and inside her where it was safe . . . and so warm.

And then she was before him, like a ghost coming out of the mist, and he stopped and stared, thinking that he'd imagined her, until she whispered his name, slid her arms around his waist, and laid her cheek against his chest. Instinctively, his arms went around her, and when he heard her breath catch on a sob, he buried his face in the curls atop her head and began turning her around and around in place, swaying to the music and the rhythm of their hearts. Tilting her chin and aiming for her lips, he spoke aloud in the darkness that which was too difficult to admit in the bright light of day.

"I love you, Rebecca Hill, more than you will ever know."

He wasn't certain, but he imagined that he heard her whisper "thank God" right before the kiss.

Her feet were on solid ground, but in Jackson's arms, she still soared. The pressure of his mouth upon hers ran the gamut of emotions, from desperate to demanding, and Rebecca would have given him her last breath, had he but asked.

His hands moved across her body, reacquainting themselves with the places that made her tremble, and those that made her cry with pleasure. When he cupped her hips, pulling her closer against the ache in his groin, her sigh was lost in the fog around them. They moved as one, back and forth, to and fro, rocking with the slow, soulful rhythm of the blues.

The song ended at the same time Jackson's patience ran out. The pause between the music was long enough for her to feel his heart thundering behind a wall of muscle and bone, and for him to feel the rapid rise and fall of her breasts beneath his fingertips.

His touch was tender as he felt his way across her face, threading his fingers through the damp, tight tangle of curls around her face.

"Will you come upstairs with me?" he asked.

Rebecca's laugh was just short of a sob. "Do you think you can find the way?"

His mouth was a whisper above her lips. "Who the hell knows, Rebecca? I've been lost all my life. Maybe we can find the way together."

She inhaled the sweetness of his touch and his kiss, savoring the minuscule droplets of water upon his skin, and then slid her arms around him, tracing the paths of the scars on his back that were an intrinsic part of the man.

"Like you said, Jackson, it's always better with two."

The levity surprised him, as did her willingness to jest about something that had just yesterday made her blush.

His voice was full of laughter, but his words were soft and so very sweet against her ear.

"Woman . . . are you trying to seduce me?"

"Just take me to bed. We'll figure that out later."

He grabbed her by the hand, turned and, with unerring instinct, led her straight to the steps.

"You go first, honey," he said. "That way I can catch you if you fall."

Her heart tugged at the poignancy of his words. *If I fall. Oh Jackson, you're always the anchor. Wasn't there a time when someone else fought your battles . . . or have you always been alone?*

She paused at the bottom step, letting herself lean against his strength, absorbing the sweetness of his vow, then moved up the stairs one step at a time, moving her hand along the rail and judging the location of the next step with the toe of her shoe. When she reached the landing, she turned in the mist and slid her hand back along the rail until their fingers connected.

"We made it," she said, guiding him the rest of the way by pushing back the door and turning on a light.

Seconds later, Jackson had locked the world out and them inside. He turned the volume on the radio down low so that the song was nothing more than a whisper, and the music that led them was what was in their hearts.

"Lady, sweet lady," he whispered, and began stripping her of her clothes.

When there was nowhere left to go but to bed, Jackson lifted her into his arms and carried her there. As he removed another foil packet from the bedside table, she closed her eyes and waited. It was almost time.

A fine mist clung to her body like a second skin, and when he joined her on the bed, parting her legs with his knee, it was like sliding across, and then into, silk. Jackson groaned in ecstasy as she encompassed him and knew that for a while, he belonged.

Rebecca sighed, shifting slightly upon the bed and moving to give him room, then, wrapping her arms around his shoulders, she urged him deeper until there was nowhere left to go.

Locked in place, they stared deep into each other's eyes and then smiled as it began.

Slow and steady . . . rocking to and fro.

It seemed as if the motion were perpetual, that there was no deviation from the rhythm other than a flare of nostrils, a swift intake of breath, and an occasional moan as the fire between them began to catch. Then without warning, urgency overtook reason and there was no time left to linger.

A flash fire came and went, leaving them breathless and blind to everything but the flow of blood through their bodies and the pounding of a heartbeat in their ears.

Just before dawn, Rebecca awoke to Jackson's hand between her legs and his mouth upon her breast. Hours later, she would still remember what it had been like to see sunlight streaming through the window and across Jackson's body as he moved within her.

The following weeks were a time of reprieve. Long days in which Jackson and Pete slowly reclaimed the camaraderie they'd known before his heart attack, followed by even longer nights in which the lovers shut out the world and made one of their own. But with their history, it stood to reason that it wouldn't last.

"Nice weather for October, isn't it?"

Rebecca smiled at her father's question and nodded. It didn't really need a reply. Being with him in an amiable mood was a rarity.

"Daddy?"

"Hummm?" Daniel's answer was slightly absent as he propped his feet upon the porch rail and laced his fingers across his full belly.

"I'm glad you came to dinner."

"Me, too, sweetheart," he said, and winked. He could still taste the roast and potatoes that she'd fixed for him. And the pie. Strawberry pie was his favorite. He didn't know where she'd found fresh strawberries in October, but he was glad that she had.

A door slammed across the driveway and Daniel frowned as Jackson Rule came out of the apartment and took the stairs down, two and three at a time.

"In an awful hurry, isn't he?" Daniel asked.

Rebecca smiled. "For him, that's pretty normal."

Daniel didn't like the sound of that. She seemed too comfortable around him these days.

Jackson waved, and then jumped into Rebecca's pickup truck and took off down the driveway in a cloud of dust.

"Where's he going?" Daniel asked.

Rebecca shrugged. His Sunday afternoon trips were a mystery to her, too. She wished he trusted her enough to tell her. Maybe one day. She sighed. And maybe not.

"Rebecca . . . ?"

She sensed the ease with which they'd been visiting was about to come to an end.

"What?"

"Why is that man still here? I understood the need for temporary shelter, but it's been over a month. Surely he could find residence at a more suitable place."

"Of course he could," she said, surprising him with her answer. "But then how would he get to work? His motorcycle was destroyed in the fire. He hasn't discussed finances with me, but I suspect that he would not be able to get to work if he moved back to town."

"But I don't think . . . "

"Daddy . . . "

The warning was there, if he would only heed it. Luckily, he did.

"I'm sorry," he said. "I'm not trying to tell you what to do."

She grinned. "Since when?"

His answering smile was sheepish. "Well, almost never."

Rebecca laughed. "Don't worry, Daddy. I'm just taking life one day at a time." Then she stretched and yawned.

Daniel glanced at his watch, trying to decide if he had enough time to swing by the shelter and check on Taylor Monroe.

"I hate to eat and run, honey, but I think I'll be going. I need to visit some people."

"Like the child at the shelter?" she asked.

He nodded.

"Jackson says you've worked wonders."

In spite of the fact that the compliment came from Jackson Rule, Daniel smiled, pleased with himself and with the child's behavior.

"I'll admit it wasn't easy, but he's learning to trust. And the oddest thing—Jackson gave him something to grow. I think it was a stroke of genius. He watched that pot and the bulb that he planted like a little worm waiting for an apple. When it sprang through the soil, he was absolutely ecstatic. He's really quite a nice child . . . when you get to know him."

Rebecca hugged her father. "And you're really quite a nice father . . . when you aren't trying so hard."

Daniel said nothing but seemed pleased by her praise.

"I guess I'll be going now," he said.

Minutes later, he was gone, leaving Rebecca alone. She wandered back into the house and stood alone in the middle of the living room, trying to find a direction for her scattered thoughts. Finally, she yawned again, stretching as she did to loosen a pulled muscle in her back, and then kicked off her shoes as she headed toward her bedroom.

Maybe she was coming down with something, she thought, as she crawled into the middle of her bed and curled up with her hands beneath her chin. She felt so tired and achy.

It was her last conscious thought.

Worry was heavy on Jackson's mind as he turned off of the highway. It was odd, he thought, how he used to feel so empty after leaving Molly behind, but these days, coming home to Rebecca seemed to make it easier. As he parked, he glanced down at his watch, noting it was almost four o'clock, and wondered why Rebecca hadn't come outside at his arrival.

A frown creased his forehead as he started to unlock her front door and then realized that it was open. It was unlike her to leave a door unlocked.

His footsteps echoed within the silence of the house, and twice he thought about calling her name aloud. But when he walked into her bedroom, he was glad that he had not.

A wave of love so strong that it was staggering gave Jackson pause. He stood within the doorway, watching her sleep, and all the while wondering why a woman that beautiful would even give him the time of day.

He crossed the distance between them in three strides. Leaning over the bed, he brushed a wayward curl from her forehead and touched her arm, testing the surface for warmth. He frowned again. She seemed too cool.

At his touch, she shivered, then moaned in her sleep, and Jackson lifted a blanket from the back of a chair and swaddled her as one would a child, tucking her in from chin to toes.

The warmth penetrated her sleep, and Rebecca's eyelids fluttered in confusion.

"Jackson?"

"Go back to sleep, baby," he whispered, and feathered a kiss across her brow.

"Tired . . . so tired," she mumbled, and then her eyelids fell shut.

As he watched her sleeping, worry began to surface. In all the months that he'd known her, he'd never seen or heard of her taking a nap in the middle of the day. Of course, he reminded himself, they'd been together little over a month, but still . . .

The thought stayed with him long after he'd gone upstairs to his apartment to change, and then again, until just before dark when he saw a light come on in her house. Only then did he relax and tell himself he was making a big deal out of nothing.

A week later, and right in the middle of making out bills, it hit her. Shock was followed by panic. It had to be a mistake. Rebecca grabbed the calendar from her desk and began counting backward . . . then forward . . . then backward again.

Her voice was shaking along with her hands as reason surfaced.

"Oh God, oh God, oh God!"

However, talking to God didn't help. He had nothing to do with this situation, as Rebecca was in no position to be calling this an immaculate conception.

"But how?" she muttered, then rolled her eyes and buried her head in her hands. Then she realized that was a stupid question.

The how was the easiest part to answer. Even the who. It was the when that was making the room spin. Every time they made love he grabbed one of those damned foil packets and . . .

Memory surfaced.

"Oh."

She sat up straight in the chair.

"Oh no."

She'd followed him into the bathroom and all but dared him to say he loved her. Shouted at him to admit the truth of what they felt for each other. And what they did after.

That had been six weeks ago. How could she have been so careless? The answer to her question sauntered into the office.

"Hey, darlin', is there anything you need?"

Her eyes were wide with shock, her mouth slack. *Need? From you? No, I pretty much think I've taken enough already.*

"Uh . . . I . . ."

"Rebecca?"

She jumped, and the pen in her hand rolled onto the desk and off onto the floor.

Jackson picked it up and tossed it on the desk. "Are you all right?"

"Sure," she said, and then cleared her throat.

My voice squeaked. What if he noticed? She took a deep breath and tried to focus, but she couldn't quit thinking about her discovery. It explained so much about how she'd been feeling.

"So . . . do you?"

"Do I what?" she muttered, and thought of what his child would look like. It made her smile, which, on the heels of her stupid question, made even less sense than the way she was behaving.

Jackson grinned, and ran a hand through his hair in frustration. "Damned if I know, honey. After this stimulating conversation, I forget what the hell I was going to say, anyway."

He pivoted and started back out the door when she called him back. He could no more have ignored the soft plea in her voice than he could have quit breathing.

"Jackson."

He turned, waiting for her to continue.

"Would you mind very much if I asked you to kiss me?"

It was the last thing he would ever have expected to hear her say, especially here at work, and when Pete could come in at any given moment. But refusing Rebecca was not something he was capable of, and so it was with great pleasure that he opened his arms.

His mouth was soft and then hungry as it slid across her lips and centered. She leaned into him, wanting to be one with him, and settled for what she got.

"Ooh damn," Jackson growled, as he finally turned her loose. "I don't know what got into you today, but hold that thought, baby. I'll settle with you tonight, okay?"

"Okay." *I know what got into me . . . you did.*

When the door closed behind him, she wrapped her arms around herself and spun in a tiny little circle. She should have been in a panic, knowing what was ahead of her, knowing the problems this was going to present. But for the life of her, and the one that was within, she couldn't do anything but smile. She probably shouldn't. It would be simpler if she couldn't. But come hell, high water, and her father's wrath, she was going to have Jackson's baby.

And there were things she needed to do.

She reached for the phone book, her bills forgotten in her haste to find the number of her gynecologist. One hasty explanation and two minutes later, she headed out the door in search of Jackson and Pete.

"Where are you going in such a hurry?" Pete asked, as Rebecca came flying around the corner of the greenhouse.

"Jackson, I need you to open up tomorrow morning. I will not be here until sometime in the afternoon."

Jackson was slightly shocked, but nodded in agreement all the same.

"And Pete, I assume you'll be here, too. I'd hate for Jackson to be on his own. People are starting to pick up bulbs and such for winter planting."

Pete scratched his head. Rebecca was sure acting strange. "Yeah . . . sure, honey. I'll be here."

"Good. Then that settles that," she said, and left as suddenly as she'd arrived.

Pete stared at the space where Rebecca had been, long after she was gone. "What do you suppose that was all about?" he finally asked.

Jackson shrugged. "Beats the hell out of me."

They looked at each other and then grinned.

"Women," they said simultaneously, and then laughed before resuming their task.

Rebecca pulled at the gown flapping around her knees and then gave up and clasped her hands together, waiting for the doctor to make his diagnosis.

"I'm guessing around the sixth of June," he announced.

"I always wanted to be a June bride," she said. "Never gave much thought to being a June mother. I guess there's a first time for everything . . . right?"

The doctor looked startled. Rebecca grinned. Finally, he laughed.

"You never have been one to do things the traditional way, have you, girl?" And then his smile disappeared. "Planning on getting married anytime soon?"

Her attitude was defensive and she knew it. "I don't really know," she said. "Does it matter?"

"Now, don't get on your high horse with me," he said. "I was thinking of what your father is going to say."

It was exactly the wrong thing to have said to her. Her face flushed, and her eyes glittered angrily. "You know, doctor, that's always been my problem. It was never, 'Rebecca, do you want to play this . . . or do you want to do that?' No . . . it was always, 'What is your father going to say if you do?'" She took a deep breath and led with her chin. "And do you know what else? I didn't once think of rules and propriety when this happened. I was thinking with my heart."

The doctor patted her on the shoulder. "That's as it should be. I'm sorry, I didn't mean anything by my remark. For now, I want to see you on a monthly basis. See my nurse, she'll give you a list of things to do, as well as a dietary chart. The further along you get, the less tolerant your system will be of certain foods. And exercise. Get plenty of rest and exercise, hear me?"

Joy in her condition resurfaced. "I hear you, and I will."

"Good. You can get dressed. Nurse will be in shortly with your information."

The minute he was gone, Rebecca was scrambling into her clothes. She couldn't wait to get home and tell . . .

She froze, a button half in and half out of its hole.

"Tell who? And say what? 'Jackson, you're going to be a father'? Or maybe I should call Daddy and say, 'Hi, Grandpop.'"

She leaned against the wall, contemplating the carpet as all the excitement in her news slowly died.

Jackson had the right to know first, and he was the last person she'd tell.

She finished dressing on a sadder note.

She knew he loved her. But would he stay with her forever? She refused to use this baby to keep them together. Either he cared for her alone, or it wouldn't be enough.

16

The fire was missing from Rebecca's eyes as she moved from day to day in a state of grace that couldn't last. The more time passed, the less time she had to confront the men in her life. And come what may, it was going to have to be done.

Jackson watched her when she thought he wasn't looking and worried that her problems were because of him . . . of their relationship. He feared she was either sorry she'd started it, or was distressed over the reaction she knew her father would have if he knew the depths of their love.

Pete knew something was wrong as well, but from where he stood, he had little right to say or do anything except be there for her if she needed a friend.

Daniel, however, had no clue that anything was wrong. All he knew was that for the past two months, Rebecca had been a different woman around him, and in his eyes, that was good. He had hated their disagreements, and having her quiet and compliant was like an answer to his prayers.

And so the men who loved Rebecca dealt with the changes in her in different ways, but it was Jackson who had the most to fear . . . and the most to lose.

o   o   o

Rain peppered the windshield as Rebecca sat inside the cab of her truck, waiting for Jackson to come out of the bank. Closing time had come none too soon for her this Saturday. She stretched her feet closer to the heater that continued to pour out warmth and sighed as she feathered her hands across her belly.

Soon I will be able to feel you in there, she thought. A shiver of delight . . . and of fear . . . made her draw her jacket closer around her. *Please God, I've never loved a man like I love Jackson. Don't let this baby ruin what's between us.*

Water running from the cab and down the windows blurred and distorted the images outside. Colors were the only thing distinct enough to detect, and yet when Rebecca looked up toward the bank and saw a tall figure pause in the doorway before leaping out into the rain, she knew that it was Jackson. There was something about the way he stood, and the angle at which he held his head.

I wonder if our baby will have that mannerism. She smiled to herself. She hoped the baby wouldn't inherit her father's propensity for meddling.

And while she watched him sprinting toward the truck, she suddenly realized that while their child would know one grandfather, the man she loved had killed the other one. It was a sobering thought, and one, at this point, she didn't want to contemplate.

"Man, it's coming on down," Jackson said, as he slid into the driver's seat and slammed the door behind him.

Rebecca frowned as she brushed at the rain on his sleeves and on the thighs of his jeans. "You're soaked," she said. "You're going to be sick."

Jackson's eyes lit up from the inside out. He would never get enough of, or get used to, having someone care about his welfare. "Here's the deposit bag," he said. When she reached for it, he pulled her across the seat and stole a kiss.

His mouth was cool and wet, and Rebecca eagerly took what he offered. He laughed when she wrinkled her nose at the water that dripped on it.

"Here, baby," he said softly. "Let me dry that little bit of nose real fast before it washes off my freckles."

She grinned. "*Your* freckles?"

"Mine. All five," he said, and just to prove he could, kissed her again, only this time, lingering long enough that when it was over, they wished they were somewhere else besides the interior of a pickup truck, on a busy New Orleans street, in the middle of the rain.

"Jackson . . . ?"

"What, darlin'?" he whispered, and feathered a fingertip down the tilt of her nose.

"Will you love me forever?"

Her question startled him. And what frightened him even more was the look in her eyes when she asked.

"I don't know what your forever means, but I can't imagine my life without you, if that answers your question."

Her eyes were wide, her lips just a shade too firm, as if she was holding herself in to keep from crying.

"Is something bothering you, honey? You haven't been yourself for weeks."

A spurt of fear surfaced. "Something? Like what?"

"I don't know. Like regret for our relationship. Like wishing you'd never met me. Like . . . "

She flew across the seat and into his arms, dodging gearshift and steering wheel with surprising skill.

"No! Don't ever . . . ever . . . let me hear you say something like that again! If I had my way, I'd be wearing your ring on my . . . "

She froze, stunned by what she'd admitted, and then felt her heart break as he looked away.

"If wishes were horses, then beggars could ride," he muttered. "I've wished for so many things in my life that didn't come true, that I've long since given up believing in miracles."

When he looked back at her, his eyes were a reflection of the weather outside. Cold and wet. "And . . . it would take a miracle to fix my life. I'm not fit to be anyone's husband. I told you before, if we're not careful, loving me will ruin you."

"No! Losing you will ruin me. Loving might . . . just might . . . keep me from going insane."

It felt as if someone just kicked him in the gut.

"God, Rebecca, you take my breath away."

Her voice was shaking as she tried to explain, wishing she had the guts to just blurt out the fact that she was carrying his child. "Yes, well, now you know how I feel when you walk into a room. Or when you smile at me. Or when you turn over in the night and pull me closer to you. I can't think of ever losing that. Do you understand me?"

"No, I will never understand a woman like you loving a man like me. Do *you* understand that?"

"But I . . ."

He shook her gently, and made her look him squarely in the face.

"I killed a man, Rebecca. And not just any man. I killed my father."

Her lips twisted bitterly as she restrained a cry, and when she would have closed her eyes and turned away, he caught her chin between his fingers and made her face him once again.

"Don't turn away from the truth, Rebecca. Look at me! Now what do you see?"

I see the father of my child. "I see love."

He sighed and pulled her closer, nestling his chin in the curls atop her head.

"I know, sweetheart. I know. That's something I can't hide, especially from you. God help us both, because I don't know how to make you see."

Long minutes passed while Rebecca drew comfort from the strength of his embrace. Finally, it was not enough. She slipped out of his arms and onto her side of the cab and began buckling her seat belt.

"Jackson?"

"What, darlin'?"

"Let's go home."

Home. A simple word with a wealth of meaning.

Jackson complied, and for a while that night, in each other's arms, it seemed as if there could be a solution to their problem. Surely, an obstacle such as theirs could be conquered if love was this strong. But that was before Jackson's phone call the next day. Before Rebecca overheard just enough to break her heart, and not enough to understand.

Their Sunday dinner was quiet. In fact, one could have called the atmosphere between Jackson and Rebecca strained. It was almost time for him to make his mysterious weekly disappearance. She kept waiting for him to ask for the keys to her truck as he had every Sunday afternoon since the fire. But he hadn't said a thing about it other than absently to ask her what she planned to do after dinner, and remark on the fact that she looked a little pale.

"Would you care for some dessert?" Rebecca asked. "It's chocolate cake."

"I don't think so, sweetheart," he said. "Maybe later."

Without waiting to see if she was having any, he began clearing the table. Rebecca wanted to scream . . . to shout . . . to make him talk, make him mad, make him react in some way other than this cold, almost impersonal manner.

Rebecca was in the middle of loading the dishwasher when Jackson came into the kitchen with an armload of dishes.

"This is the last of them," he said.

Here it comes, she thought. *Any minute now he's going to ask if he can use the truck.*

"I need to make a phone call. Do you mind?" he said. "It's local."

"No, go ahead," she said, and tilted her head toward the wall phone by the door.

All expression slid off of his face, leaving him with the eyes of a stranger. Inadvertently, Rebecca shivered.

"If you don't mind," he said, "I'll use the phone in your bedroom. That way you won't have to try not to bang pots and pans, okay?"

She shrugged and turned back to the sink. *Don't make a big deal out of this. Everyone is entitled to privacy.*

Jackson hated himself for the lie. *Why can't I just tell her?* he wondered. *Why can't I just open my mouth and tell her about Molly?* But the moment he'd thought it, he knew his own answer. Tell her one thing, and something else might slip out. Then if she knows too much, someone could get hurt . . . someone like Molly. And then it would all have been for nothing.

He went into the bedroom and dialed the phone, waiting impatiently as the hospice finally answered, and then again while Dr. Franco was being paged. He'd already made the decision not to go to Azalea Hospice today, and to spend it with Rebecca instead. And so he waited, and more than five minutes passed before the doctor came on the line.

"Dr. Franco here," he said.

"Hey, Doc, it's me, Jackson Rule. I was just calling to check on . . ."

"My God, you must have ESP."

Jackson frowned. "Why?"

"Because, I was just coming to call you. Your sister has asked to see you."

Jackson went cold. All at once. From the inside out.

"Oh my God!" He swallowed twice before he could gather his wits enough to continue. "What the hell are you saying? Why would she just *ask* to see me? What have you told her?"

"Look, it's too complicated to explain over the phone," the doctor said. "But it's what we've hoped might happen ever since the day she saw your picture in the paper."

"But why now?" Jackson asked.

"As I said before, I'll explain when you get here." Then

Franco paused, wondering if he'd read Jackson Rule wrong after all. "You do want to see her, don't you?"

Jackson groaned. "Hell yes. I love Molly. No matter how sick she is . . . or how hopeless her case continues to be. If she spends the rest of her life at Azalea Hospice, I don't care. Nothing is going to change what I feel for her. Being able to see her again was what got me through the years at Angola, for God's sake."

"Fine. When can you come?"

Jackson glanced at his watch, mentally calculating the time it would take him to get there.

"Thirty . . . maybe forty-five minutes."

"I'll be waiting," Franco said.

Jackson hung up the phone and then bounced from the bed with a light in his eyes and a smile on his face. Rebecca was standing in the doorway, her eyes wide. She was just seconds away from hysteria, but Jackson didn't recognize the emotion, only that she was there.

"Honey! I didn't know you were there."

"Obviously," she said, and tried not to scream. *He loves Molly? Who in God's name is Molly? And Azalea Hospice? My God, what have I done? What have I done?*

Blind to everything but the excitement of finally getting to see and talk to his sister, he blurted out the thing Rebecca most feared to hear.

"I need to borrow your truck."

"Why am I not surprised?" she muttered, and grabbed for her purse on the bedside table, digging through the contents until she found the keys. She tossed them toward him.

He caught them in midair and then swung her into his arms, kissing her firmly upon the lips, still unaware that she wasn't responding normally.

This may be my chance, Jackson thought. *If Molly is asking for me, then maybe there's a chance we can be a family again. I want Rebecca to know her, like she was before, not after . . .*

His thoughts ended abruptly. He'd lived too long in the past. God willing, maybe he would have a future after all.

"I don't know how long I'll be gone, but when I get back, we need to talk."

Rebecca's thoughts were in turmoil. *Oh, Jackson, if I've been nothing more than a substitute for the real thing, then we're way past the need for words. We needed to talk a long time ago.*

He ran a finger beneath her chin, studying the dark shadows beneath her eyes and the weary droop to her lips.

"Why don't you take a nap while I'm gone?" he suggested. "You look worn-out."

She laughed, but it was not a happy sound. Jackson, however, was too high on his news to hear anything but what was on the surface.

"Be back later," he said, and slammed the front door behind him as he ran for the truck.

Rebecca stood in place for a long, long time after he was gone. It was only after her legs began to shake that she crawled into bed and pulled the covers around her. Dry-eyed and sick at heart, she rolled into a ball and contemplated the stupidity of woman to ever risk loving man.

What was even worse was, she could just hear her father saying, I told you so.

Dr. Franco's office was warm, too warm. The windows overlooking the lawn were slightly fogged as the cool November air whistled around the corner of the building outside. Jackson sat with his back to the door, facing the doctor's desk, paying only moderate attention to Dr. Franco's explanation for Molly's sudden turnaround. Little of it made much sense, and none of it mattered. The only thing of any consequence was that an aide was on the way to the office with Molly.

Jackson alternated between elation and fear. If his presence destroyed what was left of his sister, he would never forgive the doctor . . . or himself. Yet the promise of reclaiming what was left of his family was overwhelming. Fifteen years . . . yet if she recovered, it would all be worth it.

"So let me do most of the talking, and we'll see how it goes," Dr. Franco said.

Jackson blinked, aware that he'd missed most of some sort of plan being concocted. But before he could ask what he'd missed, a knock sounded on the door behind him, and he found himself holding his breath as Dr. Franco motioned for him to stay seated and then called for them to come in.

"Molly's here, Dr. Franco, just as you ordered."

"That's fine, just fine, Charlotte. Why don't you wait outside until I call for you, okay?"

The aide nodded and stepped aside as Molly Rule came through the door, unaware that anyone was seated in the high wing chair facing the window on the other side of her doctor's desk.

With just enough of the look of a lost child to remind a viewer of her defect, she slipped into the room. Dark hair caught up in some frivolous ponytail, her slender figure casually dressed in a green sweater and blue jeans, she was still her usual, elegant self.

"Dr. Mike! Guess what? Cook made your favorite dessert today and you missed it."

Michael Franco groaned. "Not custard pie?"

Molly's delight was plain as she laughed aloud. "Yes, custard pie . . . with nutmeg sprinkles. Warren Milham stole four pieces off a tray and then ate them all before Antoine caught him. It was so funny."

Jackson doubled his fists and took a slow, deep breath, bracing himself for the moment when he would be revealed. She seemed so normal. The conversation so ordinary, that, for a moment, he could almost convince himself that there was nothing wrong with her. That the last fifteen years had been nothing more than a horrible mistake that some state health care worker had made. For one second, he almost wished he hadn't come, that this day was still some unnamed day in the future. But it wasn't possible. Not now. She'd asked, and he'd come. Just as he'd always known it would happen.

"I'm sorry I missed it," Dr. Franco said. "But I was busy try-ing to work out the details of your last request."

Jackson heard Molly squeal, and then clap her hands in delight.

"You mean . . . are you saying that you found my brother? Oh, Dr. Mike! How can I ever thank you?"

"So you still want to see him?" Franco asked.

"Oh yes, more than you can imagine." She started toward the window, as if thinking that she might see him arrive, when Dr. Franco grabbed her by the arm, afraid that Jackson's pres-ence would be prematurely revealed.

"Molly! Wait!"

At his touch, she flinched and then blanched as a shadow passed over her face. Her lips went slack as she wrapped her arms around herself and started to moan.

"I'm sorry," Dr. Franco said. "I didn't mean to grab you, dear. Let's take a couple of slow, deep breaths and calm down, okay?"

Dear God, Jackson thought. *What's happening to her?*

Molly shuddered, blinked, and then complied with the doc-tor's request.

"Are you okay?" Franco finally asked.

"I'm fine," Molly said, as if nothing had happened, and it was then that Jackson knew. On the outside, life for Molly might seem normal. It was when the past intruded that she was unable to cope. And Molly hadn't just been touched in the past . . . she'd been used . . . brutally and repeatedly, by the man who she'd called father.

"Molly?"

"Yes."

"You remember when you said that you wanted me to find A. J.?"

"Yes, oh yes!"

"And do you remember how I told you that he wouldn't look exactly as you remembered? That a lot of years had passed since you two had seen each other and that he would be different?"

She laughed, and Jackson's belly turned. *Please God, don't let me mess this up.*

"He can't look all that bad, Dr. Mike. He was a handsome teenager. Girls were crazy about him, you know. He looked like a movie star, with all that black hair and those blue eyes." And then she frowned. "I hope he hasn't gone bald. His hair was so black . . . and so pretty."

What fantasy world is she living in, Jackson wondered. *I don't remember all that many girls. All I remember is being afraid to go to sleep at night and afraid to wake up.*

"But he has changed. He's not a teenager anymore, remember?"

Molly nodded. "I know, I know. But it hasn't been that long." And then her face fell, and a sudden look of confusion swept across her eyes. "Has it?"

Dr. Franco took a couple of steps backward until he and Jackson were looking eye to eye.

"Now, Doc?"

Franco nodded.

Jackson said a prayer, spun the chair, and then stood. At first, all he heard was Molly's swift intake of breath, and then he stepped around the desk and paused, waiting for her reaction.

"Hello, Molly, honey. Long time no see."

The light in her eyes died. All at once. Without warning. He could see her mouth moving, but no words were coming out.

"It's me, honey. It's A. J. I sure have missed you."

"Molly, remember . . ." Dr. Franco said in a low, calming voice. "A. J.'s not a boy anymore, he's a man."

She began pulling at the pockets of her blue jeans and then crossed her arms across her breasts. Clutching the collar of her sweater, she started to moan.

Jackson looked nervously toward the doctor, waiting for his signal . . . any signal, that would tell him this hadn't been the worst mistake of his life.

"Molly, remember when we used to . . . ?"

Jackson never got to finish.

Molly threw her arms up before her, as if warding off blows, and then staggered backward until she met the wall. A high-pitched, keening cry came up her throat and out into the room, making the hair stand on the back of Jackson's neck.

"Doc?" Jackson asked.

But Dr. Franco motioned for Jackson to stay put and let nature run its course.

"Dear God, Molly, don't cry," Jackson whispered, and took a step forward, with his hand outstretched. "It's me, honey. It's A.J . . . your brother."

"No!" she screamed, and began circling the room backward, making sure that she kept distance between herself and the apparition that had come back to haunt her.

"Look out!" Jackson shouted, as she staggered against the desk and fell backward onto the floor. When he would have jumped to her assistance, Dr. Franco stepped between them, again, stopping physical contact.

"Get away from me," she screamed, as she dragged herself to her feet and then ran as far into a corner of the room as she could get. "You're dead! You're dead!" Again she wrapped her arms around herself, and this time, started rocking to and fro in place, slinging the long hair of her ponytail in and out of her eyes in self-flagellation.

"Stanton is dead . . . he can't hurt me . . . he can't hurt me," she said, as she banged the back of her head against the wall.

"Molly! Stop it!" Dr. Franco ordered in a swift, no-nonsense tone of voice, and Jackson breathed a slow sigh of relief when she seemed to respond. "This isn't a ghost. And he isn't your father. It's your brother. It's A. J."

She looked up at Jackson, but her eyes didn't focus. She was too lost in the past and he knew it.

"Stanton?"

"No, Molly, it's me, A. J. I grew up, remember? It's been a long, long time since you saw me. I just got older."

She started to talk in a low, stuttering monotone. "No . . . no . . . no, Stanton. You can't fool me again. I'm not a little girl anymore. I'm a big girl. And daddies aren't supposed to hurt their girls . . . daddies aren't supposed to . . . to do those things . . . It's not nice to touch me there."

"Dear God," Dr. Franco muttered. In all the years of therapy, she'd never revealed what she was hinting at now. "If only I'd known. If only she'd said something like this sooner, maybe . . . "

Jackson was getting scared. Too much was coming out too suddenly. If Franco let her continue, she was going to say too much.

"Doc, let's just call this off. Right now. Before it's too late for her to . . . "

"No!" Franco said. "She needs to let it all out before she can heal."

Jackson grabbed the doctor's arm. "No, wait," he begged.

But it was too late. Jackson's touch upon the doctor's arm was little more than a brush of skin against fabric. Nothing like restraint. But the motion set Molly in a rage that startled them all, and sent the aide who was standing outside the door running into the room. Molly came at Jackson screaming . . . with both fists doubled.

"Don't touch him!" she shrieked. "You won't touch anyone . . . ever again. I killed you once. But you didn't stay dead. Get away from him or I'll kill you again."

Oh God, she said it.

As she came at him like a madwoman, he caught her on the run, and when his arms closed around her, she threw back her head and began to scream. The cries echoed in his head and in his heart, and he let her wail until her voice was hoarse and her eyes were nearly swollen shut from tears. Then and only then, did he press her cheek against his chest, and rock her where they stood.

"Cry all you want, Molly. Cry for the both of us. I'm not going to hurt you, sweetheart. I'm not Stanton. He's dead and gone."

And as he talked and rocked, he got sick to his stomach. As sick as he'd been the day Stanton had died. The day he'd come home early and found his sister in a state of near unconscious-ness with Stanton on top of her, using her as if she were noth-ing but a thing to satisfy his physical needs. He shuddered at the memory, remembering their ensuing fight . . . and then waking up to find Molly standing over Stanton's body with the shotgun in her hand . . . and the blood . . . and her screams.

His reverie ended as her head suddenly rolled back. "Molly?" She went limp in his arms.

"Here, let me help you," the doctor offered, but Jackson waved him away and picked her up himself, carrying her to the chair in which he'd been sitting, then cradling her in his lap because he couldn't bear to let her go.

"I've called for a physician," Dr. Franco said softly, as Jackson held her in his lap.

"What the hell is he going to do for her now?" Jackson growled, as he looked down into Molly's pale, tear-streaked face. This woman was almost a stranger to him . . . and yet there was enough of the girl that she'd been for him to hold with a degree of comfort and familiarity.

Dr. Franco sat down on a corner of his desk, staring at the siblings in the chair in front of him with amazement. "You didn't kill your father, she did . . . didn't she?" he asked.

Jackson glared at the aide who was still in the room.

"Jackson, it doesn't matter anymore," Franco said. "You don't have to protect her any longer. She's admitted aloud what she hasn't been able to say all these years. She killed him. Not you. Don't take that away from her. It may be what saves her."

Jackson's head dropped against the back of the chair, unaware of the panoramic vista through the windows before him. He was too locked into the horror of their past.

"Why did you take the blame?" Franco asked, amazed that a boy of sixteen would willingly do that.

Jackson's eyes were hate-filled and glittering with rage. "Because if I'd come to in time, I'd have done it myself. Because I wanted him dead. Because she'd suffered enough."

And then he took a slow, shuddering breath. "And because I hadn't taken care of her like I promised I would."

The doctor was puzzled. "Who asked that of you? Aren't you several years younger than she? Wouldn't she have been the one to do the caretaking?"

"We couldn't depend on Stanton. I was the man of the family—Laura said so. And then she died, so it was my job to take care of Molly."

Franco's hand was gentle on Jackson's shoulder as a doctor came into the room, accompanied by several orderlies.

"No, Jackson. It wasn't your job, but I will admit, you were . . . and you are, quite a man. What you did in the name of duty . . ." He shook his head, too moved to finish. "All I can say is . . . it's quite a statement for brotherly love."

17

It was nearly six o'clock in the evening, and Jackson had been gone over five hours, which was at least three hours longer than he'd ever been gone before.

The rest Rebecca needed had never come. Once she'd gotten past the shock of what she'd heard him say, she'd alternated between pacing the floor and going on a cleaning binge. Neither had alleviated the misery that was keeping her company.

Three times in the last thirty minutes, Rebecca thought she'd heard him driving up, and each time, it had been her wishful thinking . . . or the wind . . . or a truck gearing down on the highway far beyond her home. And each time she'd come away from the window a little more disheartened, a little more panicked.

What if he doesn't come back? What if . . . ?

The phone rang, interrupting her thoughts and sending her running to answer.

It will be him, she thought. He's probably had engine trouble, or maybe a flat.

"Hello!"

The breathless quality of her voice was lost on Pete as he shouted into the phone.

"Rebecca! Turn on your television now!"

"Pete? Is that you? What's the big . . . ?"

"Do it!" he shouted. "Any local station. I think they're all out there."

"All who? Out where?"

"For God's sake, girl! Just do it!"

Her first tinge of worry came when he disconnected so rudely. It wasn't until a picture of Jackson's face flashed on camera, and she heard an on-the-spot reporter shouting into his microphone, that she fell into the nearest chair and started to shake.

" . . . the biggest story since . . .

The reporter's voice faded in and out of her consciousness. For a time, her entire focus was upon the man on the screen.

"Oh my God," Rebecca moaned, and clutched her arms around her middle.

" . . . is expected to make a public announcement any moment. All we're waiting on is the doctor's okay. As we told you earlier . . . it's an unbelievable story of love and devotion that . . . "

Rebecca grabbed onto the arms of her chair to keep from collapsing onto the floor. The phone rang again, but she ignored it, unable to move, let alone speak.

She closed her eyes, willing herself not to faint, and when a local news woman began summarizing the history of Jackson Rule's incarceration, Rebecca froze . . . and listened . . . and died just a little bit more inside.

"Damn it, Molly, no!" Jackson begged as he paced the doctor's office. "You can't do this, not after all you've been through. What if they arrest you? What if they make you spend the rest of your life behind another set of bars . . . with an entirely different set of inmates?" He was ready to go on his knees before his sister, who had been transformed by his reappearance in her life. "You do not . . . you cannot . . . know what that is like."

Molly Rule stood firmly by the decision that she'd made only hours earlier, and to Jackson's dismay, her doctor was behind her one hundred percent.

"I have to tell, A. J. I won't live with the guilt of knowing that when I lost my mind, you also lost your freedom . . . not to mention your good name."

Jackson groaned and hugged her again, as he had over and over for the past three hours. When she'd come to, it was as if another woman had awakened in his arms. Her eyes were still swollen and tear-streaked, but the vacancy in them was gone. He could tell, simply by looking, that the Molly he'd known and loved was back. The doctor called it hysterical amnesia. Jackson called it survival.

But if Molly followed through on her threat, he feared it would be her undoing.

"A public announcement? They will crucify you!"

Even though Molly's voice trembled, her words were sure. "I don't care," she said. "Your arrest was all too public. I intend that your vindication be the same. Besides, Dr. Franco told me everything you'd done to protect me."

"It doesn't matter what they want to do to me," Molly argued. "You should have told the truth when it happened."

"And listen while they made you tell the world what that son of a bitch was doing to you? I don't think so."

"It couldn't have been any worse than what I did to you by going nuts."

Jackson's eyes glittered, like pieces of ice. "You don't know what you're saying . . . but I do. They'll drag out every sordid, sorry-ass thing that Stanton did to you, and then put their own sick twist into it for kicks."

Molly groaned and covered her face. Listening to what A. J. had done on her behalf was still too painful to contemplate. Having to remember aloud what she'd spent half of her life trying to hide might kill her . . . and then again, it might not.

Dr. Franco interrupted. "That was then, this is now," he said. "Incest and sexual abuse, especially against children, were rarely discussed in the seventies, but it's big news these days. God help the man who stands accused today, because the public will destroy him before he's proven innocent or guilty. I'd say that the odds are that your sister will never spend a day in jail."

Jackson cursed, then paced, then begged some more, but it was to no avail. The lawyer for the corporation that owned Azalea Hospice had already been called. He'd agreed to be Molly's temporary counsel. He had then called the media, leaking enough information to get them out in full force without revealing all. That fact, alone, was Molly Rule's to tell.

A knock sounded on the office door, and then an orderly entered.

"Dr. Franco, they're waiting."

Molly spun, her hands clasped like a child about to walk on stage and recite her piece. Jackson glowered, wanting to grab Molly and run.

Michael Franco silently gauged the behavior between brother and sister and decided that whatever happened out there, none of it could be as damaging as the secrets they'd each been living with.

"Tell them we're on our way," he said, and then held out his hand. "Molly? Are you ready, dear?"

Jackson stepped between them, his arm sliding firmly around Molly's shoulder. He might be younger, but he was by several inches the taller and by far the stronger. And she was *his* sister.

"I'm going with you, Molly. If it gets to be too much, just lean on me," Jackson whispered.

Tears pooled and her chin trembled as she accepted her brother's gentle kiss on her forehead. "I always have, A. J. That's what got us in this trouble."

Dr. Franco felt torn for them both. Jackson Rule . . . ever the man of the family.

o   o   o

A loud thump at Rebecca's front door, accompanied by a series of muffled curses, sent her stumbling from her chair to see what was wrong. The newscaster was still repeating the bits and pieces of the background information they'd unearthed in their archives while waiting for the actual press conference to begin, but the facts where few and far between. Most of their dialogue was based on old, but similar, cases of child abuse and sparse information on Jackson Rule during his incarceration in Angola State Penitentiary.

"Rebecca! Open the darned door."

Pete!

The door swung inward, leaving the pair face-to-face. He thought about hugging her until he saw the look on her face, and settled for just being in the same place at the same time with her. If she came unglued later, at least she wouldn't be alone.

"Did you hear?" he asked, as he pushed his way past her toward the living room.

"Hear what? The fact that police are swarming all over Azalea Hospice and they're dredging up old history on Jackson, yes. As to why it's happening . . . no."

"That's what I figured," he muttered, as he studied the blank expression in her eyes. "Sit down, girl, before you fall down."

He glanced toward the television and grabbed the remote. The volume elevated as he pressed the button, and then the camera suddenly panned the group of four who were coming out of a doorway.

"Oh God, Pete. I may not survive this. I didn't know about her, I swear I didn't," Rebecca moaned, imagining herself the other woman.

Pete snorted. "Hell, none of us knew he had a sister. I don't know what the big secret was for, but I bet we're about to find out."

Sister? Molly is his sister? Thank the Lord! It was all she had time to absorb before a man introduced himself as Dr. Michael Franco and began to speak.

"Ladies and gentlemen, as Molly Rule's therapist, I am advising you ahead of time that this is not a question and answer session. She has something she wants to say to all of you." Dr. Franco looked at Molly and smiled gently. "Actually, she wants the world to hear. So you will listen, but I'm asking you to adhere to her wishes by not interrupting during what she has to say.

"During a face-to-face meeting with her brother, Jackson Rule, which was their first in more than fifteen years, Ms. Rule experienced a recurrence of memory that was witnessed by more than one employee of Azalea Hospice. My colleagues and I have attributed her condition to hysterical amnesia, and as she speaks, I think you will understand why. You will all receive a written statement, prepared by our administrator, which will enlighten you on the reasons, and the treatments, for which Molly Rule has been kept here.

"So, ladies and gentlemen, I give you Molly Rule."

Nearly blinded by the lights aimed toward the podium, Molly couldn't actually see where people were positioned, or even how many were out there. In a way, it made what she had to do all that much easier. If she didn't have to see their faces, then she wouldn't see their disgust or their horror when she said what she had to say.

She looked at Jackson only once, and could tell by the expression on his face that if she wanted to, he would be more than willing for her to back out now—never to say the truth aloud. But Molly had lived in a state of denial her whole life. It was past time to tell.

And so she squeezed her brother's hand, then tilted her chin just the tiniest bit as she stepped up to the bank of microphones sprouting from the podium before her. Her voice was shaking, but her words were clear. There would be no more misunderstandings where she was concerned.

"My earliest memory is that of my father, Stanton Rule, slipping into my room at night and fondling me. I don't know how old I was, but it was before my brother, A. J., was born, and there are only four years separating our ages. Years later, I remember thinking that if I held my breath long enough, I could die, and then it would never happen again. But that's a difficult way to commit suicide." She paused, and there was a slight, wry smile on her face. "And I was only seven at the time."

The silence beyond the lights was so perfect that Jackson could almost believe there was no one there. He gazed at the profile of his sister's face, almost waiting for a breakdown . . . but it never came. And as she continued to talk, he began to understand Dr. Franco's reasoning for allowing her to speak. The longer she stood there, the stronger her voice became. It was then he realized how healing a simple truth can be.

"I don't know if my mother ever knew. I know I didn't tell. Stanton's threats were too real. When I turned nine, Momma bought me a training bra and, the same day, Stanton took my virginity. He said it was to celebrate my growing up. I knew it wasn't right, but I didn't know how to stop him. He was so big . . . and so strong."

A slight gasp from somewhere behind the lights was followed by a small, but distinct sob from one of the onlookers. Jackson gritted his teeth and stared at a point just above the brilliant horizon, unaware of the rage and hate painted upon his face. He'd seen his father in action only once, but it had been enough to want him dead. He didn't want to hear about the years of Molly's suffering at that man's hands.

"By the time our mother died, I was well-used goods. I believe I was about eleven, maybe twelve, but I can't be sure. After a time, the years all sort of ran together. The only thing I knew for sure was that the bigger and older my brother A. J. became, the more afraid Stanton was that I'd tell him. It wasn't something he ever said, it was something I just sensed. I think that's why he beat A. J. so often. He wanted to keep the upper hand."

Jackson closed his eyes and swallowed the knot in his throat, telling himself to focus on what Molly was saying, and not what had happened in the past.

She took a deep breath, and then grabbed onto the podium with both hands.

"There were so many ugly incidents between my birth and Stanton's death, that they don't bear repeating. Besides, you came to hear the end of the story, didn't you?" At this point, her strong voice wavered, sounding just a little bit uncertain.

"It all started because I thought I was pregnant with my father's child."

Jackson visibly staggered. *Dear God . . . Molly!*

Molly heard Jackson move, but to finish this, she couldn't look back. "It made Stanton furious. He told me it was all my fault. That I should have been more careful. Then he decided to beat it out of me. I don't remember much other than the fact that the beating culminated with a rape that left me close to unconscious. I suppose he thought that since I was already pregnant, it was too good an opportunity to waste. I do not remember A. J. coming home and catching my father in the act, but I remember coming to and seeing them fighting, and realized what must have happened."

Unable to let her stand alone any longer, Jackson stepped up to the podium and slipped an arm around Molly's shoulder. She fell back a bit, and let him be her strength.

"You can stop any time you want to," he whispered.

She shook her head and then turned back to face the lights.

"When I came to my senses, A. J. was unconscious and Stanton was a bloody mess. It must have been some fight. I wish I'd seen it."

Her slight attempt at humor was lost upon the silent reporters, who stood transfixed behind their cameras, listening to a true tale of horror. More than one was teary-eyed, and several were openly crying. It was impossible not to be moved by Molly Rule's recital of her life.

"He told me to clean myself up. I saw what he'd done to my brother. I knew that when A. J. came to his senses, it would start all over again. So I went and got the shotgun instead." She took a slow, deep breath and bowed her head. Her hands were fixed, her knuckles white as she gripped the podium to keep from falling. And then she looked up.

"It was easy. Had I known how easy it would be to kill a devil, I would have done it years before. When I aimed it at him, he laughed. When I cocked the hammers on both barrels, I remember that he started to swear. I don't remember much after that. Only the blood . . . and A. J. taking the gun away from me. Then I started to scream . . . and scream . . . and . . ."

"That's enough, Molly. That's enough." Jackson said, and started to pull her away.

She shuddered, and then shrugged out of his arms as tears began to fall down her cheeks.

"I wanted you to come, not to hear *why* I killed Stanton Rule, but that my brother did not. I swear by all that's holy, that I didn't know he'd taken the blame. I would never have let A. J. go to prison for something I did." She grasped Jackson's hand and pulled him to her side. "I didn't know where he'd gone. Until this morning, I didn't even realize so many years had passed." Her breath caught on a sob. "I guess I just . . . lost myself . . . and that's all I have to say."

Complete silence reigned for about ten seconds, and then it seemed as if all hell broke loose. In spite of Dr. Franco's requests for no questions, they came from everywhere. It took Molly unaware. Jackson reacted by dragging her from the podium and back into the building, leaving the doctor and the administrator to answer what questions they chose.

But Molly had not left her troubles behind her. The police were inside, waiting for her. For Jackson, it was the last straw.

"What the hell do you want?" he growled, and pushed Molly behind him.

A man, who introduced himself as the hospice lawyer, emerged from the group.

"We've been negotiating Molly's situation," he explained.

Jackson's anger erupted. "Situation? Exactly *which* situation would that be? The one regarding her life of physical and sexual abuse . . . or the rape that drove her mad?"

There wasn't a policeman among them that could look Molly Rule in the face. None of them wanted to be here.

"Don't worry, Mr. Rule," the lawyer said. "They're not taking her anywhere. She's going to stay here for the time being. I seriously doubt if a single charge will be filed . . . however, you have to realize that the men are only doing their job. After all, she did just confess to a murder."

"Jackson . . . let them alone," Molly said.

She laid her head against his chest and he wrapped his arms around her. She sighed. No matter what else happened, telling the truth felt good.

Dr. Franco appeared, quickly taking charge of the situation. For the first time, Jackson and Molly were left alone in a corner of the hall to talk.

"I can't believe how you've grown up," Molly whispered, wanting to trace the shape of his face, yet not trusting herself to remain calm. The resemblance between her brother and Stanton was too real to ignore. At least this soon.

"I can't believe you either," Jackson said.

"Where do you live?" Molly asked.

At that moment, Jackson remembered Rebecca and groaned. "Damn, I should have called Rebecca."

Molly saw the light in his eyes and smiled. "Is she your wife?"

The shock on Jackson's face was too real to ignore. "Hell no! Men like me should never get married."

Molly frowned. "It sounds to me as if you could use some therapy, too. There's nothing wrong with you. And after this, the stigma of being branded a murderer will be gone. You're just a survivor, like me." She laid her hand on his arm. "Do you love her?"

"With all my heart."

"Does she love you?"

Jackson looked away. "Yes, I think, too much."

Molly slipped her arms around her brother's waist and hugged him again. "No, A. J. There's no such thing as too much love. Now, go home, make your peace with your lady, and let yourself be happy. For me . . . and for you. Will you do that for me?"

Jackson groaned. "You ask too much of me, Molly."

"No, A. J., you don't expect enough for yourself. Now go home. Call me tomorrow. I would like to meet the woman who stole my brother's heart."

It took Jackson forever to get off the grounds without being followed. And when he cleared the front gates of Azalea Hospice, it felt as if the weight of the world had lifted from his shoulders.

Pete was the first to speak. "I will be damned," he muttered, as Rebecca aimed the remote at the screen and then watched it turn dark. "Have you ever heard the like? Imagine! Giving up all them years of your life to keep a secret!"

Rebecca felt sick. For what Jackson had endured, and for what his sister had been forced to do in the name of self-defense. Hearing the true ugliness of abuse firsthand was overwhelming. Knowing the people who had suffered it, almost too much to accept.

"So . . . what are you going to do?" Pete asked.

Rebecca turned toward him, her tear-glazed face a study in confusion.

"About what?"

Pete shrugged. "Oh . . . I don't know. About everything, I guess."

"There's nothing to do, Pete. I loved him before I knew. I love him still. Hearing everyone else tell me he's suddenly a good guy doesn't make me feel vindicated. I already knew that. I just wish I'd heard it from him first."

Pete's eyes boggled. "Love? Are you telling me that you two really have something going?"

"Something going?" Her laugh was weak as she thought of the child growing within her. "I know how I feel. I'm not real sure about him. I do know that he was willing to give me up to keep a secret."

Pete's face fell. There was true pain in Rebecca's voice, and even the tiniest bit of envy.

"I don't know what's in that boy's mind," Pete muttered. "But from what we just heard, I can understand why he wouldn't want to talk about it. Hell! Didn't you see his face when they did those close-ups? He didn't want to be there. And he didn't want her baring her soul to the world, either."

"I know," Rebecca muttered.

"Think about it, honey," Pete warned. "He had two choices. Tell you the truth and destroy his sister. Or keep the lie . . . and destroy himself."

She groaned. "It just wasn't fair."

Pete nodded. "No, it wasn't. But I doubt that Jackson's had one whole day of fair in his entire life. Why would he think it should change?"

"Go home, Pete. I need to think."

"You could call your father," he said.

She rolled her eyes.

"He *is* a preacher."

"But he's also my father. He's never been able to separate the two," she said. "I'll be fine. I just need some time."

Pete shrugged. "Whatever you say, honey. I guess I'll see you tomorrow?"

"I don't think I'll open up," she said. "I'm afraid our customers would be looking for something besides plants."

Pete slapped his leg. "Dang. I hadn't thought of that. I'll put a sign out front at the store on my way home if you like."

"Thanks, Pete. I'd appreciate that."

And then Rebecca was alone with her thoughts, wondering how Molly Rule's revelation was going to change all of their lives.

°   °   °

After all her worrying and waiting, she was in the kitchen and missed seeing Jackson drive up. One minute she was getting a drink of water, and the next thing she knew, she heard the front door slam.

She set the glass in the sink and turned, uncertain how to react, or what to say until he walked into the room.

The harsh glare of artificial light revealed more than Jackson would have liked for her to see. Molly had given him a reprieve, but nothing mattered if Rebecca was unable to forgive him for the lies, and he could tell by the look on her face that she knew.

"Rebecca . . . honey, I know I should have called. But everything happened so fast. And then Molly wanted to . . . "

Rebecca flew across the room and into his arms. "Hush," she whispered, and captured his face with her hands. "Just hold me."

When his arms wound around her, and his hold tightened, Rebecca knew that it was going to be all right. The desperation with which he held her was obvious. She'd seen his pain for herself. And he'd come home . . . to her. Nothing else mattered.

"I thought that you would hate me," he whispered, and dug his fists into her hair, holding on to Rebecca as if she were his lifeline.

Her sigh was soft against his cheek as she lifted her mouth for a kiss.

"I did, for about a minute. After that, I just prayed that you'd come back to me. I loved you when everyone else wanted to hate you, Jackson. I loved you when you wouldn't love yourself. Within hours, you are going to be a hero. The whole world is going to love you now. I was afraid you wouldn't need me anymore."

"Wouldn't need you any . . . ?" He groaned at her stupidity, and then his mouth descended.

Rebecca gasped as his lips raked her neck, then her chin, then centered upon her mouth. His body trembled beneath her touch, his heart thundered against her breast. And when she whispered his name, he spun with her in his arms and headed for the nearest bed.

The room was dark, but they didn't need light to see with their hearts. Clothing and inhibition were removed as their need for each other increased. Suddenly, Rebecca felt herself being propelled backward, only to be anchored by the descent of Jackson's body upon hers.

When contact came, he grunted, aching with the need to belong, but suddenly he remembered he wasn't wearing any protection.

"Oh damn," he groaned, and rolled off to the side. "Hold that thought, sweetheart."

Now's your chance, Rebecca thought. *Tell him the truth*.

But the impulse quickly came and went. It wasn't the right time. He'd had far too many revelations to deal with this day. Learning that he was to be a father might be one too many.

"Look in the drawer," she said. A minute later she heard the sound of a wrapper ripping open.

"Sorry, sweetheart," he whispered, as his hands slid back across her body in the dark. "There's no need to bring another innocent life into this rotten world."

As his mouth slid down her belly, then past the point of no return, Rebecca gasped, but not because of where he'd gone. It was because of what he'd said. And when her heart began to hammer in rhythm to the stroke of his hands, she began to cry. But not from the pleasure his touch evoked. It was from fear. She carried a child it seemed he might not want.

How did one reconcile this deep a love, and that deep a hate? Rebecca didn't know how to reach him, and it seemed that he was too far gone to help himself.

18

Jackson stepped out of the shower the next morning with a frown on his face. Rebecca's prediction had been right. Overnight, he had become everyone's hero. The phone calls started before daybreak and hadn't stopped yet. At first, he'd tried to be cordial, but the more insistent the reporters' questions became, the more terse his answers. By the third call, he'd lost his patience . . . and his cool. To save them both, Rebecca had turned on the answering machine, turned down the volume, and let whoever called, say what they would. As long as Jackson didn't have to hear it, he was a happier man.

Dripping wet and disgusted with the world in general, he combed his thick, wet hair away from his face and started to reach for a towel, when Rebecca appeared in the doorway with one in her hand.

With an unembarrassed smile on her face, she leaned against the wall, with a towel dangling from her hand, and appreciatively eyed the wet man standing on her bathroom rug.

Jackson had to grin. The preacher's daughter was just full of surprises.

"Well?" he finally asked. "Do I dry, or do I die of pneumonia?"

Her eyes were twinkling when she handed him the towel. "It seems such a shame to cover up so much interesting territory."

"I could give you a private showing," Jackson offered.

She sighed. "I don't think that's such a good idea," she said. "Daddy's on his way over."

"Hell." The frown was back on Jackson's face as he started drying with fervor.

"No, Jackson, don't do this anymore. It's time he knew the truth. Besides, now he has nothing left to complain about."

Jackson rolled his eyes at the naïveté of her remark. "Darlin', you don't think like a man; therefore, you cannot know what it will do to him to see a bare-assed man in his little girl's house."

"I'm not a little girl, and I don't give a fig now, just like I didn't care before. You're the one who wouldn't let me tell. If I'd had my way, the whole world would already know that I love you."

"Just because I've been vindicated as a murderer, doesn't change the ugliness of my past."

Rebecca looked him straight in the eye. "I don't want you different. I love *you*, not someone else. I'm sorry as I can be that your childhood was so awful. It breaks my heart just to think about it. But I love the man that you became because of it. I just wish you knew how to love yourself as much as I do."

With that, she marched out of the bathroom, leaving him alone with the truth. A long moment passed, and then he remembered her father's imminent arrival and bolted out of the bath to get his jeans.

Minutes later, all dressed except for a shirt, Jackson wandered into the kitchen.

"Rebecca, I can't find any of my T-shirts."

"They're probably in the dryer," she said. "I'll check. Why don't you go get the paper while I look?"

"You did my laundry?"

"It was self-defense," she muttered. "When you didn't come home, I got nervous, then I got scared. By the time I figured out what was going on, it was either throw them and you out, or wash them."

He stopped her as she passed, and planted a swift, rueful kiss near her ear. "I'm sorry," he whispered.

"Don't be sorry," she said, and then grinned. "Be thankful that they are clean, and not out on the front lawn."

He laughed, and headed for the door to get the paper as she disappeared into the laundry room. When he opened the front door, a man jumped from a car and came at him on the run.

Had he known company was coming, he would have dressed for the occasion. As it was, his bare-chested, just-showered appearance gave the reporter the scoop of the day.

"Mr. Rule! What were you thinking the day you were arrested? Weren't you afraid to be imprisoned with all those hardened criminals? What was your life like behind bars?"

Jackson froze. "What the hell are you doing here?" he growled. "This is private property."

"My name is . . . "

"I don't care who you are," Jackson said, taking a couple of steps forward. "I'm not talking to any more reporters. Now get out of here before I call the police."

The reporter shoved a tape recorder in Jackson's face. "Did you ever witness any of your sister's abuse? Do you know what happened to the baby she was carrying?"

He already knew that Molly had lost the baby during the first week she was hospitalized, but in no way did he intend to share that, or any other information about their lives.

"You are a slug," Jackson whispered, and started backing the man toward his car. "Why would you ask a total stranger such personal questions? Why don't you get a real job, and stop making a living off of other people's pain?"

"The public has a right to . . . "

"Not my business, they don't," Jackson growled, answering him before the statement had been made. "Now git."

Then he turned his back on the man, as if he were of no consequence, and went back to the door.

The reporter's eyes widened as he saw the old scars on Jackson's back. He knew he was seeing, firsthand, the depth of abuse that Jackson Rule had suffered as a child.

What he did was instinctive. A reporter's final proof that would confirm a story. He lifted the camera hanging around his neck, focused the zoom lens, and then snapped. Once, twice, then a rapid succession of pictures in graphic detail, mirroring the breadth of Jackson's shoulders, the trim, hard lines of his body, and the tracks that a madman had left behind.

Jackson heard the sound, and spun, giving the reporter one last final picture. The look on Jackson's face was full of anger and warning. The reporter grinned. He already knew that it was Jackson's resemblance to his father that had triggered Molly Rule's memory. This would be the perfect lead for tomorrow's front page news. The reporter could see the headlines now.

LIKE FATHER . . . LIKE SON?

"I'll get a raise for this, for sure," he muttered, and jumped into his car and drove away.

Unaware of the damage that had already been done, Jackson picked up the paper and walked into the house.

"At least he's gone," he muttered, and then heard another car pulling up.

He turned to look and then met the startled gaze of the man behind the wheel. They stared, one into the other's eyes, and it was Daniel Hill who was the first to look away.

"Rebecca, your father is here," Jackson shouted, then left the door open and disappeared from sight.

Rebecca came on the run, anxious that the two men she loved most not get into an argument. To her dismay, Jackson was gone. There was nothing to do but make the best of this mess. When her father came to the door she took his coat and hung it in the closet as he shut the door behind him.

"Daddy, I got your message. I'm sorry I didn't answer when you called, but this morning has been hell."

Daniel nodded. Despite the oath, the word hell was probably quite appropriate. He'd been stunned by last night's newscast, and even more so by the story in the early morning paper. All he could remember was the way he'd judged Jackson Rule, even though time and time again the man kept showing his true self. Daniel had come to the conclusion that he'd been ignoring the signs God had been giving him.

"It doesn't matter," Daniel said, and tried not to think of the implications of a half-dressed man in his daughter's house this early in the morning. "I came to see Jackson."

Rebecca frowned as she apologetically touched her father's sleeve. "Daddy, I don't think this is such a good time to . . ."

Daniel bowed his head. "No, Rebecca, this is the perfect time. I am ashamed of the way I've behaved. I need to ask his forgiveness."

Jackson came into the room, pulling a clean T-shirt over his head and combing his hair with his fingers. Although Rebecca's father seemed sincere, Jackson's sense of self-preservation made him keep his distance. Even now, when it would seem that all of his troubles were behind him, he'd spent too many years being let down to count on a break.

"You don't need to apologize for anything, preacher," he said shortly.

"Yes, I do," Daniel insisted. "I've prayed about it all night, and the conclusion I came to about my behavior isn't a pretty one."

"The situation itself was pretty ugly," Jackson said.

Daniel wouldn't desist. "No, let me say what has to be said." He took a deep breath, then turned away from Rebecca, unable to look at her when he said it.

"At first, I was afraid of you . . . for Rebecca's sake. When I saw how diligently you worked, and how many times you came to her aid, I realized that I was no longer afraid *of* you, I was afraid that you would take her away from me.

"And then there was the shelter. Hearing all those people praise a man I had judged and found wanting made me ashamed of myself. And when you asked me to help a child instead of yourself, I knew you were a worthy man. I just couldn't bring myself to admit it."

Rebecca gasped, but Daniel continued.

"It's true. I was jealous of you. And that's a terrible sin. I could see Rebecca's growing feelings for you. I didn't want her to love you more than me. I'm sorry . . . so very, very sorry for all the times I hurt you. Will you forgive me?"

Jackson was stunned. He'd expected the man to do anything but humble himself in such a manner.

"Rebecca's lucky to have a father like you," he finally said. "And I think she knows it. As for apologizing to me, I expect it could go both ways. There's a pretty big chip that rides on my shoulder. I expect I more or less asked for a lot of what I got. I'll forgive you, if you can forgive me."

To Rebecca, it looked as if her father wilted with relief, and when both men silently shook hands, she wanted to throw up her hand and shout for joy. *Now is the time*, she thought. *Now is the time.*

Tell them your news.

But sanity intervened before she opened her mouth. All too quickly, she remembered Jackson's words. *There's no need to bring another innocent child into this rotten world.*

Tears clouded her vision as she turned away, digging in her pocket for a tissue.

"Is anyone ever going to eat what I've cooked?" she muttered.

Jackson slid an arm around her shoulders as she blew her nose.

"What's the matter, honey, put a little too much pepper in the eggs?"

She grinned through tears and poked him in the ribs. "You are too funny for words," she said, then remembered her father, who was still waiting for absolution. "Come on, Daddy, you can referee while we eat."

Daniel Hill's smile was wide and genuine. "No arguing while you dine," he said, as he followed them into the kitchen. "Your mother never allowed fighting at the table."

During breakfast and the visit that followed, Jackson let himself be absorbed by the father and daughter kinship, and for a while, pretended that he might really belong.

By noon, the gate leading onto Rebecca's property was swarming with reporters and camera crews, trying to get a glimpse of the man who'd given his all in the name of brotherly love. But thanks to a sign that Pete had put up, TRESPASSERS WILL BE PROSECUTED, they were no longer appearing at the house.

Daniel made himself useful by fielding calls, then left to run their errands, leaving his daughter and Jackson alone to make plans.

Jackson sat on her bed, watching as Rebecca stood before her mirror, braiding her hair. "Would you like to come with me today?"

She looked up and met the reflection of Jackson's gaze.

"To Azalea Hospice?"

He nodded.

Rebecca watched the expressions changing on his face and wished she could read his mind.

"You want me to meet your sister?"

Now confusion was in his voice, as if he didn't understand her hesistance. "Well, yes."

"So, is this sort of like meeting the family before you pop the question?"

That she'd startled him was obvious. That she was probably way out of line, and pushing limits that Jackson should have been the one to set, was also true. But Rebecca was operating on a different schedule than the rest of the world. Her time and her options were dwindling by the week. Before long, the baby's presence would be obvious. Already, some of her clothes were becoming too snug.

"Rebecca . . . I haven't . . . "

She fastened the end of her braid and then looked away, unwilling to face the hesitancy in his eyes.

"Never mind," she said. "It's not really my place to say that, is it?"

Jackson caught her as she turned away.

"Don't doubt that I love you," he said, and pulled her down onto his lap and buried his face in the sweet-smelling curve of her neck. "Don't give up on me, honey. For the last few months, you're all that's kept me sane."

"So, does this mean you don't need me anymore?"

Jackson sighed, and wrapped his arms around her. "No, baby, it just means that I'm still screwed up."

Join the club, she thought, and swallowed a bitter laugh as his mouth swept across her face and centered upon her lips. The urgency of his kiss was too real to misinterpret, and Rebecca relented, returning the passion, touch for touch. When they paused for breath, and to right themselves with gravity, Rebecca cupped his face with her hands.

"Maybe you should go without me."

Jackson groaned, and stole one last taste of her lips. "I will learn to get things right, I swear to God," he whispered. "You've got to trust me . . . and give me time."

Something I don't have enough of, Rebecca thought, and then unwound herself from his arms and out of his lap.

"The keys to the pickup are on the coffee table in the living room. I'll turn up the volume on the answering machine so that I can hear your voice, so call if you need me, okay?"

"I will always need you, Rebecca."

"I know," she whispered. "I'm sorry I'm being impatient. It's just that . . . "

"What?"

She stood in the doorway, absorbing the man she'd come to love and contemplating his reaction if she just said it all now. Finally, she shrugged.

"Nothing. I guess it can wait one more day."

"What can wait?"

She smiled. "You better hurry. You'll probably have to dodge half the county out there, as it is."

"Damn," he muttered.

Then he left, and Rebecca was finally alone, save for their baby, who was growing within.

They'd gone from a night filled with passion to the morning from hell, which started with the newspaper on Rebecca's front porch. Horrified at the headlines, she debated about trying to hide it from Jackson, and then knew that would only compound his reaction later. When he came in the kitchen and sat down at the table, she handed him the paper, trying for a casual, would you look at this, attitude, which unfortunately, he could not possibly share.

LIKE FATHER . . . LIKE SON?

Jackson stared in horror at the two pictures side by side in the middle of the page. One was an old file copy of his father that the papers had used for weeks after he'd been murdered. The other was of Jackson that the reporter had taken yesterday. The faces were so similar that it made Jackson sick, right down to mirror expressions of barely hidden anger. He saw himself in Stanton a thousand times over.

"Son of a holy bitch."

Jackson's reaction was exactly as Rebecca had feared.

"Isn't that stupid?" she said, and kissed his cheek as she read over his shoulder. "Physical resemblance is expected within families. It's the character and personality that make each person different."

Jackson's stomach rolled. "What if it's not just physical?"

"Lord love a duck, Jackson," Rebecca muttered. "How old are you?"

Startled by her question, he answered without thought. "Nearly thirty-two."

"So, how often in those years have you gotten drunk and beaten someone to within an inch of their life?"

"Well, never, but I've been behind bars for more than half my life. Who's to say what might . . . ?"

"Pooh, that's an excuse. If you were anything like that man,"—she pointed to Stanton's picture—"then I'd guess you would have been what you were no matter where you were living."

He frowned. He'd never thought of it exactly in those terms.

"And what about all of those children at the shelter? Do they turn you on?"

His face turned red with anger and shock. "Hell no!"

"Then I rest my case. You are nothing like your father."

She continued to press her case, because her whole life rested upon his understanding of himself. "Would your father have saved a woman from being run down? Or assaulted? Would he have cared about a friend enough to administer CPR? Would he have stayed in a burning building to rescue a helpless child, or would he have saved his sorry hide instead?"

Jackson didn't answer, and in frustration, Rebecca ripped the paper from his hands and threw it on the floor.

"Look at me, Jackson! If you aren't brave enough to trust yourself, then trust me to do it for you!"

He groaned, then pulled her into his arms, burying his face against the softness of her breasts. When she combed her fingers through his hair and then tilted his face to hers, he was humbled by the love in her eyes.

"Do you love me, Jackson Rule?"

"Yes, dear God, yes."

"Will you love me forever?"

He smiled slowly, remembering another time when she'd asked that same question, with the same tone of desperation.

"Forever."

She sighed, and then buried her face in his hair.

"Promise . . . no matter what?"

Jackson frowned. Something was warning him that all was not right with Rebecca.

"Honey, what's wrong?"

"Are you going to see Molly today?"

He nodded. "The district attorney is going to announce his decision as to whether to prosecute her or not. Her doctor and the lawyers all swear it's simply a formality, that they aren't about to crucify a woman who's already endured what she has."

"But you need to hear that for yourself, don't you?" Rebecca whispered.

"Yes."

She smiled. "Then go. When you come back, we need to talk."

Jackson stood up and pulled her into his arms. "Are you sure you're okay?"

Rebecca rested her cheek against his shirt and let herself relax in the comfort of his arms.

"As long as you come back to me, I'll always be okay. Now eat your food before it gets cold. I've got a million things to do."

He frowned. "You aren't going to open up the greenhouse are you?"

"Oh, it's already open, but I'm not going," she said. "Pete and Daddy are at the helm. It should make for an interesting day for the both of them."

Jackson grinned. "Maybe he'll convert Pete."

"Or vice versa."

The thought of Daniel Hill becoming as mouthy and cantankerous as Pete Walters made them both laugh.

When she was certain that Jackson was gone, she began flipping through the yellow pages in the phone book, running her finger down the listings until she found what she wanted.

"Harley-Davidson, this is it." She punched in the numbers, then counted the rings. And when a man answered, she began to talk.

"Do you deliver?"

The minute Jackson walked into the room, Molly's eyes lit up. It was the sign that Dr. Franco had been waiting for. If she could look at Jackson and see her brother and not the man she had killed, then she was well on the way to recovery.

"A. J., you came," Molly said.

Jackson ruffled her ponytail and then kissed her on the cheek. "You knew I would," he said. "Couldn't let you hear the good news all by yourself."

Her smile wilted. "If it's not good news, I don't care—not much, anyway. All that matters to me is clearing your name."

Jackson thought of the hateful twist that some of the media were already putting to his "good name" and wanted to laugh. No matter how white a fence is painted, inevitably, the dark gray wood will one day show. He had a feeling that he would never be completely clear of the dirt Stanton Rule had left behind.

"When are you bringing Rebecca to meet me?" Molly asked.

Jackson looked away, aware that it was his fault she hadn't come before.

"Soon."

"How soon?"

He sighed. "One thing hasn't changed about you. You're still persistent as hell."

"What's wrong, A. J.?"

He shrugged. "Nothing."

"Oh right! And we're both candidates for the Nobel Peace Prize."

Jackson grinned. The Molly he knew and loved was definitely on the mend.

"So, what's wrong?" she persisted.

"I haven't asked her to marry me yet." He looked away, choking on the fear that lived within him. "What if someday I turn out like Stanton?"

Molly gasped. "Have you lost your mind? Why on earth would you think something like that?"

"Look at my face," Jackson said in a low growl, unwilling for the men on the other side of the room to hear their conversation. "Who's to say that I'm not like him in a thousand other ways as well?"

"I'm to say," Molly cried. "Stanton would never have done what you did! He would never have sacrificed an hour of his life in the name of love, let alone fifteen years. My God, A. J., did prison completely scramble your brains?"

"Probably," Jackson muttered. "Now hush, here come the suits."

Molly tensed as she turned, and then her brother's hand slid across her shoulder. At that moment, she knew that whatever happened, she would never regret it a day in her life, because she was already free of the lies.

Jackson burst through the front door with a smile on his face.

"They aren't going to prosecute!" he shouted, as Rebecca came into the living room. He swept her off her feet and danced her around the room, unaware that she wasn't exactly participating in the act.

"That's wonderful," she said, and hugged him when he finally set her back on her feet. "I'm so happy for her."

"Me, too," Jackson said. "She deserves some good luck." And then he thought of the last thing the doctor told him before he left. "Honey, did a Dr. Franco call? He was going to check on something and then give me a firm date as to when I could take Molly off the grounds for a visit. He says since she's been out of circulation for so long, she probably needs to work her way slowly back into the real world."

"I don't know," Rebecca said. "I heard the phone ring several times while I was in the bath, and then I forgot to check the messages. Maybe you better play them back to see."

"Coming with me?" he asked.

"In a minute," Rebecca said. "I need to put these letters in the mail before the postman comes by."

He went toward the kitchen while she headed out the door.

The day was stingy with sunshine. It kept coming and going behind a bank of clouds as Rebecca walked across the yard to the end of the fence. She looked up at the sky, and then shivered from the chill, wishing she'd put on a jacket before coming outside.

Far down the road, she could see the hordes of reporters still camped at the gate. Knowing there were probably a hundred cameras with telescopic lenses trained on her face, she resisted the urge to stick out her tongue and settled for a quick sprint back into the house, instead.

As she entered, she could hear the answering machine while Jackson played the messages, and pictured his face as each request for an interview from some media source came and went. It was when she heard the one for her that she started running, but it was too late to stop him from learning what he should already have known.

Miss Hill, you missed your prenatal visit yesterday. Please call the doctor's office and reschedule as soon as possible at 555–4400.

In the midst of writing down the number, Jackson's hand stilled. *Prenatal?* And then Rebecca burst into the room.

"Jackson, I . . . "

The look on her face was enough to make him panic. "What the hell was that all about?"

The room began to tilt beneath Rebecca's feet as she faced the fact that she might lose him. But when Jackson started toward her, she held her ground. She wouldn't run from the truth, or from Jackson Rule.

"Talk to me, Rebecca. Tell me it's not what I'm thinking."

"I can't do that," she said.

"You're not pregnant."

"Are you asking me, or telling me?" Rebecca muttered, as anger began to surface. How dare he resent what she viewed with such joy?

His eyes widened as he raked her slender body with a new, and appraising, look, afraid to let himself believe that this was not a disaster. "Oh my God. I was so careful. I never meant for you to . . . "

"Well, I never *meant* for it to happen either," Rebecca said, "but it did, and I will not be sorry that a new life has come out of our love."

He felt breathless, and at the same time, a little angry that he'd had to learn this from an answering machine. And then his sense of fair play reminded him that she'd learned his secrets in a similar way. Finally, he asked.

"Were you ever going to tell me?"

"Yes."

Again, anger surfaced, and this time, it was revealed in the tone of his voice.

"For God's sake . . . when?" he cried.

"When I thought you were ready to hear it. When I knew you would be listening to me, and not some ghost from your past."

The thought of what she still didn't know about his life before made him sick with worry. Her world was so normal . . . and good. His had been so twisted . . . and ugly. Until his death, Stanton Rule had been Jackson's only role model. What kind of a father could he be when the only one he'd known hadn't been fit to bury? In a new spurt of worry, he started to pace.

"Have mercy," he muttered, and grabbed the morning paper from the table nearby. "Look at this, Rebecca! Look at him . . . look at me! Don't you see the implications? And I'm not referring to a physical resemblance anymore. I didn't have someone in my childhood teaching me how to become a man, because it took everything I had just to survive. What if I do everything wrong? Do you want to put yourself . . . and a baby . . . through that kind of hell?"

Rebecca slapped the paper out of his hands. "That's a tired, worn-out excuse, Jackson Rule. You're not your father. You're you! I fell in love with you long before I knew you were innocent of what you claimed to have done."

"What if I let you down?"

"What if you don't?" she countered.

She knew that he loved her, but the fear on his face was all too plain to ignore. She took a deep breath. It was time to lay down her cards. With a silent prayer that she was doing the right thing, she pulled a key out of the pocket of her jeans and threw it at him from across the room.

"Here, catch!" she said.

He grabbed it to keep from being hit in the face, and then stared down at the familiar logo on the leather attached.

"What is this for?"

Rebecca took him by the arm and pulled him through the house, dragging him out onto the steps and then pointing at the shiny new Harley-Davidson motorcycle partially hidden behind a stand of lilacs.

"It's for you," she said, aware that her voice was thickening with tears she couldn't hide. "It's for you to run with, Jackson. There's your chance. All you have to do is get on that bike and ride away. Maybe if you ride far enough and fast enough, you can outrun your past . . . and our love. If you don't want me and our baby, then fine! The next time I fall, I'll pick my own damned self up or find someone else who will. I don't need a man who doesn't need me!"

And then she walked back in the house, slamming the door behind her.

The key warmed in his hand as he stared at the bike. Long after she was gone, her words still rang in his ears.

Don't need her? Hell he wasn't even sure he could face another day without her.

Didn't want their child? Just the thought of a baby crying for a father who never came was enough to make him sick with longing.

The next time she fell? That was the one that did it. She belonged to him. If she needed picking up, then by God, he was going to be the one who did it!

He clutched the key in his fist and walked back into the house. She was standing in the middle of the kitchen, and he could see her shaking from where he stood. While she watched, he dropped the key in the middle of the table then started toward her.

"I want to work with abused children," he said. "That means I have to finish college."

A joy she'd never allowed herself to experience started to spread throughout her body. "Okay . . . then you're fired. Go enroll."

When he was so close he could smell the lingering scent of her shampoo, he added, "I can't turn my back on Molly. Not now. I'm all she has."

She could feel the heat from his body. When she looked up, the blaze of blue fire in his eyes made her weak with longing.

"I think my garage apartment is about to become vacant. Maybe she'd like to live there."

Jackson groaned and then dropped to his knees, wrapping his arms around the back of her legs and laying his cheek against the flat of her belly.

"My God . . . my God . . . my baby," he whispered, and held her tight.

Relief was so overwhelming that Rebecca started to cry. Gently, she stroked the top of his head as if he were a child. "If you'll let me, I'll love you both until the day that I die."

He was shaking, both with fear and with longing, as he took a slow breath and then stood. Struggling with words he'd never dreamed of speaking, Jackson cupped his hands at the back of her head, urging her closer.

"I know that," he said softly. "I don't deserve you, lady. But God help me, I don't have the strength to let you and the baby go. Rebecca Ruth Hill, I love you madly. Will you please, before I lose my mind, say that you'll marry me?"

She went limp in his arms. "Yes, yes, a thousand times yes," she said.

Overwhelming joy centered within him, melting the last of the ice around his heart, as he tilted her face to meet his kiss.

"I'd settle for just the one," he whispered, and tasted her tears on his lips as he swept them across her face.

Rebecca stilled, then, clutching fiercely at his shirt, she started to shake him.

"No, Jackson! Never settle. You gave up half of your life in the name of love, and for that, I will admire you forever. But it's time that you take what you want . . . what you deserve."

"I want you, Rebecca, and I want to watch our baby grow up. I want Molly to be happy. And I want your father to marry us."

The moment it was said, he caught himself holding his breath, afraid that he'd asked too much.

Rebecca slid her hands up the front of his shirt, then wrapped them around his neck. She looked up, unaware of the tears still running down her face.

"Thank you, my darling," she said softly.

"For what?" Jackson asked.

"For always knowing the best way to my heart."

Jackson wrapped her in a fierce, unyielding embrace as he absorbed her love.

"You made it easy, sweet lady."

She smiled. "How so?"

"I would have been a fool not to see it. You kept showing me the way."

Epilogue

The air was warm. Too warm for the cap and gown he was wearing. But at this point, Jackson wouldn't have traded it for anything. For the last two and a half years, he'd sweat everything but blood for the degree he was about to receive. Another hour or so of heat shouldn't matter.

The speaker on stage droned on and on about the challenges awaiting the new graduates. Jackson smiled to himself. He'd already faced and survived more challenges than most of these people would see in a lifetime. But none of it would have been worth a damn without the family he had today.

He turned his head, again, searching the sea of faces high above the floor of the convention center where Tulane University's graduation ceremonies were being held, looking for Rebecca and Danny. They were up there somewhere, along with the rest of the family.

Although Danny was not quite two years old, Rebecca had insisted that he be present to watch his father walk across the stage to accept his diploma. Struggling with a lively toddler in this kind of crowd would be difficult for Rebecca, but he hadn't had it in him to disagree. She knew how much this day meant to him. Having everyone that he loved present to see his achievement was the best gift she could give him, and he'd accepted it in the spirit with which it was given.

Family. For Jackson, it was a simple word rich with meaning. It represented knowing that he was loved and accepted, and the comfort of having a place to call home.

He shifted in his seat, turning his attention back to the rows of students among whom he sat, and staring at the eagerness on their faces and the joy in their eyes, knowing that a long-awaited goal was only minutes away.

Hope was on their faces. Hope and a trace of fear for the unknown. Molly was a little bit like these students. Now and again through the last two years, he'd caught a glimpse of hesitation in her eyes, as if she didn't dare trust the world not to slap her down. But thanks to the unexpected and unabashed adoration of Clark Thurman, who, upon meeting his sister, had fallen hopelessly and quietly in love, she was becoming more and more confident with each passing day.

Jackson went to bed each night praying that there would come a day when Molly would trust enough to be able to return Clark's love, but for now, hope was enough to get them through.

He thought of Rebecca's father, and knew that it was a true miracle that they'd all come to a comfortable peace among themselves, and of Pete, who'd remained a true and steadfast friend.

And then, when he wasn't listening, the audience suddenly broke into loud applause. Startled by the noise, he realized that the speaker had finished. It was time.

Elation raised the pitch of Rebecca's voice. "Oh look! It's finally starting!" she said, shifting the sleepy baby in her lap, and watching as the long-winded speaker finally sat down. Her pulse accelerated as the students began filing out of their chairs in alphabetical order and started walking across the stage to receive their diplomas as their names were called.

"Want me to take him?" Daniel asked, and held out his hands, more than willing to hold the child who'd stolen his heart.

She glanced down, noting with relief that Danny was now all but immobile, sucking his thumb and clutching his blanket as he leaned against her breast. "Thanks, but he's quiet now. I don't want to mess with a good thing."

Molly gave the tall, sandy-haired man in the seat beside her a quiet smile, and then whispered in Rebecca's ear. "Clark and I could take him outside for a bit if you think it would help," she offered.

Rebecca shook her head. "No way, Molly, I wouldn't have you miss this moment for the world."

Molly studied the shape of the baby's small face, gently stroking his hair as he slumped in Rebecca's arms.

"Danny looks so much like A. J., doesn't he?"

Rebecca's heart filled as she gazed down at the child in her arms. "Like a carbon copy . . . right down to the big blue eyes."

In an unusual show of affection, Molly leaned over and kissed Rebecca's cheek.

"I always wanted a sister. You're the best thing that ever happened to us, you know."

Surprised by the unexpected compliment, Rebecca's eyes glazed with unshed tears. "I'd say that the feeling is mutual."

Clark slipped his hand across Molly's arm. "Look, dear, he's at the steps!"

All their focus turned toward the podium. Without thinking of those behind her, Rebecca suddenly stood. Her heart was pounding in her throat, and her throat was thick with tears, but she was determined that Danny see what his father had accomplished. Even though he would be too young to remember, his father would not forget.

"Look, Danny! See Daddy?"

Upon hearing his favorite person's name being called, the toddler roused in his mother's arms, staring with sleepy confusion across a sea of unfamiliar faces as his father's name ricocheted within the convention center walls.

"Andrew Jackson Rule!"

The name echoed within Jackson's mind as he exhaled slowly, then started across the stage, his gaze fixed upon the man at the podium who was waiting to shake his hand. His steps were long and measured, just as they'd been on the day he'd walked through the gates of Angola State Penitentiary. Only this time, he wasn't walking into the unknown. And this time, he was not alone.

"Congratulations, Mr. Rule," the dean said, shaking Jackson's hand, and handing him the diploma with practiced ease.

Jackson tightened his grasp on the leather case that would ultimately hold his degree. And then he paused and looked up, wishing he'd at least determined Rebecca's location before the program began, wanting to share this moment with her.

During the round of general applause, he thought he caught a glimpse of white in the sea of colors, and his gaze shifted a bit to the right. Rebecca was wearing white. And then he saw her, far up in the balcony, standing and waving. He knew it was her, although he could barely discern her dark red curls, the smile on her face . . . and their child in her arms. A sudden film of tears blurred his vision. She held his reason for living.

On the day of their marriage, Jackson had made a silent pact with God that he'd spend the rest of his life making sure that no child of his had cause to hate or to fear. And now, on this day, he'd just earned the right to help children, other than his own, learn how to forget and forgive those who'd destroyed their own youth.

He lifted his arm and waved, lightly at first, and then with joy and with vigor. Life had come close to beating him down. And then a preacher's daughter had done what no one else would do. She'd thanked him, then trusted him, then loved him with all of her heart.

He walked off the stage toward the rest of his life.

Escape to Romance
and
WIN A YEAR OF ROMANCE!

Ten lucky winners will receive a free year of romance—*more than 30 free books*. Every book HarperMonogram publishes in 1997 will be delivered directly to your doorstep if you are one of the ten winners drawn at random.

Harper
Monogram

Don't Miss DINAH McCALL'S
Stunning Debut

DREAMCATCHER

Amanda Potter escapes her obsessive husband
through the warm embrace of a dream that
draws her through time. Detective Dupree
knows his destiny is intertwined with
Amanda's and must convince her that her
dream lover is only a heartbeat away.

And published under her own name,
Sharon Sala...

DEEP IN THE HEART Stalked by a stranger, Samantha
Carlyle returns to Texas—and her old friend John Thomas
Knight—for safety. The tender lawman may be able to protect
Sam's body, but his warm Southern ways put her heart at risk.

LUCKY Despite her vow never to be with a man like her
gambling father, Lucky Houston is drawn to Nick Chenault, the
owner of a Las Vegas club. Only by trusting Nick can Lucky put
the past behind her and discover a love that can conquer the odds.

DIAMOND Legendary country singer Jesse Eagle knows it's
love at first sight when he sees Diamond Houston singing
in a two-bit roadhouse. He is willing to risk his
career and his reputation to make Diamond his own.

Harper Monogram

THE BEST IN THE
ROMANCE BUSINESS
EXPLAIN HOW IT'S DONE

A MUST FOR ROMANCE
READERS AND WRITERS

edited by
Jayne Ann Krentz

Nineteen bestselling romance novelists
reveal their secrets in this collection of essays,
explaining the popularity of the romance
novel, why they write in this genre, how the
romance novel has been misunderstood by
critics, and more. Contributors include Laura
Kinsale, Elizabeth Lowell,
Jayne Ann Krentz, Susan
Elizabeth Phillips, Mary Jo
Putney, and many others.